Island Madness

Other books by Tim Binding available in Picador

A Perfect Execution

TIM BINDING

Island Madness

PICADOR

First published 1998 by Picador

an imprint of Macmillan Publishers Ltd
25 Eccleston Place, London sw1w 9nf
and Basingstoke

Associated companies throughout the world

isbn 0 330 35035 8

Copyright © Tim Binding 1998

The right of Tim Binding to be identified as the
author of this work has been asserted by him in accordance
with the Copyright, Designs and Patents Act 1988.

This book is a work of fiction. Names, characters, places,
organizations, and incidents are either products of the author's imagination
or used fictitiously. Any resemblance to actual events, places, organizations,
or persons, living or dead, is entirely coincidental.

3 5 7 9 8 6 4

A CIP catalogue record for this book is available from
the British Library.

Typeset by SetSystems Ltd, Saffron Walden, Essex
Printed and bound in Great Britain by
Mackays of Chatham plc, Chatham, Kent

This is for Titch,
an example to us all,
with love and admiration

One

The Battle was over. Fortress Stalingrad was no more. What remained of the great army huddled broken, like its commander General Paulus, bereft of speech, squatting in cellars or flooded foxholes, unable to comprehend the savagery of their downfall and the enormity of their betrayal. Flying to the island with the plane's mid-afternoon shadow racing over the deep green waters of the Channel, it was hard for Lentsch to believe that at the other end of the continent men that he had known, men who were so used to victory, men who knew the worth of themselves and the army in which they served, had been left to die in the frozen ruins of their invincible dream. It was not simply the totality of their defeat but the manner of it. Travelling back from his leave Lentsch was returning with tales more terrible, more desolate, than any he had heard before, tales that he was afraid to impart to anyone else, lest they infect the island with an ineradicable melancholy.

The encirclement had come in November, from a Slavic enemy whose numbers seemed unimaginable. Where had they sprung from, these winter blooms, appearing from the east with names He had believed to be long extinct? As each division had been identified and marked on His map they were stared and marvelled at as a botanist might gaze at some unidentified flower, half unbelieving that such plants could resurrect themselves so quickly from such poisoned wastes. Surely that division had perished at Kiev, this one annihilated north-west of Kalatch? But along the banks of the Don and the Volga they had risen again, springing up in numbers undreamed of, strangling those who had thought to clear the ground of their despised vegetation with fresh shoots of implacable strength. And thus had His army been surrounded and ordered by Him to hold fast, even though common sense dictated that it escape, push the growing entanglement aside and reach safety. Generals had flown out and pleaded with Him to let them attempt a breakout, but His answer was always the same. He must not leave the Volga, He could not leave the Volga, He shall not leave the Volga. To leave the Volga would be a humiliation, to leave the Volga would be a disgrace, not solely for Him but for the whole of Germany. The Sixth Army must hold fast. And now they were gone and the world in which they had lived had gone with them. One hundred and forty-five thousand dead and ninety-one thousand captured, a catastrophe of biblical proportions. And here was Major Lentsch, flying to another of His obsessions, another Fortress in the making.

All through that winter men had been pouring in onto the island: engineers from Belgium, skilled construction workers from France, men laden with theodolites and drills who bored holes and tapped rocks and drew their indelible marks in the sand. There seemed no end to them. Down in St Peter Port the harbour was jammed with trawlers and tugs and great floating cranes, their necks bent double in search of their prey; metal rods, barbed wire, timber, and cement – always cement, the essential dust of His creation, cement in the flat-bottomed barges which wallowed their way from Cherbourg, cement stacked twelve feet high on St Julian's Pier, cement hauled round the island on the narrow-gauge railway built for its exclusive use, to be mixed and poured and moulded into the fertile shapes of war. A military chastity belt of His design had been fitted around the island's most tender regions, so that like a jealous lord He could prevent any violation of His fresh, plump property. But still He wanted more: more concrete, more guns, more men. In all of Western Europe there was nothing that glittered in His mind's eye more brightly than the Channel Islands. *Inselwahn*, they called it. Island Madness.

Though the north of Guernsey is blessed with longer, sandier beaches, it is the tiny bays of the south, hidden by steep paths and high ferns, that form the island's sparkling garland. Flying towards Jerbourg Point, Lentsch could see the coves in which he had bathed so often, Corbiere, La Jonnet, Petit Bot Bay, and then, as the plane banked north, came the long gabled roof of the Villa Pascal that looked down on the most delightful of them all, Saints Bay. As they passed over the house Lentsch noticed that the French windows had been thrown open while above, in continental fashion, the bedding hung out of the bedroom windows, even Albert's. The house looked as still and as perfect as ever, but for the first time Lentsch saw it all in blocks of colour: the shining white of the stone, the patchy greens of the lawn, the red-ochre cliffs spattered with a dark fuzz of olive and beneath it all the burning blue of the swollen sea. He imagined the brush strokes he would be unable to accomplish, the skill that had guided Cézanne's hand. It *was* true what he had painted, what others had seized upon. He had always believed that it must be, despite the strident arguments which were now ranged against him and his kind. Now, unexpectedly, Lentsch had seen a glimmer of it for himself. From this plane, of all places! He said nothing to his companion, but raised the roll of canvas to his lips, as if in silent homage. These few acres had held him in their captive embrace for over two years, and every inch bore memories: the grass where they held their comic games of polo, with him and Zep as the horses and Molly's straw hat as the prize; the jetty where first he had taught Isobel to dive; the rocky path down which they had all skipped encumbered in fancy dress; the ledge underneath the old tower where he would sit and paint. How fortunate it was that there should have been a war strong enough to carry him this far. On one rare occasion, when he had been invited to dinner at Isobel's house, he had told them that when it was all over he would like to live here. She had looked at her father quickly, but neither had said anything. There was no need. They both knew what was meant. He was not the enemy. He was a soldier, that was all.

Though the sky above was still clear, clouds were banking up to the north-east, promising an evening of rain and harsh wind.

Lentsch had felt the beginnings of it tugging at the wings of the plane ever since they had taken off. He had not expected to arrive this way, but had bumped into Ernst in Granville market while haggling over the price of an under-the-counter round of cheese. Lentsch had stuffed it into his greatcoat pocket hoping that Ernst hadn't noticed, but there was nothing to worry about. Ernst was returning from one of his frequent conferences at Cherbourg. Speer had been there! Speer, Reichsminister for Armaments and Munitions, Director of the Organisation! Ernst could hardly contain his excitement. In an uncharacteristic display of generosity he offered Lentsch a ride in his plane – a Focke-Wulf 189.

'It's not right, Major,' he had said, clasping Lentsch in a boastful embrace, squashing the illicit purchase in the process. 'Surely a man of your position can persuade von Schmettow to place an aircraft at your disposal. We'll radio ahead for your car.'

His startled owl-like features flickered in self-congratulation. Lentsch had given him the weakest of smiles in return. It was not Ernst's charm that cut the ice with the Military Government over in St Germain. However, as Guernsey's head of the Organisation Todt, the ever-expanding construction arm of the Wehrmacht, he had a greater authority to call upon. Civilians might laugh at the sight of the State Labour Service parading up and down the Esplanade, gleaming shovels at the ready, but the truth was that Ernst could have anything he liked. On the few times he had been invited to the Villa, Lentsch had noticed him looking over the house with a nakedly acquisitive eye. Though his headquarters were to be found in one of the grandest house of them all, Saumarez Park (and making a pig of the grounds according to Albert, a much greater crime in his book than any vandalism committed on the building), he himself lived in a rather modest bungalow at the back of the town. Still Lentsch was grateful for the lift. A six-hour crossing from St Malo in choppy waters with sullen members of the Wehrmacht brooding over the latest news was not what he had wanted. Better to listen to Ernst and his miraculous feats of engineering.

Ernst leant over and tapped him on the knee, pointing down to where Albert held his daily battle with the moles.

'By the way,' he shouted over the noise of the engine. 'Some artillery fellows will be coming over to your place in the next couple of days. To take a look at the lawns.'

Lentsch felt a tug of unease. 'The lawns?'

'Yes. There is a feeling that we require another battery post in that area. The bay in general is not sufficiently protected.'

Lentsch looked back to the wide sweep of Moulin Huet. It was empty save for a lone fishing boat making its weekly licensed lobster trawl along the coast. It might be one of the most secluded parts of the island, suitable perhaps for a reconnaissance landing of two or three, but it would be suicide to attempt anything on a larger scale.

'Protected from what?' he shouted back. 'Nothing of any size could land there. The coves are too small, the paths too narrow. Besides we have one gun emplacement on the other side.'

Ernst nodded in agreement.

'Precisely. If on that side why not yours? We don't want any gaps to be found when . . .' He stopped and looked at Lentsch hard.

'When the invasion comes?' Lentsch suggested. Ernst shook his head at the impossibility of the thought.

'When it's finished,' he offered lamely.

'Why not lower down?' Lentsch argued. 'You could dig into the cliff more. Up there you wouldn't see so much. Besides,' he gave a wan smile, hoping to rekindle Ernst's goodwill, 'it would ruin the view.'

Ernst attempted an unconvincing look of sympathy.

'I can see that. But digging into the cliff would take more men, more materials. It would take longer. I have to balance these things.'

Lentsch looked out in dismay. It would not simply spoil the house, it would break the spell woven around it. Suddenly the plane's engines cut out and in the silence he was standing by the French windows smoking a cigarette, listening to Isobel's clear laughter rising up from the beach. With luck he would be seeing her tonight. He tried to think of what he might say to her, how eager he should appear. He'd had a good three days in Paris, washing away the hold of her in as many nightclubs as one man could take, but once back home he could not wait to return. He had listened to his mother and sister, feeling increasingly awkward and irritated, as if they had no right to tell him of their hardships, the rationing, the bombing raids, the barely articulated feeling of gloom. He felt strangely unaffected by it, as if it had nothing to do with him. The war might ebb and flow across continents, but it hardly seemed to matter. Only Guernsey existed. Guernsey was the best place in the world.

The plane coughed, as if to remind him of Ernst's threat.

'Well, I shall put up a fight, I can promise you,' Lentsch told him vehemently. 'There are plenty of other places to choose from. That's if it's necessary at all.'

Ernst tapped his briefcase as if he had the plans already under lock and key. 'I understand how you feel, Major,' he said. 'And if I lived there, I too would do everything in my power to keep it just so. But as it is . . .'

So that was it. Ernst was beginning to flex his muscles. This was going to be how it was from now on, the army pushed aside in favour of those who held everything but their own prejudices in contempt. Lentsch tried to hold his ground

'As you say. Unfortunately there is no extra room.'

Ernst smirked.

'In war,' he said simply, 'people come and go.'

The plane slithered recklessly down the grass runway. For a moment Lentsch thought that they were going to crash into one of the Junkers parked at the far end. The brakes didn't seem to have any effect at all. Ernst, catching his look of horror, affected a blithe indifference.

'Happens all the time,' he shrugged. 'They have to mow the grass extra close because it grows so fast overnight. Once a month a plane crashes.'

Ernst jumped down and sped off without another word. Lentsch hauled his baggage out and followed. On the roof of the heavily sandbagged terminal stood a sentry, stuck there with legs apart, like a decoration on a wedding cake. Below, in front of the car, waited Albert. Though in his late fifties when he had first started to work for him, Albert had possessed the wiry strength of someone twenty years younger. Now he was beginning to look his age, but his skin still retained that depth of colour that only a man who has spent his working life outside can obtain. Lentsch promised himself that this month he would get up the nerve to ask Albert to sit for him. He was dressed as awkwardly as usual: baggy brown jacket, woollen waistcoat and a pair of dress-suit trousers with a velvet stripe down the outside leg that had once belonged to his former employer. His blue beret was draped over his head like a three-egg omelette. Most men were expected to show due deference to their German masters and lifting one's cap, even raising it the slightest fraction, was considered a sufficient demonstration, but not Albert. Lentsch had never seen him without it, not even when he had roused him out of bed in the middle of the night. Zep was convinced the man was completely bald, but Lentsch wasn't so sure. A bald pate would not worry Albert unduly. It was a definite state, a fact of life, a badge of hard-won honour. A thin straggle of something blowing across the top, however, he would not appreciate, for like many men who feign indifference to their appearance, Albert was vain. One had only to look at the shine of his shoes or the fussy knot of his tie to know that. And anyway, as Lentsch had pointed out to Zep, he went to the barber's once a month.

Albert opened the door but made no attempt to help Lentsch with his luggage.

'I didn't expect to see you here,' Lentsch told him, as he laid his bags carefully on to the back seat. 'Where's Wedel?'

Albert pointed to his stomach.

'The runs,' he said. 'He went mushroom picking yesterday and came back with a basket of toadstools. I told him not to eat 'em but would he listen? "At home we eat all sorts," he boasted. He

7

tried to get Mrs H. to have a few but I warned her off.' A smile of grim satisfaction crept over his face. 'Been up all night. Bent double. He's better now though. Except for the squits.'

'The squits?'

'You know.' Albert made an appropriate noise.

'Ah, yes. The squits.'

Albert coughed. 'We all got something wrong with us these days. I've sprained my ankle and got this throat I can't get rid of, Marjorie's got the shingles and half the girls in Boots have been going in and out of the pox doctor's clinic faster than a spring tide. Well, they're not handling my prescriptions any more, I can tell you that.'

They drove off. As they turned out onto Forest Road Albert tugged at his beret, as if acknowledging the sentry's salute. It took Lentsch by surprise. Was he merely being insolent or did he see himself as a quasi-official now? He soon got his answer. A kilometre down the road the car started to edge steadily to the left. Lentsch put his hand on the wheel and eased it firmly over to the correct side.

'Sorry,' said Albert.

'It's quite all right,' said Lentsch.

'Habit of a lifetime,' Albert went on.

'But you couldn't drive before we came,' Lentsch reminded him.

'It's in the blood,' Albert countered. 'Like the sea.'

'You couldn't swim either.'

'Nor can I still.'

They turned onto the Rue des Escaliers. A short journey down and then out along the cliff. Five minutes at the most. He wondered if she would be there to greet him. He looked over at Albert's face to see if he could detect her presence. Nothing.

'I have brought you something,' he said. 'Here.'

He fished out a small packet, wrapped in tissue paper. Albert took a hand from the wheel and held the parcel up to his ear, shaking it gently. There was a metallic rattling inside.

'What is it, then?' he asked, easing it into his jacket pocket. 'Gramophone needles?'

Lentsch shook his head. 'Razor blades. Fifty. All new.'

'Fifty?' Albert was pleased. He rubbed his face in anticipation of his first fresh shave of the month. 'That should keep me going for a bit.'

Lentsch was grateful he did not say 'until it's all over' or 'until we throw you out', though he knew that such thoughts must be on his mind. As a trusted member of the household Albert listened to the BBC as often as they did, standing at the back of the living room, hanging on to every word booming out of the huge radiogram. That was one of the reasons why he was in such demand. With his sources Albert had an invitation to tea at someone's house every day of the week.

The car bumped down the narrow road, high hedges and ferns on either side. Then, as it began to climb again, Albert put his foot down and they were out on top, out along the narrow pitted track, past the high gates and onto the thinly gravelled drive, moving up through the lime trees to the Villa's front entrance with its white pillars and grey stone steps. Passing the pebble-dash lodge Lentsch could see a bicycle propped up against a half-stacked pile of wood under the porch by the front door. Smoke rose up from the building's squat brick chimney. Four o'clock in the afternoon and Marjorie had lit her fire already. She would have to be reminded once again about the need to conserve fuel, though he understand well enough these unnecessary acts of defiance. Being forced to swap places with her caretaker was not something a woman of Mrs Hallivand's background forgot lightly.

Like many houses looking out to sea, the rooms were set in reverse order, the utility rooms, kitchen, storerooms, washrooms placed at the front, while the main rooms, the library, the dining room and the drawing room, were found at the back. Dividing the two were the stairs to the cellar, the main staircase leading to the first and second floors and the billiard room. The house was quiet.

It was obvious there was no one there to greet him. He had expected someone, Zep or Molly. Even Marjorie could have put in an appearance. Lentsch felt cheated. He had brought gifts for them all, three hours spent in Granville hunting for presents he knew they would appreciate – dance records for Isobel, a twelve-year-old Armagnac for the Captain, a pair of silk stockings for Molly and a traveller's set of Guernsey's most famous author, Victor Hugo, for Marjorie. Dropping his bags on the tiled floor he strode down the hall and flung open the doors to the drawing room. The armchairs and sofa had been shoved back against the walls. The radiogram from his study had been moved in, his box of seventy-eights on the floor beside it. So this is what they got up whenever he left. Albert stood in the doorway, trying to hide an expression of guilt.

'You should have cleared up,' Lentsch told him. 'I don't mind parties while I'm away, but . . .'

Albert limped in and in a slow, deliberate move, pushed the sofa further back.

'It's for you,' he said. 'They're planning a little get-together. I wasn't meant to do this until later, but I promised Mrs H. I'd go to town before the shops shut. She's got some shoes that need mending.'

Lentsch felt his spirits soar, though he tried not to show it.

'Who's coming? Do you know?'

'The usual crowd. The Captain's organized it all – he and Miss Molly.'

Lentsch walked into the hall, picked up the receiver and gave the number.

'You're not meant to know,' Albert warned. 'If the Captain finds out I've let on . . .'

Lentsch winked.

'Don't worry. I . . .' One ring and someone had lifted the phone. He turned quickly, waving Albert away.

'Yes?'

She'd been waiting for him! He kept his voice as light as possible.

'Isobel! It's me. I have just returned. I was hoping to see you. Tonight, perhaps?'

She spoke quickly. 'I can't, not tonight. I'm sorry.'

Lentsch smiled to himself. He could imagine her, standing over that glass-topped table in the drawing room, looking round to see if her father was in earshot. Soon she would pick up the receiver and move over to the staircase. It was where she loved to sit, talking, reading, painting her toenails. Her hair would be bunched back, her legs bare. He tried to sound disappointed.

'Never mind. I am sure I can find something else to do, down at the club perhaps.'

There was a silence at the other end.

'Isobel. Is everything all right?'

'Yes. Quite all right.'

'Your father – is he well?'

'Yes. He's dining with Major Ernst tonight.' She lowered her voice. 'Across the road.'

'In the Major's house?'

'Yes.'

'And you will be all alone?'

'No, no. Some friends are coming over.' She was finding it difficult to lie, bless her.

'And did you miss me?' he asked.

'Not as much as I had thought.'

Lentsch closed his eyes. It wasn't the reply he had expected. He didn't know what to say.

'Oh. I had hoped . . .'

She corrected herself.

'I did miss you. It was just I did other things.'

He teased her some more.

'If I cannot see you tonight, how about tomorrow? Perhaps we could go riding. I have not taken Wotan out for weeks now.'

'Wotan. Such a ridiculous name for a horse.'

'To your ears, perhaps. For us it is a strong name, a strong name for a strong horse.'

'A beautiful horse,' she agreed.

'I thought I might take him over to Vazon and stretch his legs. Why don't you come too? I could call for you in the morning.'

'Don't you have work to do?'

'On Sunday?'

'You shouldn't neglect your duties, Gerhard, even for your horse.'

'That is exactly who I should neglect my duties for. My horse is the second most important creature on this island.'

Lentsch could hear her laugh despite herself.

'Father will be gone all afternoon,' she relented. 'Call for me then. Look, I've got to go.'

'Oh. Until tomorrow, then.' He shouted the last sentence to an empty line.

Albert was waiting in the drawing room, pretending not have heard a single word. Lentsch put his hand round his shoulders and walked him through onto the veranda.

'Let us walk around the garden,' he suggested. 'Have you time? How are the moles?'

'Three while you were away.'

'Three? Pretty soon you will be able to make a coat,' Lentsch joked.

'Pretty soon we'll be eating them. Our rations have been put back again. Is it any wonder we're all dropping like ninepins. And we had another blessed break-in last night.'

'Another? The third in how many months? Have you told your nephew?'

'What can he do? It's not us locals, Major. It's the foreigns. They're all over the place.'

There were sixteen thousand foreign labourers on the island, part of His vast army of slave workers, men stolen from the captured lands of the continent and put to work for the Organisation Todt; in Germany they worked in factories, built roads, mended railways. Here they were building the Western Wall. The whole area around the old quarter of St Peter Port was filled with them; Spaniards,

Poles, Russians, and a huge contingent of North Africans. The Kasbah, Albert called it.

The two men walked to the end of the lawn and looked out. The boat had gone now, and the bay's still emptiness accentuated its deep beauty. Since they had placed even further restrictions on civilian movement there were parts of the island which grew more sacred by the day. Lentsch shivered. Ernst's threat came ringing back at him. He pointed across to the squat bulge of concrete billowing out of the cliff on the other side.

'The artillery want to get their hands on this,' he blurted out. 'Another one of those somewhere down here. Can you imagine it, with paths and cables and bunkers for the men. Not to mention the noise.' He held his hands over his ears. 'It's Major Ernst, you know.'

'What is?'

'The house. He wants to live here too.'

'But there's no room. Not with you and the Captain and everyone.'

Everyone was Bohde, the island's censor. Albert did not like Bohde ever since he had caught him in the fruit garden stuffing himself full of loganberries.

'He will try and get rid of one of us,' Lentsch explained. 'Make me look not capable in administration, or the Captain's security procedures, perhaps. Something like that. Still, for the Villa, for you and Marjorie, it might be for the best. That way, there would be no new battery. Of that you could be sure.'

Albert did not know what to say. Like Lentsch he saw himself as the Villa's guardian rather than its occupier. Change, however, was never welcome. Lentsch tried to reassure him.

'Don't worry. It might not come to it. But the lower part of the garden, after the roses, where we play the polo. This I think we should dig up and make for some potatoes and vegetables. That way the garden would not look so . . .' He searched for the correct word.

'English?' Albert ventured.

'Privileged,' Lentsch countered. 'I'll get Helmut to start as soon as he's back on his feet.'

Lentsch turned and they started back to the house.

'It's good to be back, Albert. Good to see Saints Bay again and the house. And you, of course.' He paused for a moment, unsure of how to continue. 'Things back home are not so good. My mother and sister are very much afraid. Bombs, you know. We did not expect it in Germany.'

'No.'

'On homes and churches. We did not expect it.'

'No.'

'We call them Meier raids, on account of Goering's boast. "If an enemy bomber reaches the Ruhr, you can call me Meier!" We have Meier raids every day now. Not much of a joke, Albert. Not for my mother. Not for anyone.'

'No. I can see that. Still . . .'

'We only have ourselves to blame, you're thinking?'

'Not you personally, Major. I've never thought that.'

'But as a people?'

'Well, I'd have to, wouldn't I? We were all getting along fine before all this. Still, I don't wish any harm on anybody.'

Lentsch was silent for a moment. That wasn't true at all. Everyone wasn't getting along fine before all this. There was a time when everything had been terrible. And then, the soul of a nation had been woken, practically overnight. It had been marvellous! How could he explain?

'And you,' he asked suddenly. 'You are well? Have you heard from your daughter?'

Albert shook his head. 'I was hoping I might have got a postcard through the Red Cross. Last week was the anniversary of Mum's death.' He began to cough. Lentsch looked down in case the old man was trying to hide his tears.

'I'm sorry,' he said. 'I did not know.' Albert, shaking his head, dismissed his condolences.

'She would have hated to see the place as it is now. All the guns

14

and barbed wire. But I do miss our girl. I still don't know if I did the right thing, staying put while she left with the rest of the evacuees. She was late in our life, was Kitty. Sometimes I wonder if I'll ever see her again.'

Lentsch was anxious to cheer him up. If there was going to be a party tonight he didn't want Albert's long face spoiling it.

'Course you will, my good chap,' he breezed, clapping him on the back. 'The way things are going it might end quicker than any of us think.' Changing the subject, he added, 'Has anything else happened while I was away? The Bloody Boiler behaving?'

'The Bloody Boiler's been going since early this morning, Major.'

'Excellent. I shall go for a bathe, take a bath and, if the weather holds, maybe sketch for an hour.' He pointed to the Martello tower on the opposite side.

'Same view?' Albert asked.

'That's just it, my friend. It is never the same.'

Albert waited as he disappeared into the house, emerging a few minutes later in civilian clothes with a towel under his arm. He watched as Lentsch ran down the path, his body hidden by the tall ferns. It was the one thing he could not understand about the Germans, this obsession with fitness and the outdoors. The Major had reached the shoreline and was walking along the rim of the bay in his bare feet, his shoes hanging round his neck. Climbing onto the jetty he stripped off and dived in. He might not be blond and six foot tall, but he was lean and fit and held himself like a man with strong blood in his veins.

A car spat up the drive, brakes, doors and horn sounding all at once. Albert recognized the mixture. Captain Zepernick, driving with the top down. 'Only a plague of locusts, a forty-degree frost, or the certainty of sexual intercourse in broad daylight will make me put up the hood,' the Captain had once joked. From the hurried demand of his footsteps coming down the red-tiled hall, Albert could tell he was not joking now.

'He has returned?' he demanded, stepping out onto the veranda.

Albert pointed to the sea.

'Did he see?'

Albert nodded. The Captain cursed in German. It was not *Donner* or *Blitzen* or that other word which Miss Molly once whispered in his ear in front of the whole company trying to embarrass him, but it was a swear word nevertheless. Albert wished that one time one of them would say *Donner und Blitzen*, if only to satisfy himself that those words were real words used by real Germans in times of anger and frustration, but though he had cooked their meals, served their drinks, ironed their shirts and stood by their side for the past two years listening to them carrying on like spoilt little madams, he had never heard one of them say it, not even when the weather was there to give them their cue. It annoyed him that they should be so wilful and choose not to do what was required.

The Captain had reached the beach and was calling out to the Major as he tried to run over the shifting shingle.

'That's right, me old china,' Albert said, looking down. 'You tell him. Donner and Blitzen. Double donner and double blitzen, with the best porcelain whistling round your ears.'

Down on the jetty the two had met up. The Major stood quite still, his towel hanging limply at his side. He would be frozen when he got back. A hot bath with a glass of brandy on the side would be what was required. Albert turned back, shaking his head. Major or no Major, he could at least cover himself up.

Two

It had been warm that day, the first for weeks, but now the wind was getting up again, coming in from the north, with a chill in its heart that only an island feels. Inspector Ned Luscombe was waiting for the post when he heard George Poidevin heaving himself up to the office with another tale of woe weighing down his lumbering frame.

The police station had expanded in the last few years but it was still primitive compared with what he had been used to. On the ground floor stood the cramped reception area, with its counter and one long bench opposite and a picture of the old king hanging crookedly on the wall. Behind it was the Sergeant's room and adjoining it, with a door leading to the washroom and the yard, an even smaller room where the police doctor used to examine the drunks. There was no cell. The prison was only forty yards away. Privacy was at a premium too. Before the war, whenever anybody was arrested, a crowd used to gather on the pavement outside to listen to what was being said. It was a foolish man who confessed his sins in Guernsey's sole police station.

There were two other floors, reached only by the outside steps that ran up from the yard. The top floor was let out to the Guernsey Amateur Dramatic and Operatic Society. Below that was Ned's own office, as big as the rest of the station put together. Though he'd put down an old carpet to dampen the sound of the men playing cards down in the back room, if he'd been sensible he would have hauled it above his head and nailed it to the ceiling. They were a keen bunch upstairs and practised regularly. *Babes in the Wood*, *Private Lives*, *Full House*: Ned knew them all off by heart. In the middle of the room stood a large table with a long drawer underneath one side, the only article of furniture in the entire building which possessed both a lock and a key. In the far corner stood a coal stove, its cracked lagged pipe leaking a continual thin spiral of smoke. Two chairs, a filing cabinet and a torn map of the island held together with glue and brown paper were the only other furnishings. One telephone upstairs, one telephone downstairs, a spare bicycle and the Yellow Peril pressed into spasmodic service after their brand-new five-seater had been requisitioned by the Geheimnis Polizei. That was it.

George Poidevin, foreman for one of the island's leading construction firms, was a pasty man and indignation quivered on him like cooked fat on the bone. He lived above a small grocery shop which his wife ran, close to St Sampson's harbour. Recognizing his malevolent wheeze Ned had hastily checked his desk to ensure that nothing of any note lay for George's greedy eyes to devour.

'George,' Ned said gaily. 'What brings you here? Come to turn yourself in?'

George wheezed his way over, put his hands on Ned's desk and panted across the stained woodwork. His breath smelt of strong sausage. The man had been eating meat!

'Do you know?' he said, blinking hard. 'Do you know what they've just told the wife?'

Ned shook his head, hoping that George's weight might prove too much for the table's tired frame. Its legs were splayed out like a dog caught on an iced pond. When it fell apart he intended to chop it up for firewood.

'No,' he replied. 'I don't know. What have they told her? Something interesting? Eva Braun's favourite recipe?'

George leaned further across, resting his weight on his ten fat fingers. The table creaked. The right far leg slipped further out. Ned prayed. A little further, a little further.

'They've only issued instructions that they be put on heavy workers' rations, that's all. Can you believe it! The bloody nerve!'

Ned wasn't sure what he was talking about.

'They, George? Who's "they"?'

'Them whores! Them bloody whores. There's my femme working all the hours God sends her and Elspeth wearing her pins to a frazzle counting out their useless money and does either of them get heavy rations? Does they buggery. But it's all right for these French mamselles, flat on their backs all day.'

It was all Ned could do to stop himself from laughing out loud. Another brothel had opened in January. There was the officers' one over at St Martin's, a spacious affair set in its own grounds, filled, it was said, with cancan girls from Paris; the one for the Todt officials halfway up George Street; and now a couple for the troops over at St Sampson's. In the afternoons you could see the men standing patiently in an orderly queue stretching halfway round the little harbour, smoking treasured cigarettes or exchanging the odd rueful joke, hands in pockets, buffeted by the winds, just like the rest of the population waiting for the bread shop to open. It always made him smile. Even the Germans had to queue for something. Now that the weather was getting better, when they weren't working the girls would start sunning themselves out on the roof, gazing out to where their homeland lay. Last year George had marched to the Feldkommandantur and complained that his wife could see them through their bedroom window.

'And so she could,' Ned had once told Bernie, laughing, 'but only if she stood on a chair.' Ned rubbed his chin hard, trying to prevent a repeat performance.

'Well, it's hard work,' he told George cheerfully. 'There's what, fifteen girls next to your place? Another fifteen down the road. With seventeen thousand troops to cater for that's a lot of jiggery pokery called for. If you work on the principle that the average soldier expects to drop his trousers at least once a fortnight, that means that those girls have to accommodate eight thousand five hundred every week. Which means,' he did a quick sum on a sheet of paper, 'two hundred and eighty-three each a week or forty-seven a day. Forty if they work Sundays.'

George Poidevin was not amused. 'It's a disgrace,' he fumed.

'You know what I said to them? I said, "Put it in writing and see what the States say. I'm not having my wife doling out heavy workers' rations to French tarts without the proper papers."'

Rumour had it that George Poidevin had once tried to slip the girls an extra loaf in return for a weekly you-know-what, and every one of them had refused. Ever since then he had been their implacable enemy.

'They won't put it in writing, not an order like that,' Ned told him. 'But they'll make you do it just the same. Let's face it, we'd all like extra rations, whatever we do. If those girls can wangle it, good luck to them. They don't last long, you know. Not with the wear and tear they have to put up with.'

George had more to tell.

'And that's not all. You know what Monty Freeman's been told? Only to keep the bank open an extra hour on Fridays so that those trollops can waltz in and deposit their money without causing offence to us locals. That's where my Elspeth works. Least she's no Jerrybag. When I think of some of our girls . . .' He stopped short.

'Thanks, George.'

'I'm sorry, I didn't mean . . .'

'Let's forget it, shall we. Is that all you have to tell me or is there a purpose to your visit?'

'I wondered if you'd had any news about the break-in.'

Van Dielen's yard had been broken into the night before. Sergeant Tommy le Coeur had found the fence smashed in. Nothing much stolen. A couple of containers broken into, the little office ransacked of its precious supply of tea and sugar. Papers strewn everywhere. Ned regarded him with reproach.

'George, I reported it to the Feldkommandantur. Take it up with them. The foreigns are no concern of mine. My advice is to forget it. Nothing'll come of it. If you want to stop it happening again, put a dog in there. Something big and hungry that'll bite the bastards.'

Ned shooed him away before Bernie came with his usual bag of treats. The less people knew about that little enterprise the better.

Bernie brought them over once every two days or so, under cover of a normal delivery. Since his garage business had slumped, Bernie had landed a job as part-time postman. It suited his lanky frame. It used to be said that Bernie was the only mechanic on the island who could lie underneath a car with his head poking out at one end and his feet at the other. There weren't many tall men on Guernsey. Not until they came. Bernie followed fast in George's footsteps.

'How's business?' he asked, slumping the oily bag on the table.

'A few break-ins over at the Vale. A fight outside the Brighton. The only bit of excitement was when old Mrs Rowe stopped Tommy in the High Street the other day and asked him if he could show her the way to the black market.'

Bernie smiled. It was a nice story, even if it wasn't true. Taking off his cap he scratched his head. His spiky hair was more suited to a lad of fourteen than a grown man nearing his thirtieth year.

'I heard there was a run-in between some artillery men and a couple of the foreigns, and,' he said, 'someone got thrown out a window.'

'A gunner?'

'No. Just a foreign.'

Ned dismissed it from his mind.

'Not a dicky-bird this end.' He patted the bag.

'About twenty this week, I reckon,' Bernie ventured out loud. 'Should be stood up against a wall and shot, the lot of them.'

Ned walked Bernie back down the stairs. Outside two young girls in white socks and raincoats, hats jammed firmly on their heads, were coming up the road pushing a heavy battered pram. Every day there'd be a bunch of them hanging around the State food stores, darting in and out between the horses' hoofs and the cartwheels, picking the loose potatoes or turnips that had rolled down into the gutter. Bernie held his cap out as they went by.

'Come on, missy,' he teased, bending low. 'Just one measly spud.'

The girls giggled past, the pram bouncing precariously on the cobbles. Bernie turned to leave.

'Fancy a pint later on?' he asked. 'I'll be at the Britannia.'

One of the oldest pubs on the island, it was one of the few out of bounds for the soldiers. A session in there and you came away feeling almost normal. Most did, anyway. Since his unwanted appointment no one seemed to want to talk to Ned any more. Except Bernie. Ned shook his head.

'Better not. I've got a late shift on tonight.'

Bernie, cap back on his head, stuck his hands in his pockets and left, whistling. Back in the office it was time to go through the mail. Though Ned kept his office to himself, when it came to going through the anonymous letters they all took a look. Ned called them up. Peter came first then Tommy, his hands black with grease.

'The Peril still not going?' Ned asked.

Tommy shook his head.

'Perhaps Bernie should take a look,' Ned suggested.

Tommy had his pride. 'There's no need for that. I can fix it.'

'That's what you said last week.'

The sack was still damp from its journey along the seafront. Ned untied the knot and gave the sack a shake.

'About twenty, I reckon,' he ventured out loud.

'How do they do it?' Peter asked, stroking the down on his ginger lip. Last year Ned had seen him playing hopscotch with his younger sisters on the sands at Vazon Bay. Now his outsize adolescent feet lay squeezed into a pair of second-hand boots that had once been the property of one of the policemen currently serving two years' hard labour in Caen prison.

'Jealousy and fear,' he told him, 'that's how. Plus a few old scores to settle.'

'But how do the Post Office tell them from real letters?' Peter persisted.

Tommy pulled ostentatiously at the corners of his whiskers, as if the thickness of his own beard was evidence of how much such a baby-faced novice had to learn.

'They're not that difficult to spot,' he said, warming his backside on the stove. 'They're nearly always written in capitals – to disguise the handwriting – and they're all addressed to the Feldkom-mandantur.'

'There's more to it than that,' Ned added. 'There's a meanness that marks them. That's the thing they can't disguise. When you see them, lying there amidst real letters, love letters, bills, notes of condolence, they stick out a mile.'

He tipped the bundle out onto the table. They were, as Tommy had predicted, all addressed to the Feldkommandantur, scrawled in furtive capital letters, sloping across the surface as if trying to evade the shame of their intent, envelopes, lined notepaper, pages torn out of a child's scrapbook, folded and stuck down and sent with malice in the heart, most with no stamp. But today Tommy was proved wrong. As Ned stirred the pile with his fingers he uncovered an envelope addressed to him, in handwriting he recognized only too well. How many other notes had she written to him, smuggled out from the fierce protection of her father's house, left in the crack in the wall by the drinking fountain or under the whitewashed stone on his parents' front path? Why, he even recognized the way she underlined his name, three straight lines underneath one another, each shorter than the last.

'Good God,' he said. 'I'd never have thought it.'

'What?'

'This is from Isobel, Isobel van Dielen.'

He tore open the envelope. There was no signature, but it didn't need one.

'She wants to meet me, that's all.'

Tommy looked over his shoulder. 'That's all? You jammy so and so.'

'No, it's nothing like that,' Ned told him, but his heart was hammering otherwise. Yes, it could be like that. It could be.

*

They had met on the quayside waiting to embark, her wide-brimmed hat blown from her head and he catching it in the air as it rose to sail over into the dark waters of the harbour. She was

23

nineteen, he twenty-seven – she on her way back from finishing school and he back on leave after his first tour as a CID officer in the Southampton police force. Though younger than him, she was the more at ease and, liking his short crop of crisp, curly hair and the bend of his mouth, unashamedly took the lead and asked him, in light of his catch, if he was a cricketer.

'A policeman,' he had replied hesitantly, fancying his chances but unsure whether it was wise to tell her the truth so early on.

'A policeman!' She had laughed.

'Yes. You find that funny?'

'No.' She threw back her head and laughed again. 'Well, yes, as a matter of fact I do. A policeman!'

'There's nothing wrong with being a policeman, is there?'

'No. But surely not on Guernsey?'

'As a matter of fact, no. But why not?'

'No reason.' She laughed again. It was a laugh that was used to hearing itself, natural and confident, part of her speech. 'Have you ever talked to any of the policemen there? They're not the brightest of fellows, you have to agree.'

Ned felt obliged to defend his compatriots.

'There's not much call for Bulldog Drummonds on our side of the water,' he answered.

'So you came to England.'

'That's right. Lots of thieving and murder to keep me busy here.'

'Murder!' She gave a little shiver, although she was neither cold nor frightened. It pleased her to move in such a way, a kind of parade of what he was to her and what she might be to him. She had restless good looks, with light coloured hair, a wide mouth and eyes that darted this way and that. Though she spoke as if she was English, her skin was of a foreign colour. There was heat and distance to it, a touch of leather to the texture. She was nearly as tall as he was and stood close to him, closer than a young woman should, squaring up to him almost like a man. She fixed him with her blue eyes and shook the set of her bobbed-cut hair, intent on discomfiting him further.

'Have you ever . . .?' She wrapped her arms under her breasts and shivered again. She was captivating. She smiled at a passer-by.

'Only one.' Her theatricality irritated him, so he added, quite truthfully, 'Killed by a horse.'

'A horse!'

'Struck him on the head. With his hoof.'

'Probably being mistreated, poor thing. I hope you didn't arrest him.'

She put her hand in front of her mouth, laughing at her own joke. His mother used to tell him that girls who put their hands in front of their mouths were not only common but most probably deceitful as well, but the manner in which she pressed her fingers to her pursed lips did not seem to indicate either of these character flaws. It was simply shamelessly seductive. Assuming that she was a tourist, and anticipating the possibility that his leave might be brightened by this unexpected opportunity, he turned the hat in his hand.

'So this is yours?'

'It was on my head, if that's what you mean.'

'It's a man's hat.'

'You think I stole it? It's my father's. *Was* my father's. I persuaded him to let me wear it.' She took it from him and set it at an angle on her head. 'Looks better on me, don't you think?'

'That depends. I've never seen your father, have I? I don't even know his name.'

'No?' She took the hat off and turned it over and pointed to the marking on the label.

'His initials, see? You know what they stand for.'

Ned peered and blushed violently. He hardly knew where to look. The girl smiled victoriously. She'd enjoyed the joke many times before.

'Van Dielen,' she said, laughing at him again. 'Nothing else.'

'Van Dielen?' He could not keep the note of surprise out of his voice.

'That's right. Why? Has he broken the law?'

No, he had not broken the law, but as soon as she mentioned the name he knew that despite the island's size she was lost to him. So he wished her a pleasant summer and walked away, watching her later as she presented her first-class ticket for her private cabin, while he, an old hand, walked briskly to the wooden seats around the funnel, and sat, with his greatcoat over his knees, waiting for the hour of midnight to strike, when the hooter would sound and the sea would churn. He could have chosen to go inside, to have a few drinks and a rolling kip on one of the hard slatted seats, but he preferred it out on deck, where he could sit, nursing his thoughts, travelling through the windy dark to the dawn outline of his home town.

Ned knew of the van Dielens. The whole island knew of the van Dielens and to whom they were related. Mr van Dielen, half English, half Dutch, had made his money first from construction work in the Middle East, and latterly in the great road-building programme snaking its way across Europe. Returning to England, hoping to capitalize on his expertise, he had found that he no longer cared for his abandoned homeland, not because it was strange to him, but because it was revealed as all too familiar. His life abroad had been lived as an outcast stuck in an outpost, out of sorts with his surroundings, forcing changes on a sleeping landscape, but England seemed unable to wake to his and others' futuristic call. Coming back with an attractive wife and a marriageable daughter he discovered that all that was required of him was that he should settle in and build bungalows and mock-Tudor suburbs with perhaps a new ladies' room for a country railway station thrown in for good measure. There was nothing in England's architectural plans that loomed large and impossible and wondrous to behold, nothing that sliced through the earth changing its people for ever; and as for the dinners and the young men he was expected to entertain on behalf of his daughter's matrimonial expectations, it was difficult to fathom which he detested the more, the stuffed game he forced into his mouth or the stuffed shirts who produced barking buckshot out of theirs. So he settled on Guernsey, which was of

England but not English, where the policemen acted under English law but the climate did not, where the signs were in English but where the natives, bred to bear a naturally taciturn disposition, spoke a language he could choose not to understand; above all a place where his wife and daughter could use the moneyed high life as a springboard to all the other social ports of call and from where the rich pickings of his continental business beckoned.

And so, being an engineer, he built a house to suit both his temperament and his purpose, combining in its design his intense desire for solitude with a showman's desire to display his architectural talents to the full. Ned knew the building well, for his father had been one of the carpenters contracted in to lay the floor. It stood, not on one of the grander roads leading out of St Peter Port, nor in the quieter more expensive reaches to the south, but on a dusty back road wedged in a dip between two hills, cramped for space and overlooking a row of undistinguished bungalows, surrounded by a riotous, unruly garden, with plants pushed into the earth to let do as they please; rot, run riot, fill the air with maddening seed, it did not matter to him, as long as they formed some impenetrable barrier between him and the road beyond. Through this fairy-tale tangle could be seen the front of the house, bulging out like an unwanted pregnancy, awkward and eye-catching, with plate-glass windows running from floor to ceiling. 'Wouldn't catch me living in it, not even if you paid me,' his father used to say. 'A shit in a showroom would be more private.' The van Dielens moved in three months after completion, in May '38, surrounded by pink walls and tubular furniture, with rugs instead of carpets, something hooded, straight out of a blacksmith's, in the middle of drawing room instead of a proper fireplace and, most peculiar at all, no curtains. Suspended above the grey metal window-frames hung reels of grey slatted metal blinds which, when lowered, shook and rattled at the slightest provocation and were only brought into use when decency demanded. Certainly Mr van Dielen didn't care to use them, propped up at the curved cocktail bar he had built, sitting there alone surrounded by dancing semiquavers and empty high stools. In the evening those who walked past would see him swirling something thick and cloudy in a strangely shaped glass, thinking about his dead wife, who lay in the cemetery half a mile away, drowned not two months after their arrival and his daughter, whom he hardly knew, packed off to finishing school. But, it was supposed, the house had done its job, and worked, like its owner, on some unfathomable law of incongruity: the long balconies and wide windows protected not by locks and curtains but by brambles and palm trees and rash-inducing rhododendron bushes; a house closed to all, yet with the owner perpetually on view; a man who talked to no one, but who himself was a constant talking point.

And they all talked about him, there was no doubt about that; what he was like to work for (firm but fair), his trips abroad, his determined, lonely life. He had bought out three concerns on Guernsey by then, a builder's yard, a brick works and a contracting firm, and within six months had put two more out of business. He was a small man, small and intense, with a stooped back and dark eyebrows and a clipped moustache which worked up and down. He walked, said Ned's father, like a clockwork toy, as if someone had just wound him up, oblivious to his surroundings. You half expected him to topple over, or stumble up against some unopened door, legs still whirring. He was always in a hurry, no time for idle chatter, just an awkward muttered greeting, head back down, and the sound of his breath rushing past. When he was here he could be seen in his green Norfolk jacket, marching his wicker basket down to the market to place a spider crab or small live lobster on top of the rest of his meagre shopping before pushing his charge back up Victoria Road and home. That was another conundrum that was brought to his account. A builder of roads and bridges, he owned no vehicle and had no garage built for one. Ned's old school friend Bernie le Cocq had tried to interest in him in one of his machines with a free bicycle thrown in for his daughter, but he would have none of it, telling Bernie in a curt letter that as he had his legs and his daughter, when she was here, had her horse, he would be grateful if he kept his suggestions to himself, a letter which Bernie had placed in the little office above his garage, next to his postcard of a fleshy French girl dressed in fat suspenders. So he had his legs and Isobel her horse – which is how Ned met her the second time, as he hurtled down on the butcher's bike he had won years back in a raffle, shaking down the steep dry rut of water lanes, his legs splayed out, his eyes closed, gathering glorious speed remembering those summer rides with Bernie and Veronica Vaudin, until he heard the scream and opened his eyes to see a horse, a bloody horse, standing stock-still with a girl upon it, up in the stirrups, crying out in fear that he might harm them both. He wrenched his hands sharply to the right and ended up capsized upon the fern-thick bank with his legs in the air, his spine jarred and a bicycle wheel humming in his ear. Only when the horse moved closer, prancing nervously on the stony ground, did he realize who the rider was.

'Why don't you look where you're going,' she shouted, adding in a quieter aside, 'Oh, it's you,' from which Ned could tell, even from this undignified position, that she was not utterly displeased to see him again.

'You had your eyes closed,' she continued. 'I watched you coming down. I thought, surely he'll see me, surely he'll open his eyes.'

'I was going swimming,' he said, as if this was going to excuse him.

She turned in her saddle and looked down towards the bay. 'The tide's out.' She paused, weighing the propriety of her next remark. 'Is it safe out there? I ought to try for a swim some day.'

Ned, who knew of the circumstance of her mother's death, stood up awkwardly before her.

'She was one of those people who thought life would never harm her,' she said. She glanced down at his legs. 'Are you a good swimmer?'

'Fair. Canoeing's my speciality.'

'Canoeing?'

29

'Yes. In a canoe.'

'Can you, you know, do that thing where you roll under?'

'That's easy. The thing is to keep calm. Not be afraid.'

'I was never afraid of the sea, until now. Would you take me swimming one day? I could hire a bike.'

They had met two days later. Ned had bought a new pair of swimming trunks, to replace the ones he had worn since he was fifteen, woollen things a mother would buy, woollen things a mother had bought, and though he had never seen cause to replace them before, he saw he was a fully fledged man now, and would have to appear as such before her. He had gone down to the Pollet and the men's clothing store. Mr Underwood's stock was narrow, a choice of three; red, black or red with a daring white stripe down the side.

'I don't see what the fuss is about,' the proprietor had argued, as Ned held each one up to the light. 'No one's going to see them once you're in the water.'

He chose the striped pair and put them on underneath his trousers to minimize the embarrassment of changing in front of her. She turned up in a pair of loose cord trousers and a hacking jacket, London-bought, or from one of the classier shops over in St Helier. Acutely aware of their differing circumstance, he threw off his collarless shirt and worn flannels before she'd even crossed the beach. While she undressed he stood by the water's edge, skimming stones with an exaggerated intensity until she skipped past and walked in up to her waist. Her costume was blue. Her legs were white.

'Don't let me go out of my depth,' she called out, gasping as she settled in and Ned called out that she was not to worry, that it was shallow for a good long distance, and that the sea was still and the tide weak and that he was beside her, which in a moment he was, looking at her strong shoulders and her auburn hair, noting that she was not a swimmer of Veronica Vaudin's capability, but a competent one. He led her out slowly, feeling the pull of the waves as they washed in. Looking back he saw the wide expanse of sand

and the steep wooded hill behind, and at the top, in front of the long green lawn that hung over the lip of the hill like a green tongue, the Villa Pascal.

'That my aunt's house, isn't it?' she asked, following his gaze. 'I've never seen it from this angle before.'

He waved his arm.

'See that man up there, pushing a barrow. That'd be my uncle. Worked for them twenty years now.'

'Your uncle!' She turned in the water. 'Marvellous!'

They were a long way out now and the water was cool and glittered a still light blue.

'Daddy doesn't know I'm doing this,' she called out, floating on her back, 'and when I get back I shall have to take a bath and wash my hair to keep it from him. He wouldn't like it if he found out.'

'Why? You're not doing anything wrong,' Ned said.

'Oh, but I am. I'm in the sea for one thing, and I'm with you for another.'

'Well, I won't tell. And you're much too smart to get caught, I'll be bound.'

'He's a watchful man,' she replied. 'He notices things without you realizing it. He is a surveyor, after all.' She kicked her legs in a plume of water.

'Try standing,' he said, and, realizing what he had done, feeling nothing but a current of cold water pulling at her feet, she struck out for the beach, arms flailing, eyes tight. Once near the shore she walked out quickly, shaking the water from her hair. Ned followed. They towelled in silence

'You shouldn't have done that,' she said. 'It's not like getting back after falling off a horse. She drowned.'

She gestured to him with her hand and he turned to face the sea, which had brought them together and now, like the immutable tide, was pulling them apart. He listened to the hurried sounds she made as she changed, the squeak of her costume as she pulled it down, her quick, strong breath as she rubbed herself dry, the noise of the sand as she lifted her feet into her clothes. He wrapped his towel around him and wriggled out of his trunks, conscious of drying himself between his legs.

'You can turn round now,' he heard her say. Her hair was wet and fuzzy and the dark hairs on her arms stood out.

'What about tomorrow?' he asked.

'I don't know.'

'I won't let it happen again,' he promised.

'You'd better not,' she replied and together they walked back up the steep hill in silence.

'In the afternoon, then,' he said when they reached the top. 'When the tide's coming in.'

'Perhaps. As long as Daddy doesn't catch me out.'

But catch her out he did, a week later, her hair stiff from the salt water, a damp bathing towel tied to the rack above the rear mudguard and the architect of her treachery riding alongside. Her father stepped out from behind the gate and pulled her off, his dark eyebrows and dark moustache joined together by lines of antici- pated anger. He held her by the arm, squeezing it hard. His voice was agitated and clipped, with a curious self-questioning cadence to it.

'You've no sense, girl. Isn't your mother's grave enough that you should want to follow in her footsteps? And where did you get this?' He picked up the bike up from the road.

'I borrowed it.'

'Borrowed it, you say? One horse is not enough for you, then? Never mind what it costs to feed and house a horse and have its feet shorn. You have to have a bicycle as well.'

'No, Daddy, it was just . . .'

'And where did you keep it all the while? Did you hide it from me? Hide it from your own father. Your only parent.'

'No, Daddy, I . . .'

'Borrowed it. Yes, I heard. Borrowed it. Well, well.' He turned on Ned. 'And for every borrower there has to be a lender, does there not, a lender prepared to lend. I presume I have you to thank for lending my daughter this, this, bicycle.' He turned the handle-bars to and fro, as if testing the steering.

'Daddy, this is—'

'No matter that the brake pads are defective and it quite lacks a rear reflector. No matter that these lanes are steep and narrow and riddled with ruts and potholes, such that cause bicycles to buckle and riders to fall, and that unlike the rare times when she chooses to sit upon her horse, here she lacks any protective headgear at all, you thought—'

'It's not his fault, Daddy.' Isobel broke in again. 'I asked for his help, that's all.'

'Asked his help! You might as well have asked him for a broken neck and had done with it.'

Ned stepped off his bike. 'She's been safe with me, I can promise you, Mr van Dielen.' He held out his hand. 'Ned Luscombe, sir.'

Van Dielen gave him a long look. 'Luscombe. I had a man who worked for me once with that name.'

Ned felt relieved. 'My father, sir. He was one of the chippies working here. Laid the floor, I believe. He's not working much now. Lung trouble.'

Van Dielen nodded. 'I thought I recognized the name. Well, Mr Luscombe, let me inform you that from now on your family's name is of only interest to me in that I never want to hear of it again. Particularly when it has the misfortune to have the Christian name Ned placed in front of it. Do I make myself clear? If I catch you near my daughter again I'll put the police on you and have you arrested.'

Tempted though he was, Ned did not confront him with the obvious retort. Isobel put her hand to her mouth, as she had on the boat coming over, and flashing him a quick look of guarded humour, turned away. Ned busied himself with the discarded bicycle to prevent himself from further stoking the man's ire. Two days later she sent him the first of those hurried notes of exhorta-tion, dropped through the letter box, instructing him that he was to be on the beach at six thirty the next day, and because of what had passed they broke into laughter the moment they met and then almost immediately fell silent, because she was where her father had forbidden her to be, with the man he had forbidden her to see, the sound of the swimming sea reminding them of their former conspiracy. They moved towards each other quickly and kissed, and with time running out became lovers without hesitation and without caution, on the soft belly of a damp cave.

'Your father does not like me,' he said, shaking the sand from his clothes.

'He doesn't like anyone much,' she told him lightly, as if it were a small idiosyncrasy, like not eating meat or fearing mice. 'We don't do as we're told.'

'We?'

'Humans. We don't always run to plan.'

'Neither do roads and bridges all the time, I suppose.'

'Yes, but you can mend a road, pull down a bridge. He can work it all out on paper beforehand. We don't obey such laws. We're not predictable that way.'

'Oh, no?' Ned said and pulled her close again.

'Well, some things are,' she agreed. 'Why do you think I wrote you the note? Just to go swimming again?'

For the remainder of his leave the notes came whenever the opportunity to meet arose. There was no real need for them. It made their affair more their own, more fun, that was all. They would meet down by the water lanes or in the abandoned semaphore station where watchers once stood, expecting Napoleon's army, and occasionally, when she was at her most defiant, her most wilful, her most erotic, she would instruct him to present himself at the house, where he would be charged to seek and find her, in the soft clearing in the broad-leaved wild of the back garden, idly flicking through fashion magazines halfway up the stairs, or waiting in her own room, where to his constant agitation they would challenge the restless noise of the blinds with a restless rhythm of their own.

He tried to keep the romance quiet, but it was hard on an island

Guernsey's size. Though his dad thought it was simply holiday skirt he was chasing, Mum knew better. She could tell by the manner in which he parted his hair and walked out of the front door with a clean handkerchief in his pocket every morning that this wasn't a two-week excursion, that this could be for all seasons. She kept quiet, ironing his shirts, brushing down his only jacket with a damp sponge, watching him set off down the lane through the kitchen window, hoping that his heart wouldn't break, hoping that she was worth it. Uncle Albert was the only one who found out. He came across the two of them early one evening. They had their arms locked around each other, hardly able to take one step forward without the propulsion of another blind embrace. Albert was carrying an unwieldy bunch of delphiniums, destined for his wife's grave, and was masked from view until it was too late to hide.

'You sure you can manage that?' Ned called out, embarrassed that his uncle should have caught him out, and Albert, recognizing his employer's niece, wiped his hand on the side of his trousers and gave him a look which asked the same question.

'This is my uncle Albert,' Ned warned her, moving her forward, 'the one I told you about.'

She took his hand.

'It's you who I have to thank for my tummy troubles, I believe,' she admonished, and when Albert looked nonplussed, added, 'The loganberries! Up at the Villa!'

Albert smiled. 'And I thought it was them pesky birds,' he said.

'No. Just me. Ned here will have to arrest me,' and she took hold of Ned's arm and hugged herself against him.

'Looks like it's you who's got him under lock and key!' Albert told her. Ned blushed.

'I have that,' she boasted, adding, 'You won't tell them, will you?'

'Them, miss?'

'Our elders and betters.'

'Nothing to do with me, miss, what you do.'

'Then I shall call you Uncle Albert too,' she promised him, and picking out one long stem for herself, kissed him on the cheek.

'He's a great man,' he told her, as they watched him walk slowly away. 'We used to go rabbit bombing together.'

'Rabbit bombing, what's that?'

'You never do that? Bit of old pipe, a cup of sugar, some weedkiller, shove it down the hole, and boom!'

She put her hand to her mouth. 'That's horrible! The poor rabbits.'

Her horror was genuine. Ned changed the subject. He had told her too much.

His leave was soon over. After he returned to the cramped CID office in Southampton the letters came first from St Peter Port and later from Zurich, where she went for the winter. A week before Christmas they arranged to meet in London, she on her way back home, he on his day off. He waited for her by Eros in clothes bought, like the swimsuit before, especially for the occasion, but the moment he saw her stepping out of a cab, he wished he had not come. His suit was cheap and awkward while her clothes fell about her as free and as light as a summer rain. They were neither sure enough in their affection nor experienced enough as lovers to take themselves to a London hotel and order up a room, but instead repaired to a tea house and sat with their love affair lying broken on the table before them. Theirs had been a holiday romance, nothing more, he the native, she the tourist, despite her claim to the contrary, and it was foolish to pretend or hope otherwise. To hide her discomfort she talked of how she'd just learnt to ski, what fun it was and how he must try it. He wondered whether she knew the gulf she was digging between them. They parted, promising to meet again in St Peter Port for the New Year, but December ended and the old year was washed out and they did not join hands to watch the new one surge in. He went over to Pleinmont with Bernie, and she? why, thanks to Mrs Hallivand's introductions she had made something of a hit that winter, sprinkling her elusive charm over the season's parties like a rare flurry of Guernsey snow.

Coming back from their celebrations, he and Bernie decided to take a New Year dip and hurried down to the bay. It was one of those frozen nights, clear and utterly still, and though they stood on the jetty and dived in, it was all they could do to turn and strike out for the shore before the cold seized their limbs and dragged them down into its liquid heart. As they rubbed themselves down, Bernie pulled out a half-pint of plum brandy and took a swig before passing it over. Up above were the lights of the Villa Pascal, as keen as any lighthouse. At that moment the doors were flung open and they could see, racing along the sloping lawn, four figures with flaming torches in their hands, running round the garden in crazy circles. Three men and a girl whooping and laughing, the men calling her name, imploring her to dance, to kiss them each in turn. 'Come on, Isobel,' Ned heard. 'Forfeit! Forfeit!' and laughing she broke free and ran back in. The men followed, the windows shut. The shrieks and laughter were banished in an instant.

'Someone's looking to have a good New Year,' he said bitterly, and Bernie, watching for a moment, clapped him on the back.

'Us too, Ned. Us too,' and together they walked back to Bernie's house. Ned left the island three days later thinking that he would probably never see her again, that she would marry soon and settle in London or wherever her husband's profession took her, while her father remained a lonely and broken man. Six months later his dad had died. 'Four days. That's all I need,' he had told his superiors, and on the boat over, a small kit bag on his shoulder, he had directed a pair of unprepared holidaymakers to Bernie's mother's guest house. They and he were there still.

*

Ned put up the envelope in his pocket and picked up another handful.

'Well, now,' he said, speaking out loud. 'Let's see what other malicious rumours are abroad this bright and lovely day.'

Three

Captain Zepernick balanced the 78 on his head while Molly reached up and placed the bottle in the centre of the record. With his infectious grin and carefree manner no one would have taken him for the head of Guernsey's Secret Police.

'Shall we dance?' Molly said and held out her arms. Zep put his hands on her tasselled waist and starting to dance, called out, '*Der Wein ist suss, nein?*'

When in mixed company, they spoke English for the most part, for the benefit of the girls, unless it was an obscene comment or to do with military matters, a needless precaution in either case, for most of the girls understood a good deal by now. That was to be expected. What surprised these men, still dressed in their once-feared uniforms, was how quickly the women had embraced their way of life, aping their manners, sharing their interests, even imitating the rhythms of their speech. All the girls spoke English as if they were foreigners themselves; out riding, playing tennis, at the card table; even in the abandonment of the bedroom, those declarations of sexual ardour were announced with the breath of the Fatherland on them. But sometimes the men reverted to their own tongue simply to remind themselves who they were and why they were here. It was so easy to forget. Here were no partisans, no sniper's bullet singing out from behind a wall, no troop trains blown to pieces: at worst just a muttered, sullen acquiescence, and at best the warmth of the Gulf Stream, the round of beaches and the spread of girls on which to exercise one's limbs.

The Captain advanced carefully across the floor, Molly wriggling slowly in his grasp. She leant back and shook her shoulders. The bottle started to rock.

'Take care,' Bohde called out. 'You'll break it.'

Lentsch waved the warning away. 'Never mind the wine,' he urged. 'It's the record you must be careful of. Hold her still, man! Hold her still!'

Molly held out her arms and shimmied in defiance, laughing as the record began to slide forward over the Captain's head.

'Come on, Zep!' she cried. 'Straighten up!'

The bottle crashed to the floor. The record dropped into her outstretched hands. Standing by the door Albert turned and went to fetch a bucket and mop. Molly advanced upon the Major.

'Sorry about that, Gerhard,' she said, holding the record out in front of her. 'Blame Zep, not me. His mind must have been on something else.'

'I am sure of that,' Lentsch told her. 'You make it so hard for all of us.'

They had met at the Casino earlier that evening. Formerly a hotel on the Esplanade, it was now Guernsey's most favoured club, where officers were permitted to entertain civilians. A gaming room could be found at the back, as could a small, unpleasant restaurant. The rooms above, each furnished with a bed, a washbasin and a wooden coat hanger, served primarily as rudimentary quarters for when the drinking had taken too heavy a toll, and at other times for perfunctory and indiscreet sex. Many used it for the former, few the latter. It was not done to be seen coming down the club stairs with a local girl following in your tread. The equilibrium of the island demanded, on the surface at least, that its womenfolk be treated with respect.

The focal point of the club was the long room at the front which overlooked the port and the sea beyond. In the summer, when the windows were thrown open, Lentsch and his friends would sit deep in the leather armchairs, their feet on the window sill, drinking *Sekt* and watching the endless harbour traffic and the determined scurry of civilians, trying to keep their spirits up. But tonight the curtains had been drawn and a fire blazed at the far end. It was comfortable in there. Tankards with their decorated tops hung along the length of the bar, imported beer racked up behind. Pictures of smiling maidens advertising Leica cameras and Junker's water heaters were propped up behind the bar, while the walls were decorated with photographs of units celebrating the comradeship of war, cooking up a rabbit stew outside a Normandy farmhouse, standing atop a K18 outside Dieppe, horseplaying on the boulevards of Paris. Pride of place belonged to gilt-framed reproduction of Padua's *Leda and the Swan*, Leda's shameless nudity stretched high above the fireplace. Those who could drain the club's two-litre glass boot without drawing breath were hoisted aloft to plant their kisses on whatever part of her body they chose, though out of all who had attempted only Zep and a fighter pilot, long since downed, had achieved that honour.

From the raucous laughter that burst forth as he walked in, Lentsch could tell that everyone was determined to put the events of the past month behind them, everyone that is except Sondeführer Bohde, who sat under the portrait, reading some directive or other, his upturned nose twitching in the air. The Captain was there too, standing up at the bar, one foot on the rail, stirring a bowl of ruby-red punch. Watching him, ladle in hand, exhorting a young navy officer to take a cup, it seemed to Lentsch that the Captain grew younger, taller, more handsome and more self-assured by the day. He was what every officer of the new regime aspired to be, a law unto himself, backed by the precedence of naked power and charmed good looks. Last summer he had scandalized Bohde by driving around the island late at night, lights blazing, wearing nothing but a pair of shorts and a cap, Molly and various hangers-on piled in the back, breaking all the curfew, blackout and speeding regulations known to man.

'It's not right,' Bohde had complained over breakfast. 'Here am I, trying to impress upon the population the importance of rules and regulations, and there is the Captain tearing about as if he is on holiday!'

'But he is on holiday,' Lentsch told him. 'We're all on holiday. That's the trouble. We've been here so long it's metamorphosed into a way of life.'

'Well, I'm not,' Bohde had shouted, 'and neither is my blue pencil. I shall write to Headquarters.'

Bohde had thrown down his napkin and, spluttering with impotent rage, stomped off upstairs to sulk. Everyone liked Zep, with his practical jokes and his generosity and his treasonable imitation of Dr Goebbels, who, to Bohde's fury, he had nicknamed Mahatma Propagandhi. Bohde could rail as much as he liked. He couldn't get close to Zep and he knew it.

Seeing Lentsch walk in, Bohde pulled himself up from his chair and trotted over, carrying a sheet of newsprint in his arms as if he had come to show off his first-born. Without asking Lentsch if he had enjoyed his leave, he thrust the precious burden under his nose.

'Tonight's issue,' he announced proudly. 'I have just been putting the finishing touches to the latest episode of *A Journey Through Medieval Germany*. As you can see, I have reached the Imperial city of Frankfurt am Main. With my imaginary knapsack and sturdy companion by my side we sit down at a modest inn and introduce the reader to Goethe and Schiller as well as invoking the glories of the Roman past. Also autobahns. Not bad for five hundred words.'

Lentsch glanced at it quickly.

'The woodcut is very good,' he offered. 'But do you think it wise to talk of this "splendid meal of sausages and hard-boiled eggs"? Most people here haven't seen a decent piece of meat for months.'

Bohde beamed.

'But that's exactly my point, Gerhard. That's what they have to look forward to when the war is won. German culture and plenty of German sausage.'

Lentsch studied Bohde's face to see if he could detect any hint of humour, but Bohde was already on his way back to his seat. It was unfortunate for the island that Bohde was not only responsible for censoring its two newspapers and reading matter, withdrawing books deemed offensive to the German people in general and Him in particular, but also for organizing the variety shows and films for the troops. Frivolity was despised by Bohde. Since his arrival, low comedies, musicals and risqué nightclub turns had been replaced by military bands, lecture slides and *volk* festivals. The illegitimate birth rate had gone up too.

Zep slapped a hand on his shoulder. 'So how was home?'

Lentsch put on the best face he could muster. 'They are learning to live with it,' he said. 'I did not stay all the time there. It was difficult, with Gretchen so close.'

Gretchen was the girl he was to have married, the girl who would have been his passport to promotion. A Party girl with a Party father.

'So you are still determined?'

Lentsch nodded. 'I am still . . . Is she here yet?'

Zep shook his head.

'You think I am a fool.' Lentsch issued an observation rather than asked a question.

Zep smiled at his friend. 'No, just foolish.' He waved his hand in the air. 'All this. It cannot be permanent. Even we cannot conquer Paradise.'

Molly was shown in wearing slinky russet red. Lentsch couldn't recall a time when he had seen her wearing something ordinary. She would be better liked if she did. Long and cold, that was Molly, perfectly poised, with white tapering hands and a hard questioning mouth. Slim, almost breastless, there was not a man in the room who was not hypnotized by her supple, dangerous beauty, who did not long to chance fate and hold her in a deadly embrace, to kiss poison's mouth and survive. Lentsch could see why the Captain had kept her for so long. She set him off perfectly; carefree, hedonistic, without a thought to the fault line that ran alongside her charmed life. She would jump it when the time came. And if she didn't make it to the other side, well to hell with it. That seemed to be her attitude. She had been with Zep for a little over a year and, generals and visiting admirals notwithstanding, ruled their social gatherings with wit, ruthlessness and sexual bravado, seeing off any competition with a lightning, almost erotic, ferocity. Being attached to the Captain had given her power once she could have only married into and she revelled in its enveloping authority. 'I blitzkrieged them all, darling,' she had boasted once. 'The Tennis Club girls, the bridge set wives, the Saturday morning golfers. Now if they want any social life, any fun, they do it through me. There's a price to everything in this world.' Tonight she had brought a friend, Veronica Vaudin, who, she claimed, 'was just dying to meet you all', which usually meant someone who, if not single, had become available and was looking for a protector. Handing her coat over to one of the stewards, Veronica bounced across the floor if she was made out of India rubber. She was a compact young woman exuding a cheerful domestic good health, with strong, muscular shoulders and a luxuriant bosom. The Major wondered idly where she had been these past two years; working her way up the ranks, perhaps. She clearly wasn't from any of the better families, she was too familiar, too forward, too ... too obvious. Veronica, Molly told them, was a leading light in Guernsey's theatrical community. Since the occupation, amateurs such as she had turned semi-professional, and now she was a regular performer at the Gaumont. Veronica held out a bare bangled arm and grinned up at his patient face.

'You should come and see our next production,' she said lightly, brushing back her flaming red hair with a brightly painted finger. '*April Frolics*, it's called. Vocalism, dancing, nigger minstrels. Just the thing to ease your troubles.'

Lentsch nodded politely. He remembered her well. Two Christmases ago, as a goodwill gesture, the Feldkommandantur had decided to fund the Christmas pantomime given by the Guernsey Amateur Dramatic and Operatic Society. Lentsch had been the guest of honour. Marjorie Hallivand, in her capacity as treasurer, had sat next to him.

'This play,' she had informed him, in a tone that reminded him of his mother, 'is a particularly *English* affair, as much a part of our culture as the *Just So Stories* or *Alice in Wonderland*. But whereas Alice has to burrow underground, here the children fly across the rooftops.'

Lentsch had nodded earnestly. He was familiar with those tales of perilous childhood, of boys and girls lost in forests, captured by witches, devoured by wolves.

'To the moon?' he ventured.

'To Neverland. Where Peter Pan lives.'

'Ah, Pan. Half goat, half man.'

'A boy,' she said reproachfully, 'though he is always played by a girl. It's a tradition of British theatre. You'll see.'

The opening scene had been set in a children's bedroom with huge bay windows that looked out upon a scene of huddled rooftops. It was curiously reminiscent of his own childhood bedroom, his bed on one side, his sister's on the other. Gazing out on to the badly hand-painted backcloth it seemed almost as real as the view he had grown up with, his grandfather's army trunk by the window, the bricked stable yard below, the surround of fields, and beyond, in the patient distance, the hidden rustlings of the marshland, wet and secret and spiked with reeds, where he and his father and would lie waiting for bloody battle to rage; the baying dogs, the smoking guns, the flurried splashes of the thick green water, and at the end, the winged custodians of this elusive paradise laid out in blood-spotted ranks on the soft green bank of moss. But however far the two of them had paddled into the still waters of the marsh's domain, however many birds they downed or wounded and watched spiralling out of sight, it was clear to him that they never managed to breach the marsh's true sanctum nor exhaust the dazzling plumed legions that rose in chorus to protect it. Thus he had grown up believing that he lived close to a fairy land, a place possessed of both a magical past and a visionary future, from where men blessed with supernatural powers would rise up through the mist to capture him and take him back to their watery redoubt, an impregnable, inviolable fortress, where some hard-won glory reigned in a state of permanent ecstasy. He lived with the possibility, nay the need, of transformation and recognized the demands that would be made by whoever had the will to wield such a transcendental sword. A leader! A visionary! A man blessed with powers that went far beyond those held by ordinary men. He existed, of that he was sure. He had always existed. In earlier times he had been called King Arthur, Siegfried, and come the future He would take on other names, hold other courts, fight other battles. For the moment He lay dormant, waiting to be woken in times of utter crisis, when the world had descended into chaos. There was, Lentsch knew, a heavy price to be paid before admittance into such exalted company; much to learn and much to sacrifice. In times of doubt, when the world did indeed appear irretrievably doomed, he would open up the old trunk in the now abandoned nursery, and take out the book their nana used to read to them, *Struwwelpeter*, and look at the pictures of unworthy children engulfed in fire, their thumbs snipped off by the man with flaming orange hair, his huge gleaming scissors dripping bright with their fresh and foolish blood. 'The door flew open and in he ran, the great long-legg'd scissor man.' Such cruel power! Such inspiring terror!

Lentsch had sat in the dark and rolled his thumbs together, waiting for this Peter Pan. He could not understand why he had to be played by a woman but when she swung through the bedroom window, clad in a tunic of brown and green, he knew the reason. It was a typically British affair, an erotic fantasy based on denial and repression, where the body's natural beauty had been gagged and hidden from view. He studied the girl's form intently as she began to stride about the stage aping the thrust of virility with what she took to be a male stance, hands on hips, legs apart, head up. She was a rider, he deduced, with rider's muscle in her flanks and long hours in the saddle giving spread to her rear. After searching for something (he could not quite determine what), she fell asleep. Lentsch was just about to ask Mrs Hallivand to explain, when another figure thundered in after him waving a tinsel wand. There was no ambiguity as to her sex.

'That's Tinkerbell,' Marjorie Hallivand whispered. 'A fairy.'

Lentsch tried not to laugh.

'A little . . .' he gestured carefully with his hands, '. . . full for a fairy, don't you think?'

Marjorie placed her hand on his arm. 'According to the author, Tinkerbell is slightly inclined to embonpoint.'

'Embonpoint?'

'Generosity of the bosom. Veronica is simply made for the part.' She sniffed. 'A little overenthusiastic, our Veronica. But she means well.'

'Ah.'

'But we have some nicely brought up girls here as well,' she emphasized, like a guide describing a favoured resort, a claim she would not have made so lightly had she foreseen the change of circumstance the next two years would bring. 'Most of the girls here are very *natürlich*, very slim. It was a holiday resort you know, before . . .' Her voice trailed off.

And will be one day again, according to Bohde, Lentsch had felt like telling her. After England had fallen and the war in the East concluded, this would be where tired soldiers of the Reich could come and recoup their strength. Guernsey would become a giant holiday camp, with beaches to bathe in and horses and nice slim girls to ride on. It was all nonsense, of course. England was not going to fall. Not now. Guernsey was Germany's island of dreams. Neverland.

Mrs Hallivand had turned and, lifting the coat from her lap, revealed a small box of chocolates.

'I've been saving them up for a special occasion,' she confessed. 'I know it sounds silly, but I feel like I'm at a first night at the opera.'

She opened the lid and peeled back the crinkly black paper. Lentsch floated his hand across the three rows, pretending to choose one to his liking. There was an increasing air of intimacy about Marjorie which he found disturbing. Though he had taken all that was hers, her house, her furniture, the source of her family's fortune, and though on clear evenings she would sit by her narrow stone window and hear her husband's enemies drinking their way through his wine cellar, it was clear that for all that Marjorie Hallivand enjoyed his company. They were of the same class, after all, shared many of the same interests. He remembered her expression of relief mingled with admiration when he had first stepped into the Villa's library and remarked on the three Russell Flints hanging on the walls, two portraits of gypsy women bathing and a landscape.

'Surely they suffer too much light here,' he had said, putting out his hand as if to protect them.

'That's what I've been telling Maurice for years,' she admitted, standing next to him. 'The middle one is Northumberland, you know. On the east coast.'

'Ah, the east coast. I sailed there once. Norfolk. With my father.'

'I have another nude of his upstairs,' she told him. 'Smaller. I don't suppose I could take it with me?'

Lentsch had carried it over that very afternoon, wrapped in sacking, and had spent an hour with her while they found the best place to hang it. Standing back they looked at the young woman's body with detached frankness.

'He gets the texture of her skin so very well,' she ventured. 'The fullness of her young flesh, almost aching to be touched. It is difficult, to get that feeling.'

The Major shifted in his shoes, determined not to be embarrassed.

'The breasts are a little too stylized, don't you think? A little too perfect, a little too ...'

'Pert?'

'Exactly.'

'Young girls tend to be like that, though, especially the models he used. I knew her, you know. Quite a heartbreaker in her day. Lovers by the score. Of course, in those days, that was what Paris was for.'

'Paris?'

'It's where I learnt about life, Major, where I learnt how to live it. You know it?'

'Certainly I know it. After Berlin, Paris is my favourite city.'

Mrs Hallivand clasped her hands. 'It's so long since . . . You must tell me all about it,' she determined. 'And in return I shall tell you all about . . . all about the House!'

Lentsch did not understand.

'Hauteville,' Mrs Hallivand explained. 'Victor Hugo's old house. I am a trustee.'

She had taken him there straight away. The interior had been maintained exactly as it had been left it in '78 – dark and heavy like a museum, with an echoing silence embedded in the walls that only long-stilled buildings can maintain. Threading their way through, Lentsch felt as if he had landed upon a treasure island and been led to a hidden chest which, when opened, revealed jewel upon jewel. She showed him the Gobelin tapestries, the table belonging to Charles II, the fire screen made by Madame de Pompadour. She led him before the great bed built for Garibaldi, but never used, and invited him to lie on its untouched length. Together they climbed up to the small glass house at the top where in each of the two corners facing the sea stood a little table where the author had written, always standing. Lentsch could hardly bring himself to speak.

'This is wonderful,' he exclaimed.

'Isn't it.'

'Wonderful. You could do anything here. Write books, paint, rule the world.'

'Oh, we don't want any rulers of the world here,' Mrs Hallivand had chided him. 'We've got enough of those already, haven't we?' She caught her breath, startled by her own indiscretion. 'Perhaps I shouldn't have said that.'

'No, no,' he assured her. 'You can say anything you like to me. But there are others, though, to whom you should be more circumspect.'

'Circumspect.' She repeated the word. 'Are you as good with your own language as you are with ours?'

Lentsch would not let the compliment deflect him from his warning.

'My fellow officers, Captain Zepernick for instance.'

'But he seems such a charming fellow,' she said. 'So polite.'

Lentsch shook his head.

'He is not?' she questioned.

'Oh, yes, he is,' Lentsch assured her. 'But don't let that deceive you. The Captain is from the new ruling class. He belongs to a different party than you or I. He is good company, but everything that takes place must do so on his own terms. If you are in his circle you are safe. If not . . .'

'I never ask to be admitted into circles,' Mrs Hallivand told him, regaining the dignity of her class. 'I accept or I do not. Now,' she said, waving her hand around the room, 'what are we going to do about all this?'

The Major had hesitated. There were favours to be gained here to be sure, ones that could carry him far beyond these waters. He could have the place stripped within the hour, packed and crated and shipped off to Karinhall with his compliments. He would finish the war under the protection of the crown prince, drinking and hunting, taking his pleasure while others died. He closed his mind to the suggestion almost in the instant it was made. There would be no collection made from this plate. No visitors either. He would keep it hidden, locked away for as long as it proved possible. Only Mrs Hallivand would be allowed in, once a week, to clean and dust and to ensure that the building stood in good repair. Otherwise an imposition of quarantine. It would become a symbol of the Occupation's benign intent.

A week later he had presented her with an inventory of the whole place and invited her to the first of their Sunday lunches, where they would sit opposite each other, in a strange parody of host and guest, both amused by Albert's uncertainty which to serve first, and talk of the worlds they had left behind; she, of life as an embassy child, her wild years in Paris, the world war death of her first husband: he of his father's estate outside the old town of Celle, the cold turret high up in one corner, where he would stand motionless, waiting for the calling geese to fly past, and later, of his life as a German officer. Books, music, tales of adventure and indiscretions, she revelled both in the telling and the listening. As a diplomat's daughter she understood the laws by which he was governed, the nature of the oaths he had taken, the unforgiving principle of duty. She moved in the same knowing circles, had witnessed the same peccadilloes, the same falls from grace. She could outmatch him in tales of ambassadors and heads of state. And when the brandy had taken hold and Albert had retired, he could confide in her, talk of his home in Hamburg and the fear he held for his mother and sister, the fear he held for Germany.

At the end of each evening he would escort her back to the lodge and stand in the porch while they wound down the last conversation of the night, their spirits freshened by the night air. She was drawn to him, he knew it, and these occasions, as she hovered by the studded door, turning back for one last word, or stretching up for that final quick peck on his cheek, he sensed that it only needed one stay of his hand, one murmur from his lips, for her to fall into his arms. He found the idea both absurd and disquieting. She was attractive, there was no doubt about that; bright, vivacious, determined never to be shocked or outwitted, slim and fit, slightly given to bone, with those quick bright movements that are the hallmark of the petite, but as far as he was concerned she was attractive only as a youngish aunt might be – untouchable – bearing scars of a sexual history fashioned in a different age, and her insistence on this coquettish intimacy he found increasingly discomforting. To embrace Mrs Hallivand, feel her lonely lips seeking his, to undress her, to be present when that repressed passion had died back once more, would only cause them both intense embarrassment and regret later on, even though there were times, at the end of a particularly enjoyable evening, when he half desired it himself. So he flirted with her politely, always perfectly groomed, always exaggeratedly correct, and she, sitting at the end of the table, matching him drink for drink, tale for tale, argument for argument, followed his movements, his eyes, the corner of his mouth, the dance of his hands, with undisguised pleasure.

'I am so glad about the war!' she had once confided. 'It's the best thing that has happened to me on this island, and I don't mind who knows it.'

'Marjorie, this is treasonable talk,' he warned her, amused and flattered by her outburst. 'You mustn't let Bohde hear you. He'll make you put it in writing, splash it all over the *Evening News.*'

Mrs Hallivand waved him away. 'I wouldn't mind! You've no idea what it was like beforehand, the company I had to keep. Men who wouldn't know Stendhal from Stalin, wives whose idea of a social gathering was some dreadful little drinks do with cheap punch, meat-paste sandwiches and pineapple chunks stuck on cocktail sticks.'

'But surely your husband . . .'

'A seducer in a stuffed shirt.'

'I'm sorry.'

'Don't be. It took him off my hands. It wasn't the seductions that really grated, rather his choice. If I'd done the same at least it would have been for someone worthwhile. Not that there was much chance of that happening here. More life in one of our tomatoes. God, I was half asleep before you came. You've woken me up, Gerhard. I'll not be able to go back to sleep again.'

That first Christmas pantomime, Mrs Hallivand's face had been lit up with barely contained excitement, her lips following every line, her hands clasped together whenever a joke or special effect hit its target. She held on to his arm, laughed behind her handkerchief, patted herself under her breasts, as if the thrill of it all were enough to make her faint. She stuck another chocolate into her mouth and without looking, reached over and popped one into his mouth. He was astonished at her boldness. Was that why he had been invited? Outside he could hear the sound of soldiers marching past and boats hooting in the harbour, but for the audience it was as if that world had ceased to exist. Yet Lentsch was not slow to see that for this production Neverland had taken on a very Guernsey-like aspect, with its pretty painted backdrop of an old castle overlooking a tree-lined coast. The pirates, clearly the villains of the piece, judging by the boos and hisses that greeted their every appearance, were of an uncharacteristically military bent. There was something peculiarly British about the crocodile too, not simply in the bowler hat it had tied on its head, but in the manner in which it managed to devour large numbers of these unwanted brigands at regular and increasingly popular intervals. Trust Marjorie to use her self-assured arrogance to orchestrate this display of theatrical defiance. He was glad he had seen it before Bohde, though. Bohde would have closed the show and slapped her down with a hefty fine.

It was only after the play had been going for a half-hour, as Peter Pan swung out across a paper lagoon, that he realized who the young woman was. Lentsch leant over to Marjorie and whispered: 'That girl. Who is she?'

'That?' She turned and faced him full on. 'Just my niece Isobel. Quite the silliest girl in the island. Doesn't know one end of a book from the other.'

'Your niece? I am sure I met her, last winter, while on leave. In Switzerland.'

He had been jumping off a ski lift and had slipped badly, swearing loudly as he fell. Sprawled on the ground, he had looked up to see a hand reaching out.

'Keep your knees bent,' she had told him slowly, shaking her head, taking him for the novice he was not. 'Glide,' and with that she had turned and pushed off down the slope. He would have liked to have followed her, but he was with a party of his own. It didn't matter. That night, in the hotel, he had walked into the lounge bar and spotted her sitting in the corner with a group of other young women, gazing out of the huge window which looked out upon the Jungfrau. He had gone over and introduced himself and asked, by way of thanks, if he might be allowed to buy her dinner. Though her eyes told him that she would have liked to accept, her face travelled in disappointed explanation to where an older woman sat, watching her every move.

'I would probably get expelled,' she said.

'In that case I shall have to kidnap you,' he said, determined to offer his charm for capture. 'It would be a good to be court-martialled for such a crime.'

She began to blush, the glow stealing over her as soft a pink as the setting sun sweeping across the distant mountain.

'Perhaps we might meet on the slopes tomorrow?' he offered. 'I promise only to fall in your arms,' but again she denied him, saying that this night was their last. For a brief instant, as she lowered her eyes on those words, he had hopes, but then he heard her companions giggle and, with the older woman sitting in the corner, he knew that it would not happen, and that perhaps he did not wish it either.

'I am sorry,' he said, 'to meet you at the end of your holiday,' and she, safe in the knowledge that she was immune to his advances but quite prepared to flirt, replied, 'I am not on holiday. I am at school.'

He took the bait readily enough.

'I thought all schoolgirls wore uniforms,' he mocked in a deliberate tone of seduction.

'Uniforms are for children and grown men playing silly games. Not grown women. We have better things to do.'

'In our country,' he said, 'women have only three things. *Kinder, Kirche und Küche*. Children, Church and kitchen.'

She gave a little shudder.

'I don't think I would like to be a German woman,' she said, 'if that's all they do. Must be terrible for them, poor things.'

He shook his head.

'It is a good time for us now. There was too much bad things in the world. Too much . . .' he rubbed his thumb against his fingers, 'greed from the bosses, too little work for the ordinary man. Too much uncertainty. Capitalism. Communism. That is all finished now. We work as one. The women too.'

She glanced back at the chaperone. 'You sound like our Miss Gatting. She's taking us there next term.'

'To Germany?'

'Yes.'

'May I ask where?'

'Munich.'

'Munich! It is where I am stationed.'

He had given her his address, but by the time he returned to his barracks he had forgotten all about her. And here she was again, swinging across the stage in black stockings and bells, with a purple cap upon her head.

'You met Isobel?' Mrs Hallivand sounded slightly put out.

'I know. It is so strange. I am sure it is her. Perhaps you could invite her to one of our lunches.'

Mrs Hallivand looked doubtful. 'Her father is very protective. Before the war I would have said too protective. But now?'

Lentsch waved away her objection. 'No, no. I would like to meet her. Introduce me after the performance.' His voice was drowned out by another burst of applause. Another pirate had been eaten. He lifted his programme in the air. 'And Mrs Hallivand.'

'Yes?'

'After today no more riding boots on the pirates. No more arms in the air as they go under.'

But that night, behind the stage, Peter Pan had led him to Neverland too, and like the lost boys whose hands he shook so solemnly at the curtain's call, he never wanted it to change. Standing at the foot of the garden, looking down on the wheel of gulls calling over the swollen sea, at times he could feel himself wishing that the war might never end. Yes, he missed his homeland and the beat of his birthright, yet every journey he took home was made in fear, not simply because of the danger, or the irrevocable signs of destruction taking hold in Germany's soul, but fear for what might happen here in his absence. For unhappily Guernsey was not isolated from the world's misfortune. It lay upon this turbulent sea, soaking up the waters of war as quickly as a sponge. Three weeks he had been away. Three weeks. A lot could happen in Neverland over three weeks. Parties, chance meetings, a crocodile's jaw quickly snapping.

★

He shook Veronica's hand. The bangles on her arm clanked discordantly.

'I am delighted to meet you,' he told her. She dropped her eyes and gave a little curtsy, which embarrassed him. Her embonpoint was certainly getting a good airing tonight. Zep, unable to ignore his natural inclination, clicked his heels and bowed low in order to take a closer look. Lentsch could see his nostrils flare as they approached the landing zone. Molly stared ahead, furious. Poor Molly, for all her sculptured poise nothing could disguise the fact that she was helplessly in love. When her guard was up, the hard quality of her character surfaced and split her haughty composure like fissures on a rock. Lentsch had told Isobel to warn her that Zep was here to have a good time and didn't give a jot for the lot of them, but if she had said anything Molly hadn't taken any notice, or couldn't help herself. And why not? Zep would be kind and generous for as long as it suited him. As Molly had once said, when they had been arguing over the dangers of fraternization: 'Well, what else are we supposed to do? Stay in purdah until it's all over? What's the point of that? All the good ones will have been snapped up by then.'

'Yes, Molly, but what if we lose?' he had asked.

She looked at him as if he had blasphemed.

'Then I'd have to pack my bags and skedaddle,' she said. 'But you're not going to. Not if you play your cards right.'

'Not if He plays our cards right,' Lentsch had corrected.

Molly stood on her heels and kissed him a little too near his mouth. At that moment the huge boom of a gun sounded, very near, momentarily silencing the crowd. Someone drew back the curtains. Another made a nervous joke. Molly had clutched at Lentsch's arm.

'What in Heaven's name was that?' she said, staying close. She wasn't frightened but she made use of it.

'Battery practice,' Lentsch told her. 'Miles away.' Molly made no attempt to move away.

'I thought Isobel might be with you,' Lentsch said, unlocking himself from her grasp. Molly took the hint and backed off.

'You'll have to wait, Gerhard,' she warned, tapping him on the lips. 'Trouble at home.'

Molly grabbed hold of Veronica's hand and pulled her across the room. Dr Mueller arrived, armed with a fresh batch of nurses from Bremen, their noses red with cold. Their first time abroad and loving every minute.

'I hope you have brought your pyjamas,' Zepernick told them as he handed out the steaming glass cups. 'Otherwise no admittance to the party later on.'

Mueller ushered his flock over to where a group of officers sat. The English girls watched with guarded interest. While they regarded German men as their equals and allies, they looked upon the women as the enemy, inferior, untrustworthy and a threat, though usually there was little cause for alarm. There was a definite pecking order here, based on rank and class, that applied to both sexes and both nationalities. As a rule the German officers preferred English girls. German women, here as nurses, translators and administrators, were strictly temporary; 'cannon fodder', the soldiers called them. It was not unusual for a man with strong appetites to use a whore for immediate gratification, a *mädchen* for weekends in France or an evening at the Regal watching a German film and a long-standing Guernsey girl who could give him hope and stability and a sense that somehow the war had already achieved a purpose.

Bohde stood up and shook hands with each of the nurses in turn. Lentsch couldn't hear what was being said, but Bohde appeared to be explaining something, quickly and earnestly. Some expressed surprise, others giggled; one simply walked away. Most of the them turned to Mueller for confirmation. Bohde started writing their names down in a little notebook he produced from his pocket.

'What the hell's he up to?' Lentsch said. 'He's surely not asking them all out.'

'Typical,' Zep mocked. 'I must try it out myself. Seduction by name, rank and number.'

The evening was starting. The room was filling up. A voice called out for the glass boot. Lentsch looked over. A young captain from artillery wanting to show off to his new chums. No chance. Someone started playing an accordion. Another started to sing. Lentsch turned to Zep and shouting above the noise, told him the dread news.

'Ernst wants to get his hands on the place.'

Zep looked amused. 'What's wrong? Worried he'll catch a dose in one of his own brothels?'

Lentsch shook his head. 'Not here. The Villa. I came over with him on his plane.'

Zep nodded. Lentsch wasn't surprised. Zep knew most things. Underneath his bonhomie lay a still and watchful mind, poised to strike without a moment's warning, though what aroused Zep to this action Lentsch found hard to determine: duty, irritation, boredom? Or was it simply the need to devour – like a man's need for regular sex? Certainly Zep's appearance after dispatching one of his victims was almost post-coital; happier, fresher, more relaxed. If anyone could deny Ernst his goal it would be him.

'He made a point of telling me,' Lentsch went on. 'If we don't find room for him, he'll try and get rid of us. And if that doesn't work he'll concrete the place over. Just to ruin it.'

Zep seemed unconcerned.

'Well, why don't we accommodate him?' he suggested. 'We could always get rid of Bohde. Ernst can't be any worse than him.'

Lentsch disagreed.

'I'm not so sure,' he argued. 'Bohde maybe a bore, but he's quiet enough.'

Zep snorted in derision, but Lentsch was not to be put off. 'We don't know what Ernst might get up to,' he insisted. 'Isn't there any dirt on him you could dredge up? Stop him in his tracks.'

Zep ignored him and looked around the room. Molly was introducing Veronica to the artillery officer, holding his arm while she accepted a light for her cigarette. Zep's face hardened for an instant, and then he asked the first thing that came into his head, simply to regain the momentum of conversation.

'Good flight?'

Lentsch shrugged his shoulders, but, remembering the landing, said, 'Tell me. Are you aware that civilians are trying to undermine the safety of the airport?'

Zep grinned. 'You mean the runway?'

Lentsch nodded. 'Ernst muttered some nonsense about grass growing overnight.'

Zep nodded. 'The groundsmen have been cutting the grass extra close so the wheels find it hard to grip. So we've had . . .' He banged his hands together.

Lentsch was worried.

'Shouldn't something be done about it? That's exactly the sort of thing Ernst would report back like a shot.'

Zep shook his hand.

'I let them cut it like that when nothing important is coming in. We have lengthened the runway anyway. That way they think they are doing something for their country. They keep their self-respect and in all other matters regarding the airport do as they're told. That way everyone is happy.'

Lentsch was unconvinced. 'But surely it might encourage them to do something worse.'

Zep disagreed. 'Never. They know what would happen if they did.' He sliced his throat. 'The lot of them.' He banged his glass down. 'Come on, Gerhard. Tomorrow we think of how to put a spoke in Ernst's wheel and other matters. Tonight we drink and make love.'

They had finally got back to the Villa at eleven o'clock. Albert

was in the drawing room standing guard over the food – two
rhubarb pies, a plate of corned beef sandwiches, three cold chickens
and a bowl of baked potatoes with a jar of gooseberry jam by their
side. Before the girls trooped off to the billiard room to change,
they had all crowded round stuffing themselves as fast as they
could. Lentsch went up to his room to fetch his round of cheese. As
he came down the stairs he saw Veronica slip one of the potatoes
into her handbag. Encouraged by her success she leant in and
grabbed a chicken leg. Stepping back she raised the meat to her
mouth before letting it fall. As her hand moved to close the clasp,
she turned suddenly to where Lentsch stood, watching.

'Whoops,' she said. 'Greasy fingers.' She picked it out. 'You
want?'

Lentsch put his cheese down on a small table and took it from
her without a word. Perfume rose off her like tar in a heat haze.
He held the leg out to her half-open mouth. Leaning forward,
she bit and wrenched and chewed as he held it firm, and then,
defiantly, bit again. Her lips were wet and fat and without guile.

'Here,' he said, handing her the cheese. 'Before the others get to
it,' and he turned, so that he would not know, one way or the
other, what she might do with it.

Out in the hall again he picked up the phone and gave the
operator Isobel's number. He let it ring for a minute or more. There
was still no reply. Bohde came down the stairs smelling of hair oil.

'Girlfriend flown the coop?' Bohde asked in malicious innocence.

Lentsch changed the subject.

'What was all that about, back at the Casino,' he asked, 'with all
those nurses Mueller brought?'

'Ah.' Bohde gathered himself up. 'It's to do with my research.'

'Research?'

'I am making a study of the German breast. In art and life. I
have asked them if I may not take certain measurements. They are
not only nurses, you know. They were all in the League of Girls.'

'And they've agreed?'

Bohde nodded.

'As young Germans with a healthy outdoor look on life, they understand the purpose behind my project. It is nothing to do' – he raised his eyebrows as if he had found some pornographic postcards hidden under Lentsch's bed – 'with smut. It will all be carried out under proper conditions. I have promised them that when applying the tape measure I will wear gloves. Warmed beforehand, of course.'

'Of course.' Lentsch couldn't stop himself from smiling.

Bohde retreated a step to gain height.

'I knew you would poke fun, Gerhard,' he shrilled. 'Which is why my findings will not be carried out here. Major Ernst has very kindly lent me the use of his garden. It is very private there. He is lending me some of his foreigns for comparison, too.'

Lentsch felt a sudden chill in the air.

'Ernst? What's Ernst got to do with it?'

Bohde's smile was the epitome of complacency. 'He is as committed to the protection of the German form as I am. He was one of the key speakers in the Naked and Education Congress of '38. Together we hope . . .' He faltered.

'Yes?'

'To further the cause of Naturism. This . . .' he swung his arms out, 'could be its home.'

Lentsch was appalled. Ernst had got one foot in the house already.

'I didn't know you two were so well acquainted,' he said coldly.

'We have much in common. This afternoon he came back specially to chair an illustrated discussion on communal nudity and the pubescent male child.' Bohde thrust himself forward again. 'The genitals,' he said, patting the front of his trousers, 'once they become hidden under woollens and such, find it difficult to distinguish between that . . .' he nodded in the direction of the drawing room, 'and the correct thing.'

'What's wrong with the women here?' Lentsch protested. 'There're all white, Anglo-Saxon.'

Bohde looked at him smugly.

'But they are not German, Major, and therefore, whatever their "credentials", they cannot be of the same quality. If this is true of art and music, which it certainly is, it must be true of life itself. You should come to one of our lectures. They're really most instructive.' He sidled past into the drawing room.

It was one o'clock now and the party showed no signs of flagging. Veronica wore plain pink flannelettes while Molly was dressed in a pair of purple silk pyjamas tucked into a spare pair of Zep's riding boots. Bohde lay in an armchair with one eye open, watching Wedel dance with one of the few nurses who, despite Zep's strictures, was still dressed in her uniform. Of Isobel there was no sign. Lentsch sat disconsolately on the sofa, his head swimming with an evening's drink and music he had not played to her. He turned to Veronica. He wasn't sure what he wanted now. Hilde Hildebrand's voice came on the gramophone, her low confessional soaring into that empty space of helplessness. *Liebe Ist Ein Geheimnis*. Love is a Secret.

'Isobel is not coming,' he announced. He felt he had said it before, but it needed to be said again. 'I had things to give her,' he continued. 'Records of Teddy Stauffer and Zacharius.' He stopped for a moment. He had so looked forward to talking to her and now she was not there the conversation was bursting out of him whether he liked it or not. Perhaps this woman would understand.

'Zacharius is our own Stephane Grappelli,' he told her slowly. 'He was taught by Kreisler, you know.'

Veronica did not know, nor had she ever heard of Kreisler, but she nodded all the same. All she understood was that Lentsch was feeling sorry for himself. If she managed to lift him out of his lovesick gloom, who knows, he might forget Isobel altogether. At times like this a girl's fortune could change overnight if she picked the right moment. But she would not do anything yet. First he had to sink a little deeper into despair.

'My father has many Kreisler records,' he continued wistfully. 'Brahms, Beethoven...' He looked across to where Bohde lay before raising his voice. 'Even Mendelssohn.' He lurched back onto his original tack. 'Do you know, Veronica, the leave before last I saw Django Reinhardt. I was this close.'

He stretched his hand from his nose to hers. She leant back and rolled her pyjama top back up. Lentsch saw she had managed to insert a glass bead into the dimpled flesh of her belly button. Veronica caught his stare.

'Do you ever go dancing?' she asked, sticking her leg out and wriggling her toes. 'I bet you know some wonderful clubs.'

He brightened at the recollection of them.

'I do!' he exclaimed, as if they could hop in a taxi and be taken to one there and then. 'Paris, Berlin, Munich.'

'Before all this happened that's what I wanted to do, branch out into clubs. Dancing and singing.'

'Singing?' A note of hope rose in his voice. He could understand so little tonight. 'You are a singer too?'

'Light operatic,' she explained. 'Of course it would have to be different for clubs. Different clientele. More sophisticated.'

Now he remembered. She was a singer! He beamed at her. 'There is a song named after you, you know,' he said, clutching her hand. 'Such a song!'

Veronica did know. Nearly every German who tried to put his hand up her skirt had told her that there was a song named after her.

'You don't say,' she said. 'Do tell.'

'A very famous song. "*Gruss und Kuss Veronika*".'

'I don't know if I want to be grussed. Even by an officer.' It had always raised a laugh in the past. Lentsch tried to ignore the flutter of her eyelids.

'No, no,' he insisted, pointing across the room, momentarily glad to evade her eyes, 'I have it somewhere. You must hear it.' He lurched across the room, bumping into Zep and Molly locked into a slow embrace. Squatting down by the radiogram he started to leaf through his box of records. It was hard for him to lift each one out and focus on the label, harder still for him to prevent them slipping out of their sleeves. Finally he found what he was looking for and held it up triumphantly.

'Veronica! "*Gruss und Kuss*",' he called out. 'You listen.'

Ignoring Zep and Molly's protests he changed the record and hurried back. As the music started he took up Veronica's hand again and began waving it in time to the music, lost in its jaunty refrain. Veronica started to hum along. It was that sort of tune. Lentsch was entranced.

'You know it already! You may keep it if you like.'

She squeezed his hand. 'I'd love to, not that I deserve such a present.'

'Isobel is not present.' Lentsch blurted out. 'She should be here.'

'Well, I'm here.'

'Of course you are. Everyone is here, all the *Swingheimes* of Guernsey.' He waved his hand across the room, knowing before he opened his mouth again that he was about to speak foolishly. 'You are very lovely. Like a picture. I would like to paint you. Perhaps tomorrow?'

Veronica held her breath. She could push it a little further and suggest that she stay the night, or thank him for a perfectly lovely evening and go home. She would have liked to stay the night, if for no other reason than to have a good look upstairs and a decent breakfast tomorrow, but she had the feeling that in his present condition come the morning he would regret it. She should leave and wait for him to call on her. The trouble was he was so drunk he probably wouldn't remember asking her, but there was just a chance. It was worth the risk. If he and Isobel were splitting up . . . There were not many better prizes on the island than Major Gerhard Lentsch. She patted his hand.

'Of course you can. One more glass of champagne and then you must get Herbert to drive me home.'

'Helmut,' he corrected. He struggled to pull himself upright. 'Champagne and brandy. That's what I need. Is what everybody needs.' He raised his voice. 'Wedel, bring me the bottles. Veronica is having another drink and then she has promised to dance for us. A dance like they do in Turkey. All belly.' He patted her stomach.

'Gerhard, darling,' she said, sufficiently pleased with herself. 'I shall do no such thing.'

Lentsch's face grew serious. 'Then you shall walk home without a pass and be arrested and brought before the magistrate. And I shall instruct him to be very severe. A fine of what . . . what do you think, Bohde?' he called out. 'Bohde!'

Though he had drunk enough to be unable to utter another coherent word until morning, Bohde had enough training to recognize the voice of a superior officer. He dragged himself out of his slumber and began to blink.

'We need your advice,' Lentsch explained. 'What do you think the punishment should be for a young English woman out on the streets after curfew, dressed only in her very finest bedclothes, and,' he shouted, deciding to let the room know her little secret, 'with this in her satchel?' He snatched her bag and brought out the cheese. 'See?'

Hearing the others laugh Bohde puzzled for a moment, concerned that if there was a joke to be had, it should not be at his own expense.

'Ask him,' he said slowly, eyeing the swaying couple with obvious distaste. 'Black marketeers are his concern.' Zep, his head buried in Molly's neck, elected not to hear.

'There's no point in asking him,' Lentsch argued. 'He's worse than all of them put together. As far as the Captain is concerned there should be no curfew at all for girls over sixteen. Isn't that right, Zep?'

Zep looked up. 'No curfew for good-looking girls,' he countered. 'The rest should be deported to Alderney.' He laughed. 'Ugly girls for the Todts and the turnip-eaters. Pretty girls for us. An island of nothing but pretty girls.' He turned his attention back to Molly, opening her jealous mouth with a hard kiss.

Lentsch turned back to Bohde. 'See what I mean? The man's no use at all. So what's it to be, Bohde?'

Bohde sat up and stared over from across the room. There was no pleasure in his face, not even a trace of an alcoholic leer, which was what Veronica expected from men in his state. She started to fidget with the tassel of her pyjama cord, feeling uncomfortably naked beneath her costume. Bohde lit his cigar slowly and bunching his fingers round the thick stem held it out in an almost obscene manner. The room had gone quiet.

'I would fine her one hundred Reichsmarks,' he declared finally.

A chorus of disappointment was thrown round the room. Only Bohde could think of something so prosaic. He held up his hands. The mutiny ceased.

'And as it is unlikely that a woman of her means could find such a sum,' he continued, 'I would make her . . .' he made a crude sucking sound with his pursed lips while twirling his cigar in the air, '. . . and so forth on a couple of these. Flush her innards out. Then we'd see what else she'd stolen.' He sank back into his chair.

'That's the only way you'll ever get anyone to smoke them,' Zep called out.

Veronica sat, staring unhappily at the floor. Lentsch attempted to lift her spirits.

'Don't worry, my dear. Bohde has no sense of humour. I know exactly what I would do.'

'And what would that be?' she asked timidly.

'Confiscate your pyjamas!' He slapped her thigh. 'Now go on. Make me happy. Dance.'

In the hall the phone started to ring. Lentsch started up, thinking it might be Isobel, but Helmut was already out of the door. Watching Veronica cavort round the room, showing her stomach to the half-bored remnants of the night, Lentsch couldn't help but contrast her with Isobel. She would never demean herself in this manner, and he would never ask her to do such a thing. Her flirtations were of a different class altogether. The other girls looked on, uncertain whether Veronica's performance was undermining their status or improving it. Their faces were nervous, intent, looking for signs, conscious of their precarious position and what might be expected of them. What was it that brought them here? Lentsch wondered. What did they hope to get out of it? Was it simply that they imagined that they were hitching themselves to the winning side? At first perhaps, though not now. Albert maintained that it was the uniform. Was that it? Certainly it was more attractive than that sad brown affair the British were forced to wear. Some women might be drawn to it, but so many, so readily, so often? Molly had told him, in a moment of disarming frankness, that it was down to the physical stature of the men themselves. 'You're all so much *bigger* than what we're used to here,' she had yawned, delighting in the offhand crudity of her remark. 'It's such a change to have a man who doesn't look like some troll from the Hall of the Mountain King. Compared with what we're usually saddled with, you lot look like gods.' Gods! As usual, Molly's remark was not completely flippant. Though in reality they were nothing special, just ordinary soldiers possessed with ordinary charms, capable of ordinary cruelties, to begin with they must have appeared to be quite extraordinary – conquerors of Europe, sublime in their authority, correct in their conviction, tall and tanned and sounding the death knell of corrupt cultures.

As if on cue the girls began to turn away from Veronica's embarrassed contortions, in preparation for their own nocturnal manoeuvres. With their stomachs full of food, their vanity flushed with drink and their limbs loosened by the persuasive decadence of America's forbidden music, they were ready to lead their escorts to the promised land. Lentsch looked on, mesmerized by the brazen quality of their several embrace, tired of the weary predictability.

Helmut returned and whispered something into Zep's ear. Dropping his hold on Molly, he hurried out of the room, leaving her standing there, discarded and alone. That was Zep all over. When it came to his work, nothing got in his way. The nurse dancing with Wedel nodded in her direction and whispered something uncomplimentary. The two of them laughed out loud. Lentsch made a mental note to see that she was never allowed in again. He wasn't going to have some nurse from Bremen insult one of his guests, however Teutonic her physique. The music came to a halt. Veronica's dance was over. She had done her best but towards the end hardly anyone had taken any notice. Zep came back, his greatcoat over his arm. Ignoring Molly he stood before Lentsch and said simply, 'I have to go.'

'Trouble?' Lentsch asked, not caring whether there was trouble or not.

Zep opened his palms. For a moment conversation ceased as all eyes fell on this young man, in so many ways the epitome of the Occupation. Wedel looked longingly at his new conquest, his prospects fading fast. Zep shook his head and winked.

'You stay here,' he told him. 'No reason for everyone's evening to be spoilt. I'll drive myself. Tell Albert he need not wait up for me either.'

Molly walked over to the drinks cabinet and poured herself a large glass of brandy. She knew better than to protest. She would simply curl up on the sofa and wait for his return. One of the unwritten rules in the house was that no matter whose girlfriend you were, there was never any question of going upstairs without an escort.

Veronica came over and taking Lentsch's hand bent down towards her host.

'Was that Turkish enough for you?' she asked. Lentsch knew what was required of him.

'Delightful,' he said.

"Every Little Movement Has A Meaning of its Own," she told him stupidly, feeling herself slip out of control.

'What?'

'It's a song, a silly song. "Every Little Movement". I could sing it for you if you like. In private.'

Almost without thinking she slipped his hand inside the loose fold of silk. She held herself still for a moment, letting him feel the weight and hang of her, then took a deep breath.

'I think we can excuse Herbert any more driving duties tonight, don't you?'

Four

There were three of them coming up the cobbled street, Tommy le Coeur, Peter Finn, and the German. Ned stood motionless in the dark doorway and switched off his torch. Two hours earlier the streets had been thick with soldiers, waltzing around the town with beer on their lips and girls on their arms. Now it was half-past twelve, the island suspended once more in the dark waters of the curfew hours, its girls either safely home or stretched out on some requisitioned bed. The German was a big man on his way back to the *Soldatenheime* and as he stumbled along bawling an incoherent lullaby, one hand draped around Tommy le Coeur's neck, sparks flew out from under the metal caps of his regulation boots illuminating the road beneath him.

Ned watched as the two policemen led the man up the street towards the Old Government House, now a residential club for officers. Tommy and the new recruit were taking good care of their charge and Ned was surprised by their display of concern. He followed at a distance, hugging the other side, his outline hidden by the wall's deep shadows. Left to himself the man would have crawled back rather than walked, but between them they managed to keep him upright. When they reached the marble steps outside the building they eased him up slowly, pausing on each lip as the man tried to reason with his sense of balance. At the top of the steps they let him go. He stood there, swaying back and forth, confronted by the impossible conundrum of the dark revolving door.

'Straighten him up a bit, Peter,' Ned heard Tommy ask.

Peter grabbed hold of the man's collar and pulled him upright.

'That better?'

'Just the ticket. Hold still a moment, sunshine.'

Tommy span on his heel and crashed his fist into the man's mouth.

'That's for my brother in the Royal Artillery,' he shouted.

The German catapulted backwards, losing his cap as he tumbled over. Drink had anaesthetized his body. He lay in the road and started to laugh.

'*Es gefallt mir hier,*' he giggled, waving up at his new found friends. '*Es gefallt mir.*'

'That's right, you flat-headed piece of shite,' Tommy agreed. 'All fall down. Tommy help you up.' He ran down and picked him up. Ned watched as Tommy led the German back up and then hit him again.

'And that's for my cousin in the Fusiliers.'

The man tried to stand on his feet but he could not. Rolling over he crouched on all fours, panting, looking up to where Tommy stood, arms akimbo.

'You OK, mate?' Tommy called out. He jumped down and made to lead him up once more. Ned stepped out of the darkness.

'Don't be a bloody fool, Tommy,' he called across.

Tommy stopped dead, looking not like the policeman he was employed to be, alert and on the lookout, but wary and caught in the act. Seeing Ned standing there he relaxed and propped the German against the wall. There was a blossom of blood on the man's mouth and underneath his nose. Tommy straightened his own tunic and breathed on the buttons of his sleeve.

'He doesn't know shit from pudding, the state he's in,' he told Ned, wiping the row clean. 'I've been waiting for something like this for two years.'

Ned lay a restraining hand on Tommy's arm. His tunic was wet and dirty and his breath smelt as if he'd had more than a couple himself that evening.

'No more, Tommy,' he insisted. 'Now let's get him inside and be on our way.'

They half carried him up the steps and pushed him through. He fell face down on the other side and lay there, as still as any corpse. Light from a distant candle fluttered over his grey uniform. They could hear distant voices from inside, singing. They turned and began back down the hill. Ned motioned Peter to walk ahead and check the doors.

'That was a bloody stupid thing to do,' he told Tommy, when the boy was out of hearing. 'Showing off in front of him like that.'

Tommy turned and walked backwards for a few steps. 'Trust you to spoil the fun,' he complained, holding his fist underneath Ned's nose. 'That's real German blood there.' He raised his hand to his mouth, licked his knuckles and then dipped his hand into his side pocket. 'Look,' he said, giggling, 'got his wallet too.'

'What?'

'Pigskin, by the feel of it.'

Ned was amazed.

'Hand it over, Tommy.'

Tommy held it out with an ill grace. Taking it Ned flipped it open and shone his torch in. Artillery. Pay and Identity Book belonging to one Lieutenant Schade. Behind it a thick wad of banknotes. He ruffled them with his fingers.

'Must be the best part of a couple of months' pay here. If not more. And you thought you help yourself, I suppose.'

'He wouldn't know. He'd just think he'd lost it.'

'Tommy, Tommy.'

'They're the enemy, Ned. That lot could come in handy one day.' Tommy reached over and tapped it. 'And anyway, what if he had the invasion plans tucked up in there?'

Ned swung it away from him. 'Don't give me that. You did this for gain, not King and country.'

'So?'

'It's called theft, Tommy. It's against the law.'

Tommy was petulant. 'They steal from us.'

'We're not them, Tommy.' He waved the wallet in the air. 'I'll hand it in to the Feldkommandantur in the morning. Tell them you found it lying in the street. They'll probably give you a medal for honesty. That would make a change, wouldn't it?'

Tommy said nothing.

'All right?'

Tommy put his hand to his helmet. 'Anything you say. Inspector.'

Ned ignored the gibe. 'Right,' he said briskly. 'Let's get back, then.'

They walked back in silence. He shouldn't have said that. Honesty was not a word to be flung about in front of the men, not after last year. It was a form of blasphemy, like swearing in front of a nun. Last year half the police force had been arrested and charged with larceny. Eighteen men; constables, sergeants, their inspector: the Germans had been watching them all for weeks. Under cover of their night patrols they'd been breaking into the food stores and lifting whatever they could carry out. Civilian or military, it made no difference to them. Ned's predecessor, Inspector Petty, had given them a helping hand with the heavier items, loading up the old police car, the Yellow Peril, with sacks of rice and flour. When Ned had been a youngster it had been one of the seven wonders of the world, Guernsey's police car, dressed in its loud yellow coat, as noisy as a Weymouth dodgem and only half as manoeuvrable. Now it was a blaring reminder of the forces' blatant corruption and, though Ned was not touched by the scandal, he hardly dared use it. When the Germans had carried out the raid that night – on the station and the policemen's homes – they had found mountains of the stuff, tucked up chimneys, stuffed under floorboards, even buried in the trench next to the shithouse. If they had served no other purpose, the arrests had brought home to all the futility of concealment, even though it was a game most people continued to practise, including Ned himself. There *was* only the chimney and the floorboard and the trench next to the shithouse. There was nowhere original to hide anything. Too bloody small, that was the trouble with Guernsey.

If it hadn't been for that debacle, Major Lentsch would never have summoned Ned into his office that February morning and told him that as a serving CID officer on the mainland he was, as of 1 April 1942, to take charge of Guernsey's decimated force.

'But I've never worked here,' Ned had protested. 'The men don't know me. They won't trust me.'

'Just as long as you don't trust them. Yet,' the Major had said. 'There are more rotten ones in there, I am sure. The ones we didn't catch. Get rid of them and perhaps in time you will turn it into something we might *all* be proud of. Proper policemen again.'

The promise of complicity in that statement did not escape him. He took the job reluctantly. Like every other able-bodied man he needed the work and he hadn't had a permanent job since the invasion, just the occasional grave-digging assignment, and a couple of months stoking furnaces at the electricity plant. But it was true. They weren't policemen any more. They were more like railway porters, or AA patrols, fetching and carrying, saluting passing badges, at anybody's beck and call. They had lost all dignity. The islanders looked at them with a stare of undisguised contempt, not for getting caught, but for vacating the moral ground to the enemy. They had been stealing rations, food destined for ordinary men and women, food meagre portions of which they had to queue for in the cold and wet; bread, salt, tea; the stuff of ordinary life. They had even been stealing from the Todt stores for the foreigns, and though no one wanted to acknowledge it everyone knew what was happening to those poor bastards. Ned remembered walking up George Street one morning and seeing one of the whores leaning out of the top storey with a tin can dangling on the end of a piece of string. Two windows away, in the hostel, an old man was hanging over the window sill, his hands outstretched. She was fat and pasty. He was brown, with no flesh on him at all. The woman swung the can to and fro so that it might gain momentum. Backwards and forwards it went, higher and higher, until the man reached out and caught it. The woman dropped the string and the man disappeared inside. Looking across she caught Ned's questioning look and, holding an imaginary spoon, made a hurried feeding motion with her hand. Ned had hung his head and walked on.

That was all a man could do, all his skulking dignity would allow under the circumstances – to hang one's head and walk on.

Ned left the police station at about half one. Rather than take the spare bicycle he decided to walk home. It would take him a little over an hour to walk over to Cobo and Mum and Dad's house, half a mile away from the bay, once one of the most popular spots on the island, now stripped to a bare and uneasy beauty with only creaking coils of barbed wire for company. Despite the cold he had plenty to think about. The letter lay in his jacket pocket. *Must see you. Sunday morning, 11 o'clock. Usual place. Must see you.* That was all. The usual place had been by the fountain in the water lanes. Did she want to start up again? Or was this police business? Surely she didn't want to inform on anyone? Not Isobel. He had half a mind to walk over there and confront her with it now. It wasn't much out of his way.

He was standing outside the darkened house almost before he knew it. There was no point in him being there, it was far too late to go knocking on doors, but he stood there nevertheless, fingering the note, looking up to where he knew she would be sleeping. The blinds were down at every window, all except the drawing room and the bar at the bay window, the stools empty, the glasses still and polished, a decoration of despair illuminated by the moon. He stood by the gate, edging imperceptibly onto the path. He wondered whether she still left the key under the stone frog by the door, wondered who else she'd left it for since last he had lifted the base and picked it out from the scuttling beetles, wondered if Lentsch had ever brushed his hand thus.

'Can I help you at all?'

Ned span round. Mr van Dielen stood directly across the narrow road, by the gate of the bungalow opposite. Behind him Ned caught sight of a large bulky figure closing the glass-panelled door.

'Mr van Dielen.' He tried not to sound surprised.

'Mr Luscombe, is it not? Or should I say Inspector Luscombe.'

'Whatever, there's no need to be alarmed.'

'Alarmed? Indeed not. No. I am not ... alarmed.'

74

Van Dielen moved across the road in short sharp steps. Ned edged back to give the man access to his own property. He experienced the same feeling as he had felt that earlier time, embarrassed, a boy caught raiding an apple orchard.

'Quite an elevation since we last met,' van Dielen observed, taking out a large key and rubbing it with a handkerchief. 'From young man leasing unroadworthy pushbikes to young man masquerading as chief of Guernsey's police. Ah, the fortunes of war, Mr Luscombe. They cannot be all bad.'

He stood on the brick step holding the key to the light. He was the same height as Ned now.

'I was a policeman even then,' Ned told him. Van Dielen sniffed.

'Hmm. If I'd known that I might have been—'

'Think nothing of it,' Ned broke in.

'Even angrier.' Van Dielen said it lightly, an observation made for his own amusement. 'And now you are here to take your revenge. A civilian snared after curfew, apprehended in the blackout. Though I doubt if my host will welcome the complaint.' He looked back. There seemed to be a dull flickering coming from behind the bungalow's curtains. 'Major Ernst,' van Dielen told him. 'In charge of all the foreign labour. You know him?'

'Not at all.'

'An excellent man. A great organizer and a good host. He likes a job well done. He believes in . . . progress.' He patted his coat and breathed in the night air. Ned could smell the brandy on his breath. 'He has his own film projector, you know. Nature films. All perfectly decent, mind, just not my cup of tea.' He stopped quickly, anxious to divert attention from his indiscretion. 'So I'm not under arrest, then?'

Ned obliged. He did not want to be questioned too closely either.

'Not at all, Mr van Dielen. Crossing the road isn't a crime.'

Van Dielen smacked his lips.

'Ah, but that's exactly what it is at this time of night, Mr Luscombe. A crime. By rights I should be found guilty and fined appropriately. This is an island of fines. A fine for crossing the road after eleven at night, a fine for not finishing the job on time, even, I am happy to report, a fine for unauthorized swimming in the sea. A great advancement from the days of old, wouldn't you say?'

'Some rules are less important than others, Mr van Dielen. I'm not after to fine you for anything.'

'Are you not?' He peered up and down the road. 'Then what, by the grace of all that's straight and narrow, are you doing here? Is this one of your authorized smuggling routes?'

'I was on my way home and I saw a light on. Or thought I did.'

'A light, you say? It is not there now.'

'No.'

'So it went off, like a signal perhaps? And yet, the house is dark, the blinds are all drawn.'

'Perhaps it was just a trick of the light.'

'A trick of light? I suppose a light could do nothing else but its own trick, Mr Luscombe.'

'I might have imagined it.'

'Perhaps you imagined a daughter under it too.'

'I was just checking, Mr van Dielen.'

'How very intriguing, Mr Luscombe, how very lame and how very like yourself to be sticking your spoke in where it does not belong, as you might say.' He twirled the key in his hand. 'Isobel went to a party this evening. If she is back,' he pointed to the grey, lifeless window, 'she is asleep. It has been a merciful long time since she last laid eyes on your constabuleric form and long may it remain so.' He raised his hat. 'Goodnight, Mr Luscombe.'

He disappeared up the overgrown path. Ned moved on. He wanted to be home now, away from this empty world, in bed with his curtains drawn and the sky blotted out and sleep dulling his sense of impotence. He wanted to run, to hear the rhythm of his own breath in the air, hear his feet pounding along the road, but it was a foolish man who ran along Guernsey's curfewed streets. Halfway down the Rohais Road he heard a car steaming towards him. He hurried along looking for a place to shelter. This was the hour of the black-market run, goods ferried in from the harbour or any one of the hidden bays to the south, brought in under organized eyes, stored in cellars and attics and army barracks. It would be well for him to stand in the shadow unobserved and let it pass, noting the vehicle and who might be driving. It was part of the lifeblood of the island now, strong and close, like the corrupt branch of an extended family, ready to embroil its relations in its fierce and unpredictable excesses. It could never be eradicated, not now that they were beginning to feel the pinch too. His mum's Staffordshire White, Sally, had been stolen months back, her throat slit not thirty yards from the back door. Three pairs of hobnailed boots were all they found, or rather the bloody prints of them, dried hard in the mud and leading across the fields. They all knew what that meant. Soldiers. He had complained about it in his monthly meeting with the Feldkommandantur. Lentsch had promised to get to the bottom of it. He had heard nothing since.

There was nowhere to hide; a long wall loomed up above him while opposite ran a line of tall spiked railings. He wasn't going to ruin a pair of perfectly good trousers in an undignified scramble trying to get over. Anyway it was too late, for now the car came sweeping up, opening the narrow road with a reckless stream of light. This was no black-market run. To be bold was one thing, to be brazen was quite another. Ned stood motionless, hoping it might pass. He could see the dark pennant fluttering at the head of the bonnet. The car drew level and pulled up a few yards ahead. The front passenger window rolled down.

'Pass,' a voice demanded.

Ned fumbled in his pocket. Crossing the road he walked up to the window and held out his curfew permit. A torch went on in the interior of the car, wavered over the card and then came up, shining full in his face.

'Out of uniform?' he heard. Ned knew better than ask the interrogator's identity.

'No,' he said. 'If you look at the bottom. I'm not required.'

There was a stifled giggle in the back. Ned looked down. A pair of legs could be seen, stretched out on the back seat. Nice legs. Bet they didn't have a pass either.

'And no salute,' came the voice. 'Did not the Feldkommandantur order all policemen to salute German officers when they see them. It is a rule, is it not?'

Quite why he had not saluted Ned did not know. Perhaps it was out of habit. They all tried to avoid giving the Germans the satisfaction of seeing British policemen perform this humiliating obeisance. It had become a game as well as a point of honour, a petty way of subverting a petty rule. Whenever they saw an officer approaching they would turn to study a shop window, or suddenly discover that their bootlaces had come undone.

'I didn't know you were an officer,' Ned said. He was tired and he still had the best part of two miles to go. 'It's dark. Or rather, it's meant to be.'

The man ignored the rebuke.

'And who else would be in a car at one o'clock in the morning, except an officer?' he asked.

Ned could not help but correct him.

'Half one,' he said.

'Half one, half two, that is not the question.'

'No.'

'Report to the Feldkommandantur in the morning.'

'What?'

'At nine. I will see that the staff sergeant is expecting you.'

'Oh, let him off, Zep. He always was the difficult one,' came the other voice, giggling again. The legs swung down. A head leant forward. The red hair was unmistakable.

'Veronica? Is that you?' Ned looked in. She was propped up in the corner, a military greatcoat thrown over her shoulders. She drew the collar around her and shivered.

'It's me all right. And this is Captain Zepernick, Zeppy to his friends. I'm surprised your paths haven't crossed already, him being a policeman like you.'

The Captain looked at him coldly.

'We have not met,' he said.

Standing in her presence Ned felt emboldened. He had hardly seen her these last two years except when he met her on the way to a rehearsal, halfway up the stairs. She moved in different circles now, and their old easy friendship had gone. When he saw her hamming it up, bending forward over the very lip of the stage, him at the back, holding the knowledge of her within him, he saw the reason why he abandoned her. Too eager to please, that was Veronica all over, too eager to please, too quick to suggestion, too willing to open her mouth and swallow whatever morsel was dangled in front of her. It made him angry, this disregard of her own worth. But now, despite himself, he felt his old childhood friendship surfacing. She had been a good sort, VV.

'I don't suppose you have a pass, Veronica.'

'Right first time,' she laughed. The man in front turned and put his hand in the air. She stopped immediately.

'She has no need of one,' he told Ned, watching him, studying his eyes, following his every movement. Ned leant his hand on the roof of the car. There was an opening here Ned felt obliged to employ.

'Everyone needs a pass after curfew. Even guests of the Wehrmacht.'

Captain Zepernick smiled. It pleased him when others were prepared to play their games.

'Ah, but she is not a guest,' he countered. 'She is on official business.' He reached out and opened the coat to reveal Veronica's night attire. 'See? I have been questioning her. We pulled her out of bed.'

'Pushed me more like,' Veronica complained, pulling the coat back together again. 'Still don't know why he bundled me out like that. Was it something I said?'

Captain Zepernick looked back and forth, as if unsure whose conversation to augment.

'He is not content,' he said to Veronica, and turning to Ned,

79

added, 'And you, why are you on foot? You have your own car, no?'

'No. Dead as a dodo.'

'Poor Ned,' Veronica mocked, 'going walkabout at this time of night. And in those shoes. Couldn't we give him a lift, Zep?'

The Captain looked at his watch.

'No. I am late already.' He handed back Ned's curfew pass. 'And the salute. This time there is no need to report. This time, understand? *Gute nacht.*'

The car sped off. Ned continued with his journey home. Soon he had left St Peter Port and was out into the country. To the east he could see the dim outline of Saumarez Park, to the west the fresh sprawl of artillery barracks and fuel depots. In former times he would have taken a short cut through the fields, but it was not wise to do so now. This part of the island was laced with treachery, landmines and booby traps underneath the sand, razor wire along the shoreline, and inland, set in the middle of every quiet walled meadow of family farmland, a French three-hundred-pounder with a wheel-spoke of wires stretching out from the brightly painted detonator to a series of posts, nine foot high, set around the perimeter of the field. Spider bombs, they were called, ready to ensnare any unfortunate paratrooper into their deadly embrace. The cobwebs of war.

Somewhere in the dark he could hear the stamp of feet where sentries stood guard. Hugging the grass verge, careful to make no sound, Ned walked on.

*

Veronica looked up to the mirror. The Captain had barely taken his eyes off her since they had resumed their journey. In further defiance of lighting regulations he reached back and switched on the interior light so that she might be better illuminated. It would have been easy to move out of the range of his vision, but knowing what was expected from her, and deciding with a thumping heart to give it her best shot, she positioned herself firmly in the centre of the seat, arms stretched out. At the outset she had speculated on the likely reward she might obtain if the Captain should make such an attempt, which was why she had chosen the back, for what she required was for the action to impart a desire from which it might be possible to extract a long-term unambiguous intent.

She started to hum that tune the Major had played her. The Captain tapped his hands on the wheel.

'You should have given him a lift,' she said, trying not to slur her words as he pulled up a little way past the narrow gate that led to the small row of cottages and her house at the end. 'He lives just round the corner.'

'No,' he said, and slamming his door behind him, pulled hers open.

'Shh,' she scolded him. 'Not so loud. You'll wake everyone.' She tried to raise herself up but he pushed her back down.

'Be quiet, then,' he said, and began to pull at her pyjama trousers. 'This is why you were dancing for the Major, no?'

'Not exactly.' She raised her bottom obligingly.

She knew this would happen, though it came to her, thinking of other things, that had not the Captain wasted time in stopping for Ned, he might have chosen somewhere more comfortable or simply have let her off with a curt goodnight and a request to meet her some other time. It was the act of arresting movement, of playing with a man's liberty, that had goaded him finally. If anything she was surprised that he waited until he got her home.

The party had been a disaster. Veronica still did not know what she had done to upset Lentsch. Why had he suddenly found her so repellent?

'Go,' he had declared, slumping back on the sofa, snagging his hand on her pyjama top, sending one of the few fastened buttons skittering across the floor. Captain Zepernick had bent down and let it roll into his hand. She knew, the moment he held it out for her, his eyes never leaving her face, what his intentions were. So did everyone else.

'If it is not too far out of my way . . .' he had said softly, knowing such an inconvenience to be beyond the island's capabilities, and with Molly splashing out another large brandy, the Major's eyes closed to everything but his own misery and Bohde looking at her as if he would like to skin her alive and describe her discomfort throughout his printed domain, she had downed her drink and accepted without even blushing.

Outside the sudden air made her giddy. She feared she might pass out or worse, throw up, but as they descended into town, bumping along the High Street, up by the bank, outside whose premises she had accepted the pass that had led her to waste three years of her life, her head began to clear from the tart whip of the wind. Then out on Rohais the Captain swore and stamped on the brake and she felt the car swoon from the violence of the act. For a moment she panicked, thinking that he had decided to demonstrate his ruthless desire on the cold ground of some abandoned playing field, but then she saw him looking back, not at her, but at a figure walking up towards them from across the road. She knew who it was the moment he took his hands out of his pockets, sinking back in relief as, in response to the Captain's clipped demand, she heard that slow, lazy voice that had been the accompanying cadence to so much of her early life. She had always liked Ned and when they were growing up together she had thought it likely that one day the two of them might make a go of it. Indeed both families had encouraged their easy friendship, leastwise her parents and his dad. Ned's mother was a different story. She'd been nice enough when Veronica had been a child, but come sixteen she'd wrinkled up her nose and stared at her as if she thought Veronica spent her evenings walking up and down the Pollet with her lips painted bright scarlet. But by the time her nineteenth birthday had come around even she had seemed resigned to their unspoken engagement. Veronica was taking her chiropody exams (a rudimentary affair, conducted by post) while Ned, tired of odd jobs, was looking round for something permanent. They'd had a great time in those early years, her and Ned, then suddenly, twelve months back, it all changed. Ned became older, irritable, churlish at the island's meagre expectations, turning down the job his uncle had promised him working for the Hallivands in their greenhouse business, finding fault with everything around him. She remembered how they had fallen out, over a kiss. It was a reward, a trophy for a victory throw of the darts, a kiss laced with gin-and-black, pressed on the lips of an older man who had held her close in leery, beery gratitude, his audience cheering them on. It was only given in jest, a stab at grabbing the limelight before her time was no longer her own, but Ned had stomped off without so much as a flying fist. It was that abandonment which had propelled her more permanently into the arms of Tommy le Coeur not three months later, despite the tales of his drinking and womanizing that lay like well-run tramlines up and down the streets of St Peter Port. A big man, immovable like the trunk of a tree, with a punchbowl of a stomach and a crow's nest of a beard, it was hard to understand the reasons for his success and yet, tipping his helmet at her one empty afternoon as she came out of the bank on the corner of the Pollet, it was only a matter of an afternoon in the back room of the Brighton before the two of them had their respective uniforms strewn all around her little examination room above Underwood's and not a carbuncle or a pickpocket in sight, the two of them laughing at the noise they were making for Mr Underwood's customers below as she bounced up and down on his great white belly.

Zep was on top of her now, fumbling with his buttons. She could hear his boots trying to gain purchase on the road. She raised her hips but it didn't seem to help. This was no good at all.

'It's bloody draughty in here,' she complained.

'Where, then?'

She pushed him off and stood up. He pressed her against the car and put his hand inside the greatcoat. She flinched. His hands were freezing.

'No,' she said. 'This way.'

She took his hand and led him round to the end house. Down the path stood her father's shed. The lock had been broken so many times they hadn't bothered to replace it any more. At the back was a small window with a workbench running off to one side. The moonlight fell upon the pitted surface and a row of chisels above. Zep stood in the doorway, looking in, as if he were a guest being shown round a hotel.

'There is no room to lie down,' he said. She sat up on the bench, put her bag to one side and leant back against the wall.

'Pretend you're on parade, then,' she said. 'Stand to attention,' and she pulled him towards her. It was an awkward posture, where movement was dictated by the needs of balance rather than desire, hanging on the side with one hand, looking over his shoulder, hoping that they weren't making too much noise, wondering whether this was a good idea. It was why she had gone to the party, wasn't it, to bag a decent Jerry? Moving back to step out of his trousers the Captain banged his head on something hanging down from the rafters.

'Careful,' she said and reaching up took it down from its hook.
'What is it?'

She held it out at arm's length. 'A carving,' she said, 'nothing much.' She cast it to one side. 'You can come back now. It's quite safe.'

He moved up again and undid her few remaining buttons, examining what he found.

'Beautiful,' he said, meaning it.

She kissed him gratefully.

'You should have seen them when I had a bit of weight on me. Your rations have half done for our figures.'

Romulus and Remus, that's what Tommy used to call them, 'each one a helmet's worth'. That first afternoon had been typical Tommy, shrugging off his duties without a moment's thought, sitting up at the bar, enjoying his steady consumption, helmet planted on the counter, her legs swinging back and forth. Whenever the connecting door opened, he would place the helmet solemnly over his glass, not because he was worried he might get caught (Tommy had been caught dozens of times – fined but never dismissed, for he was fearless when it came to fighting) but because it amused him to lift his hat of high office and feign astonishment at what lay underneath. There was a playfulness within Tommy that cut away his years, an irresponsibility that captured her utterly, though the news that Ned had upped and joined the English police and could be seen swanning about Dorchester High Street in a uniform one size too large for him had helped. So it was Tommy who she walked out with against her father's wishes, Tommy with his unquenchable thirst and huge hands, Tommy with his delicate wood carvings and his roving eye. And for a while it worked. She thought that given enough solid sustenance from her, she could wean him off his flights of fancy. She didn't give him time for anyone else. By the time mother took ill and she was needed more at home it never occurred to her that he might return to his old ways, for it was Tommy who carved the Virgin Mary that her mother kept on her sickbed beside her, Tommy who carried her downstairs so that she might be near her garden, Tommy who pushed her along the Esplanade every Sunday, but despite all his kindness, stories came winging back of Tommy here and Tommy there, and did you see him walking out of the Normandie, one on each arm? She might have turned a blind eye had she not come across him, waiting for opening time, sitting on the stone wall carving a little lighthouse with 'To Mary-Ellen: Guernsey Memories' carved upon it. Though he promised to mend his ways, even as he was saying it his eye flicked across to a couple of trippers sauntering down the opposite road, skirts billowing in the wind. He winked at them. Just couldn't help it. So she chucked him there and then, him and his ring, and spent her time looking after Mum, cooking for Dad in the evenings and pruning leathery feet every morning from ten to twelve thirty and on Wednesday afternoons from half-past two to half-past four. She had some regular clients then, some of the island's real toffs, even Mrs Hallivand. And then Molly had arrived, right after one of Mrs Hallivand's imperial fortnightly visits. Veronica knew Molly slightly. 'Ideas above her station,' her mother used to say. 'With a figure like that she can afford them,' her da would reply. Molly had come about an ingrowing toenail, and they both stood by the window watching Mrs Hallivand sail down the street distributing nods and pleasantries to those who deserved them.

'I see you work under the royal warrant,' Molly observed and Veronica gave such a good impression of Her Majesty that Molly laughing added, 'You should go on the stage. Come round to the Society one night. Up above the police station. We need some new blood. See if you like it. Only keep that one under your hat. Marjorie holds the purse strings.' And so she did. She was good. She had the mouth and the bottle for it. She could sing too. Every now and again she could hear Tommy's laugh rise up through the floors. She still liked him. They started up again, unofficial. Nothing special. He'd been seen walking out with Elspeth Poidevin but had dropped her without warning. Rumour had it he was the father of her child, but it didn't seem to bother either of them. When he was free he'd come round Tuesdays and Thursdays, just as was she was about to lock up and as often as not she'd turn the 'closed' sign, lock the door, pull down the blind and bounce that chuckle out of him again. She looked forward to it. Better he should be like this, hardly drunk, grateful and grinning, than stumbling into their marriage bed late at night with only the curse of failed expectation to embrace. The evenings were different. She'd started going out with a different set. Molly's crowd. A bit more class than she was used to. She was earning a little money too, especially in the summer months. It was curious what people found under their socks when suddenly exposed to sunlight. She had a trickle of holiday-makers who came in the second or third day, their feet twitching on her carpet like flat misshapen creatures hauled up from the bottom of the ocean floor. And then she found another man. Son of a solicitor. A little dim but good-natured enough. Fancied himself as Guernsey's answer to Noël Coward, all cravats and cigarette holders and tennis racquets. He taught her how to play croquet and mix Pimm's No. 1. She learnt quickly. She began to read *Country Life, Picture Post*. She took the lead in plays by Agatha Christie. She acquired manners. Her voice changed, losing that slow insular edge she could hear in her parents and Tommy and all the others she had known. She could say wittier, nastier things. She saw people in the long term, what they could do, where they might be going, how she might be a part of it. She didn't want the likes of Tommy any more. She was on her way to becoming a young lady now. She began to leave her surgery early, so that Tommy would arrive to find it locked and her gone. For three weeks it worked and then he caught her halfway up the police stairs on her way to a read-through of a new murder mystery. She was going to get strangled in her nightdress. She was looking forward to it.

'Been round a couple of times. You're never there,' Tommy complained, his bulk filling the first-floor landing.

'I don't open up for just anyone any more.' She smoothed down the folds of her dress and waited. She knew what she had said. She found it rather clever.

'Not even for old Tommy?' he asked.

'Not even for old Tommy,' she repeated.

'Made you something. For the shop.'

Veronica flinched. How she hated that word.

'It's a surgery, Tommy, not a shop.'

He reached under his coat and drew out a carved wooden foot, with toes and toenails and a perfectly arched instep.

'It's a foot. See? You could hang it outside above the pavement. Like a chemist's.'

'Very nice.'

'I could help you hang it, if you like. Come round tomorrow say, after lunch.'

'I'd have to ask Mr Underwood's permission first. They're his premises, after all.'

Tommy nodded. They both knew full well she had no intention of hanging his handiwork anywhere. He looked angry.

'How's the acting going, then?'

Laughter came from above. She looked up, worried she was missing something.

'Swimmingly.'

'Swimmingly! What sort of word is that?'

'Just a word, Tommy, like any other.'

'Well, I've never heard it before.'

She looked down.

'Well, pardon me for talking.'

'I better let you get on with it, then, if it's going swimmingly.'

He turned to walk back down, and then called up again, in one last attempt.

'Your ma all right?'

She felt for him then. He had been good to Ma. More than good. He had been generous and kind.

'As well as can be expected. Come round and see her if you want. She'd like that.'

'When?'

'Whenever you want. She's not going anywhere. I don't have to be there, do I?'

'Suppose not.'

'Just as well if I wasn't. Don't want to get your hopes up, Tommy.'

'You saying there's no point in me calling round, then?'

'Not on my account.'

'Not even if my poor old feet need attention?'

'A tank couldn't harm your feet, Tommy. Not in those boots.'

He trod heavily down the stairs, looking back once in the hope that she would be standing there, looking down, ready to rush down those guilt-trodden stairs into his burly arms, but she was gone. Upstairs she read her lines and placed her white-powdered neck in Gerald's trembling hands. It was marvellous. He could hardly get his words out he was so excited. Every time she slid to the floor, his hands travelled down the sides of her body a little more slowly, and when he crossed the stage to make his telephone call he held one hand in front of his trousers in the hope that no one would notice. She did, lying on the floor looking up the length of his leg, and so did Molly, winking at her from the sidelines. There was an advert she'd seen in the *Picture Post* recently from some undergarments manufacturer which ran 'The Less a Man Feels of His Underwear the More He Likes It'. Well, Gerald was feeling his by jingo and didn't seem too upset. God knows what he'd be like when it came to the dress rehearsal. She was going to wear her new nightdress bought from down below. Just like silk it felt, made from this new stuff, Viscana, with a satin collar and blouselike bodice, tucked in at the waist and all smooth and showy at the front. Once he'd run his hands over that it'd stick out so far he probably be able to hang the receiver off the end. She started to shake with laughter. 'Keep your bust still, V,' Mrs Hallivand complained. 'You're a corpse, girl, not a badly set blancmange.' Afterwards she led him outside and with her hands set primly in her lap listened while he declared his intentions, listing his prospects, his father's business, the plot of land they owned by the golf course and the hotel he planned to build. Give me six months, he promised, and I'll be able to go to your father. You can go to my father right this minute, sweetheart, she wanted to tell him, he's not waiting on anything, but she held her peace, told him how thrilled she was (and she was, there was no doubting it), went home, and lay in bed thinking of the house she and Gerald would live in one day over at St Martins or the posh bits of St Peter Port, and how she would wake in the morning to a clear open window and a garden beneath and the sound of Gerald going off to work. He'd be no trouble, at least not to begin with. Spunk in her hand, that's what he'd be. And then, what, two months later, he was gone, not just Gerald but every man jack of them, across the water to join up. She'd been horrified. It won't be for long, darling, he assured her, it won't be for long, scrambling out of his flannels for the first and last time (a calculated surrender disguised as girlish trust), and what happens? Gerald gets washed overboard and drowns while on training! All those months wasted. Tommy imagined he could win her back with him gone. She'd seen him at Ned's father's funeral, and thrown him a discreet, affectionate wave, but the trouble was her tastes had changed for good by then. Gerald might have been a bit of a fool, but at least he had aspirations, at least he had prospects. Ned was there, home on compassionate leave. She understood him now, why he had left. They made a promise to have a drink together, the day before he was due back on the mainland. The next day the Germans came. It was bad for her at first, for she had cut loose so many boats by then. But unlike all the other men she had ever known, the Germans took care of their bodies; they liked them, liked the look of them, liked the feel of them, wanted to understand them. They were like women in that way. She learnt to adapt her practices to their requirements, just like the town's barbers. Business boomed. And as for the Guernsey Society, they had never been in greater demand. She was getting the best of both worlds. Not like poor Ned. The islanders expected him to protect them from the Germans and the Germans demanded that he enforce their rules. There he was, caught in the middle, viewed with suspicion by both sides. And how were he and Tommy getting on now, she wondered? She never had worn that nightie.

Zep put his hands under her, drawing her buttocks out into the air, sending her sprawling further back. Her head started to bang against the wooden frame. The chisels began to dance. He was in a hurry now. Putting her hands round his neck, she managed to haul herself up. It would be over soon, and he would be gone. In the few minutes left it would be important to impart to him something which he might not expect, which on reflection would remind him not simply of the fleeting desire Ned had provoked, but of a particular attraction which she alone might possess. What, though? And how to deliver it? A word, a gesture, a promise of things to come? Would the prospect of regularly betraying Molly be sufficient for his ego, or would the picture of her elegant painted face, set hard against their departure, be precisely the image to turn him against her? She pulled him close. Over his shoulder, to the side of the door, behind a pile a boxes and glass frames and old sacking she saw two boots glinting in the wan light. One of them moved cautiously. She gasped.

'You like this?' the Captain demanded.

She started to tremble, sweat breaking out.

'Yes?'

'Yes,' she said, staring hard. 'It's *gut. Sehr gut.*'

She pressed his head into her, wondering who could it be; not her father, surely. Please God, not that. Another thought brought a shudder to her. Tommy. The boots were big enough. How many times had she felt his uniform on her like this, inhaling the sour smell of sweat and spilt beer mixed with the sweet tang of wood shavings? This uniform had been dipped in a different brew altogether, cigar smoke, brass polish and on the shoulders and lapels and the collar of his shirt the scent of Molly and Molly's perfume, a cocoon of desire. That wouldn't protect him. Tommy would step out and split his skull open like a walnut, and they would have to drag the body away and bury him in some faraway field! The island would be turned upside down in the hunt for him. And Lentsch knew the Captain had left with her! She would be the first person they would interrogate. This could be the end of her life! She began to shake uncontrollably, in her thighs and her arms and the muscles deep within her belly. The Captain lifted her clear and grinning, urged her on.

When it was over he stood still, breathing hard. She did not know where to look, what her eyes might tell him. He was watching her closely. He had expected something more perfunctory. He was impressed.

'I must go,' he said eventually. 'They are waiting for me.'

She jumped down and held the coat open against him, terrified he might turn around.

'*Gruss und kuss Veronika.* Remember?' she said, propelling him gently backwards, holding him fast with her mouth and body. She could hear breathing now, she was sure of it. She reached round and pushed open the door. He was out onto the path.

'Do you like horses?' he asked. 'Riding?'

She had never been on a horse in her life. They frightened her.

'Love it,' she said. 'Anything outdoors.'

'I will send a message perhaps. To your shop.'

'*Gut. Sehr gut.*' She took his hand away from her. 'Now let me get some beauty sleep.'

She stood in the doorway as he walked back, hearing the soft clip of the door and the whine of the engine as he pulled away, remembering too late the clothing that lay on the car floor. Back in the shed she picked up a spade and held it across her chest, like a rifle at port arms.

'Is that you, Tommy?'

There was no sound. The breathing had stopped. She jabbed at the dark.

'Come on! Come on! You can show yourself now!'

She stabbed at the black air again, and this time made contact. There was a squeal and the boxes fell in front of her. She jumped back in fright. She didn't care who she woke now.

'Come on! Out with you! He's coming back, you know!'

A figure came out from behind the fallen pile, small and pale. She could smell him even in this wind.

'Pliss!'

She didn't recognize the accent but she knew who he was, or where he came from. One of the Todt workers. He stood there, uncertain, ready to run. They saw them only at first or last light, standing in the backs of lorries, or shuffling along the road with picks and shovels slung over their shoulders. Most of the time they were in the forbidden zones, building fortifications. The islanders tried to take no notice of them. They were nothing to do with them, after all. Who in the world had seen anything like them, with their gaunt stares and dark faces, thinking incomprehensible thoughts? They looked barely human as it was. Molly had told her that half of them were from asylums, the others bad people, Communists and the like. When they weren't locked up in their billets they were prowling about the countryside lifting whatever they could lay their hands on. But this one didn't look so terrible.

'What are you doing here?' she asked, as if she didn't know. He said nothing. She stood in the doorway and pointed to her mouth.

'Food? You come to steal food?'

He shook his head. As she moved to chuck him out he crouched down, raising his arm to ward off the blow. He could be no more than sixteen. Perhaps younger. It was difficult to tell with the foreigns. Must be starving to be out at this hour. She remembered the food table and how the girls had all crowded round it. They were no different, elbowing each other aside for the next greasy mouthful. It was all slave labour of sorts. She grabbed his wrist and dragging him over, pulled the cheese out from her bag.

'Eat,' she said.

He took it carefully, turning it in his hands.

'It's OK,' she said. 'Eat. It's good.'

He held it up and took a bite. He found it hard to chew and swallow.

'Drink?' she asked, tipping her hand. 'Water?'

He nodded.

'Come on, then.'

She led him along the path to the back door, where the cottage leant into the soil like an old farm labourer used beyond his years. She held her index finger to her lips.

'Shh. OK?'

The boy nodded.

'*Ja.*'

Once in the kitchen she drew the curtains and switched on the light. The boy was white from head to foot, white on his long clumpy hair, white on his hollow watchful face and white on his anxious legs. Only the cut of his muddy jacket, of incongruous quality, gave him substance, that and the dark red well of his sunken eyes. Tied round his waist he wore a grubby pair of football shorts, and his feet were planted in boots three sizes too big for him.

She cut him a thick slice of bread and poured him a glass of milk. She had always imagined the foreigns to be quick and furtive, but he took his time, eating slowly, pausing to swallow. He held the unfinished cheese between his knees. White cheese against white knees. White milk and white bread. She wished she could give him something with a little colour in it. They were long and thin, his legs, made for climbing cliffs and stealing gulls' eggs and falling off bikes. Legs like Ned once had, legs for legging it. When he had finished he looked to the door and began to rub his calves.

'You can't go out like that,' she said.

The boy did not understand.

'Clothes,' she said, slapping her thigh. '*Vêtements*. You need more clothes.' She pointed to the floor. 'Stay,' she commanded.

In the front room lay a pile of pantomime costumes she had brought back to mend: a couple of pirates' outfits, some fairies' wings, and the clothes for the lost boys. There was a pair of thick red flannel trousers in amongst them she had patched only the night before.

'Here,' she said, coming back in. 'Put these on.'

He hesitated.

She mimed for him again, tugging and straining as she tried to pull them over an imaginary pair of boots. His mouth flickered with laughter.

'Go on!'

As he took them her dad's voice came floating down.

'Veronica? Is that you?

The boy looked to run, but Veronica shook her head.

'Who you got down there?'

Footsteps came down the stairs. A short man in trousers and a shirt peered round the door. Since her mother had been bedridden, her father had taken to sleeping on the floor beside her in his clothes.

'What in Christendom is that?' he demanded.

'A foreign,' she said. 'I found him outside.'

'Trying to rob us, the little tyke. I'll learn him.' He raised his hand. Veronica caught it in mid-air. There was no power behind it.

'No, Da. Look at him. He's starving, poor little mite.'

'And you're breaking the rules, girl. You know that. Go on, sling your hook.' He made for the back door. Veronica put her weight against it.

'He's not going till he's properly fed,' she said. 'And that's that. Now get back to bed. What you don't see you don't know.'

'Get us all killed,' her father complained. 'Wake Mum up.'

'How is she?'

Her father looked at the boy, who was too frightened to move, and then at his daughter. He hardly knew her any more.

'Restless. Small wonder with her daughter coming home at all hours.'

'It's all in a good cause, Da,' she said.

'And what cause might that be?'

'Survival. More grub.'

The boy stood up and drew his jacket around him. He held his hands in prayer and bowed before them. He seemed agitated.

'*Lager Ute,*' he said. '*Lager Ute.*'

'What's he saying?' Veronica asked her father.

'That's his billet. Near the Todt Headquarters. He'll need to get back there before it gets light.' He held up his hand. 'I don't know why I'm doing this.'

He moved to the side dresser and bent down. They heard the clatter of the bread bin. He came up holding a paper bag.

'Egg and tomato pie. Mrs Luscombe brought it round this afternoon.' He broke it in two and stuck half in the boy's pocket. 'Now vamoose, before you get us all shot.'

Veronica took the boy to the door. She tapped her wrist.

'At night,' she said. '*Nacht.* This door. Open.' She swung it to and fro. 'You *komm hier.* For food. Yes?'

'Yiss.'

'Good. *Sehr gut.*'

The boy smiled quickly again. She took his head and held it against her. He turned, and ran out into the dark.

Her father was sitting at the table, smoking the stub end of a roll-up.

'Dangerous game you're playing, girl,' he said.

'Him? He won't talk.'

Her father shook his head.

'Not him. I mean that.' He pointed to the greatcoat. 'No good'll come of it.'

'No? What about you up at the airport?'

'That's different. Working for them is one thing. We've no choice in the matter. Having . . . relations is another.'

'Well, excuse me for living. And where do you think those fighters are going? Butlin's Holiday Camp? You can see the bombers circling waiting for their escort, for Christ's sake. That's what you're doing, Dad. Helping bomb London.'

Her father's face darkened with anger.

'You don't know the half of it, girl. I know what I'm doing and I know what you're doing. You should have stuck with Tommy le Coeur. There'd be none of this nonsense then.'

'Tommy was going with every tart he could lay his hands on!'

'Well, you must have given him a taste for them, that's all I can say.'

'Da!'

'I mean it. Thank God your mother can't see it all.'

'I'll move out if you like.'

'It might come to that.'

He trudged back upstairs. Veronica opened the back door and walked out into the garden, down to the field at the end, wondering if the boy had got back home safely. Home! She sighed at the impossibility of the word and feeling the tears rise up, held on to the railing and let her body shake.

*

Reaching the top of the hill Ned stopped and looked down. Though the moon shone full, it was a winter moon, one that bled the island of all colour. On the shoreline, a mass of shapes stood out against the sky, a gravel digger, its half-open jaw towering over the silhouette of a Henschel locomotive with its string of empty wagons. Closer by, the pocket of houses where he had been brought up, once whitewashed every year, but now left to fade in tired sympathy. No one painted their houses any more. Guernsey had a new shade now, occupational grey.

But beyond the bay sparkled. No blackout could hide it tonight, and as it danced, deep and dark, it seemed to restore to the island that sense of floating space that he had long forgotten existed. For a moment he could remember what it had been like before the grey, when the island had rung, not to the sound of marching feet and strident songs, but to sounds that had been banished by decree, sounds an active people made. For they did nothing now except shamble from one day to the next. He stood and listened. Even the tone of the sea had been changed! He could remember how it had been, the rhythm he had slept and woken to, not this slap, slap, slap, as it met thick concrete walls, but the sucking wash of it as it beat its way, back and forth, over the long expanse of pebble and sand. Time was when he would have gone down and dragged the canoe out, now one of the few craft on the island that hadn't been confiscated or broken up. Not that he'd hidden it, that was the beauty of it. It was a foldaway canoe called a Folboat, eighteen foot long, light but strong enough to carry a load of around 700 lbs. Dismantled it looked more like a camp bed than anything else and with the paddles hidden among the pitchforks they hadn't given it a second glance. He'd seen an advert for it seven years ago. 2/6 a week it cost to buy then and he'd done it with the help of dad and a loan from Uncle Albert. He used to take it out regularly on spring nights like this, skimming over the huge stillness of the world, dipping in moonlight on the empty sea. In the summer Veronica came too, the two of them skirting the mute cliffs and motionless bays before she slipped in, swimming on top of the great swell, challenging the cold currents while he described safety's circle. The island had been theirs then; they had the strength and skill to possess it, to feed in its deep waters, to embrace its age with their surging youth.

An owl called, reminding him of other hoots and chants that

once broke this hushed night air; singing his way home with Bernie, their stomachs awash with beer; the skinny-dipping squeals a whole group of them had enticed once out of Veronica and Bernie's girl and the young Elspeth Poidevin and how they had run back across L'Ancresse Common with freshly glimpsed secrets to take to bed. Everyone grew older, he knew that, and he knew too that it was not the passing of his youth that he regretted, but that it should pass into this, where their movements were constricted not by the island's history or their own stubborn prejudices but by a homeland which had ceased to exist. For where were they now? What identity did they possess? They listened to the wireless, waiting for messages of hope and exhortation, but though London sent an armada of them to the other occupied countries, none were directed here. England kept quiet about the Channel Islands as if she were punishing the islands for letting the side down. 'England expects that every man will do his duty', that's the phrase he had been taught at school. But what could they do here, with no place to hide, living amongst an enemy who was polite and considerate and bristling with power?

He was careful to make little sound when he got home, but the walk had wakened him, and he did not feel like sleep. He felt hungry and in need of company, and so he knelt down and talked softly to the dog. Jimbo raised his head in attentive affection before settling back to sleep. On the stone shelf in the larder lay five turnip cakes Mum must have made that afternoon and beside them a pile of oatmeal biscuits. There was no bread. The four eggs meant that the chickens were still laying; meant that the chickens were still there. Ned had moved them into the washroom at the back, and though the kitchen smelt of them a little, at least they were safe. He took two eggs and bit into a biscuit. He hadn't eaten properly the whole day.

The iron stove had gone out hours ago, but it would not take long to light. Before the Occupation it would have been kept on all night, burning coal that Dad would have brought back from the builder's yard, but they hadn't had any decent stuff since '41, just wet sludge from Belgium that seemed to generate everything but heat. Their supply of wood was running low, though they had yet to decide whether to demolish Sally's old pen and use it for fuel. He opened the front of the stove and shoved a couple of small logs on top of a small pile of kindling. Pulling the pan down from its hook, he cracked in the eggs and waited for the heat to come through. There was still some tea in the caddy left over from Uncle Albert's weekly visit, and though he felt guilty making a pot solely for himself, he put the kettle on. He needed some comfort.

While the eggs were cooking he moved into the other room and sat in the armchair where Dad used to sit bathing his feet, waiting for his supper. Though the light in the kitchen was weak, it shone clear through. Ned couldn't help but look. This was where he had been brought up, this tiny cottage, the downstairs room, the kitchen, the outside lav and the two rooms upstairs. He had been right to get out, whatever Dad had thought, and now he was back again. Back and alone and without a future. How familiar it looked, and yet how strange that this might turn out to be his whole life; the red carpet brought back from one of the big houses before he had been born, the French clock Grandad had rescued from some sinking tramp steamer, the warped sideboard with the ashtray from Portland Bill on it, Mum and Dad's wedding picture propped up behind. What else? A square table, a clean grate, a mirror with the silver backing coming off, the lighthouse doorstop and three easy chairs. He returned to the kitchen, put the pan on the table, pulled the *Star* out of his pocket and started to read.

Like everyone else he took little notice of the news, for that came firmly under the censor's control: reports of Lord Haw-Haw's latest broadcast, exaggerated claims about their military successes and feeble attempts at ingratiation. Instead he turned straight to the back page. At the top right-hand corner, Conversation Lesson No. 204. Tonight's was typical. *Was halten Sie von diesem Bild?* What do you think of this picture? *Ich bin kein Kunstkenner.* I am no connoisseur. *Sie sehen doch, was es darstellen soll.* Yet you see what it is supposed to represent. *Es stellt eine Dame dar, die Klavier spielt.* It shows a lady playing the piano. Now, how do you like it? *Nun also, wie gefällt es Ihnen?* All very well and good, although Ned couldn't see the point of the third remark. Either it showed a lady playing a piano or it didn't. However that was nothing compared with the last phrase. *Das kann ich nicht sagen: ich bin taub.* I cannot tell: I am deaf. What should he make of that? What it a mistake. Did they mean to write 'I cannot tell: I am blind'? Or was it a joke? He could imagine Sondeführer Bohde beside himself with merriment over that one. However, 'What do you think of this . . .?' was useful. *Was halten Sie von diesem . . .?* He said it out loud and then looked down to the advertisements. The Trade Cards. The Island's Market Place. The Entertainments. In far left-hand corner, he read the usual: *Wanted. Blacksmiths, Bricklayers, Stone masons, fitters and quarrymen of all classes. Apply van Dielen. 30 Victoria Rd.* Opposite were tonight's exchange offerings. *Two Tennis racquets with presses for offer of tobacco. Write 'Ping'. Dog soap and shampoo for best offer cigarettes, write 'Bob Martin'. Gents shoes Sir Herbert Parker make for sugar or useful commodities.* And in the centre another announcement: *Chiropody. Miss Veronica Vaudin is pleased to announce an extension of her opening hours. Mornings 10–12.30: Afternoon 2.30–4.30. Monday – Friday. By appointment only.* Ned leant back in his chair. Veronica had worked hard for her qualification. His mother hadn't approved of that either. 'Feet!' he remembered her saying. 'Fancy having a daughter-in-law in Feet!' 'Just the job if Ned joins the boys in blue,' his dad had retorted. 'She can massage them of a night,' and he winked at him, man to man, as Mum had banged her temper round the kitchen.

There was nothing in the paper for him. A few bantams for sale, that was all. He placed the pan in the sink and stepped outside. Almost immediately he was aware of a stealthy rustling noise in the field at the back. At first he thought it might be a fox padding along the undergrowth, but despite its stealth it was too clumsy a sound to be made by made four legs. Two legs then, moving towards the back of next door's garden, oblivious of Ned's presence. A soldier with a loaf of bread in his hand? A foreign with one of next door's chickens under his arm? He moved to the gate leading to the back field, ready to pounce, when he heard the sigh of a voice he recognized.

'V, is that you?' he called, moving quickly up to the gate.

A sniffling and then the voice whispered back. 'Ned?'

She stepped into the moonlight, her arms holding her coat tightly round her body. Her hair looked almost silver.

'Got home safely, then?' he said.

She blew her nose and laughed. 'In a manner of speaking. Sorry about the lift.'

'That's all right. I fancied the walk. How's your mum?'

'Not bad. Dad's his usual handful, though. I needed to take a breath of air.'

He nodded, unable to think of anything else to say, feeling the awkwardness between them. Once they had been so at ease with each other. They were standing in different territories now.

'I thought I heard something,' he said. 'No one's been trying to break in round you or anything?'

'No, don't think so. What's there to steal? Anyway, the night's too bright.'

They both looked up. They were alone, under the stars again.

'We'd have gone canoeing,' Ned said, 'on a night like this.'

'You would. I'd have stopped in. Too cold for swimming.' She shivered, as if the coat was giving her no protection at all. 'I'd better get back in. Busy day tomorrow.'

'Yes, I read your advert. You must be doing well.'

'Not that. I've got rehearsals all day. You coming to see us?'

'Perhaps. If I have the time.'

'You always used to.'

Ned turned and looked out over the grey field. He didn't want to look at her any more. 'There's a different audience there now, V,' he told her.

'Only in one half. You don't have to sit with them. They're quite separate.'

'When they choose to be.'

'You can't blame them for wanting company, Ned. We all want company.'

'So I saw.' He regretted saying it the moment it left his mouth.

'You been talking to my father?' Veronica's whisper rose in intensity. 'You crossed me off, remember.' She paused. 'God, listen to the pair of us. To think we could have been married by now.'

'You'd have regretted it.'

'Possibly. Possibly not. You would, though. You had other ambitions. Well, they haven't come to much, have they? You're stuck here, Ned Luscombe, whether you like it or not. So make the best of it. Like we all have to.' She started to walk away.

'V, I didn't mean . . .' But she had gone.

It was cold in his bedroom, cold and uncomfortable. Outside the wind was picking up again. Across the landing he could hear Mum snoring. At least she was safe in bed. She'd taken to sleepwalking in the last few months. Three to four in the morning was the chosen time. Usually he'd be alerted by the sound of her stumbling into a chair; once he'd woken to find the kettle singing its heart out on the stove with her gone and the back door swinging open. He'd thrown his coat over his pyjamas and followed the opened back gate and the silver trail of footsteps on the wet cobwebbed grass with his police torch. He'd found her half a mile away, walking along the hedgerows picking imaginary blackberries in her wicker basket, her nightdress bedraggled and torn, her arms all bloody from the tangle of thorns. Since that time usually he slept with his bedroom door open and the back-door key under his pillow. But not tonight. His quarrel with Veronica and the thought of Isobel had made him weary and forgetful. Tomorrow he would see Isobel again. Must see you, she had written. *Must see you.* She would confide in him, ask his help, declare . . . declare her what? He waited for sleep behind a closed door trying to picture her and what she might say, but thinking too of Tommy and letters and most irritatingly of all, Veronica swimming in the sea.

*

The Major took a last look at the drawing room, with the half-empty bottles and stubbed-out cigarette ends littering the sideboard, the parquet floor strewn with the set of Christmas paper hats and streamers that Zep had found in a box in the cellar. In the far corner he could see a nurse's skirt and jacket, her shoes laid carefully on top. Molly lay curled up on the sofa, nursing a brandy she didn't want to drink. She was just trying to keep awake, to look alive for the Captain's return. He took pity on her.

'You can come upstairs if you want.'

'What?' Molly looked up, both confused and surprised at such an unexpected proposition.

'No, no, I wasn't suggesting—' He broke off. 'I meant the Captain's room. Under the circumstances I would have no objections.'

For a moment Molly looked disappointed, not because she desired him, but because he did not desire her. She ran her hand through her hair as if to remind herself of her irrepressible allure, then swung her legs out from under.

'That's kind of you, Gerhard, but I'd better not. You might not object but Zep probably would.'

'After tonight? I don't think so.'

'But you can't be sure, can you?' Lentsch opened his hands. 'See? It's not worth the risk.'

'Some cocoa then, before I retire?'

'That would be nice.'

He marched purposefully down to the kitchen, Albert's domain. The light was bright and bare, everything washed and put away. He found the tin quickly enough, with a pencil mark on the outside marking the content level, but he couldn't find any sugar. Hadn't he asked Albert to get some? He couldn't remember.

'You're the cream in my coffee,' he sang out loud. 'You're the milk in my tea.'

Stirring the powdered chocolate into the milk made him dizzy. He walked back with exaggerated precision, banging into one of the Russell Flints before stumbling into the drawing room, holding the cups high in the air as if he were a steward keeping balance on a pitching yacht. Molly was putting away her lipstick and mirror.

'Piping hot and not a drop spilt,' he announced loudly, 'though I nearly scalded the naked ladies on the way.'

Molly took the cup without batting an eyelid. She wasn't going to make the same mistake twice. 'I'm sorry?'

'The paintings in the hall! I nearly lost my balance and poured cocoa all over the walls.'

'Mrs H. wouldn't like that.'

'No.' He swayed in front of her and took a tentative sip. 'Good old Mrs H.'

Molly was beginning to reassert herself. 'That's right,' she said. 'Good old Mrs H.' She stretched out her legs and admiring what she saw, wriggled her painted toes. 'And here am I slouched in her best furniture.'

'You knew her well before?'

She laughed. 'We moved in different circles, Gerhard, apart from the amateur dramatics.'

'Ah, yes, your plays and shows. Everyone seems to have taken part in them at one time or another, all except Albert, that is.'

'Well, there's not a lot to do in a place like Guernsey. Dressing up on stage kept us out of mischief.'

'Really?'

'No, not really. Quite the reverse, in fact. In fact I think Mrs H. thought she had to be there to see we didn't get carried away. The young flowers of Guernsey and all that. I bet she never imagined for one minute that one day I'd be a regular guest in her house, sleeping in one of her feather beds. Equality of the classes was never her strong point.'

Down the corridor they could hear laughter. Wedel was enjoying his unexpected time with the ill-mannered nurse from Bremen.

'Some people have all the luck,' Molly said and reaching down for her glass tipped the rest of her brandy into the hot drink. 'You and me seem to have missed out tonight. Yours never turned up and mine ran out on me.'

'There are always other times.'

'You hope. Take it while you can, that's my motto.' She stood up. 'Go on, then, off to beddy-byes. I'll make my myself useful down here.'

The Major lay on his bed, listening to her clearing up. He was surprised that the Captain had not yet returned. It must be important, to keep him from Molly, waiting so patiently to fill his bed. In a way he was pleased Isobel hadn't turned up. There was no delicacy to these parties any more. The way everyone was carrying on, the house was becoming little better than a brothel. He should have known it would turn out like this. He remembered the time when, unknown to her father, Isobel had stayed overnight. Zep and he had come down to a late breakfast. The girls had already left. Albert had just brought in a plate of black pudding, made from the blood of rabbits.

'Well,' Zep had demanded, helping himself from Albert's tray, 'what's she like, then?'

Lentsch had been shocked at his matter-of-fact boldness.

'Really, Zep. I don't think . . .'

Zep laughed. 'Don't look so outraged, Gerhard. Haven't you ever looked at Molly and asked yourself the same question? Of course you have.' He waved his fork in the air and leant across. 'I'll tell you what she's like. Like a good watch; well oiled, superb moving parts and keeps perfect time. If I were a generous man I would let you wear her for a while.' He looked at Lentsch, grinning. 'But I'm not.'

What would have happened, Lentsch wondered, if he had taken Molly's arm and hauled her up here without another word? Would she have resisted? Temporarily perhaps but not for long. And why not? Fear? Drunken lust? Or simply another consequence of ordinary war? And what would it have been like making love with her while listening for the sound of Zep's car coming up the drive? It would be exciting, taking her like that, wouldn't it? He touched himself. God, were they all mad?

He hung his uniform on the back of the door and walked across to the window and the dark rolling lawn beyond. He was about to draw the curtains when he saw lights sweeping up the headland. Not just one car but two, and a motorcycle as well. They bobbed and bounced in the night air then disappeared from view as the road bent inwards to the drive and the front of the house. Then he heard a car door slam shut and voices and Zep fumbling with his key. Lights came on, footsteps down the corridor. He expected them to march into the drawing room, where Molly was waiting, but they did not. They took the stairs two at a time with the Captain calling out his name.

*

Ned was woken by the sound of heavy pounding. For a moment he thought he was back in the section house with his Sergeant rattling his stick on their cast-iron beds and then he woke and saw his mother standing over him, shielding the candle flame with her bony hand. He could see the shape of her, lost underneath her flannel nightgown, and for the first time he realized how thin she had become. He rubbed his eyes.

'What's up?' he asked.

'They're at the door,' she said, and as if on cue the noise started up again, a hammering on one side of the front door and a barking on the other. Ned sat up and looked to the blacked-out window. Her shadow danced on the curtain to the rhythm of fluttering flame.

'Who could it be?' she asked, and trying to wish the answer into the world, added hopefully, 'Russians?'

Ned shook his head. 'Douse the flame,' he told her, 'and let's have a look at them.'

He slid out of bed and lifted up the black fabric and looked down. There were two of them. The Major's car stood in the road behind them. It didn't look good. He dropped the curtain.

'Germans,' he said. 'Is the radio safe?'

'Up on the chimney ledge where it always is. Oh, Ned.' She clutched at him and began to shake. Ned stroked her hair.

'Don't worry. They wouldn't send Lentsch's car just to arrest me,' he lied. The banging on the door continued, louder this time, and then, above the noise, came the call: his title and his name. A torch shone up at the window. He pushed his mother away gently.

'Go back to bed. It's best if you keep out of it.'

He slipped into his trousers and pulled on a shirt. Downstairs was damp and cold, and the empty fireplace in the front room looked bare and vulnerable. Jimbo stood by the door, growling.

'Basket,' he ordered and the dog slunk off. Checking that the curtains were well drawn, he went to the table and lit the oil lamp. The electricity wouldn't be on for another hour. A thick plume of acrid smoke rose to the black patch on the low ceiling. He adjusted the wick. Light flickered on the walls. The banging resumed.

'*Moment!*' he called out. '*Moment!*'

He walked over to the fireplace and ducking his head down reached up. If someone had denounced them they would have told them where to look as well. Before he had been dragooned into the force his mother used to hold BBC parties once a week. Everyone would bring something, a plate of biscuits, a pot of jam, a rhubarb cake, and they would drink blackberry-leaf tea listening to their guest of honour, brought out from its hiding place and set down in the centre of the table on a folded linen napkin. He'd put a stop to them as soon as he'd been appointed.

He eased the radio out of its hiding place, careful not to disturb the soot, and hurried into the kitchen. Underneath Jimbo's basket, beneath the flagstone, was a hollow he had dug a month after the Occupation. It was where he kept Dad's pistol, a relic of the old war. The Alsatian looked up and licked his hand.

'Good boy,' he told him. 'Stay there.'

He dragged the basket across the floor and lifted up the stone. The gun lay at the bottom, wrapped in an oilcloth. Taking it out he lowered the radio face down, replacing the weapon carefully in amongst the precious valves at the back. Once the flagstone was back in position he pulled the dog's basket back in place. Jimbo, hoping this was part of some new game, began to thump his tail in anticipation. Ned patted his head.

'Later, boy. Later.'

He turned on the tap and ran the cold water across his face and hands. The banging was continuous now and the front room seemed to shake with every blow. Drying his hands on the back of his trousers he ran across and opened the door. Light shone in his face. The night air stung his skin.

'Yes,' he said, 'who is it? What do you want?'

'Inspector Luscombe?'

'Yes?'

'You are to come with us. Major Lentsch requests.'

Lentsch requests. Well, that was a new one. Squinting in the light he looked at the bearer of this unwanted invitation. He recognized him, Helmut Wedel, Lentsch's adjutant.

'Wedel, is that you?' The man nodded. 'What's happened?'

'Major Lentsch requests,' he repeated. He motioned to the car. 'Please?'

Ned pointed to his bare feet and held up three fingers. Wedel nodded and walked back up the path to the waiting car. Ned ran back upstairs. His mother was standing in the doorway of her bedroom, shivering. Behind her, Ned could see the double bed and the grease spot on the wall where Dad used to lean his head for his last smoke of the day. A mark on the wall, a plot of land out at the back, and six chickens. Not much after thirty years.

'I thought I told you to get back into bed,' he said.

'What do they want?' she demanded. 'It's not yet six thirty.'

'I don't know. It's nothing you've done.' He put his hands on her shoulders. She was cold and bony and afraid. He remembered how she used to be, warm and soft and content. 'I'll be back for breakfast, you'll see.' He kissed her on the cheek. 'Now get on with you. The radio's under the floor. Just in case.'

She nodded.

Outside Helmut stood by the car smoking a cigarette. As Ned walked up, not knowing quite what was expected of him, Helmut

108

moved to the back door, wiping the handle with his sleeve. He opened the door, inviting Ned in.

'Nice auto,' Helmut observed.

It was a nice auto. It had been Bernie's pride and joy, his Wolseley, there for weddings, funerals and other days of hire, but he had lost it to them almost immediately, a month after their arrival. It had had three 'owners' up to now, Knackfuss, Kratzen and now Lentsch. Ned climbed in and looked around. They were taking good care of it. He must tell Bernie. Most cars were marked by now, dents and crumpled bumpers, or some other indication of the Occupation. It was all very well for them to insist they changed the habits of a lifetime but once on the road, cycling down the narrow lanes, it was all too easy to revert to the old ways. The proper ways. The trouble was you'd round a corner and find yourself on course for a collision with a senior member of the Wehrmacht and a hefty fine from the magistrate the following morning.

'So what's all the fuss?' Ned said. 'My mother thought you were Russians.'

Helmut laughed.

'For sure. We knock on your door politely and request to steal your food,' he joked, failing to see the piquancy of his remark, adding, equally incongruously, 'We are having bad business with the Russians.'

Not according to Lord Haw-Haw you're not, Ned thought. 'You are?' he asked innocently.

'*Ja.* Two nights they broke into the Villa. Bread, sugar, and a pie from apples. For the Major's tea.'

Ned bit his lip. 'Terrible.'

Helmut nodded. 'We sleep now with our rations in our room. Cakes, butter, sausage – all next to the hairbrush.' He fumbled in his pocket. 'A smoke, Herr Luscombe?' he offered, handing back a battered packet. Ned accepted it gratefully. He had exchanged his last coupon for a second-hand bicycle tyre.

'Thanks.' He made to pass the packet back. Helmut waved it away with an expansive gesture.

'Finish them. I am on leave next week. Amsterdam.'

Ned slipped the cigarettes in his jacket pocket. 'Nice. I'll come with you if you like.'

Helmut laughed. 'For sure. But first you have to have the right uniform. A British policeman – no good.'

'I haven't got a uniform. I'm plain-clothes, remember.'

'*Ja*, I know. A policeman without a uniform.' He shook his head, as if he found the combination an impossible one to comprehend.

'Where are we going?' Ned asked.

Helmut shrugged his shoulders and then deciding to take matters in his own hands said, 'Torteval. Gull Bay. The Dortmann Battery.'

'Gull Bay?'

The coast around Torteval was a restricted area and had been since '41 – a rabbit warren of naval gun emplacements, bunkers and anti-aircraft guns.

Helmut nodded.

Ten minutes later the car bumped up the red packed-earth drive. Light was creeping over the sea, grey and cold. On the cliff's edge stood the old red stone fort, now burdened with barnacles of roughly edged concrete. Soon the whole area would be a blaze of colour from the flowering gorse and the heather, but now there was just the wind tugging at the stunted winter growth. Wedel turned the car quickly, spinning the rear wheels on the dirt. Dortmann Battery. Lentsch stood by the sunken entrance, set deep into the rock, the cold wind tugging at his greatcoat. Beside him stood the officer who had lectured him earlier that morning, Captain Zepernick. Ned ducked into the stern breeze and hurried over.

'Major,' he shouted. 'What seems to be the trouble?'

Lentsch didn't seem to want to answer him. Captain Zepernick made to continue but Lentsch held up his hand, clearing his throat to prepare both himself and Ned for what he had to say.

'I have some news for you, Inspector.'

'Yes?'

'It is not good news. Not good at all.' He looked up, biting back the words. 'It's Isobel, Inspector.' He gestured inside. 'She is dead. In there. They have killed Isobel.'

As Ned waited for Lentsch to continue, it seemed to him that the island had been waiting for a moment like this, when the two tides of Guernsey's life would meet in an inevitable rip tide. He felt an anger rising within him, wondering what particular complicity had brought these two men together, whether it was one or both of them who might be responsible. Isobel dead! He could not quite envisage that, Isobel and death, although, until the coming of the letter, he had not considered Isobel as 'alive' for some time. She had passed beyond his world, lain with another species, mutated into an unwelcome and possibly lethal hybrid of war. The letter had made her human again, one of them. The Germans were not human. The foreigns were not human. Knowing this helped them survive.

'Isobel?' he said. 'Dead? But how?'

Lentsch hesitated, then spoke.

'She was found early this morning.' He nodded. 'Inside there.'

'Here? I don't understand. This is out of bounds.'

The Captain looked embarrassed. 'Each bunker has a shaft, for emergencies,' he explained. 'She was found, lying at the bottom of such a thing.'

Ned ran his fingers over his face. He could imagine what had happened. Caught by a group of drunken soldiers no doubt, raped and beaten to death. He thought again of that fierce little man and the peculiar personal tragedies that this island had visited upon him.

'Has her father been told?' he asked.

Lentsch nodded. For a moment Ned was nonplussed.

'Then what do you want me to do? Make a formal identi-fication?'

'Come and see for yourself,' he demanded, picking up his own.

The Captain led the way, ducking his head as he stepped through the squat entrance. Above the desk by the door ran an inscription. Ned raised his eyes to it. *Kom in unsere Kassematte, da Kriegst Du Keine vor die Platte* it read.

'You read German?' Lentsch asked.

Ned shook his head. 'Some of the phrases in the *Star*, that's all. Not that they're all that useful.'

Lentsch nodded. 'It means "Come into our casement and you won't get hit."'

Ned followed him in. Facing him was a straight corridor some thirty foot in length and nine foot high. The walls were lined with cream-painted lockers, on which were perched numbered helmets. Further down he could see the tall outline of a rifle rack. Hushed voices could be heard coming from a darkened room at the end, low and nervous. Boots rang out on metal, and as his eyes grew accustomed to the bright light, something set in the middle of the far floor seemed to swing round. A young man swam into view, leaning back on a slatted metal seat, his legs stretched out in front like a child's on a playground roundabout, his arm resting on the huge apparatus of a gunsight. Ned was looking directly into the gun room. The soldier looked up and saw Ned looking back at him. They were the same age, Ned guessed. The gunner spoke to an invisible companion. The door swung to, but did not close. Captain Zepernick beckoned him through.

'This way.'

Ned followed him into a chamber running off to the left.

'This is where the gun crew abide when on duty,' the Captain explained. 'It is where she was found.'

Ned looked round. To his immediate right running along the wall were nine bunks in tiers of three. Two more, with a field telephone at the foot of the lower one, were on the wall to his left. Facing him stood a thin cupboard; then, along the back wall, a table and stove. On the adjoining wall another steel door and next to it a fierce black contraption with concertina piping that snaked along the ceiling and out through a hatch above his head. He stared at it wondering what it could be. Lentsch caught his eye again.

'Air pump,' he said, 'for gas attack.'

The Captain coughed deliberately, as if to remind Lentsch of the company he was keeping. Ned continued with the questions.

'How many men work here?' he asked.

'Usually four, three men and an officer,' Lentsch answered quickly.

'And last night?'

'Three. Is that not correct, Captain.'

Zepernick nodded.

'The Lieutenant left last night at the start of his leave. But he is due to report in at ten o'clock this morning to arrange a passage to the mainland.'

Although military in materials and colour, the men had clearly tried to make the place as comfortable as possible. A home-made chess set with crude square-cut figures stood on a little table, while pictures of families and girlfriends were propped on a lintel above, over which loomed an elaborate cuckoo clock wreathed in heavy wooden leaves. On the inside door of the wardrobe, which was full of uniforms and boots, were pasted a collection of mildly obscene outdoor photographs, girls in suspenders, girls playing leapfrog, girls squinting in the sun with their hands coyly protecting their private parts. None of them were exactly pin-up material; they were all too thin or too short or too old. They all had that same, faraway look in their eyes, as if, despite the smiles and the poses, they were only half there. From the torn scraps sticking out from a number of drawing pins, some, probably of a more explicit nature, had been hastily removed. For his or their superiors' benefit? Whichever, by now they'd be nothing more than ashes in the stove. In the centre of this gallery was pinned a cartoon of a trouserless Winston Churchill. Winston was kneeling on all fours, the famous V of his fingers drawing into his mouth a Jew's circumcised and syphilitic penis, while, at the other end, a laughing Uncle Sam decked out in a top hat spiked with dollars sodomized him with mirth. The Jew and the American's hands met in gleeful celebration over his gross, compliant form.

The Major closed the cupboard door. He was embarrassed. Captain Zepernick crossed over to the stove. At the other side of it, at waist height, a hatch had been built into the wall. Its thick metal door hung open.

'This is the shaft where she was found,' Zepernick said, 'for escaping.' He seemed ashamed to admit that they might need such a device. Ned bent down and looked in. There was a sizeable tunnel running back, about eight feet long and three feet high, with a rung-laddered shaft at the far end. Zepernick joined him, pointing in.

'There should be two steel...' he searched for the word ... 'planks?'

'Girders,' Ned suggested.

Zepernick nodded. 'Two steel girders and a brick wall in there, all of which can be removed quickly.'

'So that people can't get in?'

Zepernick shook his head. 'Blast protection.' He lifted his hand and made a dropping motion. 'From the grenades.'

'So why aren't they there now?'

Captain Zepernick snorted, a mixture of laughter and impatience.

'Soldiers! They love to break the rules. In an emergency they want to get out as quickly as possible.'

'So it's kept empty?'

'No. They keep wood for the stove. Enough for every night. Then they don't have to go so much to the storeroom. Yesterday, however, they had cleaned it out. They knew there was to be an inspection. It was quite empty.'

Ned put head in and looked around. Though the walls were of concrete, the flooring was metal. He banged it with his hand. It reverberated like an echo chamber. Re-emerging he said, 'Surely they would have heard something?'

Zepernick shook his head. 'Yesterday evening they had a long practice. Setting targets with the new range-finding tower. Loading and firing drills. For night attack. Perhaps you heard? Until eleven o'clock. And afterwards the cleaning.'

'And this lieutenant, he wasn't here for this practice?'

'He stayed until the last. A few minutes before nine, I understand.'

'And none of them came into this room?'

'Only to make coffee, and cook.'

'And the lieutenant?'

'Schade? I do not know? You will have to ask him.'

'Schade?'

'Yes. You know of him?'

'No, no. Just want to make sure I get the name right. So when did they find her?'

'At half-past one. She was dead already.'

'And when did they last look into the hatch?'

'At eight approximately.'

Ned stood up and dusted his knees.

'And when did you arrive?'

'Soon after.' He took out his notebook again and made a great show of turning the pages. 'I arrived at ten minutes past two o'clock exactly. After taking Miss Vaudin to her home.'

Ned looked at him. It couldn't have taken him longer than five minutes to get here from Veronica's. He had been with her a good thirty minutes. Ned ignored his smug triumphalism.

'Before we came in, Major, you said, "They have killed Isobel." What did you mean? The gunners here?'

The Major dismissed the suggestion with a wave of his hand.

'I should have thought that was obvious,' he said. 'One of you, one of the islanders must have killed her. For her . . .'

'Yes?'

'You call it collaboration.'

'People called it a lot worse than that, Major.' He paused. 'But if she was found in here surely that points to one of your men?'

Lentsch stared down at the floor. Captain Zepernick broke in.

'If she was killed by a soldier, do you think they would have left her here?' he said. 'Do you not think they would have thrown her over the cliff, or taken her somewhere not so embarrassing?'

'But civilians would have to know of the escape shaft's existence. This area has been out of bounds to us for over eighteen months. How do you explain that?'

Captain Zepernick shrugged his shoulders.

'What about the Todt workers,' Ned persisted, 'the foreigns? We all know you can't keep them under control.'

The Captain was growing impatient.

'It is not the Zwangsarbeiters or our men that should concern you. There is something else.'

He ducked out of the door and into the corridor. Ned hesitated. He did not want this. He had told Isobel the truth when they had first met. He had seen only one body and that an accidental death, not one silenced by malice.

'In here,' Zepernick announced. 'The ammunition room.'

Ned followed him into a chamber running off to the right. Painted on the walls leapt a fresco of firs and ferns and glades of stolen light. Brown bears peeped out of clumps of trees, deer drank from ponds and through the branches flew woodpeckers and ducks.

'It is beautiful, is it not?' Lentsch spoke softly behind him. Ned turned, startled. 'The men miss their homeland,' he explained, both proud and apologetic. 'Go to any German barracks and you will find the same. It would not be so in England, I think. In Sandhurst or Aldershot.'

Along the walls, against the delicately drawn grasses, stood racks of artillery shells, stacked lengthways like a woodcutter's supply of winter logs. In the middle of this military glade lay a figure: Isobel, gaily clad in a calf-length tunic of fringed green, palms down by her side. Her skin, where it was visible, her arms her legs, the still divide of her breasts, was blue. Her mouth was strangely open, as if frozen in a cry or expectant of a lover's kiss. He bent down and saw the reason why. It was held open by a quantity of what looked like pale butter. A horrid thought came into his mind and his eyes travelled to where the outline of her hips could be seen, before questioning the Captain with a look.

'Just the mouth,' the Captain replied.

Ned looked closer. It had been squeezed in. He could see the indentations of a man's knuckles.

'What is it?' Ned said, touching it gently. 'Butter?'

'Cement,' Captain Zepernick said, embarrassed. 'And much sand. In her nostrils also.'

Ned lifted her arm and placed it across her chest. It was the first time he had touched a dead person and though he trembled to touch her, not remembering her exactly, for there was no time for that, but recognizing the shape and stretch of her, he found it easier than he had imagined. She still felt like Isobel. Her skin was paler than Isobel's, that was all. He put his hand gently on her belly. The cold seemed to radiate through the thin cloth. She looked frozen.

'It's the wrong time of year to be out wearing something like this,' he said, fingering the strap of her dress, straightening it back over her shoulder.

'Peter Pan,' Lentsch said, standing behind him.

'What?'

'It is the tunic she wore when we first met,' the Major told him. 'That is why she is wearing it.'

'She was destined for the Major's party,' the Captain explained.

'What party?'

'For my return,' the Major said. 'It was a surprise.'

Ned got to his feet. Suddenly from across the corridor a whirring noise started. The cuckoo clock sounded seven times. They stood still, arms behind their backs, heads bowed, as if the last post was sounding. As the echo died down Ned bent down again. There was a speck of something caught in the depths of her hair. He held it in the air.

'*Was halten Sie von diesem?*' he said. The others stopped. He could hear them holding their breath in surprise. The Captain took the strand from his grasp.

'From outside?' Zepernick suggested. 'As they carried her up the cliff path?'

It was Ned's turn to shake his head.

'This isn't grass,' he said. 'This is straw. From a farm or a stable, perhaps. Had she been riding that day?' He looked at Lentsch.

'Not that I am aware of,' he said.

The three gunners who had found her, Kanoniers Rupp, Bauer, and Laurer, were country boys all, with country boy's hands and country boy's complexions. They had seen nothing, heard nothing. They had manned their gun like honest soldiers. That was all they understood, the rest was hopeful bewilderment. Unlike the officers their grasp of English was slight. They looked at their boots, watching each other out of the corner of their eyes for signs of betrayal. Clustering round the little table like young birds in a crowded nest, opening their mouths in an anxious chorus of demanding innocence, it was impossible to hear their story straight, and Ned was sure that that was what it was, a story, but even when sent out of the room and brought back one by one, standing before the two men who could banish them to the Russian front, they managed to maintain their faltering innocence. But there was a tale they were not telling, this fearful little group, something which had taken place within this cramped and claustrophobic room, with its folded blankets and polished boots. He could catch it in the inadvertent looks to the absent Lieutenant's low bunk, as if they expected the black field phone on the wall near his pillow to spring into accusatory life; he could follow it by the uneasy order that informed their rest room, the stubby chess pieces sitting neatly in their squares, the uncluttered, half-used mantelpiece, the bare space under each set of bunks. All barrack rooms display a certain scrubbed solitude, Ned knew from his own experience, but there was a degree of latitude allowed in such quarters which had not been prevailed upon here. It had been sterilized, wiped clean. Something had gone on here, though Ned was sure it was nothing to do with Isobel. But their fear, their theatrical outrage at her intrusion, puzzled him. It was as if her presence threatened to shed an unwelcome light on some other activity. Perhaps the iron air filter doubled up as an illegal still. Perhaps they'd uncovered a coven of pederasts. Perhaps the missing Schade, lying in a drunken stupor in the Soldatenheim, could enlighten them.

Before driving to van Dielen's house, Ned asked to be taken back home. He wanted to tell Mum the news before Albert arrived with it tucked under his arm. She hadn't gone to bed. She was in the kitchen counting out the food stores, checking them off in the little pocketbook she kept in her apron. She did it every morning, and most afternoons too. She heard him come in but barely turned from the pantry door.

'Only an ounce of butter left,' she fretted. 'And no more coming till next week. And that tea your uncle brought round. It's half gone already. It's too much, really it is.'

Ned led her out of the pantry door and standing by the porcelain sink told her as best he could. He hardly knew what to say. His mother had never met Isobel. She had never even talked about her. When he had been seeing her, he had been doing something that was not simply on his own but outside his mother's understanding. They had seen his mother once, him and Isobel, walking up past Isobel's house, taking Dad his tea when he was working overtime on some renovation work for the museum. She had been clothed as she was now, in an old shirt and a long faded blue skirt with sagging pockets at the front, her bare arms swinging her thick calico shopping bag, her large and ruddy face set to the task ahead. Her footsteps were solid, like her shoes, her strength harnessed to the necessity of work, so different from the demeanour of the young woman beside him. It was not simply a matter of age. The distinction between them would remain whatever their times in life, even if it were his mother who had been the girl and Isobel the older woman. Suddenly he had not wanted to belong to his mother or any of her kind. He wanted to lay claim only to Isobel and all the other Isobels of the world, young or old. He wanted to inherit their muscle, their skin, their light unsullied timbre. He stepped back behind a bush and pulled Isobel after him.

'Shh,' he warned.

'Someone you know?' she teased, and breaking out of his grip she stuck her head through the leaves. Ned pulled her back again, this time more sharply.

'No one special,' he said, planting the lie on her warmth of her throat, and dragging her back against him. She stuck her feet out willingly as he hauled her back to the clearing. 'An old busybody, that's all,' he scoffed and laying her on the ground had stirred her stomach with his foot.

'I know all about busybodies,' she grinned. 'There's my aunt for a start. God, my aunt. Tries to run my life.' She scrambled up on her hands and knees and, crawling over the grass, called out, 'Ahoy there, Mrs Whoever-you-are! Someone here says you're an old . . .'

Ned covered her giggling mouth and turned her over.

'Be quiet now,' he said, pinning her loose arms high above her head. 'It's my mother. All right?'

'I know,' she boasted. She bounced her hips against him. 'I'd like to meet her.'

'Not now,' he said, untying the belt of her jacket, conscious of their desire.

'Later, then.'

'Why? I've got your father to steer clear of. Now you've my mother. We're evens.'

'Not really,' she told him, looking down at his insistent hands. 'You couldn't charm my father however hard you tried. But I could charm your mother as easy as pie.'

Her jacket and blouse lay open. He was barely listening.

'You could?'

'Yes. Don't you know? I can charm anybody I want to.'

Now when he tried to form her name in front of his mother and place it alongside the other word filling his mouth, death, it was as if he were acknowledging for the first time the strength of his failed affection, the bitter ground that he had trodden upon.

'Isobel. It's Isobel, Mum. She's dead,' he said, stumbling over her Christian name as if he had no right to use it. 'Killed.' He felt himself blushing. It was almost as if he were admitting to the deed himself.

'Isobel! Dead!' she said, echoing her son's own exclamation. 'But how!'

'That's what they want me to find out,' he replied, walking out into the front room, indicating the Major, who stood awkwardly in the light of the doorway. He turned and lowered his voice. 'I just came back to let you know I'm all right. I'll have a quick wash while I'm here. There's no telling how long they'll keep me.'

Ned went upstairs. The Major, conscious of the silence and the requirements of his upbringing, took off his cap and advanced. Ned's mother stepped into the room and faced him. In the kitchen the dog growled, and as she looked back, ready to draw attention to him as a means of conversation, she noticed the half ring of dirt on the flagstone. Ned had failed to put the basket back in its proper place. The circle of dust proclaimed their duplicity like the cheap sparkle on a brass wedding ring.

'Stop that nonsense,' she scolded quickly and shut the door. 'He still hasn't got over this morning,' she explained, adding, 'You gave us all a proper fright.'

The Major bowed his stiff apology. 'I did not mean to alarm you at such an hour.'

Ned's mother sniffed. It was not the time that mattered.

'We're all early risers here,' she told him, in a tone one might tell a stranger the nature of one's religion.

'He has told you the news?'

'Yes. Dreadful.'

'I need his help, Mrs Luscombe.'

'I can see that.'

'I must take him away again.'

'To the house, yes.'

'You know it?'

'Dad helped build it before he passed away.' She saw the Major's quickly masked look of incomprehension. 'Ned's father,' she explained.

'Ah.' The Major looked relieved. 'He died recently.'

She nodded, wiping her hands on her dress.

'It must be hard for you,' he continued, anxious to win the battle of apologies. 'Your bereavement and then us here, the two things so close together.'

'Well, you coming took my mind off Dad going, I must say.' She heard Ned moving about upstairs. 'And he'd be back in England now, learning foreign ways. So I've got you to thank for that as well.'

Lentsch opened his hands.

'You see. Even the German army has its uses. But I must warn you. He is still learning foreign ways.' She smiled despite herself.

Ned's clattered down the stairs. They stepped back.

'What?' Ned said, ducking into the conversation. His mother, fussing through her embarrassment, handed him his coat and shooed him out of the door.

'Mind your manners,' she reminded him softly, but he was already out on the path. The Major bowed his head and followed. She stood in the doorway, still wary, shaking her head, remembering not the blank look of sorrow she had seen on her son's face not five minutes earlier, but that former time, in the coming of the last New Year, when Isobel had given him up, that resolution week Ned had spent drinking, long and deep, behind the closed doors of the Britannia and the rogues' bar halfway down Hauteville, the same ill-lit, damp back room where he had thrown Veronica over, the product of another imagined slight. She had seen the weakness of the male sex in him that week, for he had done the thing that a thwarted man does, treating the world as if he was its only deserving occupant. Though he had shown an indifferent face to his mates, what a spoilt complexion surfaced when only his mother and father were present! Even at the New Year's Eve party over at Bernie's house, it had been Ned's private bitterness, uttered quickly in his father's ear, that had soured their celebratory drink, rather than the rattle sounding in Dad's chest. 'Happy New Year, son,' Dad had offered, clinking his ruby glass, a gesture to a continuity he knew to be illusory, and Ned dismissed the attempt with an impatient snort, and, grabbing Bernie by the arm, had declared that the two of them were going out to wash the bastard past away, downing whatever was in his glass, not the mulled beer on offer, but something strong and vicious, in three savage gulps before escaping to a chorus of drunken cheers. He was too busy inhaling that spiteful strength from the room to notice how Dad had flinched, conscious of the gathering speed of his mortality and the burden it placed on them all. A carpenter all his life, clever with his hands, by then he could barely climb the stairs unaided, one of the many handicaps he had tried to keep from their son, not for fear of worrying him, but in an attempt to maintain his own fragile pride. The first full day of Ned's visit, Dad had woken to bad lungs, hawking bloody lumps into his fisted handkerchief, and as she had helped to dress him, with him sitting on the edge of the bed, an unlit roll-up stuck on his lip, panting as she pulled his trousers over his legs, the bedroom door had swung open. Across the passageway Ned sat on his bed in a cruel parody of their hidden pantomime, and for a moment the two men looked at each other. What an unwelcome mirror they both saw. Then Dad had pushed the door shut, and with his temper let loose from the slam of it, shoved her down onto the floor. From then on, during Ned's stay, sheer bloody-mindedness had willed his body to confront tasks that had been beyond him the six months previously; carrying potatoes in from the outhouse, gathering fallen logs in the garden, even working the wet sheets through the mangle out in the yard, both of them knowing that when Ned returned to the mainland this need for exertion would pass. And so it proved, but not simply passed, for this impetuous gesture had evaporated what small reserves of energy Dad had left, and with the damp weeks of January seeping in the cold and clammy bedroom walls he took to his bed again. Yes, she would mourn the passing of Isobel, not simply for the brutality of her death, but for what it might do to her son. He had abandoned both family and faith in his careless pursuit of her and with the news he had brought back now, she feared he would never recover. Isobel would be preserved for ever, the ghost of her figure ready to rise up between him and the life he had yet to live.

She watched as Ned climbed into the car, easing back onto the leather upholstery as if he was as familiar with its cushioned panels and pale armrests as he was with the pedalled chair sitting on its polished pedestal in the barber's shop opposite Underwood's. Then the Major stepped in, hiding her son from view. He put his hand inside his jacket and drew out a silver case. She saw her son's hand floating over and, closing her eyes, shut the door fast, thankful that Dad had not been alive to witness such a close and crowning capitulation.

*

Ned could feel the acid rising in his stomach. He rubbed his chest, then despite the fact that it eased the pain, stopped. Lentsch was looking at him intently. Ned pulled his handkerchief up to his mouth and let the clear bile run.

'Stomach complaint?' Lentsch queried, bringing his voice under control.

Ned nodded.

Lentsch fumbled in his pocket.

'Chalk,' he said, holding out a silver case of small white tablets. 'From home.' He patted his stomach. 'I too have this malady.'

Ned chewed on the tablet.

'This is a bad business,' Lentsch said. 'I have given strict instructions. There will be no reprisals. People must know we believe in the rule of law.'

The calm of Lentsch's chill reassurance seemed to thaw a shard of frozen recklessness in Ned's heart.

'Is that why you deported all the British-born last month?' he asked.

Lentsch looked to the floor.

'Has not England interned all Germans, taken them to some place of detention, where they can be watched, kept under guard?'

'I don't know.'

'Of course they have. It is only sense. Even if you believe that they will not plot against you, you must do this. For security. Do not worry about your English friends. They will be looked after.' He took out a chalk pill and popped it into his mouth. 'Who knows? They may even get more to eat.'

Ned was annoyed. Even now the ever-present subject of food loomed large.

'But you promised us that no one would be deported. Except . . .'

He let the word die in the air between them. There had been only three of them, a nurse, a hospital cleaner and the woman who had taken a job on one of the big farms just a few months before the invasion. Ned had seen her once, herding cattle along the back lanes in the summer rain, slapping their backsides in affectionate exasperation, her determined face softened by an unhurried contentment. She'd been studying agriculture at a college in Reading and had come over as soon as she'd heard about the job. Even at the time people said she was being foolish, coming so close to the Continent, but she wouldn't listen. To work outdoors, to work with animals, that was all she wanted, and Ned supposed that once here it hadn't seemed possible that it would ever be taken from her, that she could be removed. And with her red hair and fair skin who was going to know? As long as she kept quiet and didn't show herself, as long as she called the cows, cleaned their stalls, sang to them softly while wiping down their warm pink udders, surely she was safe? And so the days became weeks and the weeks months; the cows were led out in the morning and milked in the afternoon, and in the evening the meal she sat down to was a family affair. But early last year she had been informed upon – that was the whisper, though the unremarkable ratchet of official machinery was Ned's more tutored guess. Whatever, she was gone by April, despite the farmer's pleas. The family had held a farewell party for her the night before and still talked of her and her way with his cattle, wondering how she was faring, hoping, as they had all promised themselves that tearful evening, that one day she might return. The Major grunted.

'In war it is not always possible to keep one's promises,' he admitted. 'We expected the war to be short. Now it is long. The island's significance, its specifications, have changed. To begin with it was to be an example of what the British could expect when we had won the war. This is what it will be like when you find us in the Cotswolds and Coventry and your town spa of Bath. This is what you will hear, this is what you will read, this is what you will see, marching down your streets. Though what is yours will be ours, we will respect it, strengthening all that is good, weeding out all that is corrupt. But now it has changed. The islands have become mixed up in the whole sorry plot. Now they are part of the military strategy.' He cleared his throat before changing the subject. 'There is something else I must say before we arrive at her house. Though her death at the hands of an islander would be purely a civilian matter, there is the matter of her father. Working for the Organisation Todt he holds the honorary rank of major and comes under military jurisdiction.'

'Even though he's English?'

'He is also Dutch, Inspector, and did much work, roads, bridges and so forth, before . . .' he gestured in front of him, 'all this happened. His work here is of the utmost importance. He and Major Ernst.' He crossed the two long fingers of his right hand. 'You know Major Ernst?'

'Only by sight. A stout gentleman.'

Lentsch grinned. 'You are too polite. A little fat man, who I am told has to wear a corset under his uniform. If that is what you can call it.'

Ned sidestepped as best he could.

'I wouldn't know about that. He likes to be on parade though, he and his men. Out in all weathers, gymnastic displays, marching up and down the Esplanade. They're quite good once you've got over their spades.'

He drew a picture of an upended shovel on the condensation, then quickly rubbed it out. Lentsch sighed.

'He and van Dielen had been dining together last night, reviewing the fortification plans.'

Ned nodded, as if hearing this information for the first time. 'Are they not ended, then?' he asked.

Lentsch bridled sufficiently to let Ned know he had overstepped the mark.

'The Organisation Todt does not come under my jurisdiction. It answers only to the military.' Now it was his turn to draw upon the steamed up window, and from his reluctant fingers came the overelaborated letters *Org. Todt*, with the winged eagle perched in between, clutching its founder's name in its talons. Lentsch circled it, then rubbed his picture out too, but in enmity rather than in haste. 'It is a most powerful organization,' he warned, 'and gaining strength at every turn. Major Ernst does not want you brought into this. He would like everything to be dealt with by the Geheimnis Polizei, to let the Captain go to work on whoever he sees fit.'

'And you do not?'

'The Captain is less mindful of the island's sensibilities than I. He and his men would start jumping on suspects like a pack of dogs. The goodwill we have built up over the last three years would vanish in a matter of hours. We need the cooperation of the civilian population, Major Ernst more than anyone. He cannot rely on conscripted labour alone.' Lentsch faced Ned. 'You are lucky you live here. Anywhere else in Europe and hostages would have been shot already. This is not the way for Guernsey. We must preserve what we have already achieved. Believe me, there are amongst us many who love your islands.'

Ned felt his anger rising again. 'Including Alderney?' he said. If Guernsey and Jersey could be compared to prisons, Alderney had taken on the mantle of a condemned cell. In the winter Alderney was surrounded by a low and menacing mist, keeping sound and sight at bay, but on the long nights of summer, when they went to bed with Alderney's still and distant image fading in the closing light, those living near the common claimed they could hear the faint chorus of Alderney's suffering skimming over the water. Sometimes it was low in tone, like a solitary hymn sung in an empty church; at others it was as the thrashing of tethered beasts caught in a stable fire. Lentsch was unperturbed.

'Even Athens had such places,' he reasoned. 'For every Parthenon there is a charnel house and someone to stoke the furnace; for every poet a slave, for every philosopher a captive whore.'

'Is that what your plans are?' Ned asked. 'To turn us all into whores and slaves?'

'We are all whores and slaves here, singing for one supper or another, doing as others bid us for want of courage, in the name of greed or expediency. For myself, I do not wish to see Guernsey change at all, though there are others stationed here with different plans. Help me with this and they may not have their chance.'

As they drove past Saumarez Park they came up against a column of Todt workers on their way to work, about thirty of them, boys and old men mostly, shuffling along, feet bare or wrapped in torn rags, hunched against the morning cold, each one carrying a tin bowl in their shackled hands. A Todt official marched alongside them, exhorting them to sing and to pick their feet up.

The group split in two and shuffled past. As he looked out through the windscreen Ned caught sight of a young boy, dressed in a dusty jacket and a pair of red pantaloons. With his dark eyes and his lips blue with cold, he looked more like a lost clown than a conscripted labourer. Where on earth had he got that outfit from? he wondered. Suddenly the boy jumped up on to the bank scrabbling about in the grass. Two others followed. The Todt official, pulling at his belt, sprang forward and began to beat them apart with a home-made whip fashioned out of a stick and four strands of leather. As they clambered back down Ned could see the boy had the best part of a dead rabbit in his hand. He held it triumphantly in the air before sinking his teeth into it. Ned could feel his stomach turn. The boy raised his head and looked into his face. There was no expression. Ned looked to the floor. Lentsch stared straight ahead.

'Animals,' they heard Wedel mutter. The column moved on, out of sight.

Five

You could barely see it from the surface, though there were plenty of clues to tell you that there were more than moles working away under the soil: the endless supply of trucks moving along the connecting roads, the brute mouths waiting in the woods to swallow you up, the bare-bricked ventilating shafts set in the middle of vacant fields. If you put your head down one of those dark, plummeting holes you could hear the sound of hard-pressed men shouting and grunting behind the grind and clank of wheels, sniff the dank smell of oil and earth and, yes, the wet slippery scent of fear rising out. Then you would might know that beneath the buttercups and tufts of couch grass lay the largest and most complex structure existing in the whole of the Channel Islands. Ah, the solid rock of Guernsey.

He found that by lying on his back and pressing his feet against the roof of the tunnel he could push the cart along the rails like the old man had suggested. The old man had lived on the canals, and in the early days, when they'd had the will to talk, he had told him of his years working on the coal barges, crisscrossing Europe and the long low tunnels that ran through his working life.

'Me and the wife would lie on the barge roof and walk 'em through,' the bargee had recalled. 'No matter what the weight. Longer than the night itself some of them tunnels. We'd take a rest halfway and lie there in the pitch dark, not a sound around us, except the water dripping and the craft nudging one another. Maybe the splash of a rat somewhere.' He'd poked him in the ribs. 'It's where all our sprats got started. Didn't matter how dark it was. We knew what we was looking for.'

Walking the wagons was tough on his legs, but it saved his arms for the shovel work at the end. Cement and brick going in, granite going out. Of the two operations, pushing the wagons out was the more dangerous, for the track sloped down towards the entrance and unless checked the wagons could pick up a dangerous momentum of their own. Crushed legs, crushed hands, broken ribs, a punctured gut – the wagons had taken their toll. A hospital, that's what they were building, a hospital with kitchens and laundries and everything, even a cinema, though at the moment it was just rock and soil and the reverberation of a hundred hammers. Two long corridors they had hacked away, and in between, connecting them, a series of long domed rooms looking more like catacombs in a cathedral, where stone plinths covering the crumbling bones of ancient saints should reside, than dormitories built to raise the wounded from their beds. Not that he would ever lie on one of them. There was only one sickbed waiting for him. Collapsed from exhaustion? Sling him in the back of the truck. Back broken by a fallen roof? Sling him in the back of the truck. Blinded by blast fragments, coughing up too much blood, arm wrenched out of its socket? Sling him in the truck. And if he survived the day? Put him on the boat to that other island from where no one returned. They would die here, he knew it, wither and die and be chucked away, tipped out over the cliffs like so much rubble.

He had been working the tunnels for three months now in numbing twelve-hour shifts, twelve hours on, twelve hours off. Up at first light, a hard tear of bread, a bowl of cloudy water speckled with torn cabbage leaves and unwashed potato peelings, perhaps a strip of dog in the bottom, and then out in the half dark, with the overseer alongside them, whipping the air with his little tin pipe, deformed merriment playing down the narrow streets, their uniform a mixed bag of rags, here a long nightshirt hanging down over a municipal trousers, there a string vest behind a railwayman's jacket, baggy linen trousers and calico shirts and flat caps atop every one, appropriated headgear of the defunct Czech army.

It was cold and weary, marching along with the wind from the coast adding a final chill to their bones. He'd never seen the sea before he'd been sent here. Two years and he still hated the sight of it. Last summer one afternoon they'd been let loose on one of the long beaches past the harbour, but though the rest had run down to the water's edge, jumping and splashing and pushing each other as if they were on holiday, he had stood on the shore, unable and unwilling to move. It scared him, the sea, so huge and cold and without remorse. Not like the river by his village, and the towpath where he'd gone fishing with his dad, the cows mooching up and down in the meadow behind them. They'd shot them all that second afternoon when the other soldiers came, the dogs, the pigs, the cows, shot the lot of them, casual and laughing, as if they were out for day's fun at a distant country fair.

So here he marched, with the weight of the sweeping sky calling to a stilled life beyond, no not marched, but shuffled in a frozen shivering sleep, ragged arm to ragged shoulder, ragged shoulder to ragged arm, feet black and raw and wrapped in blood-hardened rags, with the road bright and shiny from the night and the distant sound of the great green water sucking at the island's heart: up the hill, past houses and cottages and hidden lives which he could guess at all too well. Were these the whitewashed walls behind which he had once lived, this cracked smudged pane of glass the window looking into his own forgotten life? Was this the meadow, this the pond, this the deserted apple grove where once his family's pigs broke ground? Was that creaking iron pump, so sturdy in its stone casement, the pump under which he pushed his dirty truant face, that the handle, that the gush of water washing away, what, his mother's ire, his sister's gibes, his father's loud lament? As they reached the lip of the hill, and started down into that deep valley, half running, half stumbling, clanking like a medieval siege machine with the tin cups and billycans hanging from their sides, it seemed to him that the closer they came to the great dark hole the lusher the valley grew, as if God Himself was taunting them, showing them all the green wonder of the world before bidding them to depart. Thick ferns rose up out of the wayside grass, buds of he knew not what had pushed their way through the dark soil, the lattice of bare branches now replaced by a canopy the colour of succulent evergreen. And then, as it appeared that the road was leading them ever deeper into this impenetrable fertility, came the clearing, a bare slice of burnt and flattened ground, announced by black-lettered noticeboards peppered with exclamation marks and protected by wire fencing twelve foot high. Waiting behind the opened double gates, in two long rows, stood the guards, bristling in their brushed uniforms, barking at them as they trotted past, towards the iron grille and the grinding lorries and the great maw of a mouth beyond, ready to swallow and chew and spit them out, digested.

They went in slowly, some directed to the wagons, some to the lines of pickaxes and shovels leaning up against the wall, their handles still greasy from the night shift. The air was chill and damp, and his clothes stuck to his skin almost immediately. Water dripped from the roof, mud slid under his feet. Though electric lights were slung along the walls it took time to appreciate the length and breadth of the gallery and the dark brilliance of the imagination that had created it. Moving along that first long corridor, hewn of granite, the traces of past pickaxe blows pressed like fossils into its slick black walls, the tunnel stretched beyond the limit of light and dark into a stone labyrinth of implacable strength. There was no beginning to be found here, no end, such was its depth and its vast disdain for life. Though he knew that he had been banished to fashion a terrain upon which his life might come to a flickering halt, he felt that unwittingly he had uncovered a land of dim eternity. This was not simply a man-made device. This was a vision of a world to come, beyond man's calling, God's gift to a cursed world, a place of unspeakable holiness. He had been driven into this darkness, to fight amongst his brethren, to jostle and squeal like another lost rat, gnawing at the earth's heart, and here, he had concluded, was where he belonged. Up top he was nothing, a number to call, a mouth to feed, a back to beat. Up top there was air and sun and the sight of the world. It was too bright, there was too much colour, too much light. The day hurt him, hurt him for what he had lost, though he saw only the dawn grey and the blood dusk of it now, and he was glad of that. Down here, with nothing but echoes of his fading memories to remind him of his fairy-tale past, it was easier to dwell. Down here doom and hope mingled like blood and sand, with sudden milky mists rising from the floor to hide him from their most searching gaze. This was of its own. Here he would make his mark, searching for the mystery of it all, and they knew it not.

For the past three weeks he had been engaged in building a connecting passage between the hospital and what would be ammunition stores, with an escape shaft set halfway between, some seventy-five feet high, an iron-rung ladder strapped inside. It was hard work, with falling roofs and unexpected subsidence taking their toll, but despite the danger it was along here, in a dark abandoned recess, now hidden behind one of the giant air filters ranged along the main corridors, that he had fashioned his tiny room, four foot high and three foot square and lined with sacking. To begin with, he did not know what he would do with his invention, nor why he had spent back-breaking minutes furiously hacking at this illegal excavation, for it was not an escape route leading to an outside salvation, it was a cell constructed within a prison. But in the days when he had dug it out, chucking the earth into his wagon, tipping the evidence of his own private domain into the waiting lorries, it came to him that what he had created was not an exit, but an entrance, not a hiding place, but the beginnings of a state of being, and that if he were careful enough and constructed it cleverly, he could expand it, build other rooms, food stores, sleeping quarters, listening posts. He would learn the tunnel's secrets, its nocturnal habits, and adapt to its calling. He would feed and clothe himself from their provisions, take warmth from their furnaces, run wires from the generators, tap into the air compressors. He would wear a stolen officer's cap and a pair of good boots and on his leather belt would swing a torch and a dagger and a length of rope. He would fashion a new world, unsuspected and hidden, one which he would command and one which would grow in power. He would take the old man in with him. Others later on. Burrow under the whole island. When they were secure they could bring some of the whores down. Start a new civilization. Rot the other world from the inside.

He'd crept over to the old man as soon as he'd got back, wakened him with broken piece of pie held under his nose, thrusting out his arm to show off his new-found prizes.

'Look,' he had whispered, a touch a pride in his voice. 'Trousers too!'

The old man had taken the pie and held it gingerly to his mouth. His teeth, loose in his reddened gums, moved sideways as he bit into it. He worked a piece slowly round his tongue, chewing carefully and swallowing hard.

'How'd you come by all this lot?' he had asked.

'Farmhouse,' the boy had told him. 'Off a line.'

Wiping the crumbs back in from the corner of his sore stubbled mouth, the old man reached out and touched it.

'That's real quality you got there, son. Sticks out a mile on you. They'll be wanting to know how you've come by it. You'd best dirty it up some more or they'll hang you up on the hooks and beat the shit out of you.'

He'd taken the old man's advice, pushed the jacket up and down the floor, rubbing sawdust and dirt into the material. Fighting over that dead rabbit had helped.

He looked for the old man in the line of men hacking at the granite wall, but couldn't see him. Perhaps he'd been sent further in. Peter, that was his name. Same name as his father. Sonya had been his sister's. And his? He could hardly remember. He hadn't had a name for such a long time. He was just feet now, feet and arms and runny shits, all wrapped up in a brand-new coat. This would get him through the coming months. Pillow, blanket, coat. He patted it lovingly. What a night that was, the car coming quietly up that wild stretch of path, him crouched underneath the gorse hedge, the rain starting to get up. The car had stopped not a body length from him. Everything foot level. Door open. Black rain on the car's mudguards and the shine of a cape and a man's boot, stepping into the squashed wet of the puddles, door swinging open and the light inside shining on the hatted head sleeping in the back. Low mutters from the man, sensing the urgency and the hurry of it. Not hunting cats in the headlights at this hour; nerves and fear afoot, something quick and something bad. Then the man had pulled the door open and out the figure fell. With the hat and the jacket and the way the body rolled on the ground he had thought it another man at first, a stumbling drunk, but then as the hat slipped off and began to roll across the ground he saw the back of her legs and the fall of her hair. Then her face was staring at him along the spongy ground, six foot away, open eyed, bare lips grinning on her face like blade work on a pumpkin and her dress slapping in the mud like a hooked fish on a river bank. The man had chased the hat and stuffed it in his pocket and then had started to drag her off, one leg in each great hand, the dress riding up over her arse, bare and moon-white, her arms trailing high above her head, her outstretched fingers leaving trails in the flattened grass, the jacket peeling up over her, like she was one of the jig-a-jig girls, stripping for him even though his back was turned, first one arm and then the other, over her shoulders and head, blown back to the bush where he crouched, his heart tight in the grip of such close danger. Reaching one of the shafts the man picked her up and counting to himself, one, two, three, lifted her clear, her bare feet swinging over the hole, before he lowered her carefully into the deep of it. Down she went, until all he could see was her head and her mouth, luminous and vile, drowning in the night air. Then, not fifty yards away, the boom of a gun went off, and hiding his face he felt the earth recoil. When he looked again the air shaft stood empty and the man was running back to the safety of his car, bumping down the road without lights, the engine gunning out of sight. And as he crept round and tugged the jacket free it seemed to him that she had been brought to her underground tomb, not by chance nor for her captor's indecent pleasure, but to offer him the means by which he might survive in his. He knew what they had done to her, what she had suffered. He did not feel sorry for her. It was what happened, what the world was made for. All the rest was a delusion. He had seen it before. Seen it with his sister that night. One after the other they came, dropping their trousers round their ankles while their predecessor hopped back into his, laughing coarse encouragement, some queuing up for a second or third time. The officer in charge, a tall, handsome man with not a speck on his uniform, had come round to their cottage that afternoon and ducking through the low doorway, had stepped in, dusting off his cap with determined politeness. There was just him and his father and sister left. Their mother and the baby had been taken into the church, along with Grandmama and all the others. The officer had looked around the room with interest, the only room they had, and picking up a sample of Sonya's embroidery work had held it out, questioning her with a friendly look. His sister had nodded and, smiling, the officer had replaced it back on the dresser with care. Then, noticing his parents' bed hidden at the back, he had gone over, drawn back the curtain and patted the snug, high mattress.

'Good,' he said to his father. 'Tell your daughter to keep it nice and warm. This is where we're all going to fuck her tonight.'

His father had wanted to end it for them that afternoon, but there was no gun for him to do it quickly, to shoot them both and then turn it on himself, just the gutting knife and the rolling pin and Grandmama's walking stick she used to whack his legs with, and he couldn't bring himself to use any of those. So they sat, the three of them, praying and singing soft songs of their homeland, hoping that the soldiers might go away or forget. When the time had come and the officer had put his head round the corner, tapping at the watch he held in his hand, his father, weeping, had shaken his head, imploring him, pointing to her youth and the trust she had placed in his ability to protect her.

137

'Do not worry,' the officer had told him, 'I understand,' and slipping the watch back into his pocket, had taken him out and shot him underneath their broken window. The soldiers had to step over his outstretched arms to come through the door. They had come through the door all night.

Six

Wedel parked the car at the top of the road. As the two men set off down the hill a group of nurses appeared on the brow of the other side, laughing and chatting. On seeing the Major approach they fell silent. One of them waved nervously. Lentsch nodded.

The house was bathed in a blank grey daylight, the blinds drawn, the pinned-back slatted shutters rattling in the spasmodic wind. Ned hesitated by the gateless entrance. Even when he had come here before, when there had been life and brazen purpose to his visit, it had seemed to him then that despite the thought that had gone into its construction and the young woman whose willing form would lead him up the stairs or out into the lush wilderness at the rear, this was a house in which footsteps and voices and words of love would always ring hollow, one where its occupants would always appear transitory. Perhaps it was true what his old man had claimed. 'Some houses,' he used to tell him, 'are built for crime, for misery, desertion. It doesn't matter if you're a saint or a sinner, the bricks and mortar will get you in the end.'

The garden was more overgrown than he remembered, a tumble of weeds and grass. Last night's clouds had hidden the worst. Lentsch moved forward.

'I tried to persuade her to do some gardening,' he told Ned, brushing aside a drooping bramble. 'I even sent Albert over for a couple of hours, but like her father, she showed no real interest.' He held the offshoot back for Ned to pass. 'A garden should not be like this,' he called out after him. 'It does not speak well of the home.'

Ned stood before the door and reached for the knocker. Thinking better of it, he laid it gently back against the brass fitting.

'It's just possible,' he said, 'that there may be something he would not want to tell me in your presence. Perhaps it would help if halfway through you took yourself into the garden, or went off and read a magazine. Improved your English.'

'My English is not good?'

'It was a joke, Major.'

Before he could grasp the heavy ring again, the door swung open. Ned could not be sure but it seemed to him that when van Dielen saw who it was the slightest trace of a smile played across his small and careful face. Ned swallowed. He felt as if his voice were trapped inside, ashamed to show itself. Isobel's father swung the door wide. He spoke in that clear, lilting voice which seemed to mock everyone but himself.

'Here you are at last, Mr Luscombe. Uninvited as always, but this time I will concur that I cannot deny you. And the Major too. A very particular delegation, if you'll excuse the observation.'

'This is a bad business, Mr van Dielen.' Ned looked sideways at the Major, conscious of his echoing of Lentsch's earlier remark.

'A bad business.' Now it was van Dielen's turn to repeat it, and he elongated the phrase, accentuating its awkward banality. 'Is this what you've come to tell me?'

He said nothing more but stepped back, flinging his arm out in an exaggerated gesture of hospitality. Ned and Lentsch walked in. There was no hall to speak of. The front door opened on to a set of tall French windows and beyond a large drawing room. Nothing had changed. It was still as bare a room as Ned had ever seen, with glass at the back and glass at the front, with rugs and strange furniture scattered across the wooden floor. 'As friendly as a barred cage,' Isobel used to say. At the back, slowly rising to the balcony, rose the tubular staircase with its polished steel handrail. Ned could hear the fall of discarded shoes as she moved towards it, hear the soft swish of her dress against the balustrade, her bare feet squeaking on the polished wood as she climbed above. His eyes rose involuntary to the corridor and her closed bedroom door. Van Dielen gestured to the steps leading down to the bar.

'Come and join me, why don't you? My first guests of the new year.'

He led them down to where a half-empty bottle of brandy stood. Van Dielen poured himself another glass.

'A dreadful extravagance, I'll admit, but under the circumstances.' He waved it at the two uncomfortable men. 'Will you not join me, gentlemen? It is of the highest quality.'

Ned looked to the floor. The Major was unfailingly polite.

'Some other time, perhaps,' he said.

Van Dielen was in the mood for repeating awkward phrases.

'Some other time. Now there's a thing to conjure with. From which would you have me choose? The future or the past?'

Ned tried to break in. 'Mr van Dielen . . .'

'I favour the past, though whether the present past or the far-away half-remembered past, I am in something of a quandary. Perhaps that infamous bicycle ride of yours, Mr Luscombe. I should have not treated you so harshly. I can see that now.'

'Mr van Dielen, there's no call to—'

'Had I known then what I know now, I would have invited you in and given you the run of the house. Brandy, cognac, rum, they're all stocked here. You could have helped yourself to anything you liked. Asked me for a cocktail. I make very good cocktails. They all said that in the East.'

'I didn't know that.'

'And as for that bicycle. I have nothing against the bicycle so long as it is maintained in good working order. I would have bought her one in due course. It was only a matter of time. Do you still have your bicycle, Mr Luscombe?'

'I sold it.'

'We saw a tandem in the desert once. A tourer. The woman was riding in front, straining hard, pulling all manner of panniers and rucksacks strapped to the sides and back, while her man was seated

141

behind, feet up on his handlebars, reading a newspaper. How we laughed! "What a very naughty fellow," I said, "for not doing his fair share." "No, no, Daddy. That's not the point," she said. "It should be the other way around." She was only nine then and already conversant with the uses of men. Pigtails on such an old head. Do you like pigtails on a girl, Mr Luscombe?'

'Pigtails?'

'On a girl they are correct, but not on a woman, I think. On the Continent, in Germany and Austria, my own country too, they are fond of pigtails on both girls and women. Why is that, I wonder?'

'I have never given it much thought.'

'No. Well, you wouldn't, would you. But is that not true, Major?'

'Indeed.'

'The young girls that took your fancy, they had pigtails, did they not?'

'Some of them, yes, I am sure. And my sister too.'

'Your sister?'

'Yes.' The Major tapped his top pocket. 'I showed you a photograph of her once, when I came here.'

'And she wore pigtails in both childhood and . . .?' He let the word fall.

'For a time.'

'There you are, then. And Isobel, did you ever wish that she might gather her locks and wear them in plaits, like your lady-friends back home?'

Now it was Lentsch's turn to falter.

'I never imagined such a thing,' he stammered

'You see! It's true! You would have preferred pigtails! She was too knowing for you, was that it? Was that what brought her down? That she was too knowing. And here we are the three of us, who brought her such a treacherous gift.'

He took another gulp, choking as he swallowed hard.

'Forgive me. I am not a great conversationalist. I know how to talk, indeed in English and in German and my own native tongue I am somewhat gifted in mastering the technical differences of vocabulary and regulations, you understand. Where I fall down is in the thing that counts, the art of conversation. The words I produce, the manner in which they are delivered, their overall intent and appearance seem to demand the immediate cessation of that of which they seek to be a part, although I find myself unable to understand why.'

'No.'

'I am doing it now, in this very modern and open design, blocking off all avenues of conversation even as I speak.'

'This is not a time for conversation, Mr van Dielen.'

'No. You are right, Mr Luscombe. Ned. May I call you Ned? It is what she called you, after all. I am her father, am I not? Have I not that right too, even though I have been unpardonably rude to you in the past?'

'Think nothing of it.'

'You said that last night, did you not? When I met you by our front gate?'

'What?' Lentsch looked surprised.

'Did you not know, Major?' Van Dielen delighted in Ned's discomfiture. 'Last night I returned from my dinner with Major Ernst to find the Inspector here scuttling about outside our house like a crab looking for a shell.' He tapped Ned on the knee. 'You must be truthful with the Major, Ned, or he will lose his little German temper.'

'This is true?' Lentsch sounded shocked.

'I was walking home late. I thought I saw a light.'

Van Dielen leapt upon the uneasy explanation.

'The light? Yes, I remember.' He stared Ned in the face. He should have been a policeman. 'There was no light or I would have seen it too, while taking my farewell of Major Ernst. The only light shining that night was the one burning in your jealous heart.'

He caught Lentsch's bewildered expression.

'Does not the Major know of that either?'

Ned felt the sand shifting from under his feet. He was being led out of his depth. Now he knew what Isobel had felt like that on that first swim. He tried to scrabble back.

'I saw no reason to tell him right away. It was all in the past. I would have got to it eventually.'

'All in the past?' Van Dielen turned to the Major. 'Two summers ago, Major, Isobel was his dream come true and she foolish enough to embrace his advances. A summer of secret love followed, a summer of illicit swimming in treacherous bays, of bicycle rides and furtive little love notes tucked in hidey-holes.' He turned as he heard Ned's intake of breath. 'Oh yes, I know all about those infamous billet-doux.' He swivelled round to the Major again. 'But she discarded him. And he did not like that. He felt cheated and wronged and for a whole winter bored the natives with his maudlin tales of his woe.' He leant back on his stool and looked at the two men triumphantly. 'At least that is what his uncle told.'

Ned tried to set the record straight.

'It was a summer romance, that was all.'

'For her maybe. But not you,' van Dielen said, rejecting his summary with scorn. 'You always entertained the possibility that she might return. Perhaps that is why you were here last night.' He seized on the idea, fascinated with the possibility of embroidery. 'Perhaps you had come earlier, to try and plead with her.'

Ned looked down at the floor. His leg was trembling. He pressed his hands on his knees and felt the sweat trickle out under his arms. Van Dielen wriggled in his seat. The prospect of giving no quarter invigorated him.

'Perhaps she tried to send you packing,' he said. 'Perhaps you lost your temper. Have you ever thought, Mr Luscombe, Ned, that you yourself could be a suspect?'

'Mr van Dielen!'

'Ah, leave me alone, why don't you? You're no use here.'

'As soon as I am able. But there are questions I need to ask.' Lentsch rose on the signal and moving to the drawing room, started flicking through the pages of some old magazines.

'A little clumsily orchestrated,' van Dielen observed. 'And quite unnecessary. Well? What is it that we must keep from him?'

'I need to know where she went that Saturday, that's all,' Ned reassured him. 'Can you tell me her movements?'

'I would have thought you knew enough about my daughter's movements to fill your notebook three times over.'

'Mr van Dielen! You must stop this. It does no good.' Ned spoke to him quietly, though his patience with the man was evaporating fast. Van Dielen closed his eyes, nodding fiercely.

'You are right,' he admitted. 'I must stop. It does no good.' He took a deep breath. 'Early in the morning she went down to the town to collect her dress from the rehearsal room. She wanted it for the party that night. Later she went for coffee with her aunt. Marjorie telephoned her. "Summoned" was the word Isobel used.'

'When was this?'

'Midmorning? Isobel was put out. She needed to alter her costume. But duty called. She went out. She drank coffee. She came back.' He looked back to the living room where the Major gazed out over the blustery green of the back garden.

'What was she like when she came back?' Ned asked.

'I hardly saw her. As soon as she got back she charged up to her room. I wouldn't read too much in that,' he added, noting Ned's interest. 'It's what girls of a certain age do. "Do you want to bring the walls down around our ears?" I called up. Not a word. I presumed she had returned to the strictures of her hemline.'

'And you?'

'I forswore needlework that Saturday. Most of the morning I spent in my study. The dinner with Major Ernst was not only social, you understand. There were important matters concerning the island's construction programme which needed attention. Isobel and I had a quick lunch of cold meats and beetroot – how I am beginning to loathe that vegetable – and in the afternoon we went down to the old quarter to do some shopping. Then it was on to the yard. I wanted to see the damage the break-in had caused, talk to my foreman.'

'George Poidevin, I take it.'

'Certainly George Poidevin.'

'Did you find much damage?' he asked.

'Judging by George's rather hysterical ranting over the phone I had assumed half the yard had been laid to waste. As it was there was hardly anything at all, except for George's precious supply of tea and sugar. You'd have thought they'd stolen the Crown jewels the way he was carrying on. "Don't worry, George," I said, "I'll get you another packet of tea for your little wooden hut," but the man seemed impervious to my intended generosity.'

'Any cement taken?'

'Not that I know of.' He caught Ned's look. 'Yes, I know what you're thinking. But even if there was, there'd be no way of identifying it. There's more bags of cement on this island than there are toffee wrappers.'

Ned returned to the subject of van Dielen's yard. It puzzled him that Isobel had gone there too.

'A bit odd that, wasn't it, she going with you? She'd never shown much interest in the yard before, had she?'

'She went to keep me company, Mr Luscombe. Daughters do that sometimes, keep their fathers company, for no other reason. It is sufficient unto itself.'

Ned made no comment. 'And then?'

'Then we walked back along the front. Once home I went back to my study and she went upstairs for a nap. Later I went to change for dinner, she was running a bath. She helped me with my bow tie. I have never been very good at that. Before I left I knocked on her door. But she wouldn't let me in.'

'Why not?'

'She said she wasn't decent. I was always very sensitive to those sorts of things, propriety, decorum, the feelings of a young woman. I understood more than she thought, more than I let on. It is not in my nature to let on.' He took another drink, satisfied. 'So I talked to her through the door. She told me not to wait up. That she'd be home late.'

Ned balanced two beer mats together, then catching van Dielen's disapproving eye quickly laid them back on the surface. 'So you weren't worried when she didn't come home.'

'No. She had stayed over once or twice before.'

'You didn't mind?' Ned asked, aware of the hypocrisy of the question.

'In war, Inspector, behaviour that would not be acceptable in peacetime seems quite ordinary, quite understandable. Necessary, even.'

'Did she ever stay with her aunt?'

'Her aunt! She'd rather sleep next to her blessed horse.'

'They didn't get on?'

'They couldn't stand each other, didn't you know?'

'I knew they were never close, but not ... yet Mrs Hallivand invited her round for coffee?'

Van Dielen laughed.

'Isobel was funny about that. "I've half a mind not to go," she said. "Then don't," I told her.' He brushed the seat of his trousers. Criticism of others was a task demanding precision and calm. 'I've no time for the woman myself. An ageing social flirt, if you ask my opinion. "No need to bow down to the old crow on my account," I told her. "No," she said, "I think I will. Just to see her squirm."'

'Squirm? I don't understand.'

'Apparently Marjorie was desperate to be invited to the Major's homecoming.' He swivelled on his stool, spilling brandy on his trousers. 'The woman's quite besotted with him, you know. She even has embroidered a picture of him looking out over the sea like some latter-day Bonny Prince Charlie, though she keeps it well hidden. Isobel chanced upon it that morning all tucked away at the bottom of some needlework basket. We had a good laugh about that. Though she never said as much, Marjorie did not entirely approve of Isobel's association with the Major.'

'And what did you think of it, Mr van Dielen?'

'I didn't force the Major on her. Isobel would have liked him, whatever his nationality.'

'But for you, it must have been helpful.'

'Helpful?'

'For your business.'

'That was not the reason I allowed it. There would have been others who, had she shown interest, would have made it more helpful.'

'Like?'

Van Dielen gestured across the road.

'He was always inviting himself over. Isobel found him repulsive.'

'And you do not. If I remember our conversation correctly, you were quite vocal in your admiration.'

'We work well together.'

'Forgive me for saying so, but don't you ever worry what will happen when they . . .'

'Lose?' Van Dielen's voice was deliberately shrill. 'No. When this is over my skills will be needed more than ever. If not here then some other, more ravaged quarter. There will be opportunity aplenty for the van Dielens to ply our trade.'

'You speak as if there were more than just you.'

'I always hoped that Isobel might find a husband who could come into the business, bear a son who would add further lustre to our endeavours.'

'And what did she think of such an idea?'

'I never told her. What would be the point? But it was always on the cards that she might meet someone who might have appreciated the firm's potential. There used to be money here, Mr Luscombe, investors' money, bankers' money, waves of it washing in with the tide. In time I dare say there will be again.'

'An empire, then, is what you're after?'

Van Dielen considered the idea for a moment. 'The English Empire is exhausted, the German Empire stillborn and America has not sufficient moral backbone to engage in such an enterprise. Commerce, business, finance, these will be the new conquistadores, not nation states, but manufacturers, engineers. A construction company straddling Europe, Africa, building roads and bridges, towns and cities, employing thousands, its arms stretching to the furthest corners of the globe? Why not?'

'And you hoped Isobel would be part of your plan?'

'No. But she was good for the business, young, attractive, the daughter of a moderately wealthy and successful man. Clients liked coming to dinner when she was here.'

'Which is why you did not discourage her with the Major.'

'Perhaps.'

He started to drink heavily again and the dark liquid sat on his lips and swam in his eyes.

'Ask me no more questions now. I have a daughter dead, Mr Luscombe, and I need to drink to that, to take it abroad this grey windswept isle and tell her mother that Isobel will soon be joining her. I have to tell her that and then listen to her curses rising from the ground. She never wanted to be here. Every day she would go down to the sea and swim out as far as she could. I asked her one day why. "I am trying to escape," she said. I thought she was joking. She came here and she died here and now my daughter has followed in her footsteps. Leave me to my troubled peace, I implore you.'

'As soon as I am able, Mr van Dielen. It is just . . .'

'What?'

'I ought to search her room.'

Van Dielen waved him away. 'Well, what's keeping you. You know where it is, I believe.'

Ned was unable to move.

'Ach. You look so discomforted! Daughters write diaries, Mr Luscombe, diaries left in the imagined privacy of their bottom drawers. And suspicious fathers read them. You may well blush, for they were fulsome epistles. I was all for ending it there and then, if not on moral grounds then at least economic ones, but Marjorie told me to rest my peace, that by next season it would be all over. So I took her advice, the only time I believe that I have ever done so. Perhaps I should not have listened to her, after all. Go on with you, up to her room. I have matters to discuss with the Major as regards her burial.'

Her room had not changed: the long walnut fitted wardrobe that ran the length of one wall, the brightly coloured striped rug which had come from the Sudan, and in the middle of the narrow bed a pair of striped pyjamas folded neatly on the pillow. Next to the bedside table, overlooking the front road, stood the writing desk, replete with inkstand, gold-nibbed Conway Stewart fountain pen and matching light-blue stationery, with the initials *vD* embossed at the head. It was typical of the man that he should fly in the face of ridicule and be the proud standard bearer of such socially unacceptable initials. Ned fingered the mark. Above the fresh sheet lay a slight tear of paper still attached to the gum. *Must see you. Sunday morning, 11 o'clock. Usual place. Must see you.* He took the note she had sent out of its envelope and smoothed it out over the notepad. It fitted perfectly; the last note she had written, then. But written when? When she had come back from Mrs Hallivand? With her father had knocking on her door?

Putting the letter back in his pocket he pulled open the drawer. More notepaper, more envelopes; a bottle of permanent black ink, a bottle of washable blue, a box of rubber bands, a tub of glue, a pencil, a green India rubber. No diary.

Ned opened the doors to the wardrobe. Below a shelf of hats and scarves ran a long rack of clothes. Though he had seen them before, indeed had been surprised when out of their folds Isobel had sprung once, dressed in a lion's costume taken from the amateur dramatics, throwing a great flurry of muslin over his head before pushing him down onto the bed, her growls turning to giggles, he had never appreciated how many different outfits she possessed: loose summer skirts, tweedy winter ones; demure frocks for church, patterned frocks for gardens, bold frocks for parties; a black cocktail dress that seemed to have a loose body already shimmering inside; cord trousers; wool jackets; and finally a blue satin ball gown with a sequinned bow and a ready-made bust jutting out. He never seen so many clothes gathered together in one place except in a shop, and that was what they looked like here, the contents of some mainland fashion store, with matching shoes and boots ranged underneath. It was only now that he understood the requirements of Isobel's position, and her natural and disguised vanity. He had only seen her wearing one or two things, the inevitable hacking jacket with the flapping back and tight buttons, the loose cord trousers with those deep, erotic pockets into which, standing behind her, he used to ease his hands, the white blouse, the white ribbed jumper, the green skirt she favoured, with buttons at the front. He pushed the clothes back and forth on their hangers. For the most part they looked unused. It had never struck him before what a woman of substance might imagine she needed, what she might come back from town with, hang in her wardrobe and not wear. Isobel had never seemed interested in clothes, and yet here were all these, racked up for future, unplayed games. His mother had, what, two good dresses to his knowledge, one for church, one for best outings, and after that, in the top two drawers of his parents' chest of drawers, lay the skirts and blouses which, like the days of the week, came out in strict rotation. He had never supposed that his mother had given a moment's thought to what she wore, and Isobel too had appeared to harbour the same indifference. Yet one had been conceived on the bed of necessity, the other inherited through the flirtatious pleasure born of wealth. When his mother was young, had she ever wanted dresses such as these? And did she, even now? It was hard for him to imagine it.

A set of brass-handled drawers ran down one side. He pulled open the first one. Underwear. He felt around quickly, uneasy at the intimate proximity. Nothing else. He pulled open the drawer below. Brassieres, mostly white, some black and one a lurid red; lace, cotton, strapless, wired; sedate, modest, daring. He stirred the contents, feeling for anything at the back. As he pulled them aside he recognized a sturdy white one, bordered by a patterned frill. She had gone swimming in it one afternoon as a dare, and it had become quite transparent when she re-emerged. Against his better judgement he picked it out and held it to the light, remembering the smooth dampness of it and the dark rose of her flesh blossoming through. A noise at the door made him look up. Lentsch stood at the door with a glass of brandy in his hand.

'Is that strictly necessary?'

'I was looking for her hat and coat.'

It was the first thing that came into his head, but in saying it he realized that they were nowhere to be seen. 'You must remember them. She wore them everywhere.'

Lentsch nodded. 'Downstairs, perhaps?'

Ned shook his head. 'I looked when we came in.' He replaced the brassiere back with the others. One of the straps got caught as he tried to close the drawer. He pushed it back in.

'Never feel very comfortable doing this sort of thing,' Ned admitted. 'When I was a boy my mother used to take me with her when she went on her yearly shopping expedition. I'd have to stand in amongst the petticoats and foundation garments while she disappeared into the changing room. Not right, a young boy having to spend a morning surrounded by ladies' smalls.'

'Smalls?'

'Underwear.'

'Ah. Smalls.'

'God, I hated it. Why do mothers do that?'

'I don't know.'

'Didn't yours?'

'No. People would come to her, I believe, for fittings.'

'I see.'

Lentsch tried to explain. 'My mother is a sort of Mrs Hallivand of our town. Only not so formidable.'

'Just as well,' Ned replied. 'Unlucky the man that gets on the wrong side of Mrs Hallivand.' He took another look around the room.

'You know Mrs Hallivand well?' Lentsch asked.

'Off and on. Uncle Albert would bring us stuff from the vegetable

152

garden. Sometimes I'd come over and help him with the gardening, mowing, raking the leaves in the autumn. If she were about she'd take me to the kitchen, make sure I had a slice of cake, put a bag of runner beans in my hand. My mum used to say that the reason I never caught a cold was because of Mrs Hallivand's greens. It's Mum that needs them now.'

'Your mother is sick?'

'She's lost a lot of weight since Dad died.'

'Does Albert give you anything from the garden now?'

Ned was anxious not to get his uncle into trouble. 'Oh, no. He's a stickler for doing things by the book. If so much as one of his gooseberries goes missing...' He stopped, remembering an earlier conversation about thieves and loganberries. Lentsch broke the silence.

'This was her room, then. I never saw it before.'

'No.'

'You have, I think.'

'Once or twice, a couple of summers ago. Before...'

'Quite. I did not know of your former attachment. If I had, I would not have summoned you so harshly.'

'It doesn't matter. It was all over between us, like her father said. Did you hear him down there, what I asked him?'

Lentsch nodded. Another pause. He fingered the light switch, turning it off and on.

'It wasn't true then, what he said, that you wanted her back?' he said. 'That was not why you were here last night?'

Ned couldn't bring himself to tell him the truth.

'I don't know. I found myself outside her house that was all, walking back home. It was stupid, but it's what you do, isn't it? Walk where you hope she might walk, look up at a window, hoping to see a light. Even in the blackout.'

Lentsch nodded. Below they could hear van Dielen moving about. Ned walked out onto the balcony and looked down. Van Dielen was coming out of his study with rolls of transparent paper under his arm.

153

'I did love her, you know,' Lentsch said with a suddenness that embarrassed him. 'It is important that you realize this.'

Ned leant against the balustrade and looked at this man, holding his military cap in his hands like a beggar on a street.

'Does it shock you so very much?' Lentsch asked. 'That I should feel like this?'

'Of course not.'

'But that she should feel for me in this manner, perhaps. Is that it?'

'Not exactly.'

'But it is part of it.'

'It's not you or her, is it, Major? It's the circumstance.' He walked back into the bedroom. 'Three years ago it wouldn't have mattered one way or the other. Just one man losing out against another. But now it's all muddled up with nations and honour and serving one's country.'

'She was betraying England, that is what you thought?'

'No, but many people did.'

'She was a brave girl, braver than all of you, fighting for what she believed in, fighting for what she loved.'

'I don't follow.'

Lentsch took a deep breath. 'She found it difficult sometimes, feeling for me, our countries at war, of what others might think of her. I felt that while I was away something had happened that upset her more than usual.'

'I thought you said you hadn't seen her.'

'I did not. I talked to her late afternoon.' He sighed. 'I was not going to tell you this. It was a private moment, and we had very few of those. As you know I was not meant to know about that evening.' He smiled. 'It was a secret, a *Geheimnis*. It was one of our favourite songs, Hilde Hildebrand's "*Liebe Ist Ein Geheimnis*", "Love is a Secret". I rang her here, to tease her, pretending I knew nothing.' He sat down on the bed and recited their conversation as best he could.

'That was all?'

'Yes. She rang off, and though it was...' the Major tapped his knee in search of the right word, '...abrupt I did not ring back.'

'And when she didn't turn up,' Ned persisted, 'why didn't you send the car here? Or come yourself?'

'I was afraid,' Lentsch admitted. 'Perhaps she no longer wanted to see me. I had always told myself that if she became frightened or wanted it to stop, I would do nothing to prevent this. She was a young woman. It would not be right. Later I was ashamed.'

'Ashamed?'

'The parties. The drinking. Most of the girls are very ... willing. Last night with Isobel not there, suddenly they did not seem right. They were not ordinary parties any more, they were like a worship to a false god. After it was over I was glad she had not arrived. In my mind I had decided that it would be the last party.'

Ned moved to the window, rubbing the breast of his jacket. Perhaps this was the right moment to show him. He could hear the palm trees, brushing against the window. The blinds were down. He put his hand into his pocket, half drawing the letter out, but a sudden squeal from outside drew him to the window again. Ned eased the metal slats aside, their metal syncopation sending shivers of memory skittering round the room. Across the way, in the garden of the bungalow opposite, the group of women they had seen earlier were chasing each other across on the small lawn in bare feet, their army greatcoats flapping round their ankles as they ran. Reaching the far end they stood in line and turning round began to call out impatiently. Almost immediately two men appeared. Ned recognized both, Major Ernst and the island's censor, Captain Bohde. Ernst carried a huge rubber ball. Bohde struggled through the door with a black tripod and camera which he tried to balance on the uneven ground.

The girls cried out again. Bohde dismissed their exhortations with a wave of his hand, first bending to look through the viewfinder and then trotting over to where the girls stood. Holding a small object to one of them he pointed to the coat and then the sky. The girl shook her head. He repeated the performance, nodding vigorously. Shrugging her shoulders, the girl dropped the coat with a swift movement.

'Jesus Christ.'

'What is it?' Lentsch got up. Ned held his finger to his mouth and beckoned him over.

Below the girl stood in the pool of her overcoat. She was quite naked underneath. Bohde was scampering back to his camera with the eagerness of a small boy while Ernst held out the ball to the woman in mock-ceremonial fashion. She accepted the gift in like manner, the scoop of her long breasts swinging down over her arm. Her legs were planted wide apart, a triangular echo of the dark smudge of her sex. The other girls disrobed too. Standing in a circle they started throwing the ball to each other, their tanned bodies forming a series of static tableaux, now a living question mark, now a figure O. When they were finished Bohde dragged the camera closer and began photographing each girl individually. Ned felt his mouth go dry. He had never seen anything like it. Ernst was walking round with a little notebook, measuring their calves and their heads, wrapping the tape-measure against the prow of their breasts. Bohde marched into the house and returned with a tray of brandy glasses. The girls put their greatcoats back on and rubbed each other warm. Ned let the blind fall back into place. He was sweating.

'Quite a view.'

Lentsch seemed unperturbed. 'Not so extraordinary as you think. In Germany there are many who bathe like that.'

'Not much bathing going on over there, Major.'

'Bathing in the air. Back home there are whole parks built specially for it. We call it *Nacktkultur* – freeing man from the evils of modern life, coming closer to nature, improving both the body and the mind. Swimming, tennis, walking, even special inns to eat and drink. Men, women, children, all of different ages, different backgrounds. The maths professor and the factory worker. The countess and the shopgirl. It is very popular.'

Ned was unconvinced. 'Well, it won't catch on here, I can tell you. Can you see my uncle and Mrs Hallivand going for a stroll together with nothing on?'

The Major smiled. 'No. For them I think such moments have passed.'

Ned was adamant. 'I don't care who does it. It's all wrong. Measuring girls like that. Taking photographs with their legs at all angles.'

Lentsch sighed. 'You are right. For some the human form alone, the thing that has captured the imagination of countless artists and sculptors for thousands of years, is not enough. It has to be measured, placed in categories, organized into ridiculous geometric shapes. A face is no longer a face, you understand, a nose no longer a nose. They are parts of a greater scheme. This is the Major for you. What you saw there was what they term "research".'

Ned's laugh was without a trace of humour. 'If they were civilians I could have them all arrested for those photographs, let alone anything else.'

'We are a nations of camera owners. Turn a German upside down and photographs will fall from his pockets.' Lentsch leant over and pulled the slats down again. One of the girls had thrown off her coat again and was standing on the medicine ball, walking it across the lawn.

'She has great poise, that one,' he observed. 'She should be a dancer, with such balance.'

'Do you know any of them?' Ned asked him, unable to prevent himself looking again.

'They were at the party last night. Dressed,' he added.

'And Major Ernst?'

'Ernst! He was having dinner with Herr van Dielen, remember.'

'What about Captain Bohde there?'

'Naturally. First at the club and then at the Villa.'

'All the time?'

'No. He left the Casino earlier than the rest of us. He had work to do at the newspaper office. He was at the house when we returned.'

'How did he seem?'

'Bohde? The same as usual. Not at ease. He does not fit in with the rest of us.'

'I might have to question him. About the time in between?'

Lentsch thought for a moment. 'Inspector. It is better if you understand that you cannot "question" any of my subordinates. You ask. You understand the difference? Very well. We can "ask" him together. I will talk. You will listen.'

Ned nodded. The girl was walking the ball back towards the bungalow, her hands on her head. Ernst was clapping. As she drew near, he placed his hands under her arms and lifted her off. A sudden phrase, like the snatch of a song, came into his head. *She could not tell Lentsch, she could not tell Lentsch, she wrote him the letter 'cause she could not tell Lentsch.*

'Do you think Isobel ever saw anything like that from up here?' he asked.

Lentsch shook his head.

'If she had she would have told me. It would have been a huge joke to her, especially if she had seen Bohde with his camera. Bohde is a terrible old woman.'

'What about Ernst? Do you think he could have asked her to take part in this "research"?'

Lentsch shook his head again. He'd suggested it once himself, of course, that she sit for him. They were upstairs, lying side by side, in his little single bed. It was the first time they had gone to bed together in the afternoon, the first time that he had seen her naked in the afternoon light, or the morning for that matter. He was the shyer of the two, turning his back to her, folding his clothes carefully across the back of his chair while she pulled everything off in a heap and hopped straight into bed. Afterwards he lay there uncomfortably. His arm was going to sleep and his neck was caught at an awkward angle. Sensing his discomfort she raised herself up and kneeling on the foot of the bed looked up out of the window. He did not know why it should be so but it seemed to him that the light shifting over her now was quite different from the light falling on her when she had been partially clothed. Could this be true? Perhaps, unlike the moon which only reflected and never possessed, there was something within the body which made skin glow, not simply the passage of blood and oxygen but an inner light wherein the spirit lay. He recalled the day in Munich when, clothed in the mantle of disapproval, he had stood and marvelled at Gauguin's reviled dark and fleshy figures and compared them to the stillborn forms from the brushes of approved painters like Johan Schult and Karl Truppe. Their women, for all their glowing health, were rendered of the flesh, but not of the blood. Their skin was flawless, flat, denied the blemish of movement. The eyes of God had not fallen upon them. He saw that same look this morning in Isobel's dread immobility, in the strange quiet of her flesh, the imperfect whiteness of her skin, the stillness of her body. The eyes of God had left her. But he did not think of such matters that afternoon in the bare domain of his bed. He thought of the light and her movement and the impossibility of their freedom. He reached out and run his fingers down the small of her back. She turned and moved over him in anticipation. He smiled quickly, raising his hands in protest.

'No, no,' he pleaded. 'I was just thinking. If you could keep still for an hour I would like to paint you as you are now.'

'What?' She smacked him playfully on the arm. 'Where would you hang it? In the front room for all your friends to gawk at or up here where Albert would have to dust it every day? I know. You could give it to my aunt. She likes a good picture. You could tell her which bit you like painting the best. My feet. My hands. This.' She bent down and placed her breast in between his lips. Lentsch felt her desire harden in his mouth.

'But quietly,' he insisted, holding still her hips. 'Just in case.'

'Oh, I forgot. Mustn't awake Auntie from her afternoon nap.' She giggled and stretching up had proceeded to give voice to her indiscretion until he too became enveloped in its untroubled and careless cry.

Lentsch snapped back to the question.

'Ernst? No. He would not wish to anger her father.'

'And Bohde?'

Lentsch shook his head. 'He would not want to anger me.'

'What if her father had been mixed up in it? What if he and Ernst and Bohde had all tried to make her do something and it had all got a bit out of hand?'

Lentsch pulled at the blind again. The garden was quite empty now, save for the solitary tripod.

'His own daughter?'

'It has been known,' Ned told him, 'fathers offering their daughters up to friends, fathers taking daughters for themselves. Happens all the time here. Maybe there's more to what we've just seen than taking pictures. Maybe they tried to involve Isobel. Maybe she resisted.'

Downstairs the front door slammed.

'He's leaving,' the Major announced.

Ned went to the window. Van Dielen was hurrying down the pathway with a bundle of papers under his arm. Ned felt tired. He wanted to go back to sleep, to walk round to Bernie's house and get drunk.

'I understand his anguish,' the Major said, 'but he should not do that. Not without permission first.'

'Not to worry,' Ned told him wearily. 'I'll post one of my men outside. He can take a statement from him when he gets back. Right now I should go and talk to Mrs Hallivand and find out what that coffee morning was all about. He wouldn't mind me telephoning from here, would he, to see if she's in?'

'He might not mind,' Lentsch agreed, 'but there is no telephone at the Lodge. Why don't you telephone your uncle at the Villa. He will know if she's there.'

★

Lentsch dropped Ned at the Villa's gateway.

'You will keep me informed of everything?' he said.

Ned leant against the car. The letter crackled in his pocket.

'Of course,' he said.

'Wedel will deliver a special pass this evening, permitting you to be out when you please, but not, you understand, exactly where. This is a personal favour. Do not abuse it.'

Wedel winked at him as he threw the car into a gravel-spitting turn. Ned straightened his hat and stepped up onto the lodge porch. This was where Uncle Albert and Auntie Rose had lived. In the summer Auntie Rose used to sit out on this veranda, a bowl of peas or runner beans in her lap and the saucepan by her feet, watching his cousin Kitty walking up and down the drive on the stilts his father had made. Now the porch was stacked with wood, a woman's bicycle propped up against the railing. Ned knocked on the door with his knuckles. Albert appeared almost at once. His beret was a mite askew, Ned thought.

'Uncle!'

'Ned.'

'She's in, then?'

'Aye. Wipe your feet. She don't care for footmarks.'

Ned squeezed past Albert into the small passageway.

'I don't remember it this cramped,' Ned whispered.

'It's stuff from the house,' Albert told him. 'The best bits are up in Kitty's room. We moved them over the day before they came.'

He pointed to a closed door on his left.

'I was thinking. Perhaps I should come in with you. To make sure she's all right.'

Ned felt proud of him. At least there were some who hadn't forgotten how to look after each other.

'Not to worry,' he reassured him. 'I'll go carefully.'

His uncle was a stubborn man. 'Her and I go back a long way, Ned,' he argued. 'She might talk better with me by her side.'

'This has got to be official, Uncle. I can't do it with you breathing over my shoulder.'

Albert sniffed. 'As you wish,' he said. 'Come up after, if you have the time.'

It was small room, cluttered with armchairs and lampshades and small tables. Above the fireplace hung a picture – a young woman, not simply naked but enjoying it. All this painting and photography, he thought, it's just an excuse for hanky-panky. Mrs Hallivand sat by the window covered by a check rug, a large wicker basket at her feet. Ned wondered whether it still had the embroidered picture of the Major tucked in at the bottom. Though she looked tired her eyes were clear. There had been no floods of tears here, Ned reasoned, no wailings or tearing of hair. Isobel was dead and her aunt sat upright, patting the armrests of her chair, watching the nephew of her former gardener make his entrance. A cake stand stood next to her with a silver teapot on the top tier and a plate of biscuits on the lower. The sun had broken through outside but here it was dark, even though the curtains were drawn well back. Glancing out of the window Ned could see his uncle walking slowly up the drive. The fire was lit but there was no heat to it. The logs hissed, thick sap bubbling from green ends. Mrs Hallivand waved a hand in their bleak direction.

'Too young. They've had no time to weather. And how's your mother?'

It was an enquiry born not out of concern, but designed to remind him who he was, and into what presence he had been admitted.

'Weak,' he said.

She nodded. 'An affliction that has struck us all. I find the climb up from town quite exhausting these days. So.' She folded her hands neatly in her lap, settling in to the rhythm of the conversation. 'You must know this little house quite well.'

'When I was younger, yes. Uncle Albert used to sit in that very chair.'

Mrs Hallivand squirmed. 'Quite a change from my usual surroundings. Though I've grown used to it.' She lowered her voice.

162

'It took me quite a spell to dislodge your uncle's aroma. I think he must sleep in those gardening clothes of his.'

'He's of the old school, Mrs Hallivand,' Ned explained, prepared to indulge her a while longer. 'Once it's on there's not much point in taking it off. Except Sundays, of course.'

'Ah. The power of religion.'

Ned shook his head. 'Bowls.'

Mrs Hallivand smiled indulgently at Ned's joke and turned the biscuit plate ninety degrees. Digestives, those square iced ones Dad had liked so much and two Bourbons. Ned had not seen a chocolate Bourbon for three years. Quiet settled on the room. He felt obliged to offer up the statutory enquiry.

'And your husband, Mrs Hallivand? Have you heard from him at all?'

It was a dangerous question to ask on the island, had they heard from their relatives, akin to asking a hospital patient the state of their health. However, Ned could tell Mrs Hallivand wished he had not been so formally polite.

'Not from him, no. About him, yes.'

'He is well, I hope.'

'He is safe. Whether he is well I have no idea, though I dare say he is.' She lifted a sugared biscuit from the plate and bit into it. Ned wondered whether he was going to be offered one. 'However,' she continued, swallowing the morsel carefully, 'you did not come here to enquire after my husband's health. You want to know about . . .' She faltered.

'Isobel. Yes. A terrible business.'

'Yes. Poor Isobel.'

'She visited you yesterday morning, I believe.'

'For coffee. If you can call what we drink now coffee.'

'Was that a regular thing?'

'She popped in from time to time.'

'I had the impression that you had asked her specially. Your telephone call that morning.'

163

Mrs Hallivand looked surprised that Ned was so well informed.

'I spoke to her most days. She said she might call round, that was all.'

'And she did?'

Mrs Hallivand nodded.

'I didn't realize that the two of you saw so much of each other.'

'Since her mother died I felt responsible for her.'

'More than her father?'

'Her father is a man. Not the easiest of men at that. I felt for her, all alone in that house. She had lots of spirit, did Isobel, lively, undisciplined.'

'But you weren't close.'

'No, we weren't. She needed someone to keep her in check. She was young. Too young for this war at any rate. This business with the Major.'

'What about it?'

She wiped the corner of her mouth with a little white handkerchief pulled from her sleeve. As she patted her lips her eyes moved to the painting on the wall.

'His head was turned. Not just by her. By the war, by the island, by their fairy-tale life. It quite upset his equilibrium. God knows what will happen to him now.'

'You and the Major get on rather well, don't you? Uncle Albert often used to remark about your dinners.'

'Used to is the operative term. The Major has other guests on his invitation list now. No time for his older friends. I wouldn't have minded if she'd been . . .'

'Yes?'

'A little more worthy of him.'

'Did you think so little of her, then?'

'No, no. She was a lovely girl. Bright, vivacious, kind.' She handed him the plate. He wavered for a moment, then chose the Bourbon. It was soft, slightly stale. He was disappointed. Mrs Hallivand continued. 'But she had no capacity for self-improvement, no sense of place or duty. It was, "this is what I am" and "this is what I want". I had always hoped that she might develop, might mature. As it was she remained what she wanted to be, a naive young woman, blessed with good looks but unwilling or unable to face up to the realities of life.'

'Forgive me for saying so, Mrs Hallivand, but you don't seem terribly upset.'

'Of course I'm upset. But I fear she brought this on herself, riding about the island without a care in the world. They all do it, those girls. They think it all such fun. And so it probably is. What they don't realize is that the islanders will put up with just so much and then . . .'

'So you think she was killed by one of us.'

'It was bound to happen to one of them one day. And no German would have killed her. She was a popular girl.'

Ned felt himself blush.

'Do you mean she had men friends other than the Major?'

'She had a good many suitors, I know that. Before the Major she was always out riding with some captain or other. I don't believe there was anything serious between any of them, but nor did she turn them away. She liked the attention, did Isobel. It was fun to have handsome young men hanging on to her every word, bowing when she came through the door, telling her father what a charming daughter he had.'

'No angry lover, then?'

'I doubt it. She was no femme fatale, just an ordinary English girl who unfortunately saw no difference between a German uniform and a Henley boating blazer. The anger directed at her will be traced to our hearts not theirs.'

It was true. Ned had seen her only last month, riding in the back of Lentsch's staff car late one afternoon. 'Hide me, Bernie, for God's sake,' he said, stepping back, and Bernie had stood on the kerb as insolently as the law permitted and stared while the car revved its engine, impatient for the horse-drawn bus that was blocking its path to move out of the way.

'Look at her, sitting in my car, like she owned it,' Bernie

165

muttered, as they passed. 'Just you wait, mademoiselle,' he called out. 'We'll give you a ride to remember when this is all over!'

Ned pulled him back into the safety of a shop doorway. 'Do you want to get us both deported?' he said, shaking him angrily. 'What's it to you what she does? I'm the one who should be angry.'

He returned to Mrs Hallivand.

'Now, yesterday morning. Nothing was said that might make you think that she was worried?'

'Why should she be worried? She was excited about the Major coming back. She was planning a surprise party.'

'Yes, I know. But you didn't call her over about that, did you?'

'No.'

'Well, why, then?'

'It was all happening too fast between them. Too many heads in the clouds and not enough feet on the ground. While he'd been away she'd been talking about their life together. She still didn't appreciate the implications. It could never have lasted.'

'Like me, you mean.'

Mrs Hallivand brushed the crumbs from her lap.

'That never bothered me at all. Every woman should have a little adventure somewhere along the way, if for nothing more than to be able to look back on it when your husband is snoring in the bed next to yours. But this was different. I was worried that she might do something she might regret. With her father's position, it wouldn't have been impossible for the two of them to get married here, engaged at least. I tried to dissuade her.'

'And what did she say?'

'What she always said. She told me to mind my own business.'

'And then?'

'We had a little row. I went to the kitchen to get some more hot water for the pot. By the time I got back she had gone. She must have been angrier than I thought. She forgot her bicycle.'

'A bicycle? I didn't know she had a bicycle.'

'My old thing. She use to ride it back and forth, you know, on her visits. I don't think her father approved. She used to hide it in the bushes at the back of their garden.'

'She told you?'

'Albert did. He came across it while he was weeding there once. She swore him to secrecy, but you know Albert. Can't resist a good gossip.'

*

Ned walked up to the house. He'd never been inside the main rooms. He was hoping that his uncle might show him round. The front door stood half open. Uncle Albert was standing on a chair in the hall, dusting the picture frames.

'If you've come for our house guests, they've all done a bunk,' he said. He stood down. 'She all right, then?'

'Less upset than me, I think.' Ned looked around. At the far end he could see the drawing room. A tray of dirty glasses and coffee cups stood on the floor. Albert nodded in its direction.

'Haven't finished clearing up yet,' he said. 'They were in and out of here last night like ferrets down a rabbit hole.'

'Who was?'

'The Captain, the Major, the ugly one, Ernst. I was packed off upstairs. No one was allowed out until seven. We weren't told until then.'

'They were here all night?'

'I'll say. Telephone ringing, cars and motorcycles racing up and down the drive. I thought it was the invasion or summat, the way they were carrying on. Then the Major came up and told me. Near to tears he was. Her father was here by then.'

'Oh?'

'Wedel brought him over, about half five. I saw him from my window.' He pushed the duster in his pocket. 'Any idea who?'

Ned shook his head. 'Someone who hated the van Dielens? A way of getting back at him?'

'Someone who wanted to teach these girls a lesson, more like.'

'Perhaps.' Ned paused. 'Isobel came up here yesterday, so Mrs Hallivand tells me.'

Albert glanced down at the Lodge. 'She wanted to know what I was doing about supper. That's all they ever think about, this lot, what they're going to stuff themselves with next.'

'And that was all?'

'It was enough.'

He stood in the hall, unwilling to say more.

'Long time since I set foot in here,' Ned said.

'Hasn't changed much,' Albert said. ''Cept for the occupants. They don't like folk snooping round here, no more than she did.'

'We still have to know our place, you mean.'

'It's what armies are all about, isn't it. Armies and class.'

'And Mrs Hallivand? What's her place now?'

'To do as she's told,' Albert said. 'Like we all must do.' He looked back. 'You can come in the kitchen, if you like. Have a cup of tea while I wash them cups and saucers. Take some back to your mother.'

'I think Mum's got enough dirty dishes of her own, thanks all the same.'

Albert refused to see the joke. 'You know what I mean. We can spare a few teaspoons. Bit of butter too, if you've a fancy.'

'Like the old days.'

Albert walked over and picked up the tray. He looked down at the cups with cigarettes and cigar ends floating in the dregs.

'No, not like them at all, Ned. Those days have passed.'

*

Seated at the enamel-faced table Ned looked at his uncle fussing in the sink. Before the Occupation Albert would have rather died than wear an apron round his waist.

'The last time I sat here I was wearing shorts and tucking into a jam sandwich,' Ned told him, wishing that just such a treat might lie in front of him now. 'Never thought I'd sit here again.'

His uncle bent over the dirty water and stirred the crockery with reckless vigour.

'Why'd you bother with Miss Isobel, then, if it wasn't to pull yourself up by her drawstrings?'

Ned took a sip of tea. Good and strong, made with not a thought to how many spoonfuls were put in the pot. God, how long was it since he had tasted tea like this? He tipped his cup up and filled his mouth, rolling the liquid round before swallowing it in one gulp. He could feel his body reel with the rush of it, like he was swigging brandy or vodka, his eyes watering, his stomach on fire. 'I don't know,' he said, suddenly garrulous. 'I thought I was in love. I didn't think about other things. She put a spell on me.'

'Yes, well, I can't blame you there. For all her foolishness she was a spirit, there's no denying it. Warm-hearted too, considerate. Not like some of them here, treating me no better than a skivvy.'

'Albert!'

A tall woman came bursting through the spring door. When she saw Ned sitting at the table she stopped.

'Oh?'

'This is my nephew, miss. Ned Luscombe? Inspector Luscombe.'

'Oh!'

Ned got to his feet. She walked across the tiles on low heels that clicked. She was wearing a smart grey cape clasped at the top and a little blue hat perched at an angle. She held out a hand; dark red fingernails, the colour of spent blood; a ring with a diamond sparkle; perfume on the wrist. He took it in his grasp. It was a white hand, long and cold and strangely erotic, even at eleven o'clock in the morning.

'Molly Langmead,' she said.

'Miss Molly was here yesterday morning, weren't you, miss?' Albert said without looking up. 'When Miss van Dielen came by to see how we were doing.'

'Mmm.' She looked around. 'Matches, Albert, I need some matches. I've quite misplaced my lighter, the one the Captain gave me.'

Albert crossed over to the dresser and pulled open a drawer.

'We got a two-legged magpie somewhere in this house,' he grumbled, 'the number of things that go missing. Here.'

He handed her the box. Molly took out a packet of cigarettes and tapped one into her hand. 'Ah,' she said, lighting it up. 'The joys of Craven A.'

'That's a rare brand these days,' Ned observed.

'One and six each on the black market, so I'm told,' she said insolently, holding the packet out. 'Do you smoke?'

'Only what I can afford,' Ned told her. He took out his notebook. 'You saw Isobel too, then?'

She looked down, amused at his hands, patting his pockets for his pen.

'Me and Veronica, yes.'

'Veronica Vaudin?'

'Is there another Veronica in St Peter Port?'

'I wouldn't know. What was she doing here?'

'What we were all doing. Preparing for the party.'

'She was a regular too, was she?'

Molly blew smoke into the air and threw the box back to Albert. Sitting back on one of the chairs she undid the clasp and let the cape fall open. Ned fought to keep his eyes on her face. She watched him closely, to see when he would succumb.

'No, this was her first time. I thought she might enliven the proceedings. It can get a bit stale, the same people day in, day out. There were a couple of men who'd shown interest in her.'

'In Veronica?'

'Well, don't sound so surprised. Of course Veronica.'

'Who, exactly?'

'I thought you wanted to know about Isobel? All right, all right.' She looked up to the ceiling. 'Our own dear Bohde, for a start. Apparently he'd been to her about his feet and came back smitten. God, what a thought. Bohde's feet!'

Ned was worried about his own. He had to tread carefully here.

'The Major told me that Bohde doesn't approve of English girls.'

'Not approving of them and wanting to sleep with them are two quite separate matters.'

Albert pulled the plug in the sink violently. Molly turned.

'I'm sorry, Albert, I know how this kind of talk upsets you, but it's true. Bohde couldn't take his eyes off her all evening. Isn't that right?'

'Not for me to say, miss.'

She leant over and flicked ash into the gurgling water. Ned let his eyes fall. When they returned Molly was looking at him with amused satisfaction.

'Your uncle is the very soul of discretion,' she said, holding the cigarette over her shoulder, daring him to take another look. 'But it's my belief every night he scurries up to his room and writes down all our misdemeanours in some horrid little exercise book of his. Where do you keep it Albert, this tittle-tattle which will undo us all? Under the mattress? Up the chimney?'

She turned and looked at him. Albert stood there, fixed. He had been caught out, Ned was sure of it! Molly laughed and leaning across, stubbed the cigarette out in Ned's saucer. She had heavy, smoker's breath.

'Tell him not to worry. His secret is safe with me.'

Albert gathered Ned's cup and saucer from the table and ran them under the cold tap. The crockery rattled in anger.

'You're a close friend of Captain Zepernick, I believe?' Ned asked her. She smiled sweetly.

'What a very polite young man you are.'

'And he was there all the time, for the party?'

'Inspector, when it comes to parties, the Captain is always the first to arrive and the last to leave. This was his party. He organized it, not Isobel. He invited the men, I brought the girls.'

'Except the nurses from Bremen.'

'Well informed, too. Yes. Without wanting to sound at all snobby, they were there for the lower ranks, the Wedels of this world.'

'For Bohde too, I believe.'

'Isn't that a hoot! I suppose it's the only way Bohde can get anyone to oblige – to bare her all for the nation state. That's the real reason they were there that night. No English girl would submit to that, though he'd asked most of us at one time or another. Apart from the nurses, who the good Doctor Mueller organized, Zep and I were in charge. It's a talent we have. Making whoopee.'

'But Captain Zepernick left the party with Miss Vaudin, is that not right?' Ned decided to call him by his formal name. With her connections Molly could make life difficult for him, and they both knew it.

'No, that is not right.' Her voice had lost its sense of play. She got up and fastened the clasp. 'He did not "leave" the party at all. He was called away when they found her. Of course we didn't know then that it was Isobel. He gave Veronica a lift home. She lives in one of those dingy fisherman's cottages by Cobo Bay. With her mother and father. Very cosy.'

Ned refused to rise to the bait.

'And he was there in the club all the time before that, and during the party.'

'Absolutely. We got changed here at about seven and left for the club about half past. Isn't that right Albert?'

Albert nodded.

'Zep dropped me off at Underwood's. Veronica had decided to get changed in her consulting room. Her father's a bit of an old stick-in-the-mud. He wouldn't have approved of her dress at all. No back and precious little front. Even I thought she was in danger of – how shall I put it – over-egging the puddings.' She laughed at her little joke. 'We had a quick drink in one of the hotel bars along the way and arrived at the Casino around eight, coming back here at around eleven. And from then on, until the Captain left, all of us were here all the time. Albert can vouch for that.'

'You know where Isobel was found?'

'The Captain told me, yes.'

'Have you ever been in one of those bunkers? Has the Captain ever taken you there?'

'No. Why on earth should he? They're out of bounds.'

'Seeing as you're a favoured guest, I was wondering if you'd been given a special tour. If you had been there, you might have told someone else about it.'

'Why on earth should I want to see round a hole in the ground?' She looked at her small gold-chained watch. Another present from the Captain? 'Look, can we do this some other time? I have an appointment which I really shouldn't miss.'

She put her hand inside her cape and pressed it flat against her stomach, wincing slightly as she felt its swell.

'The doctor!' he exclaimed. 'You should have said.'

'No.' She sounded light, airy, full of brimming confidence. 'Underwood's. I'm having a new dress made up. My first fitting.'

'Been saving the coupons, then?'

Molly smiled. 'Something like that.'

'Something special, is it?'

'A party.' She looked around the kitchen. 'I just love parties, don't I, Albert?'

*

Walking down the drive Ned saw the Captain's car coming up the drive. He stepped on the grass to let it pass. The car slowed down, the engine running. The roof was open and the Captain held his hat between his legs. He stared forward and waited. Ned bit his lip and saluted.

'Captain.'

Zepernick leant across and waved an envelope at him.

'I was going to have Wedel deliver this today. Take it now.'

'What is it? A special pass?'

'Special pass! No! It is to do with your dress.'

'My dress? I don't understand, Captain.'

The Captain looked out to where Molly stood in the doorway. He looked at his watch and waved.

'Your uniforms,' he said. 'You and your cadets.'

'Constables.'

173

'You need to be smarter. The island does not look good with such costumes. Read.'

Zepernick gunned the car up the drive. Ned tore the envelope open. Inside was a letter headed with the Feldkommandantur stamp. Two letters addressed to him in two days, almost a record. The first paragraph was some piffle about sloppy attire; ties not straight, boots not polished, buttons hanging off the jacket. And then this:

Consequently, beginning this Wednesday, the entire police force will present itself to Underwood's the tailors where provision has been made for measurements and fittings to be taken for a complete set of new uniforms. New uniforms will be issued the following month on April 15th. They will be made in strict accordance to the specifications of British Policemen. The cost will be met from existing police funds. Any policemen found to be wearing their old uniforms after that date will be fined five shillings and suspended without pay for one week. The maintenance of these new uniforms will be solely the owners' responsibility.'

Signed, Captain R. Zepernick.

'Underwood's again,' Ned said out loud, screwing the letter into a ball. 'I'm in the wrong bloody business.'

Seven

Albert stands by the granite grave in the churchyard. In his hand he holds a bunch of wild primroses. They have come early this year and he is glad, for he would not have liked to have left without seeing the first flowers of spring peeking through one more time. It will, he reckons, be what he will miss the most, the flowers and the way they cover the island in such sudden profusion.

It is a bare, ungainly grave with a square cut of gravel on which stands a small vase. The inscription reads *Rose Luscombe, Wife to Albert, Mother to Kitty, Mum to Both*. The flowers are fresh as always, for Albert comes here every other day to replace the old with the new. Sometimes he brings cultivated flowers from the greenhouse, sometimes ones picked from the garden, and, when he can, wild flowers from the verges and hedgerows, gathered with an eye to their composition as he walks the two miles to where she is buried. There are tears in his eyes, as constant an accompaniment as the flowers in his hands, a mark of an irredeemable sorrow he carries within and which grows more acute at each visit. Alone, up at the House, looking after these strangely attractive men, his brother gone too, he feels her loss more than ever, for the island has become a contemptuous territory, both familiar and utterly foreign. It is not the wail of the siren nor the pulse of marching feet that has set his mind against his homeland, but the cries of those he has known all his life, now choking before his very eyes in a sea of greed and suspicion. Let them go under! Let them drown! He will not help them! He talks to her now, talking as he did when she was alive, for contrary to folklore it was always Albert who would return with the gossip he had gathered from the Hallivands' floor or supped down at the Britannia, while it was Rose, crippled with arthritis, who would sit in her chair and sniff, but unlike former times he takes no pleasure in his tales. He talks to her now, of the island's perfidy, of its moral loss, mentioning names that were once their everyday companions, all the time looking out to the sea, wondering where their daughter is. He knows that he will never see her again, that she is lost to him, gone for ever. He has not heard from her since she left that Tuesday before the invasion, him pushing her off, feeling the tears in the back of his throat, wanting to take her in his arms and hug the very essence of her into him, dying to tell her, as he pretended to be so unconcerned, so cheerful, that he would always love her, always miss her, fearing the very worst. As he says out loud to his dead wife lying but four feet below him, it's the not knowing where she is that's the worry. London, Birmingham, Coventry, there had been some terrible bombings over there, whole areas ablaze, and though he did not believe the ninety per cent of lies that passed for news on the front pages of the *Star*, the ten per cent of truth would be enough to blow their Kitty to smithereens. It makes him angry to think that it should have come to this, makes him want to curse, but being where he is he bites his lip. Kitty would have been safer here, he tells her, blaming himself yet again for marching their daughter down to the quayside, with a bundle of clothes in a borrowed suitcase, a set of tulip bulbs wrapped in secret in her nightgown that she might grow in memory of him, and a letter of introduction from Mrs Hallivand to the hostel at Weymouth, hoping that she might find work there. But then who knows, she might have taken up with them, like so many other girls of her age. It isn't their class or lack of upbringing that has turned their heads, Albert is convinced, it is their age. All their young life they've been told what to do, what to say, how to behave, their future set out like their mothers' and grandmothers' before them, and suddenly the plan has been torn up, and they've been handed a licence to do as they please – and fresh male company to do it with besides. And what can their elders do? The young hold the power now, and by

God they know how to use it. He has never seen women of such little worth wield such authority; a father betrayed after forbidding his daughter to stay out late; lipsticked bevies of them walking arm in arm down the Pollet, lording it over the ration queues; whole families in thrall to the eighteen-year-old who just might get her father work if they let her shame their name. There is nothing these girls can't do, except jump on a boat and leave, and the younger they are, the more shameless and ungodly their behaviour. Only this afternoon he'd seen a couple of brazen little beasts – troop carriers (it shamed him even as he spoke their epithet) – strutting past, holding their swollen stomachs out as proudly if they'd had the Iron Cross pinned upon them. 'Couldn't have looked happier if they'd been...' he draws in a deep breath, knowing his wife's antipathy to such talk, 'by — — himself.'

Albert shakes his head, bewildered at the improbability of it all. 'If you were alive,' he tells her, 'if you were alive...' But he can go no further. Instead he starts again with his other tale, the one he has held as tightly to himself these two miles as the bunch of primroses now standing in the cloudy vase, smoothing the gravel with his hand, forming shapes and patterns as he works. He has big hands, red and ruthless, hands used to the shotgun and the snare, hands used to the fork and the spade, hardened by frost and stone and the snag of summer thorn, tough hands, always purposeful but as delicate with the rabbit's neck as they are with the greenhouse seedling. There are no weeds today, no stray leaves for him to clear, nothing to interrupt his fuss, but in his agitation it is he who is disturbing the symmetry of the ground, making little heaps of stones with his hands, fashioning the square and diagonals of the English flag, marking out the single word LIDICHY before obliterating it with his hand. He has not read of this foreign place in the newspaper (which is why he spells it incorrectly) nor has he heard of it from the lips of Lord Haw-Haw or the outlawed Alva Lidell, but in recent months it has reverberated round the walls of Mrs Hallivand's drawing room, first in hushed whispers, and lately in more acerbic tones. Usually it is the Major who introduces the word, waving a requisitioned fork in the air, or filling his balloon with another swirl of Mr Hallivand's brandy, only for it to be shrugged off by a show of indifference by the Captain or dismissed as malicious tittle-tattle by the loganberry thief. LIDICHY. He writes it again and underneath adds the phrase CERTAIN DEATH. Almost immediately he smoothes the gravel free once more, fearful lest someone might be watching him, or that he might leave without remembering to erase the confession, but it is too cold, too windy and too late in the afternoon for inquisitive meddlers to be around, and besides, who would intrude on an old man visiting his wife's recent grave? He fashions the words again, speaking them to his Rose lying so close, tracing the letters he has formed as if by writing them she will absorb what he has to tell her. LIDICHY he writes, CERTAIN DEATH and then, underneath, the word DUTY. He stares at this bleak litany for a moment, silent and then rubs out LIDICHY and replaces it with GUERNSEY. GUERNSEY, CERTAIN DEATH and DUTY. He looks at his list and, conscious of the flawed logic he has imposed, shuffles his hand across the pebbles for the third time in order to place the words in their correct order. Now it appears for the last time. GUERNSEY, it reads. GUERNSEY, DUTY and CERTAIN DEATH. 'Duty and Certain Death,' he says calmly. He turns and speaks it into the wind. 'Duty and Certain Death.' He shouts it loudly so that his words are lifted into the wind and carried out over the water to where his daughter could be standing, in Weymouth or Southampton, planting those tulip bulbs perhaps, thinking of her old dad and the soil she has left behind. She cannot hear him, he knows, and he can never tell her what he has never told her, but perhaps, God willing, in years to come, his spirit will find her and whisper that he did love her and that he missed her and he died with the thought of her in his eyes and in his arms.

★

In the late morning Mrs Hallivand walks up the hill. It is for the most part a humble street, and with her frame bent by both the steep incline and the weakness of her undernourished frame she is struck, as always, by how the route to Guernsey's most famous house takes her past some of the island's most unprepossessing quarters, battered damp dwellings, built haphazardly, huddled and crumbling, punctuated by dank alleyways and dim cobbled court-yards, the smell of rot and drains and last night's urine drifting through a hum of upstairs cries. It was somewhere here, despite his initial denials, that her husband Maurice had leaned their ledger girl up against the wall, too busy inhaling the scent of his own desires to notice the stench rising from round their ankles. Was that what all her good works had been for, so that she could book Elspeth Poidevin into the Weymouth Hostel for Wayward Girls without too many questions being asked and have the baby whisked away (to a good home, she promised blithely) as soon as it dropped out of the little trollop and into the midwife's arms? Whenever she went into the bank and had the misfortune to see her grinning insolently from behind the counter an uneasy wave of guilt swept over her, for the child she had foisted on some unsuspecting couple and the mother she had denied. Not that Elspeth showed any signs of the loss, cocking her head at any man who came through the door. No one could describe Elspeth as pretty, a dumpy thing, stupid and cruel like her parents, but there was no denying that there was something overwhelmingly tempting about her, perched up on her stool, licking her fingers as she counted out the banknotes, on show and out of reach, like a flaky pastry fat with cream set out in a baker's window. At least she had kept her mouth shut. For that reason alone the fifty pounds had been money well spent. Twenty-five pounds and a job in the office for life, that's what she asked for in the drawing room that afternoon, lowering her eyes, her hands clasped over the all too apparent bulge. Fifty pounds, two months in the hostel and a job anywhere but with us, that's how she countered and Elspeth took it on the spot, knowing the strings the Hallivands could pull, the embarrassed standard-bearer of the family name pushing his hair back in the library, grooming himself for the onslaught to come.

Mrs Hallivand carries with her a large oval basket in which lies a stone bottle, a square of squashed carrot cake, a duster, a chamois leather, a tin of floor polish, a packet of fly-papers, a mousetrap and a hefty clutch of keys: a rusting iron one, heavy like the front door for which it is fashioned, and a host of smaller ones, each tied with a small white handwritten label bearing the name of its locked location: the Billiard Room, the Tapestry Room, the Smoking Room, the Library, the Blue Drawing Room, the Red Drawing Room, and so on, up to the Eyrie. She has carried this basket for twelve years, ever since her late father proposed to the Parisian authorities who own the property that she become their designated trustee. The States were willing to appoint a housekeeper for the weekly chores, but Mrs Hallivand offered to perform these functions herself, not because she liked cleaning (she had rarely lifted a duster or squeezed a mop in her life) but because she realized that such an unchaperoned opportunity would afford her an intimacy with the house's former occupier denied to anybody else. Maurice might spend business afternoons on the mainland enjoying one of his golf club wives on the second floor of the Norfolk Hotel, Bournemouth (boasting a Cocktail Bar, the Richmonde Lounge and the Norfolk Hotel Broadcasting Orchestra); she on the other hand took her pleasure alone, high in Victor's eagle nest, surrounded by memen-toes of his life and work. And what a life! It thrilled her to think of that great bearded giant looking down on the town where she now stood, washing his naked torso for all to see, the apparatus of his prodigious sexual appetite on display; servant girls, married women from the town, visiting aristocratic amours, not to mention the mistress up the road, he served them all. He did not try and hide it. He recommended sexual intercourse to his friends as a cure for headaches, depression, even constipation, urging them to act with-out delay, with whomsoever was available. Regular intercourse was a physical necessity; the smooth running of the body demanded it.

From where came the means was not the point. Sex on such a grand, lordly scale had nothing to do with infidelity or betrayal, far removed from Maurice's clumsy affairs with their candlelit dinners and false promises of love. Victor's needs were simple; an uncomplicated coupling taken when the need came upon him, like a cup of strong coffee or a brisk walk, enjoyable, invigorating, and paradoxically, however exotic the company, a profoundly solitary exercise: a prelude to the real business of the day – work. And what work! Here amongst these rooms she could finger his lines of thought, delve into the mystery of the man. Over the years, suspended in reverie in that floating room of light, she had come to believe that only she had the capacity to embrace and receive his monumental fertility. Every week she would take one of his notebooks home and place it on her bedside table. Let Maurice return from his expeditions to fall asleep in his adjoining bed, she would sit in hers and become, if not satiated, then hungrily content. She did not reproach her husband for his excesses, but not because she excused them, for she did not, but because she wanted as little to do with him as he did with her. What she had not told anyone since her arrival seventeen years ago was that once the flurry of moving to Guernsey had died down, once she had settled into the island's ways, she had opened her eyes one morning and came to the conclusion that she had made a terrible and irreversible mistake. All her life she had fought to be allied to a certain kind of uncharted freedom, a man of spirit, and now, looking up from the comfort of their then double bed, watching Maurice mouth the minutes of the golf club's last meeting, it was plain to see she had handcuffed herself to a dullard and sentenced her own free will to a life of imprisonment. Maurice was small-minded. Guernsey was small-minded. The forty thousand souls living alongside them had similar visions. Their horizons stretched no further than the rock on which they stood, a self-satisfied triangle, six by seven by nine, an immovable wedge of granite, stuck fast and impervious to change. Where was the glitter, the intrigue, where were the stakes to be played, the bolts from the blue? It was all so dull! The clubs with their empty protocol and pointless committees, the endless cocktail circuit, the spring and winter balls, all, in their proud pomposity, heartbreaking reminders of the glittering society she had left behind. When her sister had turned up she had hoped that she might be able to take Isobel under her wing, so that she could live once again a life of wit and nerve, but Isobel, wilfully indifferent to her schemes and confident in her own inherent abilities, had paid her little attention. Then there'd been that trouble over Ned Luscombe. Albert had come running to her about that the moment he found out. How could it be, he said, waving a pair of hedge-clippers in his hands, that his nephew would dare walk out with Mrs Hallivand's niece? What if it went further, what if the worst thing in the world happened and they had to get married? They were headstrong those two, from stubborn stock, Albert had pronounced, ever the gardener, adding, 'I could never be related to you, Mrs H., not even if the King himself commanded it.' She had laughed, the spell of her own horror at the story broken, for she saw at once that Isobel would never contemplate such an unlikely and unflattering alliance either. She had seen the look of incredulous pity pass over her niece's face when Isobel had first been introduced to Maurice, the celebrated stories she had been told of her aunt's glittering past transformed into insolent mockery. Ned hadn't seduced her. Isobel had seduced him, and Mrs Hallivand knew why. To get back at her. To tell her to mind her own business, that she needed no lessons from such an abject failure as her. So she told Albert not to worry, that by next spring he would be able to tip his beret and wish her good morning with an easy heart.

'Thank God for that, ma'am,' he said. 'No disrespect regarding your niece intended.'

'And none taken, Albert. None taken.'

She climbs the steps now and unlocks the heavy front door. Closing it firmly behind her, she pauses in the hallway and feels the silence fall upon her, something which the island itself once possessed, but which now she finds only within these walls. It is a curious thing, this weight of absolute security. In the early days, when she had discovered her dreadful mistake, she would throw open the windows at the Villa, and lean out, cursing this peace, as if, willing it, she might hear the old noises of city she loved, the hum of the hub, as her father had called it, winging over the water. Now, standing in its last refuge, she wishes the island's long quiet would return. It has become part of her, but though she misses it such a realization does not please her.

Though her first port of call is usually the study, from where she works her way down, today she makes straight for the Red Drawing Room, a dark, heavy room, weighted down with oak furniture. The lock turns easily and skirting round the edge she moves quickly to the window to open the centre section of shutters. Light falls in, bisecting the room, illuminating beams of dust. Through the shadows the magnificence of the room takes form, a fire screen worked by Mme de Pompadour and four gilt figures taken from the Doge's palace, the silk tapestries covering the wall and ceiling. In the centre stands the great table belonging to Charles II. In former times a pair of archbishop's candlesticks stood at either end, but these have been set down on the floor, and in their place lies a humdrum collection of bags and containers: a pickling jar full of six-inch nails, a dried milk tin packed with bolts; a closed shoebox with a scattering of sugar rounds its base, a carrier bag bulging with the same substance with the name Underwood written on the side, another, altogether more elegant, which announces that Voisin & Co. of King St, Jersey is *the* Shopping Centre of the Channel Islands; a clock; a pair of pliers; batteries from a torch. Placing the basket on the table Mrs Hallivand sets aside the tins and other cleaning paraphernalia and lifting the embroidered cloth which is tucked in all the way round uncovers a pound bag of sugar and the last packet of weedkiller left in the Lodge's outhouse. She picks up the tin and, holding it in front of her as if it were dynamite or something which might give her an electric shock, lifts the lid of the shoebox.

'I very much doubt,' she says to the self-portrait hanging above the fireplace as she pours it in, 'whether you or I have ever seen so much sugar before, even in peace time. Three ounces a week is all we get now.' She pauses and then decides. 'I don't suppose it would do any harm. And I have such a sweet tooth.'

She moves quickly to the little kitchen at the back, where in earlier times the caretaker would brew up a cup during visiting hours. There is a kettle there and a small paraffin ring and beside them stands the tea caddy with the Swiss maid and Matterhorn motif and in which lies a dwindling amount of real leaf tea. On a shelf directly above the kettle stands a sizeable brown teapot, good for four thirsty people, with a cracked lid and a spout which pours in an indifferent arc. Mrs Hallivand turns the tap and as the water is slightly discoloured lets it run for a full minute before she fills the kettle through its furred-up spout.

While waiting for the kettle to boil she walks back into the room, to the window and the view of the besieged harbour and the glittering sea beyond. The room is beginning to smell of this strange assortment of packages, a damp sweetness clinging to the silk, an odd sourness too, like stale sweat. In previous times it would have smelt of cigar smoke and port. She talks, not to her husband, nor her dead niece, nor her dead sister (none of whom she misses), but to the man whose spirit had captured her heart all those years ago but who in the last eighteen months had been supplanted by another. If only she had been younger! If only the Major had been older! It was easy to see why he had found Isobel attractive, less easy to fathom his affection. Mrs Hallivand had flirted with a hundred different Lentsches in her time. If she'd been her niece's age, Isobel wouldn't have lasted more than a week. As it was, with barely any competition in sight, she'd had an uninterrupted run, and where there might have been doubts, the language had saved her. Like any foreign man equipped with an English that was both precise and elegantly correct, when faced with a willing young woman with good looks and passable manners, the Major had taken any display of weakness in Isobel's character as simply an example of his own inadequate hold on her native tongue. And there were so many reasons why she deserved him and her niece did not. Their love of literature, their understanding of art, the intelligent delight they both took in those flirtatious conversations that only lovers can sustain. She was still good-looking, she still had sparkle and, if she chose to wake it, there still lay within her that hard, unforgiving sexuality to which so many young men had once been drawn. But the Major had chosen Isobel, and Isobel was gone and now she has returned to the man who understood her best. The Major's appeal was not only transitory, but misplaced. He meant nothing to her now.

The kettle starts to sing. Mrs Hallivand makes the tea, and using the milk from the stone bottle pours herself a cup. Bringing the cup back into the room she bends down and with her hand scoops up a palmful of crystals. It is an obscene amount to hold, to let run free. Raising her hand she lets it flow through her fingers. She thinks of all the islanders queuing in the buffeting winds, waiting for their pitiful gram of this and their pitiful gram of that. The sugar sparkles fresh and light, a radiant white in this brown and solemn room, fairy dust from an angel's wand caught in a beam from a distant star. She thinks of the long glittering evenings of her reckless youth; the murmur of voices in the ballroom below: the starched dress shirt and how it had glowed in the dark as she pressed her breasts, oh her lovely breasts, against it, reaching for one more illicit embrace. The white drifts down, to the floor and around her shoes. The light hurts her eyes. She could be skiing on the slopes above Wengen or walking barefoot on Deauville sand. She could be seventeen again, standing by the bay windows, watching the snow drift over the Parisian rooftops, waiting for her Peter Pan to lead her astray. She looks out, potion in hand, waiting for the sweet dreams of the liquid to cool.

A figure appears in the doorway. She turns.

'You're early,' she says. 'There's some tea in the pot if you want.'

'Well?' he says. 'How did it go?'

'He doesn't know anything.'

Albert grunts and walks to the table.

'Got you something.' He hands her a large tin.

'Custard! Where how on earth did you come by that?'

'Never you mind. Take it. Got something else too.' He digs into his pockets again. 'Razor blades. Fifty of them.' He pulls out a little box and shakes the contents into the pickling jar. He holds it to the light. 'This'll take the wind out of his sails.'

Mrs Hallivand holds her cup tightly.

'I'm frightened, Albert,' she says. 'Isobel has made it much more dangerous. I don't know if I can go on.'

Albert steps up and shakes her hard.

'Do as you're told, you silly woman. We've not long now.'

Eight

Five o'clock in the evening and Tommy le Coeur came back to the station in a bad mood. Van Dielen had still not returned and his feet were frozen. He showed Ned the holes in his boots.

'A lot to carry, these pins,' he said. 'No warmth to this coat either. Be the death of me, this job.'

'Your problems are soon to be at an end, Tommy,' Ned replied, handing over the Captain's note. 'In a couple of weeks' time they could run you at Ascot.'

He made Tommy a mug of tea before walking down to the Royal Hotel, now Feldkommandantur Headquarters, to tell Lentsch of the day's developments. Not that there was much. Her neck had been broken, grabbed and twisted round hard, like a gamekeeper might a bird or rabbit, that's what the police doctor had pronounced. She was still alive probably when the cement had been pressed into her mouth and up her nose, but limp and helpless, like a rag doll. Death by suffocation or dislocation? Dr Meecham hummed and hawed. He was out of his depth. Seeing as the one the Home Office usually sent was unavailable, perhaps Lentsch could send for a pathologist from France?

Outside the Royal, Wedel was polishing the bonnet of Bernie's car. Though the 'Royal' had been taken down and a German notice hung in its place Ned was pleased to see that the old AA sign still hung below the little wooden balcony. A couple of workmen stood underneath, painting the window frames. Although he recognized them, as he approached they looked to their work, ashamed for all three of them. Wedel lifted his hand in acknowledgement. Ned nodded.

'I thought you were going on leave?' he said.

Wedel winced. '*Kaput*,' he said, looking up to the first floor.

'That's a uniform for you.'

More men were working inside, ladders and buckets of white-wash blocking the corridor. A guard showed him up to Lentsch's office on the first floor. Despite the desk and two flags guarding the other trappings of authority, the dagger, the candlesticks and the ornate silver inkstand, the room, with its faded flowered wallpaper and obligatory chipped washstand tucked away in the far corner, still looked like a mid-priced bedroom with a faulty tap and a partial view of the sea. Above the mantelpiece hung the inevitable portrait, garlanded by a profusion of dark ferns woven round the frame as if he was peeking out through the gloom of a Silesian glade. Ned tried to imagine who would spend the morning fashioning such an absurd decoration. That was the difference between their two nations. Both held their leader in awe, depended on his strength and vision to carry them through, but while the British trusted Churchill, even admired him, they didn't worship him. No one would bedeck a picture of his ugly flab with bits of leaf and twig.

Lentsch appeared in the doorway, his eyes red.

'I see you are admiring Wedel's handiwork,' he said, fighting to keep his voice under control.

'What?'

'The decoration. It is our leader's birthday. April 20th. All Germans celebrate.'

Ned smiled. 'He'll be pleased, then, to know you've gone to so much trouble. Smartening the place up, too.'

'Yes. The soldiers also.'

'You're not the only ones.' Ned showed him the Captain's letter. Lentsch read it quickly.

'I did not know this.'

'Well, he wouldn't want to bother you I expect, considering.'

'New uniforms!' Lentsch walked to the window again. 'I look out here and see the same Guernsey I saw three weeks ago – and yet it is not the same. It is without Isobel. Do you realize this, that she is no longer here? The tides come in and out, the harbour unloads, birds build their nests for the spring, and yet she is not here. How can this be?' He turned back. 'It is my fault that she is dead. You believe this too, I think?'

'No, Major, I don't think that.'

He folded the Captain's letter back into his pocket, wedging it up against Isobel's. Of course it's your fault, he thought, and who knows, maybe more directly than you would have me believe. Why couldn't Isobel have gone to Lentsch? Because of the Major's involvement in something?

'There is nothing for me here now,' Lentsch continued flatly. 'I hoped that when the war was over I would return here, become one of you, watch the boats and the seasons and be content.'

'It takes a long time to become one of us, Major,' Ned told him. 'I'm not sure that I'm one of us yet. My father never thought I was.'

A silence fell.

'I would not have wanted this for the world,' the Major exclaimed, pressing his hands against the glass, 'and yet I cannot say that I wish I had not been here. I cannot say that.' He moved across to the desk and turning the picture frame over in his hands, handed it to Ned. 'See how happy she looks,' he implored. 'See how happy I made her. Tell me I did wrong.'

Ned studied the photograph. It had been taken somewhere along the water lanes, near where he used to meet her. Three perfectly pressed uniformed officers walking along the narrow lane, Zepernick, a shorter man Ned did not recognize and the Major. Captain Zepernick, gloves in his hands, was in the midst of telling a joke, the shorter man was taking a cigarette from his mouth, and on the far side Lentsch was turning to his companions, smiling at what was being said. In between him and the smoker, dressed in a short-sleeved white top and perfectly creased jodhpurs, marched Isobel, riding crop held across her breasts in a rising diagonal from right to the left. She too was turning to Zepernick, she too was smiling, but though it was the Captain's story that darted in and out between them, it was she who was the centre of their attention. Her hair was brushed back, her body brimming with a confident and irrepressible health. She strode amongst them like a circus trainer surrounded by her favourite lions. How she loved these intelligent and handsome creatures. What tricks they would perform for her! She was not afraid to run with them, to put her head into their mouths, let them prowl and parade in her unprotected company. All she had to do was to crack the whip and they competed for her sport! And in their immense power and beauty they had turned and with one careless swipe had killed her. He felt his stomach wince from a stab of empty pity, though whether for Isobel or himself he could not determine.

'Who took the photograph?' he asked, placing it back on the desk.

'Bohde,' the Major replied. 'So. Van Dielen. He made a full statement?'

'Mr van Dielen has not yet returned.'

'But it is nearly eighteen hundred already! Six!'

'I know. Still, if wants to be by himself. There's no law against it.'

*

He left the Major telephoning Captain Zepernick. The cobbled lanes in the Pollet were cold and empty. If only he had gone to her that night, as soon as he had read the letter! If only the note had been more forthcoming! His feet set a rhythm on the stones. Lentsch, Lentsch, she could not tell Lentsch. If not directly involving Lentsch, then something she dare not tell him? Something to do with an islander, something that would get whoever it was into deep trouble with the Germans. Someone close to her, perhaps. Her father? Her aunt? Molly?

The Britannia was empty save for Albert, sitting in the corner. He beckoned him over.

'Thought you might be in need of some company,' he said.

Ned pulled a chair out. 'Trust you to think right, Uncle.'

Albert waved his glass in the air. 'We'll have a couple more here,' he called out, 'if you're not too busy.'

Ned sat down. 'Heard from Kitty?' he asked, anxious to keep clear of Isobel.

Albert shook his head.

'Went to the post office yesterday. No joy. I'll try again Monday. Something might have come in over the weekend.'

Ned tried to reassure him. 'It's just a matter of getting through. She'll have written, all right.'

'Oh, yes. She'll have written, all right. Don't help me none, though, do it?'

He waited while the barman laid the glasses on the table, then leant forward.

'I've been thinking, Ned. Did you ever think, you know, to make a run for it?'

'To England, you mean?'

'Why not? Steal a boat one night. You could make it.'

'Don't know about that. Anyway, what about Mum?'

'I can look after your mother.'

Ned took a sip and looked at him.

'Anyone would think you want to get rid of me.'

'Dead right, I want to get rid of you. This business of Isobel. Could just be the start, to my way of thinking.'

'Start of what?'

Albert lowered his voice. 'Vigilantes. A warning to the rest of us. She may not be the last. I mean there's a lot of cement in one bag.'

'You know about that, then?'

'Wedel,' Albert said, as if the word tasted bad. 'More gobble than a turkey, his tongue.'

'Well, I hope you're wrong,' Ned told him. 'Any more trouble like that and we'll all be in hot water.'

'That's what I mean. There's no telling what will happen next, what madmen are stirring the pot. You should have gone with Kitty. Left us old 'uns to it.'

'And left Mum to bury Dad?'

'I could have buried your father. It's a brother's duty just as much as a son's. He wouldn't have minded.'

'I'm not sure about that. I'd let him down, going over the water. If I'd buggered off just before his funeral, left Mum in the lurch . . .'

'Your mum's known harder times than these,' Albert said. 'But she got on with it. We knew how to live then, knew what's what. All this island can do with a scrap of decency these days is funerals. And there're plenty of them.'

'Well, there's another one now.'

'Aye. Mrs H. will be in charge, so I'm told.'

'Oh? She didn't seem that bothered to me.'

Albert swirled the beer at the bottom of his glass. 'You got a lot to learn, Ned. That's just the way she were brought up. Inside's a different story. How's he taking it, her father?'

'He hasn't been seen all day. Left the house this morning and vanished in a puff of smoke. The Major's going potty.'

Albert finished his beer.

'Don't you worry about van Dielen,' he said, signalling for another. 'He'll come back.'

*

But he had not come back, that strange little man. It was days later, when the hue and cry had been taken up not simply by Ned's ill-dressed cohorts, but by the whole trembling island, that tales of his sightings were delivered piece by piece to Ned's office or, when he was not there, to the station below where Tommy bent over the counter like a schoolboy at his desk, placing his arm across the report sheet in a vain attempt to hide his near illegible hand. Many had seen him in his deerstalker hat and his Norfolk jacket, flapping at the sides, standing on the half-finished gun emplacements, climbing down the steep coastal paths, his small figure, dark and bent, as recognizable as that of the stick-twirling Hollywood tramp, gaining attention by his very avoidance of it, seen but not intruded upon; not by the soldiers scanning the horizon standing next to their Flak-30s as he paced the newly dug concrete fields testing their vulnerability with a prod of his gnarled stick, a present it was said from Dr Todt himself; not by the motorcycle patrols brewing up their lunchtime billycans while they watched his silhouette clambering over the lattice work of newly laid reinforcing rods; not by the weary clusters of labourers who leant over their spades, thankful for the brief respite, while he jumped down into the fresh-dug trenches and shored up excavations, inspecting the depth and quality of their exhaustive cultivation; not by the Spanish Republican engine driver, sweating behind his black-belching Henschel which pulled the crates bearing the van Dielen mark from St Sampson's harbour to the western coast, who raised his cap when he had first seen him at early morning light, down at the docks, looking out to the entrance through which he and his family had first arrived; not by the islanders on their way to morning service, processions of the faithful and the converted, who caught sight of him hurrying down the lanes, and who heard the news walking up those consecrated paths, who took it inside and passed it along in the sideways shuffle of the pews, whispering the deed as they rose from their uncertain prayers, some even scribbling the dread message on the back page of a prayer book before holding it out to their neighbour's troubled eyes. Murder? Aye, Murder, coughed behind handkerchiefs and sung tunelessly alongside Wesleyan rhymes; murder placed on the horsehair cassocks and proffered wafers and mouthed by silent lips in the hollow echoes of a sermon. Murder half-concealed and half-bred and brought half-awake blink-ing out into the morning light, to be passed from islander to islander, the word and the wind scattering their faith once more; murder of their own kind buttoned under their coats, murder a street away, hidden under their hats, murder of a young daughter stuffed under the benches of the horse-drawn bus and taken to town to be fed to the seagulls pecking along the promenade or tapped out by faltering fingers on the wrought-iron benches circling the empty bandstand in Candie Gardens, where the day before the band from the Luftwaffe had played tunes that Jack Hilton and Lilly Harvey had made famous all over the cracked continent. All that day did van Dielen trudge, hopping from place to place, as he might on any other normal working day, waving his pass with its picture and his honorary rank and letters of authorization slipped inside, examining pit props in the tunnels over at La Vassalerie, harassing a nervous and flustered George Poidevin in another examination of the yard, stamping along the wide northern bays, looking out to the forbidden coast beyond. He was solicitous to those he did meet, enquiring almost as a matter of politeness as to the set of the concrete or the camber in the excavations, for it was always the materials with which he was concerned, whether the cold or the heat or some other variable had compromised their quality, and when he questioned those responsible he asked them as a visiting doctor might question a patient's relatives, interpreting their layman's replies while forgiving them their foolish ignorance. Those he spoke to thought no more of it, for the news of his tragedy had not travelled then, though it seemed to follow him in his wake like the draw of a great ship, churning the settled ground of occupation for the scavengers to wheel about in heady excitement.

Ned thought he would show up on Monday, but he did not. Tommy was sent back to patrol outside the house. Ned waited in his office. A light rain settled. Halfway through the morning Ned put on his waterproof and walked over to the construction yard. He could see where the foreigns had broken in on Friday night. The fence had been kicked in not a hundred yards from a harbour checkpoint. Ned stepped in through the little door set in the high double gates. In the middle of the yard stood a small hut raised a few feet off the ground, lengths of raw wood arranged by size to one side, bundles of iron rods on the other. On the ground around a strewn, slippery chaos; boxes with their sides smashed in, machinery parts in junked heaps, a dented wheelbarrow jammed with half-opened packets of nails. George Poidevin stood on an untidy stack of wooden crates, levering open their lids with a length of flattened piping. Eleven thirty in the morning and he was making hard work of it. Ned picked his way over.

'I need to see your boss,' Ned called out. 'You seen him about?'

George wedged the pipe in the crack and clambered down.

'Terrible business, Mr Luscombe,' he pleaded. 'Terrible business. My missus is terrible cut up.'

Ned stirred a discarded coupling with his foot and looked about him.

'This the break-in I've heard so much about?' George nodded. 'Made a bit of a mess, didn't they?'

'Blooming nuisance, those foreigns. Should be kept under lock and key, not allowed to come and go as they please.' He pointed in the direction of the shed. The door hung off its hinges. 'When they broke in all the paperwork was blown to buggery. No idea what's where any more. This week of all weeks. I'm having the devil's own job.'

'So Mr van Dielen hasn't been here today?'

'Not today. Saw him yesterday though, and Saturday.'

'Miss van Dielen was here Saturday, is that right?'

George nodded. 'They came round to the house first. Elspeth told him where I was and that.'

'He wanted to see about the break-in.'

'No, he wasn't worried about that.'

'Oh?'

George drew a deep breath.

'We get instructions every Friday, see, what we're doing the next week. What deliveries to make, what materials need to go where. It's my job to sort it all out.' He waved his hand over the mess. 'I usually do it on the Saturday morning. Get a bit of overtime that way. Well, last Friday he gives out the instructions as per usual. Number One lorry on metal rod run up over to Fort Hommet. Number Two up over to St Peter Port to pick up the colours for some extra tunnel work.'

'I don't understand. The colours?'

'Each construction firm has been given a different colour. Ours is red. Every container that comes in from the mainland has the firm's colour stamped on a little square on the side. Like that one there. That way there's no mix-up at the harbour. It's all done through the Organisation Todt. They specify the materials, the time of arrival, where they have to be delivered, what job it's for. Mr van Dielen sorts it out with Major Ernst every Friday morning, and by the time we knock off, he's worked out the schedules for the next week. But that night the foreigns broke in, so instead of doing what I normally do on the Saturday I spent all morning trying to clear up the mess. Saturday afternoon I'm back at the yard writing up the roster, when in he barges, dancing up and down like he's got a banger up his arse. Forget the old running order, he says, everything's changed. It's all hands to the tunnels at La Vassalerie and the gun emplacements over L'Ancresse Bay. Everything else has to stop. And if Major Ernst changes his mind and wants us to do something else, we're not to hang about waiting for confirmation, we do it, no questions asked. Well, that's irregular for a start. We're not supposed to take orders direct from the Germans. It's against the rules. I looks at him and he claps me on the back, all friendly like, first time I've ever known him do that, and tells me to sort it out as best I can. Said he'd come round Sunday and help me out.'

'And Isobel was here with him that Saturday?'

'She were waiting by the gates when we come out. But I knew she was there earlier 'cause I heard them coming across the road. Hammer and tongs, they were.' He paused. 'Found up by the cliff, they say; horribly mutilated, that's the word. Breasts sliced off, things in her private parts,' he said hopefully.

'You heard wrong,' Ned told him sharply. 'What was the quarrel about? Did you hear any of it?'

George shook his head.

'Same old palaver, I reckon. Wouldn't do as she was told. "Once more unto the breach," he says, when we were done, her standing over there, looking like thunder at a picnic party. "What she needs is the back of your hand," I tells him. "That's what my Elspeth gets."'

'You never spoke to her.'

'No. Never have, as a matter of fact. Never will now.'

'And where were you on Saturday night, George?'

'Saturday. Me and the missus went out, first to the Britannia, then on to the Albion. Very nearly missed the curfew.'

'That would never do. And Sunday . . .'

'He was waiting for me when I arrived! Would you believe it? Went through it all calm as anything. You wouldn't think that . . . I mean, he never let on.' He coughed. 'Do you think he might, you know, have done her in himself? It's a thought, isn't it, considering he's gone AWOL.'

'Very helpful, George. Anything else?'

George looked round, making sure they were alone.

'About the break-in.'

'George, we've been through this.'

'No, no, Mr Luscombe. I wasn't criticizing. I know how stretched you are. I was thinking, well, of deputies.'

'Deputies, George. How do you mean?'

'Well, seeing as you're so busy with this murder and the Feldkommandantur not really interested, I was thinking, if you were to deputize me I could go looking for the crates myself – search houses, question folk. Like a proper policeman.'

'Forgive me for mentioning it, but didn't you have some difficulty a couple of years back with receiving stolen goods?'

'That were a long time ago, Mr Luscombe. I had bills of lading, receipts. It was what you call a mistreatment of justice.'

'Sorry, George.'

'But the break-in! No one's doing anything about it.' He looked around at the confusion. 'What about the foreigns?' he persisted. 'Has anyone searched their billets, noticed anything odd going on? Stains on their clothing, like?'

'George, what are you talking about?'

George pointed to one of the empty containers.

'Paint,' he said. 'The bastards nicked a load of yellow paint.'

'What would the foreigns want a load of paint for?'

'There's no knowing what they get up to, is there? They're parts of this town it's not safe to walk through of a night. Slant-eyes roaming the streets in little better than nightshirts.'

Ned couldn't help himself. 'So you think they've been painting the town yellow, do you?'

He walked back along the promenade. A light mist hung over the sea about a mile out. The tide was on the turn. A group of Todt workers came trotting round the corner, the rasp of their breath louder than the fall their feet, the smell of them lingering as they passed; a company of cycle infantry approached in the opposite direction, their heavy bicycles hissing on the wet road. Across the way a line of lorries were loading up on the quay and by the little sentry hut a motorcycle patrol was starting off on its hourly circular inspection, the outrider waving a rueful farewell to his mate retreating back into his warm wooden shell. Over by the harbour an anti-aircraft gun, its muzzle protected by a thick tarpaulin, was being hoisted up from one of the barges heaving on the oil-spilled water. Ned stood still and gripped the railing, the only islander in sight.

When he got back to the station he found his outside door swinging in the wind. He kicked a loose stone in temper. One of the amateur dramatics had forgotten to close it again. As he started up the stairs he heard a rattling noise directly above him. Someone was trying his door handle. He moved quietly, trying to remember which boards creaked and which didn't. Coming up level with the landing he saw Veronica pushing an envelope under his door. He rested his chin on the floor and spoke to her ankles.

'So it's you is it, writing all these anonymous letters?'

Veronica straightened up, unable at first to see him. She wore a pale blue patterned dress and a blue hat and her coat was unbuttoned, held together only by the belt. He blew up her legs. She stepped back.

'There you are. Gave me a proper fright.'

'Not like you, V, telling tales out of school.' He unlocked the door and pushed it open. The little white envelope lay on the floor.

'You'd better come in and tell me what this is all about,' he said. Veronica stayed put.

'It's not about anything,' she said. 'Just a ticket for the show next month. Thought you might like to come along. For old times' sake.'

Ned put his finger under the flap. Inside was a pink slip, smudged and badly printed. *April Frolics*, it read. *Sparkling Wit, Excellent Vocalism, Vivacious Dancing, Mysterious Conjuring, and those Irresistible Coons, the Nigger Minstrels.*

'What are you?' he said. 'Vivacious Dancing?'

'And Excellent Vocalism,' she said. Ned nodded.

'Come in anyway. I wanted to talk to you about the party on Saturday. I didn't know you mixed in such high-flown circles.'

She stood in the doorway, defiant.

'Don't you start getting at me again! You can question me all you like, but I'm not having you looking down your nose like that.'

Ned sighed. 'Sorry. Just tell me. I won't jump down your throat, promise.'

'Scout's honour?'

'Scout's honour.'

'Go on then, make the sign.'

'V, I'm a policeman.'

'Not to me you're not.'

'That's the trouble with this place. I'm not a policeman to anyone. Albert thinks of me as his brother's son, Mrs Hallivand thinks of me as her gardener's nephew, Mum thinks I still wear short trousers and you . . .'

'I think you put on long trousers too soon.'

'Thanks!'

Veronica relented. 'It's not easy for either of us, Ned, seeing what we were. But what we were is what we were. Not what we are.'

She sat down. It was strange the two of them sitting opposite each other, him with his notebook, her with her hands folded in the lap of her buttoned dress. Time was when he had held her and kissed her, when they had leant back and whispered private things to each other that made them laugh. All right, he thought, be what you are, but whether you like it or not you're also what you were. He leant back. He wanted to see her body relax and assume that voluptuous familiarity his mother had found so disturbing. He spoke softly.

'Tell me about the party, then.'

'Nothing much to tell. Molly invited me. Said it would be fun. It was all right at first, down at the Casino, but as the evening wore on and Isobel didn't turn up things went from bad to worse. By the end it was more like a wake than a party. Molly was all for sending the car over again, but the Major wouldn't allow it.'

'Again?' Ned asked quickly. 'He sent the car over before?'

'No. We drove past there on the way back to the Villa. Dr Mueller, one of the nurses in the front with the driver, and me and the Major in the back.'

'When was this?'

'Ten thirty, eleven, I don't know.'

'And?'

'The house was in total darkness. I was all for banging on the door but he wouldn't let me. Said she'd be up at the Villa. She wasn't, of course.' She paused. 'How's he taking it?'

'Badly.'

'Do you think I should go round later, to offer my sympathies?'

Ned couldn't help himself. 'You've only just met him, V.'

Veronica rose to her own defence. 'It's not like that. We've a lot in common, that's all. Singing. Music. Fritz Kreisler.'

'Who?'

'Fritz Kreisler. He's a violinist. Jazz. Quite the rage on the Continent. The Major's got all his records. He was going to lend me some for my routine. I'm getting quite popular these days.'

'On the stage, you mean.'

'Yes, Ned, on the stage. I got three encores the last time I sang Nanki Poo.'

Ned felt his displeasure rising. He'd always distrusted the exhibitionist in her.

'Don't get me wrong, but it's a very captive audience you're playing to.'

'Ha ha very funny I don't think.'

'Tell me about Bohde. He left the Casino early, didn't he?'

'I don't know, I wasn't keeping an eye on him, the little creep. But he was at the Villa when we arrived.'

'And how did he seem?'

Veronica shuddered. 'Horrible. He doesn't like us English girls. He was giving me filthy looks all evening.'

'Lots of men give you filthy looks, V.'

'I don't mean like that. I can handle those. No, this was like I shouldn't be there, like I shouldn't be alive. I put it to the back of my mind, but thinking about it now, and what happened . . .' She started to cry. Ned made no attempt to comfort her. It was his way of punishing her.

'And then this Captain Zepernick took you home.'

The cold formality of his question shocked her. She blew her nose and stood up.

'As well you know.'

'And how was the handsome devil?' He'd lost it now. He laid down his pencil and closed the notebook.

'He drives too fast.'

'You should have walked home with me.'

'I didn't have a pass, remember.' She looked out of the window. 'But I didn't need one then, did I?'

Ned riffled a penny over the back of his fingers. It was a trick he'd learnt lying on his bunk in the section house. He looked up at her, swinging her bag back and forth. It hardly seemed possible that she was the same Veronica he had known before. She held herself differently, wore a different expression on her face. There was no peace to her.

'You'd better go,' he said.

The penny slipped from his fingers and rolled onto the floor. Her voice came cold and scornful.

'Can't wait to get rid of me, can you?'

'I just don't want you to get hurt, V, that's all,' he said, bending underneath his desk. 'They're not what they seem.'

'Neither were you. Neither was Tommy. So what's new.'

Her voice seemed far away. He got up slowly, careful not to bang his head. But she had gone.

★

One foot on the stairs and Mr Underwood came running out.

'You have a visitor,' he warned her. 'I had to unlock the door myself.'

Captain Zepernick was sitting in her chair with his boots on her desk, writing a message on the back of an envelope.

'Captain!' She looked back, afraid that Ned might have followed her. She hated it when he thought badly of her. 'Is this official? Something to do with your feet?'

'With my feet, no.' The Captain swung his legs down onto the floor. 'Tomorrow afternoon. I was hoping you might come for a drive.'

'A drive? What, just you and me?'

'Yes. That is not to your liking?'

'No, no, it's just . . . what about Molly?'

He did not reply but reaching out ran his hand slowly up the back of her leg. It seemed to take a good quarter of an hour to reach its destination, stopping on the way, retracing its cruelly deliberate journey. His breath came quietly, intently. She did not move.

'You didn't expect me again?' he asked.

'I didn't know.'

'Good. I like that.' He stood up, his hand lifting her slightly. 'I liked very much the other night. Very much.'

'Did you?'

'Very much? And you too, I think?'

'Yes.' A lie and a truth in one word.

'It is unusual so early on. The way you . . .'

'Yes.'

202

'I will be here at four. If you sit by the window you will see when I arrive.'

'Will I?'

He stretched out a finger and traced the tremble of her lips.

'The mouth too next time, I think.'

'Really?'

'Yes. In my car perhaps, or a house I know. Maybe here.'

'There's no telling, is there.'

She kissed him. Captain Zepernick stepped back and smiled.

'Till tomorrow, then.'

She felt was lost and afraid, the penny rolling over Ned's cold hand. Her heart was leaden, her arms heavy by her side. She stood in dread of herself, of what she had become. She didn't want to say yes. She couldn't say no. She opened the door for him.

'Till tomorrow, then.'

Nine

He is not hot but he feels the heat of the sun. He is not thirsty but he imagines the pitiless depth of the desert on his cracked lips. He wants to embrace the world but his hands have lost all sense of touch; he wants to look out onto visions of grace but there is only a lumpen grey mass moving before him. He never loved anything as much as his constructions, never felt for his flesh and blood the way he did for his bricks and mortar. He could fashion those latter materials, mould them, break them in his hands. He could lean over his desk at night and see them outlined on the transparent paper; he could walk in loam and clay and watch the ground give birth to their skeletal form. He had not bothered with buildings to house mortal men. His were monuments to power, to organization, orchestrating the ceaseless trudge of humanity. It was movement he had craved, movement and design, and this island had seen some of his greatest creations. He had shaped the white Observation Towers in one of which he now sits; he had welded the eagles' nest gun emplacements onto the granite grip of rock; he had let loose the great swim of concrete upon the land. How he had loved those grains, the powdered weight of it lying in the sack, the thick slop of it churning in the mixer, pouring out grey and glutinous into wet, waiting moulds. What a revolutionary mixture it was, what deceptive strength lay in those unassuming seeds, how soft they seemed, how easily they hardened, what creations they spawned. And like all living things it could only spring to life after water's hydrogen kiss. In his youth he had worked on a packet steamer and had stood once on its creaking deck watching the ice world of Greenland gliding past and he knows that concrete possesses the same treacherous beauty. Like the rush of an avalanche it can cover the landscape in one swoop, obliterating dip and hollow, inventing new worlds of flattened beauty. It is hard and impenetrable but is able to bend its shape. It possesses both depth and resonance, and though he has seen instances of decorated concrete, most notably in the concrete house of Norfolk, Home Place, where the surface is studded with flint and clay tiles and local brown stone, he prefers his concrete unmasked, with only the pattern of the wooden board marking its austere exterior. Concrete should be naked, unashamed. It should stand in defiance of the elements. It is the product of a new age, a powdered miracle. Man will be dwarfed by its power, its dormant energy. They will wander among its pillars and frescos and marvel at its unremitting strength. They will stand in awe listening to the echoes of their own tiny footsteps vanish in its great booming hollows. There will be cities of concrete, he knows it, cities with stadiums and railway stations and vast temples to new religions; there will be housing complexes, ranged over the ground like the spokes of a wheel, long rows of rectangular flat dwellings, two, possibly three storeys high, each equipped with a window box and a little balcony from which mothers can watch their children pushing scooters on the concrete paths below. Planes will land on concrete, ships will dock alongside concrete. The land will be crisscrossed by great ribbons of it, on which hundreds, nay thousands, of black blunt-nosed cars will run; free movement, free power and thus freed desire. Thought as action. Action as design. It is just the beginning. In a drawer under his draughtsman's desk there lies a plan of the islands and the mainland and, joining them, two concrete bridges rising high above the sea, one from Cap de Carteret to Jersey, the other, further up the coast, from Flamanville to Guernsey, for when the war is over, those who have carried out His instructions will need to take themselves, their fiancées, their families, to a place of recreation and rest, where they may walk and tumble and gather strength. What better haven than these small islands, where everything can be tuned to their needs, Jersey for officers and high government officials, Guernsey for the other ranks? He had shown Dr Todt his design late one evening, and before the doctor could raise the obvious objection, had admitted that by its very nature the project would consume a high percentage of the labour force needed. 'But think of it,' he had declared, 'the longest bridge in the world built solely that the good and industrious might be rewarded.' Todt had warmed to the idea, reminding him of that other discussion they had taken part in, during his official visit to England in '37, and their meeting with the Minister of Transport. There had been talk of a bridge across the Channel then, and, ever the visionary, Todt had suggested that the enterprise should be seen not simply as a matter for England and France but as a European concern. The Minister had been polite but evasive, and later van Dielen realized that he should have taken this false enthusiasm as a warning against the British and their myopic view of the world. He should never have attached himself to England, he had reflected, he should have moved straight back to Europe. When they were discussing the coming weeks that night over dinner, with Ernst holding his glass in their air as if he could see the future whirling in the sparkling liquid, in a moment of rare frankness, he had shared his notion with Ernst, hoping that he might pass it on to Speer, whom he knew only slightly, but Major Ernst had looked at him strangely and said, 'What makes you think that the traffic will be from the Continent? From England I think, and not for a holiday.' He did not understand then, and he chooses not to understand now.

He has spent his days in the Observation Tower above Gull Rock, near where his daughter was found. The tower is hollow and silent. There is no one working here now, nor will there be for the next few weeks. Over at Choet it's a different matter. The watch-tower there will have men crawling in and out like bees in a hive.

There are five levels to these towers, and unlike their defensive predecessors, built in another age, they face almost exclusively to the sea, ignoring any danger that might emerge from the hinterland. Only from the roof, reached by an awkward twenty-foot climb, can one see an uninterrupted three hundred and sixty degrees. The island, say the towers, is ours. There is no danger within. Each floor looks out onto a different level of sea, viewed through long curving slits which elongate the seascape. The ocean looks wide and flat, squashed into a solid vertical plane. Paradoxically, for these are direction-finding towers, built to enhance the accuracy of the guns, the overall effect is to distort distance.

Since he has been here he has observed nothing, least of all direction. It has rained almost constantly with an accompanying thick mist. Waking that first morning it was as if he had been born again into a cocooned world of white, a fairyland of floating spirits, and when the wind came and blew away a veil or two, the water appeared as elusive, shimmering silver, chemical, amniotic. He is becalmed, floating like a baby, standing by the aperture hoping to see the soul of his daughter float past, lying on the roof waiting to hear the beat of her heart coming from the looming flap of a gull, white on the wing. He wants nothing now but for the island to have an eternal untouched life, and for him and those he has lost to be a part of that eternity. But this perturbs him, for he worries that within the structures he has built, there might lie a fatal, undetected weakness, similar to the one which must have run through his family life. Either that or the island harbours some grudge against him. But why? What has he done? Has he not woven round it a most marvellous protective shell, one which will keep the sea at bay for a hundred years? Is not the island made whole? Is it not tended and watered and kept in good order as never before? And what was asked from it in return? Nothing but that it might take his family to its bosom. He tries to remember the colour of his wife's eyes or the first time Isobel spoke but he cannot. He tries to picture his daughter as a little girl, running barefoot in an Egyptian courtyard, but though he can see the chickens scattering in her wake he cannot see her or even detect the sound of her voice above their flapping squawks.

He does not move much, except when needs must, when he crosses the room to the high narrow window at the back, under which he drops his trousers and deposits whatever he can onto the cold concrete floor. He is glad to be alone, for he has done with speech. He has nothing more to say. Time will not restore this faculty, for though time might heal a memory or set a fractured soul, time cannot shine light where no light can escape. His speech had been designed for buildings and viaducts, to describe the sweep of roads, to weigh structure in balance. He has no phrases to summon a wife or conjure up a daughter. He has used up all the words that were in his command; his vocabulary is obsolete, redundant, a faulty design. He is lost for words.

He finds it difficult to sleep at night. The damp sea air rushes in through the openings. There are scufflings and scratchings below. It is cold. Every so often he can hear the voices of soldiers in one of the gun emplacements a quarter of a mile away, a guffaw of laughter, a snatch of song. He marks the passage of time from the beam of the slit-eyed headlamps shining forth from the hourly motorbike patrols which bounce towards him along the high cliff road before disappearing down the wooded hill, only to be recaptured minutes later, out of the rear window, as they cruise up along the road that runs the length of the bay, the insect buzz of their engines fading fast. The road has its hidden travellers too, padding shadowy footfalls, or the stealthy creak of what, a handcart, a bicycle? So much dark activity.

He has not eaten for two days, but today, as he shakes out his coat, which he uses as a pillow, he discovers a large bar of chocolate within one of its deep pockets, a gift from Major Ernst, a far and distant figure who he can remember only by an overbearing shape. He tears back the wrapping and pushes it into his mouth. It is difficult to chew, for there is nothing to chew on. It is evasive like his memory, hard to dislodge: it glues to the roof of his mouth, coats his tongue and, when he attempts to swallow, large lumps stick in his gullet. Though he knows he should not, he eats the bar as quickly as he can, licking the waxed paper clean, smearing his mouth and beard. Almost immediately he feels sick. He feels his stomach lurching, feels the green bile of it rising. He feels giddy, his breathing becomes problematic, a hand is clutching at his heart.

He can smell the stink of himself and that of the room. He needs to get out, to break free. He charges down the circular steps, out of control. Halfway down he retches; he bends double; he straightens up. A great spray, sudden like a geyser, leaps forth from his mouth, splashing onto the walls and down in front of him. Then another. The volume is excessive, the noise unbearable. His hand slips on the running smear. He skids down the stairs, spraying once more, vomit on his shirt and trousers, before stumbling out into the open air, gasping, grabbing handfuls of grass to wipe himself clean. He needs to rinse his mouth out with water. Water! It is not hunger which assaults him. It is thirst.

He sets out across the scrubland, to the hill and the bay below. The dying wind tugs at his shirt. He falls a number of times, breaking a shoelace as he scrambles back up. Once on the road, he half trots down the hill, and at the bottom, jumping down from the sea wall, he starts to walk along the beach. It would be easy for him to be caught; snagged on the barbed wire, between whose lines he walks, a foot or leg blown off by one of the landmines he unwittingly avoids; arrested by one of the motorcycle patrols; shot at by one of the convoys of artillery men. But no one appears during his twenty-minute walk of the bay. It is as he suspected. He no longer exists.

At the end of the beach he crosses up over the narrow peninsula. On the other side the Henschel engine is preparing to pull its line of empty trucks on their journey round the coast. Unnoticed he climbs aboard as the train moves off. He sits on the last truck, his feet dangling over the side, looking left and right, chugging up along the coast, past the little houses and empty lanes, past the barracks and converted greenhouses, skirting round old castles and half-completed gun emplacements, the water a dazzling deep, the rocks golden like tumbled honeycombs, past Perelle Bay and Vazon Bay, past Cobo, heading north, past all the long bays of summer where the flat roads meet the long sweep of sand, past where mothers and fathers should lie up on their elbows watching children running back and forth, shielding their eyes from the fierce bright of it, past the volleyball throwers and driftwood cricket players, past kite flyers and donkey riders and dripping ice-cream cone carriers; past shrieking horseplay and awkward bathers pulling wet costumes over embarrassed skin; past sleeping pink-eyed bellies and knotted handkerchiefs; past sandcastles and rock pools and buckets filled with salt water in which wriggling things wriggle. The gorse is beginning to flower, he sees primroses speckle distant banks. He is riding a holiday train on a holiday island.

Now the train has reached Picquerel Point and forks left, past the Church at Vale and up over the common to L'Ancresse Bay. Even before he can see them, he hears the noise of them, the sound of shovels and steam and the orders of impatient men. And there they are, a great swarming mix of them, on the beach below, pulled from every spare construction site; Poles and Hungarians, from Russia and the Spanish Civil War, travellers, troublemakers, Communists, simpletons, recipients of grudges and suspected fifth columnists, all the flotsam and jetsam of decadent Europe put to work in His cause. The train is idling now, waiting for the trucks to be filled. Directly below him a party of Todt workers are leaning on their spades. He knows what they have been doing, digging out the beach for the gravel mincer standing at the far end of the bay: sand for his cement.

The guard in charge of the group is moving down the line holding a battered bucket, from which he dispenses a ladleful of water to each man in turn. They are a motley crew. Old men mostly, nothing on their arms and nothing in their eyes, but they are practised in the art of acceptance. They do not grab at it too quickly, for then they would spill most of it, but nor are they slow, for lethargy in any form annoys the guards. Each one steadies the rim before tipping it carefully into his mouth, wiping any escaping drops over the grease of his stubble. The guard seems an amiable enough fellow, nodding to one or two of the men, sharing a roughshod joke. Van Dielen jumps down. He is standing at the head of the group but not in line with it. Hearing the noise the guard turns. He sees van Dielen at right angles to the other men, facing him. He recognizes his face but no further. Van Dielen opens his mouth, touches his lips. He beckons. That's what he wants. Though he has seen the state of his trousers and his shoes, he has no way of measuring how quickly his image has deteriorated. His hair is knotted, his skin unshaven and raw, his eyes bloodshot. There is excrement down the right leg of his trousers. To keep himself warm at night he has been using empty cement sacks with which to cover himself. In the damp air the dust from inside has hardened on his hair and his clothes. He looks stronger than the rest, but the guard knows there could many reasons for this. He may be a trustee, or have influential friends in the cookhouse. He may be able to do something entertaining – play a musical instrument, for example, or dance a jig. He might have some amusing physical attribute. They had one like that over in Alderney, a cook with a cock twenty-one centimetres long, thin and tapered like a pencil. They used to get him to toss himself off into the evening soup or pay one of the whores or one of the younger foreigns to suck him off. The cook was game for it, as long as it lasted. Poor bastards went blind after making some hooch out of iodine and potato peelings, half his hut and a couple of the girls too. Didn't matter whether the slits could see or not, fact it made it funnier, them not being able to see who or what they were going to have to fuck next, but the cook and his mates were shot the next day and tipped over the cliff. But whatever it is that sets this man apart counts for nothing here. He has stepped out of line. The guard swings the bucket. Van Dielen gestures impatiently, mimicking the actions of the last man.

'*Wasser, ja?*'

Van Dielen nods.

The guard runs forward and throws the contents over him, pushing down the shingle, chucking a shovel after him. The others move back down, and with their heads down, start loading. Van Dielen follows their action; shovel in, shovel out, up in the air and throw. Shovel in, shovel out, up in the air and throw. His gravel lands short. The guard screams and shouts, sliding down, hitting him on the side with a handle of a spade. He falls. He lies there panting. The guard hits him again across the legs and walks away in disgust. The man next to him gestures him to get up, and pushing him to one side shows him how it should be done.

He watches. He shovels. He shovels all morning. He shovels all afternoon. The gravel flies through the air and lands in the truck. The truck is filled. He feels no pain.

At the end of the day the guard hands each man a stamped chit which entitles him to the evening meal. They walk back to the compound clutching them as if they were children holding tickets to a circus. The old man talks to him constantly, a smattering of English and German and another language he cannot recognize, though he does not seem to care or notice that van Dielen replies not once. A smile, a shrug of the shoulders, a shake of the head, are all he can manage, and even they are used not as contributions but rather as aids to his enigmatic silence. He is no stranger to the compound. He has passed it many times, on his way to the Manor House to see Ernst, driving past the huddles of men squatting on the scuffed earth. There are many groups such as his on the road now, trudging back to the compound, limp from the day's work. He stands in line and shuffles to his soup. It is pale and warm. Grease swims on the inside of his tin cup. He is given bread too, hard and gritty, two thin slices.

They eat before going inside. His hut has the number seven written on it. There is a door at either end and a narrow passageway down the middle. Inside men are already lying on the two-tiered level of planks. The old man steers van Dielen along. Halfway down he stops opposite a young boy curled up on the top plank. He has red trousers. His hair is white. He has a mucky old jacket round his shoulders. The old man indicates the space opposite while he slides onto the plank underneath the boy. The young boy reaches down and grabs the old man's hand. They shake. The old man pulls his hand in the direction of the newcomer. The boy raises his head, smiles and winks at him. It is a beautiful smile, calm and full of tenderness. Van Dielen closes his eyes. There is nothing of van Dielen left in him now. Everything he has known or done or said is seeping out of the very pores of his skin. He is fading fast.

Ten

Bernie leant over and, putting his glass under the brass tap, pushed himself another drink. Ned handed over his glass. They listened to the steady stream of beer foaming in.

'What time's kick-off?' Bernie asked softly.

'Half twelve,' Ned replied.

'Well, drink up, then. You don't want to be sober when you get there, do you?'

They were alone in the Britannia, and the doors were closed. They sat up at the bar, looking through the thick panes of distorted glass to the little continental square across the road. A couple of soldiers sat on the bench built around the oak, while another tried to wash his face under the pump. It was barely past breakfast.

Bernie took a tentative sip. 'Weak as water,' he pronounced, adding, almost as an afterthought, 'No news, then?'

Ned sighed. There was no news.

'How can a man like that vanish into thin air?' Bernie asked, as if a hole in the ground, a chuck over the cliff top, or little bits of the man fed to one of the hungry pigs might not have been a probable end.

'Beats me,' Ned confessed. 'I've got half the force out knocking on doors, there's military patrols beating the restricted areas, boats on the look out for floaters. Even George Poidevin has got in on the act. Everywhere I go I see him bouncing behind the wheel of their works lorry, peering over the walls, jumping down into ditches, searching for his boss. Never thought of George as a St Bernard before, though he's got the girth for it. Trouble is, apart from him and the Germans, no one wants to know.'

Bernie laid his drink on the dark polished wood.

'Stands to reason, seeing as he was one of them.'

'We've all got to live, Bernie. There's a lot of families that would have gone to the wall by now if it wasn't for the likes of van Dielen,' he said. 'He's just doing his job.'

Bernie spat the beer back in his glass.

'He's doing more than that. He's betraying his country, making money out of them fortifications.'

'And the men that drive his lorries? The electricians he employs, the plumbers? Are they all traitors too?'

Bernie was stubborn. 'It's one thing being ordered to do it. It's another lining your pocket. We're at war, in case you hadn't noticed.'

'That's just it, Bernie, the rest of the world might be, but we're not,' Ned countered. 'You might get a couple of schoolboys chalking victory signs on bicycle saddles, but what can grown men do? Blow up a fuel depot? Shoot a soldier? You know what would happen if we did, and for what? The truth is we've all got to get by the best we can, whether we like it or not.'

Bernie looked at him carefully.

'You should take a long look at yourself. You can't see it, but you're getting too far in with them.'

'I'm not in with them,' Ned said sharply, knowing it to be partly true. 'You seem to forget. Some of us have to work with them. We've got no choice.'

Bernie prodded Ned's arm. 'I know. Don't think I don't. Now drink up, there's a good chap. You and me are going to get quietly sozzled.'

'But I'm Chief of Police, Bernie. I'm not allowed to get drunk.'

Bernie leant over the bar and began to pour another couple of pints.

'Not today you're not,' he intoned. 'You're Ned Luscombe, in need of beer. Now do as I say and stop arguing.'

*

If van Dielen was on the run it was difficult to know how he had escaped with patrols out looking for him, posters bearing his description pinned on every parish noticeboard and the announcement proclaimed in every newspaper of the substantial reward available to whosoever delivered him up. Half the island had already claimed the prize. Letters, telephone calls, confidential whisperings in Ned's office. Van Dielen is hiding in Mrs Merrill's attic; he'd been seen stretching his legs up at Groper's Farm: none of it true, but in Mrs Merrill's attic they found a stack of carpets four foot high, looted from abandoned houses on evacuation day, and in Groper's Farm they disturbed three fat and unregistered pigs slumbering in an underground pen. Under the guise of cooperation people were exorcizing their grudges.

Lentsch regarded these false alarms with resigned acceptance. He was not in charge, anyway. Albert had told Ned that since the night they found her the Major could hardly manage to put his boots on the right feet, let alone administer the island.

'Going down faster than a bishop's trousers,' Albert said one evening over his third pint. 'Pitiful to see a grown man acting that way. We all have our time of trouble. Any man worth his salt shifts it on his shoulder like a sack of coal and carries on as best he can. The Major's gone weak at the knees.'

Albert had become a regular at the Britannia. It was almost like old times. It had started that late afternoon when Ned had caught him struggling up the police stairs with a bloody tree in his hand.

'Uncle, what on earth are you doing here?'

Albert rested his burden on the banisters.

'Running errands for Mrs H. like an overgrown scout. Stage prop for the spring show, she says. Weighs a bloody ton. Half the leaves have dropped off already. You any good with a paintbrush?'

'I've managed to avoid the amateur dramatics this long, Uncle. I'm not for getting to be drawn in now.'

'Well, give me hand anyway, and let's lay this bugger to rest. I'll buy you a pint afterwards.'

'Done.'

That's how it had started. Ned would come in after work, around six. Albert would walk in sometime later, waving his finger at the barman. 'Last refuge for a sane man,' he would announce. 'It's a madhouse up there.' Since Isobel's death the Villa's moorings had been cut loose. The house lay adrift in a sea of uncertainty, the captain indifferent to its plight.

'Every morning he comes down for breakfast,' Albert had complained, 'cuts all over his face where he's nicked himself shaving, buttons half undone, hair not combed proper. He sits there moving good food around his plate, like it was something the dog had sicked up, the Captain and Bohde both staring at the tablecloth, pretending not to notice.'

'At least they have some sympathy for him, even if you don't.'

'Sympathy's got nothing to do with it. They're just hoping he'll bugger off so they can help themselves to his grub. Moment he's out of the door they've scraped his plate cleaner than a sergeant-major's mess tin. Can't wait for him to go and dread him coming back. Not that he's any use in the Feldkommandantur by all accounts. Sits in his office all day staring out of the window, blubbing into his handkerchief. You see him much?'

'Most mornings,' Ned admitted. 'Not that there's much to report these days.'

'No sign of the Dutchman, then?'

'The Major thinks he might have thrown himself off a cliff, that he's lying underwater somewhere along the coast with a handful of stones in his pocket.'

Albert sniffed.

'Water would have kept him down a day or two, water would have moved him about bit, but unless he weighed himself down with an anchor he'd have popped up by now with his face half gone and his feet busting out of his boots. It's what the Major needs, though, a good ducking. That'd bring him to his senses.'

'You're being too hard on him,' Ned countered. 'He's had a shock.'

'He's a soldier,' his uncle countered. 'He should be able to cope with shocks. The Captain takes him aside every now and again, trying to talk some sense into him, but he won't listen. Won't go down to the Casino, mopes about the house playing those blessed records, wanders about the lanes late at night in his civvies. Looking to get himself shot, if he's not careful.'

'He won't get shot.'

'No? The Captain's thinks he's playing a sort of Russian roulette, deliberately going to the restricted areas in the dark. He's asked Wedel to follow him, but he just seems to slip out, unnoticed. God knows where he gets to.'

Ned knew where. He had first appeared on the Wednesday after van Dielen's disappearance, quite late, about nine. Ned was just about to go to bed. A knock on the door and there he stood, a bunch of leeks in his hand, and a large rabbit in a cage.

'I did not ask your uncle's permission,' he confessed, waving the cage in the air. 'But with your mother not being well, he will not disapprove.'

Ned had pulled out one of the last bottles of cider Dad had made, and sat him down. He sat there holding his glass, not saying a word, barely noticing what he was drinking. The crackle of the small fire made him look up.

'Your mother?' he asked suddenly. 'She is not here?'

'Upstairs. She goes to bed early. I was just about to follow, before you showed up.' Lentsch half rose out of his chair. 'No, no, Major. I didn't mean that. I'm happy to stay up. Mum has a nasty habit of sleepwalking. I should stay up, to make sure she's safe.'

Lentsch sighed. 'This is what soldiers hope to do. Kill the enemy and keep their mothers safe. You are lucky. Your mother *is* safe. Mine is not. It is only a matter of time before the bombing in Hamburg starts. I am surprised it has not already happened.'

Ned tried to reassure him. 'They're only going after military targets, railway lines, factories, dockyards. It may not mean much but they're bloody well trained. They know what they're doing.'

'That's what you hear on the radio. It is not the truth. You are bombing the ordinary houses. Germany is like a bonfire. Such terrible fires.'

'I thought your mother lived in the country.'

'We have two places. An apartment in Hamburg and a house in a village, some miles away. My sister is working in Hamburg, in administration. They will not let her go. So my mother stays with her. Once I imagined that I might be able to bring them here! I thought here was safe. I was wrong about that too. No news?'

Ned shook his head. 'I've only so many men.'

'You think he is alive?'

'I don't know. He's either hiding, kidnapped or dead.'

'Half the island thinks he killed her. They think he killed her and that we have spirited him away.' He picked up the paper lying on the floor. 'This speaks of him as our "trusted friend", of how "impossible" it would be for him to get to the Continent without our knowledge, when in fact, if he had the use of a boat, it would be quite easy under cover of darkness. It is clear what the writer really thinks.'

'I am surprised Bohde let it pass,' Ned said.

'It reflects badly on me, that is why,' Lentsch admitted. 'Bohde is testing his muscles. He wants a fight.' He threw the paper down to the floor. 'You see that this is not true, that I would not protect him.'

'You might not. Others would.'

'You are thinking of Major Ernst.'

'I'm thinking of Major Ernst. There's his headquarters at Saumarez Park. It's big enough to hide a battleship. He could even be keeping van Dielen there against his will.'

'I have no jurisdiction over Ernst. Neither have you. He can do as he pleases. Despite that I do not think he has anything to do with it. He is too ambitious to scupper his chances over a girl.'

'Ambitious men overreach themselves, Major, especially ones with a fondness for naked women in their back garden.'

'Perhaps. But Ernst would not do this other thing, put her down a shaft. It is too risky. He would throw her over a cliff, he would blame a couple of foreigns, shoot them before any one could prove otherwise.'

'Unless the father knew.'

'But then he would have told us. Van Dielen is ambitious too, but sacrificing his own daughter?' The Major sat on the edge of the armchair. 'Inspector Luscombe?'

'Yes?'

'I cannot call you this,' he confessed, 'not if we are to join, you and I. We are both too close to her for this formality, you understand. When there is just the two of us, you will have to be Ned.'

'That as may be, I'm sorry but I can't call you . . .' He stopped. He had no idea what Lentsch's Christian name was.

'Gerhard.'

'I simply can't.'

'No. I understand. Just Major, then.'

'Just Major, then.'

*

That was just the beginning. He'd come round most evenings. Ned's mother started lighting the fire early, wasting their precious supply of fuel to make the room 'look cosy when he comes'. He would bring them gifts in return: a packet of rice, a length of smoked sausage, fresh bread. They would sit at the kitchen table and eat from cracked plates, Ned's mother having to prompt her son to pass the potatoes or to cut the Major another wedge of pie, and Lentsch, conscious of this untutored hospitality, would beckon her gently into conversation, lead her to where her memories of the island's earlier times lay, offering in return stories of his own domestic past, his mother and father, the sister he missed and the eternal foolish ways of youth. There were no obvious parallels to their lives except those which made them both sigh at what it was that had turned such seeming placidity so awry; parallels of loss, of dashed expectation, of soft memories which made the austerity of the present only more intense.

'You are lucky to have your son to look after you,' he once told her. 'All sons wish this. The son that cannot feels that he has betrayed the one person he loves most in the world.'

'Go on with you,' Ned's mother had retorted. 'It's I who have to look after him,' and as the three of them had laughed Ned had looked at the Major and thanked him by his smile. Ned was amazed at his mother's transformation, the sudden lightness of her movements round the table as she served the supper, the glow that came to her cheeks as these meals progressed. She had even started to wear the second of her better dresses. If only he could touch her in this way, bring that faraway smile to her face. His mother was not in love with Lentsch, she was in love with being a mother again.

'He's a good boy,' she said once, waving to him as he closed the garden gate. Ned laughed.

'He's not a boy, Mum.'

'Yes, he is,' she replied, turning round to ruffle his hair. 'You've just got to look at the way he holds out his plate or hugs his knees in front of the fire. You're the same.'

Usually when the meal was over she went upstairs to leave them together, so that they might slowly dismantle the wall that still remained between them. Then the Major would pack his bags and leave home, and travel into the other Germany which had raised him, the one which had sent him here. Ned had never heard a man talk like Lentsch before, about who he was and why he was, and though some of it made no sense to him at all, asides and compliments to a world of which he had but the haziest conception, in Lentsch's hesitant voice he found the echo of uncertainty of his own.

'I wanted to do so many things with my life,' the Major said one night, nursing one of the beer bottles that Ned had brought up from the Britannia, 'to study, to learn about living things, to create some knowledge. And now I do this.'

He looked at his watch. 'You have a radio?'

Ned tried to keep his face expressionless.

'It is time for one of our broadcasts to England,' he continued. 'You listen, I suppose?' Ned hesitated. 'Go on, bring it out from its hiding place. I do not care.'

Ned leant into the fireplace. Small pieces of plaster fell as he pulled the wireless free.

'Plug it in, plug it in!'

'It takes a bit of time to warm up,' Ned said. 'But it's got a nice tone.'

The Major pushed Ned aside and started to fiddle with the knobs, skipping babbling voices and snatches of blurred tunes until he found the station he wanted.

'Bremen,' he announced.

The man with the long drawl came on. Though it was accepted wisdom that no one could believe a word he said, there was a certain elegance in his contempt that had an unsettling ring of truth about it. Not the military claims, which were written for him by the German High Command, but more in the depiction of the Allied command, their venality, their disdain for the common man. It was something that struck an uneasy chord on this island. He was back on his old track tonight, pouring scorn on the bloated figure of Churchill, 'the most sordid figure in British history', who had shocked his subordinates by talking to Roosevelt in his dressing gown while the President lay in bed.

'It is a clever picture to paint,' Lentsch pointed out, 'whether you believe it or not. He is suggesting a deep-seated depravity, a willingness of the British leader to debase himself before the corrupting power of America. An intellectual if not physical buggery.'

Ned said nothing. He had never liked Churchill much anyway. He wasn't alone in that either. Then the music started. It was pleasant but didn't warrant the eagerness with which Lentsch bent his head.

'Very catchy,' Ned said.

The Major shook his head vigorously, holding his hand up to indicate silence. Then the voice came, singing in soft English.

> I'm – playing with fire
> I'm – going to get burnt

> I know it but what can I do
> I know my heart must be content
> To go where it is sent,
> Although I'll repent when I'm through
>
> But what can I do
>
> I'm – playing with fire
> I'm – going to get burnt
> But I'll merry go round it with you
> When I go for my ride
> With my eyes open wide
> I'm playing with fire
> I know it but what can I do

'I prefer Anne Shelton myself,' Ned said.

Lentsch hushed him again. Then the voice returned, this time speaking rather than singing. There was a cautionary insistence previously absent, articulating every warning vowel with great care, less anyone should miss the message.

> England – is playing with fire
> She's – going to get burnt
> She knows it, but what can she do,
> She says her people must be content
> That for Churchill's sins they may repent
> When they're through
> They'll be plenty of praying to do
>
> England – is playing with fire
> She's – already been burnt
> And Egypt is troubling her too
> Sure she's losing her pride
> With her eyes open wide
> England is playing with fire
> She knows it
> Does America too?

'Charlie's Orchestra,' Lentsch told him. 'Some of the best musicians in the country. But the message! Always Churchill.

Always America. For them America is Russia's cousin, the two great enemies of European civilization. The war is not simply about territory. It is about culture, with Germany alone defending Europe from the barbarism of the East and the decadence of the West. Hitler always said he would get no help from England. England likes money too much. That is why we followed him. We had faith. We had vision.'

'And we don't?'

'You have resilience, courage and stubbornness. But not vision. Your vision was made a hundred years ago. Now you simply want to live off its fruits, to be left in peace. If we had won quickly, as we knew we could, if Churchill had been defeated, if he had been captured or exiled to Canada, if your old King had returned to the throne, accepted peace, do you think anyone would have minded very much? A few maybe. This was a reluctant war. You did not wish it.'

'You did.'

'Not with England. France there were some old scores to settle. The East, Communism, was our first enemy and later it would have been America. America wants to rule the world. It wants us to sing American songs and dance American dances. It wants us to watch American films and eat American food. We don't want these things. We have our own food, our own language, our own songs!'

'So do we.'

'Not for much longer. The momentum of all these things, your language, your music, has passed into their hands. We are German and we wish to remain so. In a way we want to stand still. America does not. America believes in movement, in the mixing of cultures; art, music, even procreation: different bodies locked in an embrace, from which is produced – what? Bastard children. Wild, beautiful children maybe, but still bastards all. America is the only nation in the world which wishes this. The only one! It wants to churn and mix, to see what happens. That is why my government detests jazz. It is just such a mixture. And in the nightclubs of Berlin, no, not just Berlin, but Paris and Rome and London, jazz is taking over. That is why they try to ban it.'

'But you listen to it.'

'Of course! I love jazz! But it is partly true what they fear. There is an American writer, Ned, called Scott Fitzgerald. You have read him?' Ned shook his head. 'No matter. He once said that jazz is sex first, and then music. And it is true. That is why the young love it. It is full of energy. It is like sex: addictive, exciting, experimental. When they cannot have sex they feast on jazz and after they have had their fill of jazz they are ready for more sex. American jazz and American sex, everything mixed up. Hitler does not want this. He does not want our youth to be seduced by foreign cultures, to breed on such undisciplined beds. He wants them to love things German. He believes in the immobility of culture. That is his misfortune, his great weakness, his misunderstanding of the modern age. He wants the roads and the cars and radio, but cannot bear the thing that comes with it, the mixing of other cultures. A nation of horses and carts, a nation with no telephones and no radios cannot mix. Their culture will stay the same. That is why our galleries are filled with paintings of old peasants and farmers' families gathered round the fire. But a nation which has aeroplanes and telephones and gramophones can never stay still. Whether it is good or bad is another matter. But it is something that cannot be stopped. Look at this island, with its concrete walls and its fortifications, trying to keep out the rest of the world. How can it? The future will not only land on the beaches or drop down from the sky. It will float through the air. We will breathe it in through our lungs, it will infect our blood. Walls keep out nothing. Now put the wireless back, otherwise I will have to report you.'

Ned unplugged the wireless and wedged it back up the chimney.

'And we did not find it there?' the Major asked incredulously. Ned shook his head. 'Hopeless!' He put his hands behind his head and sighed. 'So, tell me, Ned. Do you think we will ever find out who killed our Isobel?'

Ned took a swig from his bottle. 'No one cares, Major. The islanders don't, her father's vanished into thin air, and those Kanoniers – well, they're keeping their mouths shut, though I tell you, they're scared of something.'

'They are scared of the Russian front.'

'Maybe.'

'What about her friends? Have you learnt nothing from them?'

'You know them better than me, what there are of them. They were all at the party. Perhaps it was a bunch of foreigns after all, or a couple of your soldiers.' He felt the letter in his pocket. *She could not tell Lentsch, she could not tell Lentsch, she wrote him the letter 'cause she could not tell Lentsch.*

'Do you ever get the feeling, Major,' he said, 'that something may be happening that we know nothing about?'

The Major leant forward. 'How do you mean?'

'Well, what if Isobel had found out something, seen something?'

'I don't understand. You mean sabotage?'

'Sabotage. Thieving. I don't know.'

'There are many things that happen on this island after dark. It is an island of secrets now, don't you think?'

'Nothing out of the ordinary going on?'

'A sudden rush of foreigns coming in to complete fortification work, that is all. The military are always in a state of anxiety. The only sabotage I know of is Ernst coming round every evening as Bohde's guest and ruining my dinner. It is one of the reasons I am always here.' He checked himself. 'I am sorry. That sounds so rude.'

Ned waved the apology away. 'That must put a strain on the kitchen,' he said, remembering the man's size.

Lentsch nodded. 'Your uncle is furious. And do you know, the food has become much worse lately as a result, burnt or not cooked properly.' He laughed. 'You should tell him such tactics are useless. Men like Ernst have no palates, no taste, only appetites!' He stopped suddenly. 'Listen,' he said. 'We are not the only ones playing music tonight.'

From out of the dark came a thin piping sound, played softly, as if no one was meant to hear.

'A curfew-breaker, it seems,' the Major said. 'This is a bad neighbourhood you are living in.'

They tiptoed out. In the field at the back Veronica was standing behind a young boy, with her arms around his chest, hugging him close, his head against her breast. The boy held a tin flute to his lips and was pointing it to the ground. The two men watched as Veronica stroked the boy's head to the sad rhythm. When he was finished the Major applauded softly.

'Bravo,' he called.

Veronica gave a start. The boy slipped out of her grasp and hid behind her skirt.

'He should be in bed,' the Major scolded. 'There is school tomorrow. Lessons to learn.'

'We were just going in,' Veronica said.

'Your son?'

'My nephew,' she replied, looking hard at Ned. He said not a word. 'He stays overnight sometimes.'

'Good, good. You have sisters and brothers, then?'

'Not exactly.' She put her arms back, holding the boy steady. 'It's a complicated story.'

'Ah.' Lentsch had no intention of intruding further. 'What is his name?'

'Peter,' she said quickly.

'That tune was so pretty,' Lentsch offered politely.

'One of our old folk songs.'

'Really? To me it sounds not English at all. Almost like the gypsies.'

'Well, we're not English here, you know,' Veronica said. 'You keep forgetting that.'

'Of course. It was very nice. Here.' He put his hand in his pocket and took out a coin. The boy retreated back further in the shadow.

'He's very shy,' Veronica told him. 'Soldiers give him night-mares.'

'We must not do that. Put it under his pillow later.'

'You're very kind.'

'It is a small thing,' he said.

Veronica took the coin and shivered.

'We best be getting in, then.'

'Yes, all of us. We must all work tomorrow.'

He turned but she called him back.

'Major.'

'Yes.'

'I'm very sorry about Isobel.'

'Thank you.'

'That night. I had a bit to drink. You must have thought me very . . . pushy.'

'Not at all. I too was drinking, I think. I must give you that record I promised.'

'Oh, that! I'd forgotten all about it.'

'If you learnt that song you would become a great favourite with the soldiers.'

Ned walked the Major to his car, then scurried back through his kitchen and hopped over the fence. Veronica was standing in her open doorway. The boy had gone.

'I thought you'd be back.'

She raised her hands up to the lintel and rested her weight on it. Once they had made love like that, with her legs wrapped round him, her arms holding her trembling weight in mid-air, her body taut with the strain, both of them feverish, trying to keep a desperate balance, both longing to cry out, to bite the silence, her parents but four feet away in the room above. Young, intoxicating times!

'Cousin Peter, eh? A foreign, is he?'

'From Russia, I think. I'm just trying to make sure he doesn't starve to death. You going to report me?'

'Don't be silly, V, but you shouldn't parade him outside like that. No telling who might find out. I can't weed out all the anonymous letters, you know. And you'd be in big trouble if they caught you.'

'Do you think he suspected?'

'I don't think he cares either way.'

'What's he like then, the Major?'

'I thought you knew him.'

'I mean man to man. What's he like?'

'He's living in another world, V – where everyone is polite and well meaning. He acts like a guest, but he's not a guest and he knows it. So there's an awkwardness to it all. At the end of the day he knows however well he behaves we all wish he wasn't here. You going to the funeral?'

'Maybe.'

'Half the army's turning out.'

'Lucky Isobel.'

'Come on, V, that's not like you!'

Her arms sagged suddenly. 'I don't know what's like me any more, Ned. Don't know whether I'm coming or going, who's friend, who's foe.' She put her arms around him and started to cry. He closed his eyes and put his lips to her head and let her sobs subside.

'Oh, Veronica. What are we going to do with you?'

Frightened of being overwhelmed, she broke away and wiped the tears with the length of her arm.

'Come to the play, why don't you,' she said, sniffing.

'I don't know, V.'

'I'll blow you a kiss.'

Ned had smiled in the dark. 'All right.'

'Ned?'

'Yes.'

'Night-night.'

'Night-night, V.'

'Ned?'

'What?'

'Dream of me sometimes.'

★

Bernie and Ned arrived at the church at twelve, though it took ten minutes to reach the little gate and the slight uphill path to the church entrance. Outside the hearse and the crowd waited, the horses in their harness stamping their feet, impatient, like the townsfolk pressed against the stone walls, for the slow three-quarters of a mile march up to the sloping cemetery and the eternal view of the sea. Funerals were one of the few occasions when the civilian population was allowed to congregate in any number. Half the town had turned out, umbrellas at the ready. Though it looked fine, the weather would not hold for long. They were islanders. They knew the signs. Up ahead, all branches of the Occupation stood at the ready, the artillery, the Luftwaffe, even the Kriegsmarine. At the front stood the uniformed men of the Organisation Todt, their hoisted spades gleaming in the cold spring air. Ernst walked up and down banging his little stick. Ned felt drunk and in need of a piss.

'It's not right,' Bernie whispered, 'the old girl all alone.'

'She wouldn't have no one else,' Ned answered. 'Albert will see she's all right.'

The sound of the church organ starting up again broke the unchallenged calm. The crowd straightened up off the walls, the troops gathered themselves together. Ernst slapped his stick quickly in three successive beats. For Ned, in a moment's sudden glazed look, the squiffy reason of why he was here evaded him. Isobel. That was it. Isobel was dead! He tried to think straight, to get everything in order, but he could not. He looked about him, lost, a blur of faces sweeping by in a pool of painful light, but no one paid him any attention. It was as if he wasn't there.

Turning once again, he caught sight of Albert standing by the church door and a desperate hope surged within him. He would understand! He raised his hand in greeting, but halfway through had to steady himself. He wiped his mouth and burped into his sleeve. The man next to him moved away.

The door opened and as the bell in the round tower began its low, hesitant toll, the pallbearers brought her out. There was a moment, as they hitched their shoulders and settled into the task of carrying her wooded weight down the drive, when it appeared that no one would follow, that the church had been empty, and not even her aunt had cared to kneel before her in her death, but then Mrs Hallivand stepped out into the light. Framed in the hollow of that stone archway, her tiny boned hands clutching a bunch of violets, deriving strength from the deeply inhaled scent as she might from a bottle of smelling salts, she stood as if under sentence, as if expecting the church to crumble and fall on top of her and bury her underneath the weight of its heartless faith. Albert took her arm. She patted his gratefully.

The coffin was loaded, the sun went out, the clouds grew closer. Watching as the hearse creaked down the drive Ned couldn't help but notice that the wheels were squeaking like the spare bicycle back at the station, like the Yellow Peril's blown suspension, like the garden gate back home. That's what's happening, he thought. The island is seizing up. Butter is the only grease available to lubricate this island, black-market butter at thirty shillings a pound. Was it any wonder that so many succumbed, when they inhabited a world where a man was entitled to only four ounces of meat a week, three of sugar, one of coffee (and that a substitute of ground acorns)? How were they supposed to get by on that? The black market, that was how. There was money to be made there all right, and money to be spent, and by a breed of men who had never imagined that such a prospect might one day lie within their grasp. Tea got spooned into the pot at five pounds a quarter, a tot of whisky came from a bottle costing ten pounds and if you wanted to blow genuine smoke rings in the air you did it from leaf which cost seven pounds an ounce.

As the orders rang out and the syncopated rhythm of a hundred boots stamped down on the macadam road, the wind began to stir; a spot of rain, a stronger breeze, a sudden drop in temperature. The crowd followed, their black umbrellas unfolded in anticipation of the downpour, the clouds' black coat-tails clearly visible, sweeping in from the north. His bladder bursting, Ned waited until they had left before relieving himself behind a flying buttress, hoping no one would notice the blasphemous steam rising from this consecrated ground.

Buttoning his flies, he moved quickly up the lane, chasing the solemn beat of the band. It was the first time he had been among a crowd, and jostling amongst them, acknowledging a greeting here, stealing a glance at an old-remembered face there, for the first time he saw them as they really were. Oh, he had waited in queues with them, seen them in their ones and twos as they walked down the Pollet, shared a bench with them on one of the bus carts, but seeing them on the move, their faces anxious to devour the coming occasion, he looked at them afresh. We're starving, Ned thought, astonished. Every one of us. Not today, not tomorrow, not in a week or a month's time, but give it a year, maybe two, and half of us will be dead. He could see how the sentence had already been passed on those who lived closest to life's precarious edge, the old and the very young; how like old men the children appeared, hunched and slow, and how like children, helplessly innocent and in need of a guiding hand, seemed the old. He could see it too on the idle hands of men not yet forty, with their ragged boots tied with lengths of string and their scarves wrapped to muffle their fifty-year-old coughs and sixty-year-old wheezes. He could catch it in the worried stoop of mothers, lost in the empty hang of their dresses which their breasts once filled. He could trace it on every image he conjured up; on his mother's face as she shivered in her fleshless nightdress; in the pale determination of those two ankle-socked girls hurrying home with their potato perambulator; in the fat fingers of George Poidevin's pasty paw as he jabbed them up and down his desk. He could see it most clearly in those who stood now by the open grave, the new aristocracy of this unjust fiefdom; Major Lentsch, Captain Zepernick and Molly. He remembered the car and the luxurious spread of Veronica's willing limbs, satiated in the wrap of her Occupational furs.

As the squall grew in its strength, the crowd instinctively huddled together. Molly looked superb, black feathers and a small black veil with matching stockings and dress; a dish to be devoured. Albert reached out, holding Mrs Hallivand back as if he were worried she might be washed into the hole; the girls leant into their uniformed protection. Only Molly remained unchanged, standing coatless alongside the Captain, the rain beating against her body, flattening her fine and flaunting dress against the wet of her calves and the turn of her hips and the low swell of her stomach. The rain streamed down and still she did not move. The wind caught her veil and blew it up over her head and as she lifted her face, her black gloved hands held stiffly by her side, she licked the wet from her face and held herself out as proud and defiant and as paintedly beautiful as a ship's figurehead glorifying in the furious rage of the sea. She drew strength from this. It lifted her spirits, not because she enjoyed the spectacle, but because she *was* the spectacle. The crowd could hardly take their eyes off her.

The storm ended as suddenly as it began. The sky cleared, but on the horizon another one could be seen to be on its way. The parish priest in robes of white and blue stepped forward to perform the burial. A firing party followed and aimed its guns in the air. As they fired, nesting crows rose from the trees and broke into a chorus of protest.

'Hit some of them buggers and we could all have a decent pie,' a voice from the back called. A nervous laugh rippled through the crowd.

The guns fired again, the crows rose once more. Lentsch looked down to where muddy water was already collecting between the coffin and the sides of the grave. He mouthed some words. In English? In German? Words of love? Words of remorse? Ned could not tell. As the escort party turned and began to march away Molly placed her hand on Zep's arm and moved to follow in their wake.

'Look at that bitch,' Ned heard someone in the crowd mutter. 'We'll get our own back when the time comes.'

Molly paled while the Captain looked in vain for the culprit, but the crowd closed its mouth to his gaze. They would not give him up. Molly tried to pull her veil down, but it stuck to her face. She took off her hat and held it in front of her.

'Jerrybag!' another shouted.

A clod of earth flew in her direction. It caught a gravestone in front and scattered in the air.

'God Save the King!'

'In future,' the Captain said to Molly, in a tone designed to be overheard, 'if people can't behave themselves, we shall have to insist that such events be conducted after curfew.'

Ned stepped forward.

'All right,' he shouted. 'That's enough of that. Get off home before you land us all in trouble.' He turned and opened his hands.

'I'm sorry you had to go through that,' he said. 'This is not the place to voice such feelings.'

'And another would be?' snapped the Captain.

Ned watched as Molly and the Captain hurried to their car.

'Perhaps we should not have been here at all,' the Major said. 'Perhaps something simpler would have been more appropriate. But . . .' he directed his gaze to where Ernst was preparing to march off his men, 'we had no choice. That is the trouble in war. Sometimes there is no choice but to do the wrong thing.'

'It's not you they're angry with,' Ned replied. 'It's their own kind they hate.'

'I suppose I should be grateful, then. It makes my job easier if they hate the likes of Molly more than the likes of me. Come back to the Villa? Have a glass of something warm, after the chill here.'

Ned looked at his watch.

'I must go. Paperwork.'

'Very well.' Lentsch was unnaturally formal. 'There was one thing I should have told you. In the hue and cry it was overlooked. The lieutenant you wanted to interview. Lieutenant Schade.'

'You haven't found him yet?'

'It appears that on that Saturday he got very drunk. First at the Casino, then later on in one of the . . .'

'Houses?' Ned suggested helpfully.

'Exactly. Over at St Sampson's. He should not have been there. It is for enlisted men, but he was most persistent. There was a fight. Then it seems he went for more drinks, in the hotels along the promenade.'

'Are you saying that he hasn't sobered up yet?'

'No, no. Early the next morning he was found in the foyer of the Soldatenheim. He told them he'd fallen down the steps and hurt his head. They thought he was just drunk you understand, a little shaky, his words all together . . .'

'Slurred.'

'Slurred. So they let him sleep. Sunday afternoon they tried to wake him. They could not. Coma. This morning he died.'

Ned felt himself grow cold. The Major tried to reassure him.

'I should have been told earlier. But with van Dielen's disappearance, everyone forgot. This has nothing to do with Isobel, I am sure. The men involved in the fights will be disciplined but not charged. They were not serious. A blow to the face, a tooth loose. Brawling. The fall must have caused it. We do not wish to upset the family, so we will tell them that it was an accident.'

The Major walked away. Ned scoured the crowd for a sight of Veronica, but couldn't see her. Perhaps she hadn't come after all. Down by the car his mother was talking to Albert. He had a hand on her shoulder and was trying to put something in the calico bag she was carrying. Two times she waved the bag aside but at the third he grabbed it and thrust in his hand. She stood up on tiptoe and gave him a kiss. Albert climbed in the driver's seat. His mother waved, then gave a little curtsy to Mrs Hallivand as the car drove off.

'What was all that about,' he said, coming up behind her.

His mother patted her handbag. 'It's a surprise,' she said.

He held her out at arm's length.

'You look nice, Mum.'

'You're just saying that.'

'I'm not! You do.'

He took her arm and walked her down the road. Halfway down

the hill he stopped and wheeling her round kissed her on the cheek. His mother looked round, flustered. A couple of women walked past, grinning.

'Ned Luscombe, what do you think you're doing!'

'I'm taking my mum in my arms, that's what I'm doing.'

'I never saw such a thing. Put me down at once.' She pulled herself back, straightening her coat. 'What would your father have said?'

'We'll never know, will we.' He hugged her again. 'And next time I see her I'm going to put my arms around Veronica.'

'Oh, it's Veronica again, is it?'

'No, it isn't, but sometimes I wish it was. She was right for me. I was right for her. I should have left it at that.'

'You've been drinking.'

'So I have. All morning, as a matter of fact.'

'Drowning your sorrows, I don't doubt. If there's one thing I can't abide it's a man feeling sorry for himself.'

'It's V I feel sorry for, letting her go like that.'

'Yes, and look at her now.'

'I helped put her there, Mum. She would have been safe if I'd done right by her.'

'She's a free woman.'

'No one here's free, Mum. Not you, not me, not V, not even Uncle Albert.'

*

Ned walked back to the office. The whole affair had gone badly. The town had been out in force, their sympathy tainted by curiosity and loathing. Their true feelings regarding the Occupation, kept simmering for these two and three-quarter years under a lid fashioned from the base metals of obedience and opportunism, had broken out into the air like thick, sulphurous fumes bubbling up from some dark and murky pool. It was not simply bottled resentment which had fuelled their anger. In the shabby folds of their funeral clothes, mingling with the smell of mothballs and camphor sticks, hung the noxious fumes of self-loathing. He had sniffed it wafting in and out of the gravestones like a sea mist rolling in and out of the rocks, ready to lead them all to grief. And when the sudden squall that the sky had promised finally descended, it washed into the very pores of their skin as quickly as the poison gas that everyone believed to be stored in Alderney. It was a dangerous and intoxicating chemical the islanders had inhaled that afternoon.

He sat down and idly opened the drawer, remembering suddenly what was inside. Until Lentsch had spoken to him he had quite forgotten about the man. That's how good a detective he was. And now he was dead, his head cracked open by the hands of a British policeman. A legitimate act of war or an act of criminality? He picked up the wallet, opened the fold and laid the money out on the table. More than a Lieutenant's wages, unless he hadn't spent any money for six months.

He held open the rest of the wallet and shook out the contents. Identity card, driver's pass, a Lloyd's chequebook, tide tables, a letter from home, the postmark smudged and indecipherable. Inside three closely written pages, whether wife, mother, brother or father, Ned had no idea. There were photographs, too: one of a good-looking woman of about fifty, holding a white lapdog: another of a young man in a ill-fitting suit, a Homburg raised above his head, and the last, a skinny girl in a summer dress standing astride a bicycle, a sweetheart no doubt, in a sweetheart's pose and a sweetheart's hopeful smile on her face. Ned felt helpless in the face of such photographs. Did they know, this man, these women, that their beloved Schade was dead, that he had lost his life pushed down some pointless steps? What would they think about the war then, these people, so content, so happy? What use were pictures, except to wound and hurt? Photographs told you nothing except that you were for ever alone, for ever transient, for ever to be betrayed by those who had held you closest, for ever to betray in turn those who hold you most dear.

As he replaced the letter he discovered an extra flap running the whole length of the wallet's back, protected by a small lip of leather tucked into the right-hand side. He put his hand in. More photographs. He laid them out on the table.

Though he understood what he saw, to begin with they were recognizable only as blurred mementoes of a soldier's masturbatory life; women spread out to enliven the bored bunk hours or passed around the mess room to a chorus of obscene jokes and merry gestures. Then as he looked closer he realized that not all the photographs were of strangers. Some were of a woman he knew, and a place he knew too, though which he had recognized first, the low curved ceiling and the open iron door of the escape shaft or the fleshy arms and the shock of tumbling hair of its occupant he could not say. She was smiling at the camera, as naked as the night she had slipped into the summer sea with him and Bernie egging her on, but here her podgy arm was wrapped around Lieutenant Schade's broad shoulders and the two of them were lying back on a bed of straw. That was how Isobel had come to have straw in her hair. Not from a farm vehicle, not from a stable, but from the tunnel itself.

Ned crossed over the square and walked down Smith Street. There was a queue on the left-hand side, stretching down the hill and round into the Lower Pollet. In the bookshop window halfway down hung yet another huge portrait wreathed in yet another collection of ferns and daffodils. Scattered round the bottom were copies of Britain's worst-selling sixpenny magazine, *Mein Kampf,* an English translation available in eighteen weekly episodes. A handwritten sign informed him that in commemoration of the coming birthday there was going to be a free draw for the whole set.

At the corner he walked up the steps and pushed open the double door. Inside the bank was cool and empty and smelt of floor polish. Monty Freeman sat in his office dictating a letter. His arms stuck out from his jacket sleeves like broomhandles on a scarecrow. A suit in search of a man, his mother used to call him. A girl at the back was writing figures in a long ledger. Ned could hear the scratch of her pen. Elspeth Poidevin sat behind the long teak counter in front of a little sign which bore her name, its lettering only slightly more elaborate than her clothes. She wore a pink blouse with a high collar and mother-of-pearl buttons and a little bow in the front, tied like a shoelace. It looked easy to pull too. She was counting slowly, licking her index finger and fluttering her eyelids at her uniformed customer. Though her pink lips formed the words silently Ned could hear every syllable: twenty-five, twenty-six, twenty-seven. He walked across the echoing floor and waited behind the smartly belted tunic. Elspeth snapped a rubber band round the notes and pushed the bundle across. The notes were small and greasy, like all the Occupational currency. The officer put his hands on the counter and looked straight at her.

'I made it twenty-nine,' he said.

'Thirty,' Elspeth said. 'But I'll count it again if you want.'

'If you please, miss.'

'Oh, we aim to please. That's what we're here for.'

She licked her finger again and brought the notes back. Each time her finger flicked a note the base of her thumb pushed up against her right breast. The bow started to wobble.

'She was right the first time,' Ned said from behind. The man turned round.

'I couldn't help noticing,' Ned admitted. 'It was thirty. She never gets things like that wrong, do you, Elspeth?'

Flattery was always welcome where Elspeth was concerned, even when it interrupted performance. 'I've got a head for figures,' she admitted. 'There you are. Thirty. What did I tell you?'

The officer took his money reluctantly, like a boy who's only been allowed to fill his sweet bag half full.

'Come again soon,' Elspeth called out, and adjusting her sign, turned her attention to her back to Ned. 'Mr Luscombe,' she said brightly. 'What can I do for you?'

Ned smiled back. 'How's the trauma?' he asked.

'I'm sorry?'

'The ladies of ill repute. Still offending your sensibilities?'

She sniffed.

'Mr Freeman deals with them after closing time. That way we don't become . . .'

'Contaminated?'

'My dad told him he wouldn't allow me to work here otherwise.'

'What it is to have a father like yours. Anyway, to business.' He looked about. Monty Freeman was watching him through his office window. The girl at the back was blotting her columns. 'About the bank?'

'Yes. Come to open an account?' Elspeth suggested.

Ned shook his head and turned back to where the officer was standing by the door, pulling at the creases of his tunic before stepping out. 'I was wondering. Do many officers like him bank here?'

'A few from the Feldkommandantur, and the Wehrmacht. The long-term residents. None of the enlisted men, of course.'

'Of course. What about artillery officers?'

'I don't know, I'm sure. They're all customers to me.'

He took out the wallet and laid it on the counter.

'It's this lieutenant, see. He's lost his wallet. A lot of money in it, tucked inside one of your envelopes. Name of Schade.'

'Doesn't ring any bells.'

'Have a look at his picture. See if you recognize him.' He opened the identity card. She looked at the picture of the thickset man, grinning into the camera. An air of innocence wafted over the counter as sweet as the perfume rising from her pampered bosom.

'No, I don't think so. Jolly-looking soul, isn't he?'

'Well, he used to have lots to be jolly about. Are you sure you don't recognize him? There's a chequebook here too.'

She picked up the card. 'Come to think of it, I think I might have served him once or twice.' She looked around before lowering her voice. 'Trouble is they all look the same in their uniforms, don't they?'

'What about without their uniforms?'

'Beg pardon?'

'In civvies. Bathing costumes. *Au naturel.*'

'Bathing costumes? What are you on about?'

'It's just that I thought you might have known this fellow socially, Elspeth. In less formal surroundings.'

'What on earth gave you that idea?'

'Well, these actually,' he said, and laid the pictures before her. 'They were in his wallet too.'

Elspeth paled and clutching at the counter slipped off her stool in a heap. The girl at the back jumped up, knocking the bottle of ink over her carefully written figures. Ned ran to the side and ducked under the counter flap. The girl had Elspeth's head in her lap. Her inky footprints ran clear across the waxed surface.

'Let's get her to her feet,' he suggested. Monty Freeman appeared at his side.

'What's going on?' he demanded, then, kicking at the girl's foot, added, 'Look what you done to my floor.'

'Never mind that!' Ned shouted. 'Get her a glass of water or something.' He put his hand under Elspeth's armpit, and with the girl's help half dragged her into Monty's office. He could feel her heart pulse, smell the sudden sweat of her. Though her body was limp and her eyes were closed, she managed to keep her stockinged legs well away from any splinters. She hadn't fainted at all. She was gaining time. Shooing the secretary out Ned sat her in Monty Freeman's swivel chair before walking back to retrieve the photographs. When he got back Monty Freeman was standing outside with a glass in his hand.

'I'm afraid you're going to be short-staffed this afternoon, Mr Freeman,' Ned told him, taking the tumbler from his grasp. 'When she's back on her feet she'll be coming with me.'

'Coming with you, whatever for?' He looked over to Elspeth's vacant seat and the teller's drawer beneath. 'It's not the bank, is it?'

'No, it's not the bank,' Ned assured him. He closed the door.

He watched while she regained her composure. Her head was just level with the desk. She struggled in her seat, then reached down and adjusted the height of the chair. She made one attempt to drink but her hand shook water out of the glass. Through the window she could see the other girls gathering around where she had fallen. She looked back, horrified.

'It's all right,' Ned reassured her, tapping his pocket. 'I've got them here. No one saw them.' He stood up. 'Come on, Elspeth. We can walk up to the station. The air will do you good.'

Back in his office he pulled the chair over from the stove and indicated for her to sit down. She sat with her handbag in her lap, looking askance at the grimy walls. Ned walked to the other side and sat opposite.

'Got a cushion?' she asked. 'This seat ain't half hard on my bum.'

She wriggled impatiently. Ned couldn't help but admire her. She had some stuffing inside her still. He leant over.

'Might as well have a look in this bag of yours, since you've brought it with you. See if there's anything else of interest.'

He tipped out the contents. A bar of German chocolate, a packet of German tobacco, a little purse with two scrunched-up ten-mark notes, a bank book, a packet of hairpins, a powder compact, a mirror, and a three sticks of different coloured lipsticks. All brand new.

'Now these pictures,' he said, taking them out and shuffling them like a deck of cards. Elspeth tried to snatch them out of his hand.

'Do you mind! Them's private. You've no right to oggle at them like that.'

'I'm investigating a crime,' Ned said. 'These could be evidence.'

'Of what? They're just photos, that's all. Who I let take pictures of me is my own affair. Nothing wrong with it.'

'Actually I'm not sure if you're right, Elspeth. First, there's the question of what you were doing.'

Elspeth looked at him indignantly. 'Figure studies, that's all they were.'

'I think the Lord Chamberlain might disagree. Leaving that aside there's the question of what went on before or after and whether any remuneration took place.' He held her protestations at bay. 'And lastly there's the question of where all this took place. Strictly out of bounds, those bunkers. Do you have any idea of the dangers you were putting yourself in if the military thought you were spying?'

She looked up. 'We was just having a bit of fun, that's all.'

'You and this Schade?'

'Yes.'

'How did you meet him?'

'Conrad? I don't know. At the bandstand, I think. Or it might have been the cinema. They have these mixed evenings most Tuesdays.'

'Well, it looks like they were a great success. When did you last see him?'

'Couple of weeks ago. He's on leave now.'

'And he'd take you down there?'

'Yes. We'd have a bit of a party.'

'We?'

She looked annoyed with herself.

'Me and couple of girls from Boots, if you must know.'

'What about the girls at the bank?'

Elspeth shook her head.

'Happen often, did they, these parties?'

'Once a week, maybe. Whenever they were on duty.'

'And you'd go there when? At night?'

'They'd pick us up after curfew, up by St Saviour's Church, drop us off at the top and walk through the security gates, change shifts. Then one would pop up to give us the all-clear and we'd climb down.'

'And you'd spend the night there?'

'We'd leave early morning, when the coast was clear.'

'Bit risky for them, wasn't it?'

Elspeth brushed her sleeve. 'Perhaps they thought we were worth it.'

'And that's all that happened there – these parties.'

'It's enough, isn't it?'

'What about your parents?'

'Said I was staying with a friend. We didn't do anything bad,

Mr Luscombe.' Her nose started to quiver. 'You're not going to tell my dad, are you? He'll beat me black and blue.'

'That depends on what else you tell me, Elspeth. The trouble is, that bunker, that gun emplacement, also happens to be the place where Miss van Dielen's body was found.'

'But that can't be! Conrad would have told me.'

'Conrad's dead,' he told her.

Now she faltered. Her hands began to shake. Ned felt sorry for her. She was just a silly girl, that was all. She reached out and touched the back of one of the photographs. He felt tempted to give them back to her and tell her to go home. 'Don't worry,' he said. 'Nothing to with this. An accident.'

'I had nothing to do with it, Mr Luscombe, honest. Never even spoken to her.'

'What about the men there? Did any of them know her, do you think? What were their names, Rupp? Bauer?'

'Rudi and Co.? No, she was too posh for them.'

He nodded. He picked up the bank book and flipped through the pages. To date Elspeth Poidevin had £3,175 in her bank account. Three thousand pounds! Ten years of his pay!

'Bloody hell, Elspeth, how did you come by all this?'

Elspeth looked at the bank book as if she had never seen it before.

'Savings.'

'Savings! From what?'

'Conrad was very generous.'

'I'll say he was.' He looked back through the entries. She'd opened the account October 1940, four months after the Occupation. The entries came in regular weekly instalments, ten, twenty, thirty pounds.

'You telling me all this came from a lieutenant?'

'Well, not all, obviously.'

'Well, who, then?'

Elspeth started to fidget. 'Can't say for sure.'

'Forgive me for suggesting this, Elspeth, but you haven't been taking a leaf out of the French ladies' books, have you? The sight of them trooping in the bank with all their hard-earned money didn't set you thinking, "If they can do it, so can I"?'

She stood up, a flush of crimson racing down her neck.

'How dare you say that! How dare you!'

'Well, what else am I supposed to think? Here's the lieutenant with pictures of you that would make a navvy blush, and here's you with a bank balance that would be the envy of your bank manager.'

Monty Freeman. That was a point. He leafed through the book again. Two years, five months, 1940, 1941, 1942, 1943. At the close of December 1942 the interest gained that year had been worked out, with Monty Freeman's signature at the bottom. Monty Freeman knew of this, knew that Elspeth Poidevin was salting away more money in five months than he could earn in a year? Upright Monty Freeman? Then he remembered the swivel chair, and how Elspeth had reached down for the lever, as if she knew exactly how to use it, as if she'd sat in it many times before. Not in office hours, he'd be bound. When the bank was closed, then, and the other girls were on their way home. Elspeth Poidevin and Monty Freeman, together at last.

Calling for Tommy, he jumped the stairs and started to run down the hill. The girls were standing outside on the corner, talking to one another. Monty Freeman was shoving his hat on as he hurried down the steps. A minute later and Ned was hugging the left-hand side of the Lower Pollet following Monty's bobbing hat as he trotted past the chemist and the goldsmith, past R. J. Collins the purveyor of home-made cakes, past all those shops and shop owners to whom he maintained such an unforgiving rectitude, his hand pushing against wall and window, his coat flapping, blind to the ripples his unscheduled progress was causing.

Down near the roundabout Ned spun on his heel. Poor Monty had stopped up by the Savoy Hotel, out of breath. Ned waited a minute before turning again. Not that there was any danger of being discovered. Monty had crossed the road and was flagging a Pullman as it came up the Esplanade. He tipped his hat to the driver and settled down on the front bench.

Ned kept a good fifty yards back, walking on the same side as the bus, hanging over the railings or the sea wall whenever necessary. He didn't need to run any more. The horse buses weren't built for speed. Women passed him with shopping bags and children. Men whistled carrying tool kits and empty lunch bags. A window cleaner cycled by, one hand on the handlebars, one hand holding his ladder. Then a doctor's car. If he shut his eyes to the harbour, the seafront looked normal. Towards Spur Point the crowd began to thin out, so he crossed back to the shore side again and hung back while the old horse pulled its load round the bend and into the South Quay of St Sampson's harbour. He could see the horse's bones working under the dull skin, see the age and suffering of the beast in each weary plod. It was easier for Ned to hide himself here, for the harbour was awash with activity: swinging cranes, shouting longshoremen, guards, soldiers, ordinary civilians, all mixed together. They looked happy enough. They were work-ing, earning a decent wage, eating decent food. The bus pulled up. A woman clambered down, her pram handed down by two others who jumped down after it. A boy with a barrel hoop. His mother. Then, from the dark of the canvas, a pair of hands carrying a hat. Monty Freeman.

A minute later he had crossed into van Dielen's yard. Ned ran round and pulling himself up looked over the fence. Monty was knocking on the little wooden door, but there was no one there; he tried the handle, but someone had fitted a new lock. He sat down and squeezed his head. There was a rumble of thunder. He looked up as the light rain returned. Monty hunched his shoulders and jammed his hat down. He was going to wait.

At the end the of the harbour stood a small sentry hut. Ned walked over and showing his warrant, asked if he could sit by the window and watch.

'*Kriminells,*' he said, exaggerating his consonants.

The guards were polite, dragging a chair to the greasy window, wiping the glass clean with an oily rag. The rain outside had settled into a steady drizzle. The wind from the sea had turned the day cold.

'*Kaffee?*'

Ned took the tin cup gratefully. The two guards trooped outside, leaving the door open. He could see their capes and their boots and the butt ends of their rifles. He breathed on the hot liquid and stared out. Back on watch, the guards resumed their conversation. He could understand some of it. There was a new girl over at the local brothel. French. Young. Very good. Something about a bottle. Much laughter. Someone had managed to drop one of the new field guns into the harbour. Smashed a boat in as well. Then a complaint. He couldn't work that one out. Their boots rang against the cobbles as they passed it back and forth. For *zwei Woche*. Two weeks. *Jeden Tag*. Every day? Boots, uniform, the lot. He followed their gestures. He got it. Another inspection.

George Poidevin arrived two hours later. Ned nearly missed him. A line of trucks queuing up for the depots on the north side had obscured his view. As the last one moved off he caught a glimpse of van Dielen's green lorry before the gates were shut again. Ned turned his collar up and ran through the puddles.

There was a light in the shed now, low and flickering, and though half the window was covered with brown paper he could see the two of them moving back and forth inside. Monty Freeman was waving his hat in the air. George was trying to calm him down. Ned's arms grew tired. In about ten minutes the two of them came outside and walked over to the lorry. George clambered aboard and started throwing things out of the back.

'We'll wait until nine,' he said. 'It'll be dead quiet by then.'

'Can't we start earlier?' Monty sounded bitter.

'It's a weekday, Mr Freeman. It wouldn't be safe. Come on, help me put these out of the rain.'

Ned dropped to the ground. Waiting was not a game he was used to. In Southampton it was always a knock on the door or a quick twist of the elbow. He walked down the road to where the phone box stood. At least they still took the old currency. Ned called the station.

'Tommy? I'm at St Sampson's. By the custom hut on the south side. I want you to bring me a bike. You can ride it over and walk back. Oh, and get me something to cover myself with. It's chucking it down and I'm wearing my best suit.'

Tommy tried to be helpful. 'A cape, you mean.'

'No, not a bloody cape. I'm trying to look inconspicuous. Something from lost property, something to cover my legs. And hurry.'

Tommy arrived twenty minutes later. He had a white bundle underneath his arm. A coat. There was black lettering on the back.

'Deckchair attendant!'

'It's all I could find,' Tommy told him, helping him on with it. 'People don't seem to lose things like they used to.'

The lorry nosed out of the gate at around ten past. As it neared the hut the guard stepped out. George had all the papers ready; his driving licence, his petrol permit, identity card, the firm's accreditation to the Todt. The guard waved him on. Ned eased out onto the road and started to pedal hard. The coat was tight around the shoulders and flapped uselessly about his legs. The beam on the lamp flickered on and off but there was the grey of the sea and the light of a sullen sky to help him. The cranes were silent now, the gunboats and barges dim silhouettes. On the rolls of barbed wire hung strands of dark seaweed, dull with oil. Back in St Peter Port George swung the lorry up Julian's Hill and then turned sharp left, down the narrow alleyway that served as a rear access to the shops on Smith Street. The lorry crept along slowly, its tarpaulin sides brushing against the cobbled walls. At the end the alley broadened out into small courtyard. George wheeled the lorry round then backed it up against the back door to the bank. A jangle of keys later and the two men slipped in, Monty with a hurricane lamp in his hand. Ned counted to thirty, then followed down the narrow passageway that led to the bank. He could hear the echo of footsteps hurrying over the parquet floor. Inside the main area the smell of floor polish seemed even stronger than before. He stood in the doorway, trying to find his bearings. The counter was straight ahead of him. To his right rose the wooden partition which made up the back wall to Monty's office. On his left stood the table where the girl with the ledger had worked, and behind, illuminated in fading flickering light, an open door with a whitewashed ceiling sloping down. He could feel the cool air rushing up from the cellars below. He took a deep breath. As he moved towards the door he heard the heavy tread of George Poidevin labouring back up. Ned skipped across and hid under the shell of the hinged counter. A grunt and George stepped into the hall.

'Mind the ink.' Monty's voice was close behind. 'Here, I'll go first.'

They were carrying three of four boxes apiece, the stack higher than their heads. Monty moved forward gingerly.

'This'll take all night,' George complained.

'What if it does. I'm ruined if they find this lot here.' He squealed. 'Oh, Christ, I've done it myself now! Oh Christ, oh Christ, oh Christ! What am I to do?'

George balanced his boxes on the desk and laid down a carpet of paper.

'Walk on those,' he said, 'otherwise your footsteps will be all over the place.'

Ned let them make six journeys. That way if there was any trouble they'd be more tired than he. Not that he could envisage Monty Freeman having a go at him. George was a different matter. He was a big man but quicker than he looked. On the seventh trip down Ned followed. As he made his descent he was struck by the low metal glitter that seemed to radiate from the walls, like a thousand polished boots, a curious myriad of glossy lights. He had never considered what might be found in a bank vault but he supposed it would be notes and coins and a stack of safe deposit boxes; never a grocery store. Stacked up against the wall were fairground pyramids of cans: sliced peaches, fruit cocktails, spiced pears; cans of peas and carrots and butter beans; tins of pilchards and sardines and round halves of salmon; corned beef, jellied ham, fish paste, evaporated milk, vegetable soup, and huge buggers of apricot jam. Sides of ham and bacon hung from hooks in the ceiling and bags of flour were stacked up on the floor. Ned stood and watched. George's fat back was bent towards him as he dragged a couple of sacks across the stone flagging. Monty was stacking loose cans of cocoa into a half-opened box, methodical even in haste. Van Houten's Cocoa. Ned could almost smell the bittersweet of it, hear the drum snap of the spoon handle as it broke into the paper seal. It would be easy for him to lift a couple and take them home. It would perk Mum's spirit up no end, to hold a real cup of cocoa in her hand. He stepped out and stood under the solitary bare bulb.

'Need a hand, gentlemen?'

George took a swing at him. Ned had never enjoyed hitting a man before but he enjoyed it now, ducking from the wild blow and landing a fist in the dough of the fat man's stomach. It was the right place to hit George, in the folds of his coarse corruption, and he made the right sort of noise, a thick wallowing noise like a blocked drain sucked free. A hot wave of fetid breath washed over Ned's face as George fell against him. Ned pushed him upright and sent him sprawling back into the arms of Monty Freeman. The thin man staggered back under his weight, the two of them crashing against the sacks of flour.

'Don't hit me,' Monty Freeman squealed, his arms floundering in clouds of white. 'I'll tell you everything.'

*

They dragged it out of them that night and most of the next day, Ned and the Major, with the Captain's men working on the Kanoniers. 'Never thought I'd feel sorry for a German,' Tommy told him, in the late morning, having coming back from where the soldiers were being held, 'but seeing the state of them ... They even asked me if I wanted to join in. Held one up for me.'

'And did you?' asked Ned, remembering poor Schade. Tommy was indignant.

'I got out of it, told them I was saving my energy for this lot back here.'

This was how it worked, how George and Monty and Elspeth spilt it out, Elspeth snuffling beside her father in Ned's office, Monty Freeman babbling in the doctor's room below, staring at the white line, thinking how easily he had lost his own balance and how, unlike the transitory drunk, it was an equilibrium he would never regain. They talked freely, recklessly, in the vain hope that such confessional cooperation would somehow weigh in their favour, that they might escape the strictures of a German prison. They were wrong in that, Ned knew, but he made no attempt to dispel their straw-grabbed illusions.

The set-up had all been Elspeth's idea, George boasted, Elspeth and the Lieutenant's. Between them they had arranged everything. George supplied the transport, and the means by which to distribute the goods around the island. Elspeth provided the one thing that would entice the Kanoniers into such a dangerous occupation. Girls. The Lieutenant had elected the boat crew and obtained the goods from the mainland. Between them they had the island sewn up.

Elspeth would meet the girls on Thursday evenings after the shops closed. They'd go down to her mum's shop and have a kip for a couple of hours. There were three others apart from Elspeth, two girls from Boots and the caretaker's daughter up from the big school. They'd wake around seven, have a wash and a good tea before changing out of their working clothes into something more suitable. George would pick them up in his van at about half eight and run them over to the point. Once out on the headland it was no more than a thirty-yard dash across the scrub to where the lid of the escape hatch stood open and, skirts flapping, they'd giggle down the iron ladder to where the straw and the soldiers waited, the three gunners Rupp, Bauer, and Laurer and their fun-loving Lieutenant.

Sometimes the parties could be quite sedate. They all liked

playing draughts and as often as not they'd have a small tournament with betting on the side; the girls would darn the men's socks, play cards, sit on their knees, listening to their halting tales of home; maybe they'd sing songs, tune into the radio, spoon close up to distant band music, their arms around each other's necks, lipstick and hair cream, lipstick and hair cream, shuffling past each other like strangers on a dance floor. Later, couple by couple, they'd slip into the tunnel to make love, but by curious convention, when it came to Elspeth and the Lieutenant's turn, the others would troop out of the room altogether and wait in the gun room. Elspeth and the Lieutenant had business to discuss as well.

At other times, opening that hatch was like taking the top off a shaken bottle of pop. Then they did run riot, all bloody night. 'Like being in a cage with wild animals,' Elspeth said with some sense of wounded awe, 'you had to meet them halfway, just to survive.' Those were the nights of cheap brandy, of drinking contests and nude wrestling, of the girls marching up and down the corridor to the hoarse cheers of *linksrecht linksrecht linksrecht*, with army rifles slung across their bouncing breasts, standing to attention in mock parades before the boys took turns with each of them, on the bunk beds and in the gunner's chair, even draped over the muzzle of the gun itself. Then came the photographs. Schade had started taking them eighteen months back, just faces at first, couples arm in arm; then the odd exposed moment caught unawares, a blouse half-pulled over a head, a giggling body hastily covered by a blanket, two pairs of bare feet, then as they tried to dig out of the pit of boredom, something more deliberate, more orchestrated. The men had stuck the more innocuous on the back of their cupboard door. Others they kept in their lockers. (They had burnt all of them in the black stove minutes after Ned and the Major had left that Sunday.) By early morning the party would have subsided and they'd all be sleeping, or if not sleeping, talking quietly, couples again, lying amongst the detritus of their energy, waiting for dawn, when the cargo boat from St Malo would appear, stopping off on its way to Peter Port at the half-submerged jetty on the cove at

Gull Bay where Schade and his bleary-eyed Kanoniers waited. The girls would be in the gun room then, wrapped up in greatcoats, watching those few wallowing minutes as the boys hauled the crates off the deck and dragged them up the steep path to one of the construction sites dotted along the cliff top, before the charged run back to the bunker, where the girls would squeal with the shock of freezing hands and wind-blown faces and one final copulation, taken quickly, as one might swallow a tot of rum. Then it was dressing and clearing up, the girls sweeping out and washing up and brushing down straw-infested blankets, while the Kanoniers, ever soldiers, tended to their uniforms and the mocked machinery of war. When the coast was clear the girls were helped up the ladder and gone, running across the scrub and down the hill to the safety of George's sister. There they would change and wash and put on their working clothes which George had left there the night before and catch a bus for town. Their part was over until the next time.

'But why not ship the goods through the harbour?' Ned asked him. George was eager to take him into his confidence.

'Too risky, Mr Luscombe. Crates have a nasty habit of busting open and besides, they're always having spot checks down there. But once you've got past, no one gives them a second glance.' His eyes glittered.

George came for the crates the same day. They were safe standing alongside the other requirements of his work. He'd load them on his van and take them back to the yard. Saturday morning, alone, George would break them open. By the day's close the goods would be safely stored in the bank vault under Smith Street.

It was a sweet, uncomplicated arrangement, a simple matter of barter, no different from the exchanges offered in the evening press. Everyone got paid in kind; the girls in parties and stockings and parcels of food; the Kanoniers in girls. The boat crew got a flat fee. Monty Freeman had been doubly fortunate, lured in by exhausting after-hours intercourse in the sanctity of his locked office, and later, as the business flourished, cash too. 'He's a dirty little bugger,' Elspeth said, forgetting the bank manager's height, 'insisted on wearing those rubber counting tips we use on his fingers, you know, to touch me privates with them,' but she kept him sweet nevertheless, for Monty had been important. Monty gave them the perfect hiding place. Monty watched his bank account swell. Monty sat Elspeth in his swivel chair, wriggled his fingers and cursed his spineless luck.

That last Thursday they'd had what was going to be the final shipment for a month. Schade was due to go on leave – to Cherbourg to drum up more business. The shipment was a special one. Something they had been waiting for for a long time. There was a coyness to George's voice now, an almost childish quality.

'Special?' Ned asked. 'How do you mean, special?'

George looked embarrassed. He looked back to his daughter, who shrugged her shoulders. 'Custard,' he said.

Ned laughed.

'I know it sounds foolish, Mr Luscombe, but that's what it was. One hundred and fifty tins of Bird's powdered custard, left behind by the British Army. A hundred and fifty tins!'

'What's so special about custard?' the Major asked.

'Three years ago,' George explained, 'a tin of custard would cost you one and tuppence. Now we can get four pounds a tin. Four pounds! There's any number of families prepared to pay that kind of money, no questions asked. Important families, pillars of the community. Think of it! One hundred and fifty tins at four pounds a tin, that's . . .'

'Six hundred pounds,' said Ned quietly.

'Six hundred pounds! And all for a couple of hours' work! Why, a fighter pilot only gets three hundred and fifty for the whole blinking year.'

It had come in on a flat sea and a rolling mist, the Kanoniers carrying it up the dripping path, while Elspeth and Schade made their goodbyes. It had been a long, boisterous evening, what with Schade going and the place in mothballs, too long and too boisterous, Elspeth had told him. Look, the boys could hardly carry it up the slope they were that drunk. They were getting out of hand, reckless. They didn't seem to understand the need for caution any more. She was glad that this was going to be the last one for a while. It gave them all time to calm down, gave him time to put them straight. Schade had asked if he might come and see her before he left for the mainland, but she had said better not. It was clever, the way she'd kept the two halves apart. She didn't want anyone to see her cosying up to a uniform.

George had collected the crate midmorning. There was no need to take it to the bank. He had customers signed up for practically every single tin. He stacked the crate up with the others behind the main gate, ready for Saturday. Saturday was not about sorting van Dielen's weekly deliveries as he had claimed. He could do that Monday morning, before anyone came. But that Friday evening the foreigns broke in, turned the yard upside down. Crates half opened, shed broken into. Tommy le Coeur had found the fence smashed in around midnight. Saturday morning George appeared. He thought the custard had gone but he couldn't be sure. There was too much mess about. He couldn't look for it, not with the police stepping all over the place, asking daft questions, and certainly not later, when unexpectedly van Dielen turned up with his daughter, wringing his hands over the new roster. Major Ernst had shot the old timetable to pieces. George couldn't understand it. Suddenly it was all hands to the tunnels and the fortifications up at L'Ancresse Bay. Didn't make any sense to him.

'Do not worry about the tunnels,' Ned insisted. 'Tell us about the yard. Tell us about Isobel.'

'Nothing to tell. She mooched about the yard while we were inside going through the orders.'

'I thought you told me she waited across the road.'

'She did for a time, then she got bored. Climbed up on the crates to get a bird's-eye view of the harbour.'

'So she might have found the tins in one of the crates. She could have taken one.'

'It wasn't there by then, I'm sure of it. They'd gone. Taken by the foreigns.'

'Or someone who knew they would be there.'

'No one knew, 'cept Mr Freeman and Elspeth. Schade, of course. I couldn't do nothing that day.'

'And on the Sunday?'

'I get there early and blow me if he isn't there already. And then of course, when I hear about Miss Isobel, where she was found, like, I daren't do nothing. Elspeth tries to get hold of Schade but he's nowhere to be seen. Buggered off to the Continent. Monday morning when things are back to normal . . .'

'I see you breaking open crates.'

'That's right. Well, they'd gone by then, that's for sure. So I straightens the yard as best I can . . .'

'And in the following days scour the island for any sign of them.'

George nodded. 'I was hoping if it were foreigns that maybe they'd dumped them, not knowing what to do with them, not realizing their real value. I mean, how many of those foreigns know what custard is?'

'There's another way to look at it, George. That you saw her through the window that afternoon, saw her discover the crate. You had to silence her before she reported you to the police.' Ned didn't believe it, but he said it all the same.

'I never, Mr Luscombe. I wouldn't do that. And if I had I wouldn't shove her down that bunker, now would I? Not bring attention to myself.'

'What was she wearing, that afternoon when she came round with her father?'

'Wearing. I don't know, really I don't. Trousers, I think.'

'Jodhpurs and a filthy old jacket,' Elspeth butted in. 'Ponged to high heaven. I wouldn't be seen dead in something like that.'

Ned leant forward. 'You were at the yard too?'

Elspeth looked at her father. 'At the house. She was with her dad. "Oh, hello, Elspeth," she says, all sweet and smiling, "you're looking well. Do you ever hear about that baby boy of yours?"

looking down her nose as if she's only ever opened her legs to catch an apple.' She looked Ned squarely in the face. 'I told her where Dad was and went and had a lie down.'

'Proper shagged out she were,' George added helpfully.

★

They searched George's house. Monty's too. More food, more tobacco, a little extra cash. They took Mrs Poidevin in. She was mainly worried about her cat. Ned had taken it round to the whores next door. They seemed to like the idea. Mrs Freeman didn't have a cat. Ned didn't like to tell her, but he thought it very likely that before the year was out she wouldn't have a husband either. At the end of the day the three inquisitors sat in Ned's office, exhausted. Captain Zepernick brought a bottle of wine from the club, and sat on the edge of Ned's desk, struggling with the cork. Ned was afraid the table was going to collapse before he managed it.

'So, it was smuggling,' the Captain said, finally raising his glass in a toast. 'The eternal black market.'

'It is one of the worst crimes,' Lentsch countered. 'It upsets the island's balance.'

'Very serious.' Zepernick was smiling. 'We have a new game now. Hunt the Custard!'

'It is not a joke, Captain.'

'No, no, of course it is not a joke. But it is not a tragedy either. It is not something that puts the island's security in danger.'

Ned couldn't resist putting his pennyworth in. 'No? A bunch of local girls have punched a bloody great hole in it just by taking off their clothes!'

'Yes, but for stockings only!' He began to laugh. 'It was a conspiracy of greed, not of insurrection. So –' he tipped up his glass – 'I must go. I have another appointment.'

Ned and the Major waited while the Captain clattered down the stairs. They heard the burst of his engine as it sprang off down the road.

'Your Captain's a character and no mistake,' Ned told the Major.

'I'd have thought he'd be spitting blood by now, seeing the mess they've made for him.'

'That is the Captain's way, Inspector. He is like an animal – only one dimension – this is good, this is bad, I eat now, I fornicate now, I kill now. He has no real sense of time, of history. If he never saw me again he would not mind. He would forget me. And yet one day, if I came back, he would greet me like his greatest friend. And for Molly, poor Molly who thinks she has the measure of him, it will be the same.' He paused. 'I have reports to write now, I think. Are we nearing the end to it, then?'

'You mean Isobel? I don't know. Do you think she could have become involved in the black market?'

'Not possible.'

'Think about it. Thumbing her nose at us islanders by going out with you, getting one over on you by dabbling in the black market. The best of both worlds. Can't you see her doing it? Not for the money. For the fun of it.'

'No.'

'She could have met up with Schade while you were away. He was quite a charmer, by all accounts.'

'No. I am sure she would not. Schade was not of her . . .'

'Don't be afraid to say it, Major. Not her class? Neither was I. That's why she liked me.'

'She had other reasons for that, I am sure. But even if she was involved in some way, or had found out, what George Poidevin said is true. The last thing any of them would do would be to tip her body in the very heart of the operations.'

She couldn't tell Lentsch. She couldn't tell Lentsch. She had written to him 'cause she could not tell Lentsch. Who would it harm. Her father? Her aunt? Who? Ned retraced his footsteps, trying to put the Major in the same frame of mind without rousing his suspicions.

'Let's get back to your telephone call that Saturday. The one you made to her that afternoon. You said she was nervous, yes? You thought it was because of the party.'

'Yes. I was not supposed to know of it. I asked if I could see her that night and she said no. She found it difficult to keep a secret.'

'But Isobel had no difficulty in keeping secrets! She did it all the time with me, her aunt, her father, she loved it! She'd have been in her element leading you up the garden path for an hour or two.'

'Garden path?'

'Fooling you, Major. Pulling the wool over your eyes. That wouldn't have made her nervous. She would have enjoyed it. No, there was something else worrying her by then. She went to bed on Friday in high spirits. Early Saturday morning she hives it down here to collect the fancy dress she wants to wear. She goes back home. Mrs Hallivand summons her for coffee. Afterwards she goes up to the Villa to check the arrangements. She leaves, has lunch, and goes to the yard with her father. By the time she gets back and takes your call, something has upset her.' He paused. 'Are you coming tonight?'

'If I may.'

'Oh, you may. Mum wouldn't mind if I stopped out, but just you try doing it.'

*

He stopped off at the Britannia for an hour before going home. Albert wasn't to be seen, but at the back Tommy le Coeur sat in a corner seat with his arm round a couple of girls. The table was full of empty glasses. At least he wasn't in uniform this time.

'Inspector! Have a drink!'

Tommy lurched to his feet and propelled Ned to the bar. 'What's it to be? Beer, whisky? You like a spot of brandy, I believe.'

'They're not allowed to sell spirits, Tommy, you know that.' Ned drew him aside. 'Bloody hell, Tommy! Two at the same time, that's going a bit even for you. Don't they have any say in the matter?'

'As long as I'm paying they're happy. Anyway, young Peter's dropping in soon. It's about time someone wet his whistle. I reckon the big one just might do the job.'

'Yes, well, just you make sure he doesn't do anything foolish. He's got enough family to support as it is.' He looked the girls over. He only hoped they were over age. 'I'm sorry about Elspeth, Tommy. There's nothing I could do, you know.'

'I know. I hadn't seen her much, after we parted company.'

'Yes, what was all that about? You seemed quite suited.'

'She cheated on me, Inspector. Walked out with someone else.'

Ned nearly choked on his beer. 'Cheated on you!'

'Made me look a fool. I don't mind playing the fool, but I'm damned if I'm going to look like one.' He finished his drink in one thick gulp. 'Better get back.' He waved again. 'That's right, darling, you sit on it while you can. I'll have split you in half before the night's out.'

By the time Ned got back home, his mother had heard the news. She banged the plates down on the table.

'He's not with you, then?'

'He'll be here later. We've been busy.'

'So I hear.' She started to set down the cutlery. When the Major had first come, she used to hand it to them, blade first. 'George won't last, not in those camps they have over there,' she told him. 'Mr Freeman neither. Elspeth might . . .'

'Elspeth will bed down with the first guard she sees. Probably end up marrying the prison governor.'

'It's a death sentence you've given the others.'

'I haven't given them anything, Mother. They broke the law.'

'It could have been me,' she said.

'I don't think you would have done what Elspeth did.'

'Not if I had young children to feed? Don't you be so certain. I know of many mothers who take in their washing for some extra bread. I know a couple who take in a good deal more as well just so they can put some food in their children's stomachs. It shouldn't be a crime to sell food, to sell ordinary folk butter and sugar.'

'At her prices?'

'I'd pay them if we had the money! I would!'

She started to smash her fists on the table, the plates jumping, knives and forks clattering to the floor. 'I'd sell my soul for a pound of butter,' she cried. 'Proper butter! A pound of butter that I could spread good and thick. My soul, my heart, anything! Anything! Just a pound of butter! Anything!'

Ned made a cup of tea and took her upstairs. She sat in bed, holding it in both hands.

'Don't spill it, for God's sake,' he said. 'There's half our sugar ration in that cup.' He saw her grip tighten. 'Don't worry. I'll get us some more.'

As he walked down the stairs he heard the tap on the door. The Major stood in the doorway, a bunch of flowers and a small parcel in his hand.

'Ah, Major.' He spoke loudly. He'd drunk a bit more than he meant to at the pub. Seeing Tommy so carefree with those girls had made him thirsty. 'I was just about to have another beer.'

The Major stepped in and looked around. Usually he could hear movement in the kitchen. Usually she came in, wiping her hands on a towel in preparation for their handshake. The silence disturbed him.

'Your mother is not here tonight?' he enquired.

'She's gone to bed.'

'She is not well?' The concern in the Major's voice surprised him.

'She's tired, that's all.' Ned took the flowers and looked around for somewhere to put them. 'I'll take these up to her in a minute. They'll cheer her up.'

'I brought something else too. I should not have.' He pulled on the string, proudly lifting the tin from its brown paper wrapping. 'Cocoa. The Captain took it from the bank vaults. So I took it from the Captain.'

'As long as he doesn't blame Albert.'

'No, no. I left him a little note. He knows who the culprit is. He is in a strange mood, the Captain. When I returned he was singing in the bath at the top of his voice, delirious with joy.' He looked upstairs. 'Would your mother mind if I gave this to her myself?'

'Go ahead.'

He could hear the murmur of soft voices, and his mother's sudden note of exclamation. The Major came down with the empty cup in her hand.

'She wants to sleep.'

Ned took the cup and ran it under the tap. He waved his hand over the table. 'She hasn't cooked us anything.'

'It is of no consequence. I am not hungry.'

They walked out into the garden. The Major took out his cigarette case and handed it over.

'I always seem to be doing this,' said Ned, helping himself.

'Take them all!'

Ned closed the lid and handed it back. 'One at a time, Major. It makes me feel better this way.'

The two men laughed and walked to the bottom of the garden. The Major put his hand on the gate and blew the smoke into the clear air.

'Fantastic, he said, looking up. 'On such a night one wants to pretend for a moment that one is free, that the world is still and at peace.'

'I used to go canoeing on nights like this,' Ned confessed, 'take my girlfriend, sleep out on one of the outlying islands.' He caught the Major's questioning look. 'No, never Isobel. We just went swimming. She was afraid of the water after her mother died. I helped her get over it. That's how we . . .'

'And I taught her how to dive. She could not do that before, I think.'

'No. With me she'd jump in, both feet.'

'Holding her nose, yes?'

'That's right.'

The two men bowed to their private thoughts, then sensing each other, looked to the sky again, waiting for the conversation to take a new direction.

'Do you have the canoe still?' the Major asked. He felt Ned's hesitation. 'No, no. Do not answer me. I do not want to know.'

'You know already, Major.'

'Of course.' He dropped the cigarette end and crushed it with his foot. 'You must be clever at hiding things. I thought we had searched all your houses.'

Ned walked over and pulled it out from the back of the pigsty. He laid it out on the ground and unfolded the two lengths. The Major walked around it.

'It is quite large.'

'That's the beauty of it. Folded up it takes up hardly any space at all.'

'No wonder we missed it.'

'There was a pig here then. That helped.'

'You ate him?'

'No, you did.' The Major started to protest. 'Soldiers,' Ned explained.

Lentsch bent down and brushed the straw and dirt from the skin.

'Why don't we try now?'

'What?'

'Now. Let us row across the water.'

'We couldn't.'

'Yes, we could. You said yourself, this is a night for sailing. I want to go, Ned. For me the island has lost her beauty. Perhaps seeing it like this will restore it for me. I would like to think of the island as beautiful again.'

Ned grunted in acknowledgement.

'What if we get caught?'

'If we are stopped I shall say I was testing the efficiency of our patrols. They would understand that. Will we be caught?'

'Probably not. If we strike out past the promontory a good distance we should be all right. There's no moon to speak of and

263

we'd be very low on the water. Patrol boats would be our main worry, but we'd hear them quite some way off.'

Lentsch gripped his arm. 'Come on, then!' he exhorted. 'Put our differences aside. Circumnavigate the island, true explorers of the night.'

They hoisted it up on their shoulders and carried it out onto the road. The Major started to trot down the narrow lane. He was eager, like a child, willing danger to emerge. He is crazy, Ned thought, and I am mad to be a part of it. When they reached the beach and the long road that ran alongside it, they jumped down, resting against the old sea wall along the length of the bay. The Major started to giggle.

'If the Captain could see me now,' he said. 'A canoe! All these sentries and watchtowers defeated by a canoe!'

Half bent, they moved along in the shadow of the wall, before setting the craft down where the bay jutted out in a cluster of spilt rock. They waded out slowly, the craft bobbing under their hands, the water cold, the sand untrustworthy. Half a mile away on the opposite side they could see the dim outline of an observation post. To the west, across the sea, the sky hung low. There was nothing to see but the vast and empty dark, no sound except the lap of the waves and the long lonely wind. Ned held the craft steady while the Major clambered in, then pushed. As he fought to keep his balance he thought he was going to tip them both in the water, but then he was in, his legs tucked under the prow. He took up the paddle and sent them spinning out over the water.

'This is marvellous,' Lentsch called, holding his paddle out like a tightrope walker.

'Shh.' Ned whispered. 'Voices carry, you know. Just do like me and hope the moon doesn't show.'

It was a rolling world that Ned seemed to lead him into, and as they moved over its looming surface Lentsch felt as if they were sailing over a sleeping giant, feeling the motion of breathing deep and slow. It was a quiet world, despite the great whistling dark, without limit, without feeling, a world where there was only the choice of existence or oblivion; nothing in between. Isobel was here, riding in the stinging spray blowing in his face, and in the murky inlets that fled by, he could see the hidden marshes of his youth, murmuring with the fluttered ruffling of disturbed birds. Here, past the swept bays and scattered rocks, was a world washed free of men, a world immune to their cries; no reason here, no love or enmity; no emotion at all, except the wondrous surge of being. Was he cold, was he soaked to the bone? He did not know. He was not the Major, he was not Isobel's lover, for there were no lovers or majors on this water. Even the man in front of him, who was he? An unknown! What connection did he have with him? None! Here, no one had any connection with any one or any thing. And it came to him that he did not want to exist in any other state than this: that to ride under the stars would be enough, to ride and feel the great indifferent power of the world carry you where it would, with it having no thought to you and with you having no thought to it.

He plunged his paddle in and felt the great suck of the water hold him fast as the paddle sank and stuck like a spoon drawn through syrup. He fought to raise it. Ned looked back.

'Nice and easy, Major, that's all she needs.'

'Sorry.'

He worked the paddle lightly, trying to imitate the shadow of the man in front of him, feeling the canoe veer left and then right, left and then right, beginning to judge the depth of the blade and the swing of his arm. He was gliding forward now, gliding forward, feeling the strength of himself and his seat hard on the slatted floor, conscious of the slow welling below him and the thin, untested membrane that kept him suspended from the dreadful deep. It was black now, very black and he began to feel alone, a little afraid. Lentsch wasn't even sure whether he could see the island at all. Surely there had been a jut of rock over there? And where was the long curve he had seen and the watchtower rising above?

Ned laid his paddle across his knees.

'We can rest up a bit,' he said.

The Major span round in his seat, panicking.

'Which way are we facing?' he asked.

Ned lifted his paddle to the stars.

'North. Towards England.'

'Are we moving at all?'

'Faster than you think.'

'I feel lost.'

'You're not lost.'

'Have you ever been out like this before?'

'Since you arrived? Only once. I nearly didn't come back. Kept on rowing. But I couldn't.'

'Your mother?'

'Not just her. It was like the whole of Guernsey wouldn't let me go, every lump of rock dragging me back. I wanted to go. I could feel the current almost willing me. It would have only taken me six or seven hours. I got so far out and then stopped. I couldn't go any further. Every time I raised the paddle it was like there was this great magnet dragging me back.'

Lentsch shivered.

'It is like a frozen landscape, I think, the sea at night. There seems no end to it. If we died here, by some misfortune, though I might feel alone, I would not feel abandoned. It would be part of my destiny, to die here. But many men I know have died in seas much more terrible than this, seas of ice and frozen mud. They were not only alone. They were betrayed. Ah, Ned, the stories I have been told.'

There had been many ways to die in Fortress Stalingrad. The road to the airport had been only ten feet across at the beginning – a five-mile stretch from the circular railways to the last airfield and escape. By the end it was over one hundred feet wide, pressed thick and deep with the frozen bodies of fallen men. By day they had shuffled and crawled along, the bleeding and dying, hoping to climb their way onto one of the lone crazy Junkers that skidded in and out of their icy trap, but at night, when the planes had stopped and the road was jammed with broken trucks and smashed guns and the wrecks of planes that had not made it, they lay down and were covered by the ceaseless fall of snow. The following morning a fresh column would begin anew, walking on the far side of the newly dead, while trucks reared and slithered over those newly frozen forms, splintering their bones like glass. There was no need to feel guilt, these desperate men, seeing their comrades pressed into such ignoble service. They would be lying alongside them soon enough. And so the track ever widened. Fourteen thousand alone had died on that road. And then the airport was overrun, and they retreated into an even more desolate landscape of burnt-out villages and wrecked cellars, falling back room by room, house by house, street by street, compressed ever tighter. From the air it appeared as if a giant furnace was at work, liquid metal arcing in molten shapes of chemistry, steel shafts stabbing at the burning earth, a man-made volcano for the modern age, but inside there was only the cold and the biting wind and the limitless white of the snow. Now there was no escape, except through death and that would not be easy, He had made sure of that. Lentsch had heard of whole companies of men lying atop ice-filled trenches, too frozen to move as the tanks rolled slowly over them, their blood and organs squirting out like freshly popped fruit; of packs of dogs ignoring the stiffening corpses and seeking out only the living, to nuzzle hungrily into their open wounds. There was no war now, just ways to die: death by gangrene, death by spotted fever, death by starvation, death for the common soldier, death for the conscript, death for the general, death which left unsatisfied, sullen and without pity, to attend to the next broken soul.

Lentsch looked out across the dark rolling water. The clouds had lifted and the island lay anchored under the barrage of stars. He could see the watchtowers, two of them, rising out of the gloom and he knew that inside them, talking, smoking, watching, were men who could not see him at all. They could see nothing! They were facing the wrong way! They had built concrete walls and watchtowers and gun emplacements but they could see nothing! They had not captured this island or made it safe. Guernsey was not an impregnable fortress! The island was strong, alive, waiting for its time. It soaked up strength from the sea like a sponge; it took its breath from the air, like a great forest might. It was not an island. It was part of the world! It was part of the world, the world that gave life and death and grew warm under the sun. One day the concrete would be covered, its lines blurred, its grey white smeared with rust and speckled with green, transformed not simply by man's neglect (though that would come) but by nature's immutable force. One day men would clamber over these curiosities, as they did the tombs of Egypt or the Great Wall of China, except here they would not marvel at their primitive expertise, rather wonder how men, at such a late time in history, could deceive themselves so fully. Deceived and betrayed. And was he part of them? Had he deceived and betrayed? Had he truly loved Isobel, or simply taken advantage of his position and her father's hasty acquiescence? Was this really love he had felt for her, or was it the other thing, an older man flattered at a young girl's interest? A uniform. A manner. A holiday romance.

'We should not be here, you know,' he said.

'You've picked a fine time to tell me, Major.'

'Not here. I meant in Guernsey. We should not be here.'

'There's nothing you or I can do about that.'

'No.' He dipped his paddle in the water, and turned the canoe round. 'Let us go home, Ned. I have seen enough.'

Eleven

Veronica closed the door to her consulting room (which is what now she calls her single room, thanks to an article she read in an old copy of *The Lady*) and proceeded down the narrow and dingy staircase, nodding to Mr Underwood who stood, as he always stood, behind the glass front door which bore his funereal name, a tribute to a success and longevity which Veronica herself would like to emulate, just as she wished that Mr Underwood, so particular concerning the appearance of his own premises, would do something about the peeling paint flaking off the stairwell walls, put a bit of carpet down perhaps, but that afternoon, as she adjusted her flamboyant blue felt hat festooned with bunches of different coloured grapes, she had no time for more than a passing pleasantry which she mouthed and which he pretended not to notice, pulling his blind down firmly as she repeated the phrase. 'Turned out nicely,' she said as she pulled at her skirt through the thick cloth of her second-hand overcoat, thinking it was true. She was turned out nicely and as a matter of fact it was beginning to turn out very nicely altogether.

Zepernick was waiting in the car. She had sat in her waiting room on the bare chair staring out of the window, looking down on the shoppers for an hour, fearing the Captain might not come, and when she had seen the car park ostentatiously up on the pavement and had breathed an audible sigh of relief it had come to her that whatever happened to her now she could never join her fellow islanders ever again. It wasn't so much that she had chosen sides. It was more to do with the fact that she had widened her horizons. It was what she had been looking for all along. It could have been with Gerald. It might have been with Ned. But it had happened finally with Captain Zepernick, Zeppy as he encouraged her to call him, hastened by the need to deal with the complexity of the world, to embrace its fearful multiplicity, to step into the unknown. All those shoppers below wanted to do was to return to the world as it had been. She did not. That was what she had been trying to escape from, and with a bit of peaked cap fortune, she had broken through.

He had been calling for her these past three weeks now, like Tommy le Coeur used to, only the Captain had better taste. At first he had simply taken her for a drive, with a hamper bouncing on the back seat. It was a simple transaction. The Captain would wait patiently while she ate her fill, but the moment she wiped her mouth and threw the napkin aside he was on top of her. It was as if someone had blown him a whistle. She had toyed with the idea of taking her time, to see how long it would take for signs of his suppressed impatience to surface, but the truth was that she found it impossible to drink champagne slowly and the food, real bread, real cheese, real ham, had proved equally irresistible, though she had made certain that there was enough left over for when she got home. It was a good job the Captain didn't know for why. It was against the law to fraternize with the foreigns, and though Zep was all for flouting the law himself, he took a different view of those who broke it without his permission. Those men for instance that he'd found smuggling, he'd had them crying like children, he had boasted, shoving photographs of their sweethearts in their broken faces, telling them to take a good look, they'd not be seeing them again. Nothing like these for them any more, he had chuckled, unplucking her buttons. Not for a long time. Such pleasure in other's discomfort, she had discovered, provoked his stamina.

The Captain greeted her with an unsettling and businesslike smile before gunning the car up the hill. As she hung on to the strap she began to worry that he might be starting to lose interest, for despite her undoubted willingness and the regular availability of her charms, however hard she responded to his insistent and methodical embrace, it was difficult for her to emulate the same nervous excitement that had coursed through her body that first time in the shed. Even if she could have arranged for the boy to be hiding nearby every time it wouldn't be the same. The element of terror would be absent, and terror, though the Captain did not fully appreciate this himself, was a quality which stimulated all his senses. The boy was now as regular in his appearances as was the Captain, slipping in round the back door at around eleven o'clock, making sure he did not bump into Ned's new visitor again. The meal would be waiting for him on the starched chequered tablecloth; a glass of milk and whatever food she had managed to cobble together. If she had time she would try and pick a few flowers and place them in the centre, in an old-fashioned drinking glass, thick, with bubbles caught up its sides. To begin with he used to push this decoration aside and stolidly chew, but he had come to expect them now, settling his nose into their haphazard midst before eating, lifting out a single stem, stroking his cheek with the tapering petals once his plate was empty. For the first time in her life she had begun to enjoy cooking. Before she went to bed she would take Da's paper and cut out that evening's recipe or cooking hint – vegetable rissoles, Guernsey Gâche, frying-pan scones. She had quite a number of them now, tucked in the back of her appointment book, and when she wasn't leafing through it, or sat by the window looking out across Lower Pollet and the eternal barber's queue, wondering what the Captain might be doing and if he intended to see Molly that night, she would deal out the scraps of newspaper like a deck of cards, thinking about the 'white waif' as Da called him and the slow, reluctant manner in which he ate, as if the food's texture and taste were of such an incomprehensible nature that he needed to savour each mouthful in order to come to some elementary under-standing of its configuration. 'Pity we had to be starving before you bothered to learn how to cook,' her da had grumbled, but it was said with paternal admiration rather than displeasure, in recognition of the feminine and thus devious manner of her undoubted duplic-ity. Once home from her time with the Captain she would take out his leftovers, lay them on the table, add to them, reshape them, and have them waiting for this pale and wild creature who in turn stuffed the remnants (and like she, he always ensured that there were remnants, conscience overcoming desire) into those deep and curiously preserved pockets before bounding out into the night and the misunderstood dimensions of his billet.

They had managed to converse by now, the boy and she, though neither understood the other's language. Gestures, mimes, single words, pictures drawn upon a sheet of paper, these were their means. She would watch him as he described his church burning, his journey to Wuppertal in the freezing cattle wagons, the shape of which he had drawn on the steamed kitchen window, the temperature of which he had indicated by the rubbing of his arms. She had hunched her shoulders as he described the building of the great tunnel, its doomed height, its vanishing length, its impenetrable darkness; the carts he had to push, the pickaxe he must wield, the ache to be found in his limbs and then, cringing in expectation, she would watch as he put his fingers in his ears and threw himself backwards, mimicking the explosions, the disfigurement, the death that came rushing out of its mouth. He drew crude crayon sketches of his living quarters too, the number of his shed, the number of bunks to be found stacked inside, the length of wood on which each man was required to lie, and she, comprehending the confinement but not the squalor, had added in her mind's eye a mattress, a blanket, even a pillow to that bare picture, for it was not within her remit to envisage a place to sleep without such comforts. They taught each other words, 'bread', 'milk', 'mother', 'father'. 'Mother?' she had asked and he had drawn the church again and the fire raging without. 'Father?' she had questioned and he had pointed his arm down and had shot at the floor. She had feared to ask any other familial questions. Despite this setback they found their language entertaining as well as informative. She had begun to make him laugh. The other day she had been miming her occupation, wielding a kitchen pair of scissors, cutting imaginary toenails, holding her nose in imaginary disgust, and he had opened his mouth and laughed, not merely smiled but laughed out loud, his lips drawn back over his brown and broken teeth, his gums bleeding still from the cuts of bread crust and baked-potato skin, laughing not solely at her acting ability but at the very impossibility of her profession. It had gathered momentum, enveloping his throat and concave chest, invading his sunken belly, seizing his whole body in a lung-bursting lock. Soon he was doubled up, unable to stop, stamping his feet on the floor, banging his ribcage, clouds of cement puffing from his half-bent body, like dust rising from a worn-out carpet beaten on a line. He was swallowing laughter as a parched desert refugee might gulp down fresh water, choking on the very thing that, taken in moderation, might restore his dehydrated life. And yet it was not laughter as she knew it. It wasn't true what someone once said, that laughter is the same the whole world over. This had sounded different, more guttural, more animal: *foreign*: not hugely dissimilar to the Captain's, though his was clipped by the order of his profession and the arrogance of his age. She had picked the boy up by the hinge of his stomach and sat him on her knee on the armchair by the stove. He had quietened in calming gasps, resting his head on the same breast that the Captain had so eagerly uncovered hours before, his spittle-flecked lips wetting the patterned cloth in the same aureoled spot which the Captain's lips had marked, his hand resting underneath the swell where the Captain's hand had rested. But unlike the Captain he lay quiet, touching not her body but the humanity within it, and she had placed the palm of her hand on his white encrusted head and with her breast flowering to the wet warmth, felt herself swoon with the sudden bloom of love and loss. So she went from laughter to laughter, from secret life to secret life, from the Captain's athletic and addictive attentions in the late afternoon to the boy's eloquent and exiled embrace in the late evening, two lives buried in her folds, both there by reason of capricious war, both nurturing her own needs. And thus practised in deception and dependence she began to want for armour.

The Captain drove in silence, past the cinema with its German film, up the hill with its German signs, the iron railings of the great school flicking past, the building gaunt and empty, save for a few workmen with ladders outside. She remembered when they had marched en bloc, masters and boys, to the quay and embarkation to England and the mad chaos of those evacuation days, scenes of indecision and panic, farms abandoned, houses with their keys left hanging in the back door, cattle unmilked, roaring with pain, meals left half eaten, fathers burying the few valuables in the back garden or leading their pets to the vets (four thousand cats and dogs had been destroyed in those few days, pausing only for the lorries to take the carcasses away), radios playing to vacated rooms, a sheet left halfway through a mangle, children's scooters lying in the street; whole streets without a sign of life, as if a plague of Pied Pipers had descended and danced a whole population away. She remembered going down to the harbour that last morning, when the last ship was due to sail, working her away amongst the bad-tempered queues jostling for their money from the bank and insurance offices, emerging customers waving their twenty-pound limit in disgust, threading her way to a quayside littered with empty carts, nervous horses snorting in their harness, men trying to sell their cars for a couple of extra pounds (she had nearly bought one herself, two pounds he had been asking and she had the money in her purse, but in the interim, thinking foolishly what would her father say and where would she keep it and how could she afford to run it, someone had taken advantage of her hesitation and closed the deal for two pounds and ten shillings), a fight over an abandoned motorbike. She had sat on a coil of tarred rope and watched the pushing of backs and the spilling of luggage and the agitated cries of the wheeling gulls, and through it heard, as they all had heard, that pattering chattering sound as the children came down the road, skipping and scuffling and plodding forward with songs or sobs in their throat, two abreast, dressed in jerseys and raincoats, shorts and skirts, clutching brown-paper parcels and teddy bears, their mums and dads close by, those going with their children marching quietly behind, carrying what belongings they had managed to snatch in pillowcases and feed sacks, and those not, running alongside, calling, cajoling, darting in for a farewell kiss, pulling them out to tie a shoelace or plonk a woollen cap upon an unruly head. They had held their breath then, all of them, as they looked into this grey muffled crocodile and realized it was true. The island was losing its soul, and at that the activity resumed, more frantic, to leave this place and place one's faith on England's foreign shore. Da had wanted her to go with Kitty Luscombe, but she couldn't, not with Mum the way she was. She'd helped Kitty patch up her clothes the night before, her father fussing over her as if she were a schoolgirl still, making her check and double check whether she'd got Mrs H.'s letter safe, if her embarkation paper was in order, counting and recounting the little sum of money he'd managed to put aside. She'd seen the two of them by the gangway that day, but hadn't intruded, Albert patting Kitty on the back, then swiftly kissing the back of her hand, pressing it to his lips and then his heart before he handed her the small case and walked away. What was Kitty doing now at this very minute? she wondered. Not riding around in a two-seater convertible about to have sex with a German officer, that's for sure, though perhaps she might be having sex with someone. War and danger did that to a body, even to someone as level-headed as Albert Luscombe's daughter. It tingled the nerves, made you feel reckless inside.

The Captain changed gear and raced along Grange Road and the great houses of authority that hid behind the evergreen hedges and wrought-iron gates, then turned left down Queen's Road, sounding his horn at a weary troop of shuffling infantrymen who stood back against the stone wall as they flashed past, the Captain acknowledging their courtesy, Veronica staring ahead, pretending that she was invisible to their whistling barrack-room taunts. At the crossroads he plunged over, hardly bothering to look left or right, taking the dog-leg of Prince Albert's Road with wheels squealing. Once through the bend he pushed back the hem of her dress high over her bare knee, accelerating into the straight. She closed her eyes. She knew where they were going. It was not the quickest way, but it allowed him speed. It fed his batteries, and if there was one thing the Captain liked, it was to be fully charged up. At the end of the road he swung the car quickly to the right. She leant into him hard and stayed pressed up against him, and they turned once more, into the steep narrow street, where halfway down he parked the car in a overgrown siding off Val Fleury Close, safe from prying eyes. She unbuttoned the flap to his pocket and eased in her hand. The key lay at the bottom, long and cold. She took it out and held it up to the light. It surprised her. It was shiny and new.

'What happened to the old one?' she asked.

The Captain took it from her, smiling, and put it back in his pocket, patting its shape through the flap. He said nothing.

The car rides and cold-weather picnics had lasted a week. Then, the following Monday when she had plumped down beside him, removed her hat, straightened her dress and asked, 'Where to today?' Zep had turned the key, revved the engine and had announced, 'A surprise.' He had driven around for ten minutes, then, turning down Hauteville, had parked by Victor Hugo's house with its scrolled plaque set inside the wall.

'I thought I would give you a guided tour of the premises. You have never been?'

She had never been. What on earth would she want to go in there for?

'I'm not a great one for visiting museums.'

'No matter. It is not what we came for.'

'Came for?' she asked, though she knew well enough, had known it with sinking heart the moment he had uttered those words, and though it came as no great shock, what it was he expected from her, what he would always expect, there was a brief flicker of hope, when he leaped out and walked round to open the passenger door, bowing in that exaggerated manner, a greenhouse orchid produced from behind his back, that he had planned a small surprise for her, something intimate, unusual, which indeed he but only as to the placing of the old, familiar event. 'From the had,

Major's desk,' he smirked once they were standing in the dark and peculiarly quiet hall, waving the key triumphantly in the dusty air as if the Major were a schoolmaster and he the prankish boy.

'What are we doing here?' she whispered, blushing at her own unconvincing naivety, and the Captain, laughing, pulled her to him and running his finger in between the rim of her collar and the damp flesh of her neck, replied, 'There is no need to whisper, Veronica. We can make as much noise as we choose,' and with that started to lead her through the rooms, his hands clasped behind his back, her holding on to them like in some silly party game, the Captain releasing her now and again, like a man might let loose the slip of his dog leash, while she ran her fingers over the surface of some long gilt frame, or traced the design on some silver brocade, marvelling at the heavy shine that made every artefact appear so deep, so endless, before pulling her back en route to their destination. Finally they reached the third floor and a room entombed with dark, somnambulant tapestries, and in the centre, mounted on a pedestal, shrouded like some dormant chrysalis, stood an enormous bed. She'd seen smaller vegetable plots.

'Built for Garibaldi,' he said proudly.

Another name Veronica did not recognize.

'The father of Italy,' he told her, walking her towards it. 'The only man famous for inventing something that has not worked. This bed was made specially for him.'

'Big, was he?' she offered facetiously, nervous now to be enclosed in this heavy darkened house with this restlessly demanding man. 'Or did he move about a lot?'

The Captain refused to laugh.

'He never arrived to use it,' he said, pulling back the cover. On an embroidered pillow lay a bottle of champagne and two glasses. 'No one has ever used it. Until now.'

Veronica had wondered if that was true, wondered whether the Captain had not entertained a host of girls here.

'What, not even Molly?'

The Captain looked surprised.

'Molly? Molly would want to move in, so she could boast about it.'

It was the first time since that time in the surgery that her name had come up. She had been the reason for the clandestine nature of these meetings, at least that was what she told herself. She didn't see much of Molly these days. Molly had pulled out of the amateur dramatics the same time they'd found Isobel stuffed down that shaft, just when they had nearly completed preparations for their spring variety show. Not one but two girls short, Mrs H. had complained! It sounded especially callous coming from her, but it was true. It was going to be something special this time too, the first time she was taking the lead. The Captain coughed and stood waiting. She made one attempt at decency.

'What about Mrs Hallivand? I wouldn't like her to come barging in.'

'She comes only in the mornings,' the Captain promised her. 'No one will see. The afternoons will be ours alone to enjoy.'

And so they had. Starting in that entombed bedroom, within the week they had laid their intermittent claim throughout nearly the whole house, aping the habits of an ill-remembered aristocracy, wandering from room to room arm in arm like some landed couple viewing their priceless heirlooms, drinking champagne out of Venetian cut glass, opening shutters, closing doors, visiting every room save one at the ground level which was permanently locked and no trace of the key to be found, but no matter, there was still the thrill of sex on cordoned chaises longues or wrapped up in fifteenth-century tapestries and best of all naked up in the Eyrie, looking down over the convict island and the captured sea. How quickly the afternoons had become a fixture of their lives, as regular as the island's motorcycle patrols, transforming this dead mausoleum into a palace of their possession, to dispose of as they saw fit, their occupation metamorphosed overnight from a single to a perpetual act, stretching like elastic both back and forward in time, creating its own history, obliterating all precedents. Where routine is concerned, there is no other history; it has always been thus. And it was in these surroundings that she began to learn the nature of the Captain's captivity too, not a declaration of hopeless love (eternal or otherwise would have been welcome), no, he did not deliver that wishful confession, but instead voiced the frustrating limits of his meagre authority, his petty ambition and his fitful jealousy of uniforms other than his own. He did not vouchsafe matters of state, secrets a seductive spy might have elicited from her carefully chosen lover, nor did these revelations occur after their coupling, for after the sex (and he was relentless in that respect, like a machine, once, twice, even three times in rapid succession), like so many men, he was eager to return to the mechanics of his restrictive male life, but rather these revelations occurred beforehand, while they made themselves at home, as he tried to mask his tumescent need by trivial and domestic conversation, a deception embarked upon not in recognition of Veronica's sensibilities, but aired to convince himself that though he required that which she carried within and without her body, it was, as the matters he began to describe, a light, inconsequential thing, of no more consequence than which tie he might choose for an afternoon's petrol-defiant motoring. And so he spoke in idle earnest, hardly bothering to hear her reply, a nod, a squeeze of the hand, a murmur sufficed, as he followed his wandering thoughts as a traveller might follow one of the hidden water lanes, hypnotized by their babbling murmur and aimless direction, not appreciating where they might be leading, and to begin with, to be sure they had led nowhere but those ruthless yet renascent bouts of intercourse, from which she left tired yet triumphant. But as the afternoons passed, and the conversations resumed day after day, as compulsive as some serial in a woman's weekly magazine, he absorbed those sighs and gestures of unspoken understanding and began to recognize a part of him in her, just as while listening she became aware of a part of her within him. And because he knew he must not and could not talk of the island and its military burdens, he guarded against such indiscretions by leading her up the gravel drive to the Villa and all the intrigues

279

that ran within its walls, the various jealousies, the indiscretions, the foolish love affairs, the tempers on the stairs. She has learnt of the Villa's habits and the inequality therein; his own cramped bedroom overlooking the concrete coal sheds, compared to the Major's bow-windowed chamber and its splendid view of the sea. She has learnt of Bohde and his compulsive and unnecessary greed; his obsessive sunbathing on the roof with young men from the Kriegsmarine; the way he comes back from the newspaper office with printer's ink on his hands, leaving the finger marks of his trade on armchairs and balustrades where they can be picked up by the more fastidious lodgers. She has learnt about Molly's relentless determination, the most singular woman he has ever met, the Captain confessed, her rare beauty setting her apart from the rest of her race, but so desperate to become official that she has attached herself to his uniform as if she were its most coveted decoration, to be paraded up and down before the ranks of his peers. To begin with he enjoyed these public exhibitions as much as Molly, delighting as his fellow officers cursed his good fortune, but over the months he has come to realize that these performances incite nothing but envy, particularly amongst his superiors. There are many who would like to strip him of this lush award and pin it to their own libidinous chest, and to his horror he has beginning to understand that there are those here who have the power to engineer it. She has learnt of the Villa's comfort and its claustrophobia, the nights of desultory conversation and depressive drinking, the petty disagreements, the endless quarrels over hot water, the thefts of spoons and cutlery and china figurines which he suspects Albert of carrying out on behalf of Mrs Hallivand, not such an upright woman as everyone supposed, he suggested. Veronica listens to it all with a fluttering heart. This is a sort of treason she is hearing and she loves the sound it makes and the shapes that dance before her. An intake of breath, the way she lifts arm or shifts her body forward, and the Captain feels emboldened, seeing in them signals of later uninhibited opportunities. There is anger in his heart when he talks, anger and jealousy, and he has kept them hidden for too long. Taking them out, displaying a nakedness before her which no one else has seen, he feels the fullness of their desire growing. There is so much to describe; the raging battle between the Major and Bohde, which a month ago the censor would not have dared to fight but now, with the Major holed and Ernst steaming to Bohde's aid, a battle which could well sink him, for all the Major's experience and the seeming greater range of his guns. Ernst's men had already dug up the fruit garden, uprooting the loganberry bushes and raspberry canes one afternoon while the Major was out, burning the bushes, Captain Zepernick told her, astonished still at the naked malignancy of it, burning them in spite of Albert's protestations, thereby further fuelling the Major's towering rage, Ernst standing over the smouldering remains saying calmly, 'We are soldiers, Major Lentsch, not gardeners.' Lentsch had exploded. 'Soldiers! Soldiers! Your men have never been soldiers.' 'I wish you'd told me earlier,' Veronica admonished him, 'you could have given some to me,' and the Captain, putting his finger to her lips, told her that she was missing the point. Of course they could have been given away, of course they could have been saved. They could have been *moved*, for Heaven's sake. The Major could have been consulted. But this had been both a declaration and an act of war, like the blitzkrieg, leaving the enemy reeling, with no cover, nothing to hang on to, sapping his will as well as attacking him without warning. And the choice of location! It was like the fall of France and the little railway carriage in the forest of Compiègne where the armistice of 1918 had been signed, a deliberate humiliation, choosing the very area in the garden where Bohde had been caught, literally red-handed, a year back. This was where they had chosen to strike! 'You sound as if you approve,' Veronica said. 'I do not approve,' the Captain admitted. 'But as a military man I admire their tactics.'

Then of course there had been the question of Isobel, whose morbid and misplaced presence in the Villa was felt at every turn. To Veronica's delight she had discovered that far from appreciating Isobel, her grace and charm, her ability to bring a special lightness to the proceedings, Captain Zepernick thought very differently of her. Scheming had been the first word he used, and Veronica, her eyes wide, tried to look surprised that any woman could ever contemplate such an activity. That first meeting after the panto-mime, for instance, that was no accident; it was stage managed, he had insisted, pleased with his English pun. Isobel had known very well who Major Lentsch was. She had been shadowing him about the town for a good six months before deciding to make her move, getting her aunt to make sure he went along that afternoon so that she could be pointed out. Isobel had left nothing to chance, dressing up in a costume as figure-hugging as the ski outfit at their earlier encounter, even as going so far as repeating the instructions she had given the Major while she advised a fallen Wendy how to fly. 'Keep your knees bent,' she had ad-libbed. 'Glide.' 'How do you know all this?' Veronica asked. 'Molly,' the Captain replied. 'Mrs Hallivand confided it all to Molly at your drama society.' Mrs Hallivand it emerged had disliked Isobel almost as much as the Captain, her one redeeming feature as far as he was concerned, but they differed as to the reason. Whilst Mrs H.'s antagonism had been founded on her anger at Isobel taking the Major away from her – 'She would have liked to have seduced him herself, the old witch,' he said – the Captain's aversion stemmed from the brazen confi-dence of Isobel's class and the pleasures of a type of life which she believed to be her right. 'The Major is no different,' he argued. 'He tries to hide it behind philosophies of humanity and art, but he cannot. He was born with this sense of superiority, the same as she. The same as Mrs Hallivand. It is there for life, like a birthmark on the skin. It can never be eradicated.'

'But I thought you were friends, you and the Major,' she said, surprised in the virulence in his voice.

'Friends!' The Captain laughed and flicked cigarette ash into the air, as if to say, that is what my friendship is worth. 'He has become a danger to us all. None of us know what he will do next. He disappears every evening, no one knows where. Bohde is convinced that he is engaged in some terrible plot.'

'Terrible plot! He's with Ned Luscombe. He lives a couple of doors down from me. I see him come and go from my bedroom window.'

'At the Inspector's house?'

'I just told you. He spends most of his time out in the garden, gazing up at the stars.' Veronica paused. 'He looks lonely, unhappy.'

'The Major does not understand the meaning of this war. He would like to see it finished.'

'Wouldn't we all?' she questioned.

'No. Some of us would like to see it won. For him it is an unfortunate interlude which he hopes will not interfere too much with his comfort. So, he has the best bedroom, the study is for his own private use, though he does nothing in there except write letters home.'

'I thought that was what studies were for.'

The Captain ignored her. 'He always takes the first helpings of food, the first hot water for the bath, the first to have his tunic pressed, his boots polished, the first to have the use of Wedel.'

'Well, he doesn't have the first use of me,' she joked.

Zepernick turned on her with venom.

'No? But that was of his choosing, was it not, not yours? You offered yourself up like a bar of Swiss chocolate.'

Veronica felt her face flare. She tried to deflect the blow.

'Anyway, what do you expect, he's your superior,' she reminded him.

'Under one roof we should be comrades. But the Major does not see this. It is not only that he thinks himself better than me, but he believes that he is more cultured, that only he can appreciate the finer things. The wine in the cellar, for instance, *he* has to swirl around in his glass and pronounce good or bad, while I am expected to swallow it back in one gulp. The servant, Albert, thinks the same. And Mrs Hallivand? She can hardly bear to be in the same room as me. She tries to hide it but she is glad Isobel is dead. She has the Major all to herself now. In the afternoon the two of them sit in the drawing room like Adam and Eve overlooking some ruined garden of Eden. Ah, the Major! This island!' and he said it with a bitterness which Veronica had heard reverberating in her own inner voice, the times she had spent holding her tongue in front of Gerald, not daring to betray her life and her language, the look his mother had given her the one time she had been taken there to tea, looking askance at her shameless figure and her ruby red mouth, thinking, I know how you entrapped my poor innocent boy, you young hussy, and she, looking back defiant, had plucked at the swollen lapel of her blouse, as if to say, well, yes, that's how we *all* do it, one way or another, even a withered old prune like you, remembering too the revulsion on Lentsch's face when she had bent down and placed herself loose in his hand, realizing that she too had not forgiven him for insulting her, for pushing her away in disgust. So she had taken Zep's hand and pressed it hard against her, as if to say that's what I want you to be, that's what I want, a man who will be as heartless in love as he must be in war, who will offer me nothing but the time he is with me, understanding that that too may have its needling edge.

In the hallway the Captain propelled her to the stairs. The climb was always erotic, whoever went first. They kissed on the first landing, his mouth rough against hers, before breaking off. Up at the top the light was brilliant. The sun shone from the west down upon the steep-stepped red and ochre roofs and the hooting harbour, and to the left, tumbling down to the aquamarine sea, was the dark olive mystery of the wooded cliffs. It was an eagle's nest there were in, and they the monarchs of the sky. He had brought two bottles of German wine, white and fruity. He stood them on one of the glass cases and strode to the window, turning to her, pulling her in front of him, pressing his hardened sex up against her buttocks, kissing her neck. He put his hands round and clasped her breasts.

'Careful.'

'Great things are happening to this island,' he said, swaying into her. 'Great things. I used to think here was nothing, a backwater. But see?'

His arm swept over the panorama. She did not see. She rubbed herself against him from side to side.

'I feel like drinking,' he said. 'What a day!'

As was their custom now, they moved the chaise longue from the back of the wall, up to the glass window. Veronica sat on one end. The Captain put his head in her lap and swung his feet up. Veronica slipped her hand inside his shirt. The bottle stood on the floor.

'I am thinking of moving out of the Villa altogether,' he told her. 'The Major has come completely undone. He is to be arrested.'

Veronica pulled her hand out.

'Arrested?'

The Captain leant over and gulped down another glass.

'I cannot tell you everything. You understand this, you are not like Molly, whose mouth is almost as wide as her—' He checked himself in time, but Veronica didn't mind what he said about Molly, so long as it was uncomplimentary. 'I have a story to tell. Listen.

That morning Bohde had come tiptoeing in with Major Ernst. The two of them were carrying three pictures which Bohde had decided to hang in the hall. Portraits. One of the Air Marshal of France – 'an ugly looking bloke,' Zep conceded, one of Albert Speer, and most importantly of all – he gulped the epithet – in celebration of His forthcoming birthday. The Commander-in Chief's eyes, Ernst had pointed out, were like two bullets flashing from the muzzle of a gun. They decided to hang them in the corridor, where everyone might see them, on the bare wall facing the doors to the main rooms. They got a chair and some nails and after much banging and hammering and standing back, hung all three up, Speer on one side, the Air Marshal of France on the other and . . . in the middle. Zepernick smiled. He found the next part of his tale amusing. He took Veronica's hand and placed it back beneath his shirt. With her other hand she unbuckled his belt. He moved once, raising his hips, then resumed his story.

As Ernst and Bohde stood back, admiring their handiwork, they suddenly realized that on the opposite wall, facing the three portraits, were two of Mrs Hallivand's favourite paintings, which Lentsch had moved from the drawing room when first they arrived, pictures which were quite unfit to be placed opposite Albert Speer or the Air Marshal of France, let alone the leader of the German nation. Both of them featured girls of oriental disposition, with dark skin and slanting eyes, flaunting their nakedness by some Arabian watering hole. So Bohde called for Wedel and told him to take them down. Wedel was hesitant. More than his life was worth, he said. The Major was very particular about where those went. Whereupon Ernst flew into an almighty rage, Bohde dancing up and down the stairs egging him on. 'Do you think that it is right that our leader should look upon these degenerate deformities?' he cried, and wrenched one of them off the wall, cracking the frame and the glass in the process. Bohde, rather chastened, told him to calm down and lifted the other off its hook. Together they carried them out into the coal shed. An hour later Lentsch returned for lunch, stomping through the French windows. Though he said he'd been out swimming his breath smelt as if he'd been drinking.

'This is a bad thing to do...' and here the Captain hesitated. 'Things are happening here which need the utmost attention and discretion.' So he marched in and sat down to lunch. Bohde sidled into his chair, Ernst next to him. Not a word was spoken. Halfway through his soup the Major noticed the picture of Albert Speer staring at him through the open door. 'Who put that up?' he demanded, and when Bohde told him that it was a gift from Major Ernst he threw down his napkin and said, 'Well, I'm damned if I'm going to have his boss spying on me while I'm having dinner,' and got up to close the door, when he saw the other two. He stepped into the hall.

'"Where are the Russell Flints?" he cries.

'"The Flints?" Bohde tries to look innocent.

'"The pictures!"' Zepernick waves his hands in the air. 'He is screaming now.'

' "I had them taken down," Ernst tells him calmly. "They are not suitable."

' "Not suitable! Not suitable! Not suitable for that—" and with that he marches back into the hall, takes each one off the wall and smashes them one by one against the wall. The Air Marshal, Albert Speer and lastly . . .' The Captain shook his head, hardly daring to give voice to the blasphemy. Veronica didn't see the problem.'

'Bit over the top, I grant you, but they're only pictures.'

The Captain touched her cheek, saying, 'You must understand, Veronica, that this picture is more valuable, more sacred than everything in this house. It would be the same if one day Mrs Hallivand came to church and found the vicar with a boy on the altar. Ernst was on the phone immediately. It is very bad for the Major, considering the circumstances.'

'What circumstances?'

The Captain ignored her question. He straightened up and poured himself another glass.

'So Ernst will move in soon, Bohde hanging on to his coat-tails. I will find a smaller place, of my own perhaps. However, before I go . . .' He looked at her closely. 'I thought tonight you might like to accompany me to the Casino.'

'The Casino.' She felt her heart race.

'Yes, and afterwards, if things have quietened down, perhaps you would like to come back to the Villa. For a late supper and a nightcap.'

She could not believe it. He was asking her back to the Villa. She did not know what to do, whether to fling her arms around his neck or to appear calm and indifferent. She wanted to do both. She wanted to be calm and indifferent but she wanted to kiss him too! The Villa! Unable to resist, she leant across and kissed him, opening up the sweet tang of wine that ran loose in his mouth, pushing herself on top of him, struggling out of her blouse and brassiere, his lips travelling greedily down, sucking in great swollen mouthfuls of her as the boy intruded suddenly on her thoughts, irritating her, he has no right, this boy, to interfere with her in this way, why should she think of him when she had the Captain lapping hungrily at her breast. She had tried to persuade him to have a wash the other day, had lit the gas to her father's fury and boiled kettle after kettle, dragging the tin bath close to the fire, rigging up the little curtain that she sheltered behind when Da was around, but when she had showed him he had recoiled, not from the prospect of soap and warm water but for the danger it could bring him. 'The guards,' he said, pointing a finger to his head, indicating thought, and then of course she understood. A clean boy would be noticed, a clean boy would be singled out and strung over the rafter he had told her about, where others have been beaten, the blood running down onto the floor until sometimes . . . he dropped his head. Did he mean pass out or die? It was unimaginable. It annoyed her sometimes the way he exaggerated his stories in order to gain sympathy, yet only the day she'd seen a foreign being kicked all in a heap by one of the Todt officials before being slung in the back of a lorry and left there all day. Horrible, simply horrible, but there were bound to be one or two sadists like that in every army, and there's no knowing of course what the foreign might have done, and pushing over the loaf for the boy to cut it himself she began to question the wisdom of even feeding him, for there was colour coming back to his cheeks there was no doubt of it. Wouldn't they notice that and wonder why? Beat the truth out of him. When he had gone she had stripped off herself and sat in the tepid water, scraping the sliver of soap under her arms, thinking how it would feel to wash the dirt from him, feeling the transformation as his rough patchy skin grew soft and glowing, the stink of his imprisonment replaced by the scent of perfumed soap, his clothes, shirt, trousers, jacket discarded and in their stead Victor Hugo's silken dressing gown the Captain liked to wear.

She pulled Zepernick's head away.

'You've picked a fine night to ask me, I must say,' she murmured, banishing the boy back to his hut. Oh, the Villa!

'Why, what is wrong?'

She digs him in the ribs.

'Tomorrow, Zep! The first day of the show. You haven't forgotten, have you? You promised.'

'Ah, yes. I forgot.' He approached the subject cautiously. 'Molly will be there, remember.' Veronica stiffened.

'No, no. You are not to worry. I have spoken to her. She will be with Major Ernst that evening.'

'Ernst?'

'Yes. It is all arranged. She belongs to Ernst now. He has made it plain. If I wish to continue here . . .'

'What does Molly think?'

'It does not matter what Molly thinks. If she hadn't been so . . . visible.' He pulled her close. 'And you, you must not do this, not show your beauty to everyone all the time. Otherwise I might lose you too.' He stroked her hair. 'It is you now for me. Does that please you? And perhaps, if Molly is very upset, I could meet her secretly, like I see you now.'

'Thanks very much!'

'It was a joke, Veronica! Don't be jealous. It is not good to be jealous in such circumstances.'

He sat up and started to take off his shirt.

'The Casino will be fun tonight. I have told them I am going to try and drink the boot again. No one has tried twice and succeeded. But I will. Now come and give me a good fuck, there's a good girl.'

'The boot?'

'It's a drinking tradition. It looks easy but it is not. It also makes you quite drunk. The last fellow, Schade, fell down and cracked his head open.' He caught her look of concern. 'He was a fool, anyway. He was the one who was involved in the black market, with Herr Poidevin and his daughter.'

'Poor Elspeth, yes.'

'You know her?'

'Everyone knows Elspeth.'

'She was lucky, her and her father. If I had my way they'd be up in Fort George. They know more than they say. Not only about the smuggling. This matter over Isobel and her father. It does not fit right. Any other time and I would not mind. But with certain other events and the Major acting so strangely, it worries me. I fear they might all be connected. The cement in her mouth. Her dress. The jacket and hat missing. She wore them that afternoon and yet they have vanished. What happened to them? Is someone wearing them now?'

He moved to her once more but she pushed him away. She knew what she had to do. This would be her one chance. She could feed him this morsel in the same manner as she fed him her flesh. It would be the seal of her success, the stamp in her passport, the key to the Villa's door.

'A jacket,' she said, 'what sort of jacket?' knowing full well what the description would be, recognizing it the moment he had spoken the words, seeing it hung up over the back of the kitchen chair, seeing the smudged label underneath the worn collar, seeing – a woman's jacket yes, with the darts on the front and cuts in the side, a woman's jacket with leather elbow patches and a pretty collar and small wooden buttons.

'You know,' Zepernick said, 'her corduroy jacket. She wore it all the time, riding, walking, probably . . .' he reached out and sucked on her again, '. . . in it too,' and Veronica, regaining her composure, remembered that indeed Zep was right, she had seen it on her any number of times, up at the rehearsal rooms, slung over her shoulders or left half trailing on the floor in that careless wealthy manner she had found so irritating, an expensive coat that only the rich would treat so casually, remembering how Isobel would pick it up and hurry into it, on her way to some other social gathering to which she, Veronica, would not be invited. An unexpected surge of resentment flooded over her. She wanted to join with this man and put paid to all the years they had been excluded, denied the things for which they had striven so hard and which still evaded them, and without hesitation, knowing that she could bring it off, she prised his lips away and bent down, kissing his chest and his stomach, and told him quickly, glorying in her ability to deflect his hands and his curiosity from the warm certainty of her body. Why, she had seen just such a jacket on a boy, this very morning. 'Today! On a boy! Where? What's his name? Do you know his family?' Zepernick raised her up, firing his questions rapidly, assuming that it is a native boy she was describing, one of those miscreants who fired catapults from behind drystone walls, of all the inhabitants the most insistent in their insolence, and she, a shiver of excitement running through her, said, 'No, not one of ours, Zep, one of yours, a *foreign*,' the cold intelligence suddenly flickering behind his eyes, like the flare of a lighted match. 'A foreign?' he repeated, and she nodded. 'You know, one of the Todt workers,' conscious of her nakedness and the leeway it afforded her, making up the story as easily as instilling freshness into those tired words of lust. She could picture it in her mind's eye, see the Pollet below her and the foreigns marching past, remove the boy far from her own home and place him in their midst with his red pantaloons and his white shock of hair and the strangely cut jacket that hung down on his slender frame, describing how he had clambered into the waiting lorry parked at the end, marvelling how it was all working out in her favour, how the Captain sat up, alert, his hands pressed together as he asked, 'Did you notice the lorry number, or a name on the side?' and she shook her head, knowing instinctively that this would be an observation too far, but seeing a way out, wanting to convert her invention into something more tangible, she leant back and said, 'Funnily enough I do know where he goes, or rather where he went,' knowing full well that he was still there, was there right now as she talked, 'for I was up by St Andrew last week seeing a patient and saw him with the other foreigns up there, at the hospital tunnel at La Vassalerie Road.' As she said it, the pang hit her, wishing that the Captain had never mentioned the jacket and that her mouth had travelled the full distance and become so full with him that she would have been unable to speak of the boy at all.

'The hospital?' he said, and she, fearful for a second that she had betrayed her own complicity, that that was something she shouldn't know, added quickly, 'Perhaps he had nothing to do with it, I don't want any trouble,' and laughing he assured her, 'Don't you worry, Veronica, he'll not harm you,' but though she shook her head, saying no she didn't mean that, the Captain wasn't listening, he had forgotten her, even as he kissed her and pulled on his shirt and told her not to worry, that he'd come by soon and make it up to her, running his hands up and down her trembling front, hurrying her down the stairs as she pulled on her coat before bundling her out of the door. And as she stood there and watched as he ran to his car, as she heard the engine scream down the hill, she realized that there would be no Casino that night and no Villa, and that far from coming closer to him she had set herself apart from him again, drawn another Occupational line in the sand. She stood out of breath, alone, and looking down the hill and the little town below she suddenly saw what she had done and understood the awful ease by which one achieves betrayal.

Twelve

The Dutchman has been working for three and a half weeks now, first outside, on L'Ancresse Bay, pouring cement into the great swell of the gun emplacements, and once that had finished down here, in the tunnel alongside the boy. Though he understands only a few of the words the boy speaks – a broken mixture of English, German and what? Polish? Russian? – he has started to follow the boy, for it is he, rather than the older man (who does not have as much spare energy), who has been nursing him through these difficult days. So he stands behind this boy at mealtimes, sits opposite him in the bouncing lorry, leans his back against the same creosoted hut wall on their meagre day of rest, and now pushes the wagon that the boy has to fill with rocks and stones and clawing clumps of clay, before bringing back an empty one for him to load in return. Though the work is without pity and the tunnel without end, the boy seems to be gaining an unacknowledged authority over these excavations by the day. He takes pride in showing van Dielen the bewildering dimensions of this labyrinth, the endless series of domed rooms, the huge mysterious length of it, the great reservoir dug for the water and near the connecting tunnel, on which he is now working, the tiny room disguised by the mud-caked sheet of metal behind which they sit and drink water from a stolen canteen. The old man and the young boy have taken it upon themselves to look after van Dielen, though he has uttered not one word of thanks, nor indeed made any sound at all, even when pushing the empty wagon back up to the tunnel's head (a task which paradoxically is harder than pushing a full-laden truck down to the entrance). Indeed his lack of speech seems to endear him to them.

Perhaps they are tired of hearing their fellow prisoners' constant complaints; perhaps his silence, his expressionless face, his slow methodical gait, are welcome changes. They clap him on the back on the few occasions he has seen fit to nod and they grasp his arm when he puckers his mouth or shrugs his shoulders in answer to a question. During the hut hours, when he remains motionless and unblinking, they sit on either side of him, patting food into his limp hand, handing him his tin of watered soup, and at night they lift his feet up onto the bed and draw the blanket close. It is not that he has difficulty in moving. Once set in motion, loping along four abreast, shovelling shingle, breaking lumps of granite in the flint-flashed dark, there is a rhythm to his life that he can run to, holding his own alongside the best of them, but when he stops he sees no reason for starting again. The motor within him has seized up. Take this morning for instance. The triangle had been rung at half-past five, and the boy had swung his legs down and shaken him awake before trotting off to the line of pails. Normally the old man would get him moving, leading him outside to the assembly point, but this time he had forgotten. Van Dielen knew the rules, he had seen it happen often enough, that the last one to stumble out into the frostbitten air got his backside warmed; knew too that the later the arrival the greater the heat, and he did not wish to be beaten, no, he wanted to dig, to lose his life again in the sweet darkness of the island's heart, but he did not stir, could not; there was something about his plank of wood and the old coat that the boy had wrapped around his shoulders that night which prevented him from moving. He lay there, looking at his bandaged feet, hearing others coughing their guts out onto the sawdust floor, scraping handfuls of lice from their armpits, belching and farting and squirting excrement into the nearby bucket, before scrambling out to stand in shivering lines while the overseer marked them off: he heard it all and yet did not move. The coat was so warm, so familiar, the scent of it so heady, so dreamlike, not the immediate smell of sweat and tar and dank green water, but something else, deep within the lining and soaked into the collar. He pulled it up over his mouth and nose and inhaled. It was as if he was lying on an operating table, breathing in ether through a mask, lurid visions of lost worlds looming up as he fell into a gathering mist. There were faces floating past, eyes creased with the sun shielded by a straw hat, a head of hair in pigtails bouncing on a donkey, a woman in a white dress standing on a raised veranda, the dying sun setting her skin aflame; scenes too, bridges and towers and ribbons of road. He wanted to follow them but his feet were too far away, wrapped in lead, feet that had once walked deserts and crossed ravines, measured out metres and yards, lain in between those of a good woman, run races with a barefooted sprite. He thought he had forgotten most things but briefly he understood that he had not forgotten, simply viewed it all in a different perspective, one in which he played no part. No wife, no daughter, no name, no past. They knew him not when he was alive and he knows them not now that they are dead. His life is but a shadow, a dark irrelevance and one in which he will take no further part. But oh, those pigtails! That barefoot sprite! Then the coat was thrown aside and the blanket torn off and he was pulled to his feet and dragged out by the wrist, his left arm trailing on the floor like he was a monkey in his keeper's grip, and stood underneath the beams where the two hooks were fixed. Behind him he heard others laugh and shout words of encouragement: 'If this doesn't get him talking, nothing will', 'Bet he faints after ten', 'Don't worry, mate, it happens to all of us' – and out of the crowd the boy had stepped forward and pointing to him, had stuck his finger in his ear, making out that the explosions in the tunnel the previous day had made rendered the Dutchman temporarily deaf, and though it had not saved him completely, for by this time his arms had been raised and tied and the whip placed in the man's hand, the overseer, after shoving the boy rudely aside, had struck him only five times, the flail of leather strands, oiled and supple and fixed to a wooden handle, breaking on his back like the splutter of Christmas crackers. After a final kick in the shins and a long intimidating bellow in his ear, he was cut down, where he stood shaking while the men dispersed, before the boy, the coat back on his shoulders, returned to lead him to the waiting lorry and the day's work.

And now it is near the day's close. Soon the evening shift will come and replace them. He is pushing what will be his last but one full wagon, marvelling at his own hands and his own wealed back and the long strength of him. He knows he should be growing weaker, as are the men around him, but he is not. It may have something to do with the boy, who returns to the billet every night before dawn with hunks of bread and strangely composed pies, the cement dust which lines his pockets its gritty salt, but it is food nevertheless, wonderful food, cold and concentrated, and they chew on it, him and the old man, chew on it and gulp it down, great lumps lodging in their throats, falling asleep to the sound of it churning their stomachs, their juices working like drains. Their farts are becoming different from those of the other men, smelling of meat and vegetables and the laws of decent digestion, rather than those occasioned by sawdust and dysentery. They wake and lift their blankets and waft the meaty fumes towards their nostrils. It is a pleasure shared.

As he nears the tunnel entrance van Dielen hears commotion. Up by the black rubber doors and the great block of light that waits outside stands a group of officers. There is the large fat man who once gave him chocolate, the man who beat him, and another, a handsome man who looks in awe at the great length he has stepped into and the noise he hears bellowing from deep behind its dark and fetid mouth. The man with the chocolate is waving his stick about, pointing towards the very spot on which he stands. Indeed for a second, the two of them, van Dielen in the remnants of his Tootall shirt and Harris tweed trousers, Major Ernst in his black uniform, peer at each other before a couple of fellow workers ease van Dielen aside and start to push his wagon out to the waiting lorries. The wheels grind on the hard concrete floor. Ernst starts shouting in the overseer's ear. The handsome one walks up and down impatiently. Then the doors swing open and the wagon disappears into the crack of blinding light, and in the flare of darkness that descends, when the doors close once again and the noise ceases and he can see nothing, the conversation comes singing down the tunnel, like voices floating on a summer's afternoon across a clear and flattened sea. 'Looking for a young one,' the fat man says. 'Got himself caught up in a murder, the slant-eyed little cunt. Red trousers and a brown coat. You got anyone like that? A woman's coat, you understand, with . . .' and he cups his hands in front of his chest, weighing imaginary flesh. They laugh one and all. The overseer nods. He is eager to help. He consults his clipboard. '*Ja, ja.*'

Turning quickly, van Dielen bends into the waiting wagon and starts to push the empty cart back up the slight incline. He keeps his head down. He shuts his eyes. He pushes. He must do this, push this empty load, otherwise he might be stopped, ordered to do something else before he can warn the boy, so he pushes, hands on the wooden frame, feet planted firmly on the floor, feeling the wheels resist the slight climb, head down, closing his eyes, pushing the wagon of his dreams. The passageway slopes all the way up to the work face, he knows this and yet only now, as he pushes harder, head down, eyes squeezed close, does he ask himself why. Why should a hospital have an entrance where the corridor slopes upwards? It makes no sense, having to push casualties uphill to an operating theatre or a recovery room. It should be level. He opens his eyes and looks beyond. Yes, it does slope up all the way, not by much, fifty centimetres every ten metres perhaps, but it is enough to ensure that the iron-clad wagon can only move back up to the face after considerable exertion. He bends to his task again, and as the wheels start to pick up speed and the voices gather in crescendo he sees something else which he has never noticed before. There are gutters running alongside the foot of every wall, and not just down this passageway but in the rooms he is passing too, where the wards and the kitchens and the cinema will be built, gutters running round the perimeter of every room, as if at some point they will be hosed down, water running off the walls and over the floor. But wards and operating theatres are not hosed down. There is only one type of building he knows of that needs hosing down. An abattoir. An abattoir? An underground abattoir? Come to think of it, who would want to send convalescing men underground, where it is damp, where there is no light, where the air is stale and unhealthy, but now is not the time to question the improbability of such an elaborate and contradictory construction, hearing the stamp of determined feet behind him, one, two, three sets, the fat man with the chocolate, the overseer who had beaten him and the handsome one, all seeking out the boy, the boy who had fed him biscuits and cake and two portions of smoked sausage pie, and placed an old jacket over his cold shoulders, and as he comes up to the intersection, where he can hear him throwing rocks into the next wagon, he abandons his wagon, giving it one lucky slap, as if thanking it for protecting him this far and starts to trot, no rooms now, no gutters either, just the long corridor and the low light and his rag-wrapped feet silent on the puddled floor, and suddenly there he is, the boy, small and perfect, standing beside the battered truck, his grey-white hair glowing in the guttering dark, throwing chunks of rock, pausing to look up as he sees this figure running towards him, weighing a lump of stone in his hand as an improvised defence, then, seeing who it is, the man with no voice, throws it into the wagon, waiting as van Dielen stumbles up, out of breath now. The Dutchman grabs the coat, breathing once again that strangely perfumed material. This is his son he has in his grasp, he knows it. He wants to hold him, to tell him of their history, of the father he could have been, but there is something growing in his windpipe, an adenoidal growth, a cancerous lump, the remnants of an indigestible sausage pie which prevents him from uttering a word. He must be rid of it! He places his hands upon his throat and works them up and down over the scrawn of his Adam's apple, the footsteps louder now, up and down, up and down, feeling the pressure coming and himself rising out of the ground, bursting like a geyser, tightening and loosening up at the same time, head thrown back, eyes closed, teeth bared, coming up for air, rising out of the white whip of the waves and the black bosom of the earth.

He lets his throat free, he hiccups, once, twice, and out of his mouth comes a great steaming ball of grease and spit, spinning and hissing on the ground like a lump of phosphor, and he takes the boy and shakes the boy, pointing backwards to the stamping echo that grows louder by the second, stamping the spit silent and speaking for the last time in his life.

'They are coming for you,' he says. 'Hide. Hide now,' and though the boy does not understand it all, he hears the urgent footsteps and sees the paternal fear and recognizing both and the pointing of van Dielen's trembling arm knows that his time in this tunnel has passed. He must leave it or die.

Running back to the abandoned shaft they slip behind the air filter into the secret room and crouch there as the feet march up, the Dutchman and he, kneeling face to face in the black space. He can feel the other man's breath on his face, smell the sour stink of it, hear it too. He reaches out and puts a gentle finger on the man's lips. The Dutchman understands well enough. As they listen to the approaching footsteps the boy imagines that they are not after him at all but this strange silent creature who follows him around like a dog, but then he hears them talk of a young one, the one with the red trousers and the woman's jacket, and he knows the trouble he is in. Then the workers are counted out while they search. He can hear them banging in the wagons, chasing through every earth-shored room, shinning up the escape shafts with their hollow cries, kicking at piles of rubble, scurrying up and down, all the Todt trustees, shouting and cursing under the wet flap of tarpaulin.

The tunnel grows silent, nothing but the drip of water and the hum of the generator at the back, and down far away, the collective murmur of the next shift waiting outside. He is tempted to try his luck now, but caution prevails. They must wait until they can move under cover of noise. One last sweep and then the doors are swung back and he can hear the men shuffling in, gathering their pickaxes, the dragged shovels ringing out on the concrete floor. Now, as the waves of men ripple through, he eases back the metal sheet and crawls out, the Dutchman following. Together they run down to the connecting tunnel and the escape shaft, thirty foot high and locked from the inside by a long iron bar. They climb it easily and though the bar is stiff with the grip of a burgeoning rust he pulls it back with one sharp jerk and hoists himself out. They are in a field surrounded by other fields, two hundred yards away from the entrance with a high cover of trees in between.

He starts to move off, beckoning the Dutchman to follow him, but the man stands his ground with a shake of his head, urging him to flee, not to bother with him. He beckons again, and again the man refuses, waving him away, as if he is driving back cattle. The boy turns and starts to run and when he looks back the Dutchman has not moved still. But this time he does not shoo the boy away. He raises his hand, simply, as if holding aloft a silent thought, waves once, now blows him a kiss and then ducks swiftly out of sight.

It is a long journey, longer than he has imagined, across the heart of the island, through steep hidden valleys and slippery moss-infested brooks, running nervously along all too quiet lanes, ducking under the stretch of spider-web bombs that sing in the light breeze, the promise of a westerly wind, blowing contentedly in his face. Then he breaks out into the flat of Cobo, and twenty minutes later he is at the back of the darkened house. She is sitting at the table with her head in her hands, the oil lamp flickering with her sobs. He wonders whether that man has made her do it with him again, and it makes him angry. He bangs on the window. She looks up, frightened. Then she sees his face pressed up against the glass and she jumps up, throwing the door open, taking him in his arms, swinging him round and round as if he were a baby. He cannot understand the ferocity of her reaction, the tears that roll down her face, her damp insistent kisses, the way she turns him this way and that, hugging him at every opportunity. 'Police,' he warns her, not *police* but the German word *polizei*, and she holds his head against her and murmurs, *'Ja, ja, ja, ja,'* in such a soft understanding way it was as if she knows, knows and doesn't care. 'Friend,' she says and taps her own chest. 'You stay here now. No more digging. No more tunnel.' Then she drags the tin bath out again and while the pans warm on the stove sits him on a chair and pulls out a pair of scissors from the drawer under the table and cuts his hair, cuts it short, like it used to be. Then she stands him up and pulls off his clothes, the stench rising as each garment hits the floor, and she holds her nose again and they laugh together just like the last time, opening the little grate and chucking them in, all except the jacket which she pulled from his shoulders the moment he was through the door. And when the bath is full, she coaxes him in, first one foot then the other, stabs of pain shooting up his leg as she splashes it gently over him, on his back and arms, his chest and belly, reaching up for his neck and guiding him down so that he is kneeling, his lips touching the surface before she grabs his head and she pushes him under. He comes up gasping, frightened and she takes hold of his head and kisses the top of it, the front of her dress all wet where his face presses up against her, like some other time, long lost, by some other fire. He doesn't mind when she ducks him under again, his scalp tingling and his ears singing, and when she is done he sits with his feet sticking out over the sides, while she holds each one in turn, working her thin curved scissors underneath his black toenails. Then he is up and out, naked before her while she dries them, dusting the gaps between his toes, kissing their blistered arches. He is not white any more but a pale olive colour and there is a length to his muscle and a masculine confidence in his stature that had not been there before. He is not a boy but a young man with his hands held over himself. So she straightens up and hands him the faded pair of pyjamas and turns her head while he dresses. And when he is decent she cooks him a plate of mashed potatoes and swede and afterwards leads him upstairs and shows him the narrow bed which wobbles and smells of her, with feathers in the pillow and a quilted cover laid on top. She peels it down and pats it open and he climbs in and draws the quilt over his ears and looking at her and the enormous room falls asleep.

She sits, watching over him. He is just like any other boy. That is what he has become and that is what he must remain. Any other boy. He will not go back. She will not let him.

She walks down the stairs and out into the back field. She brushes her hair with the back of her hand and straightens her dress. She only hopes his mother has gone to bed.

Thirteen

It had been raining off and on most of the night but with the dawn came an unfettered sun and the air was full with the throated chorus of birds. The telephone call had come through late afternoon. The Major was to report to the headquarters in the morning. A boat would be at the harbour to take him to Jersey at ten. Out in the garden the foliage glistened and the path down to the cove was slippery underfoot. The spring tide had pulled the water a long way back and the dark bubbling cratered sand was alive with sandpipers and terns. As he walked out to the water the bare rocks that he passed were dark and sombre, and the seaweed, not usually exposed, a greenless black-brown, the colour of a ruined world. The ribs of a long-sunk ship poked out from the greasy mud: lumps of rusted iron lay in dark green puddles. It had the look of a scorched, smouldering landscape, as if an army had fought over it with tanks and mines and flame-throwers and, having burnt and bombed it into submission, had moved on. It reminded him of the land he had never seen, but whose contours were branded on his soul: the blistered map of Stalingrad.

He swam out a good distance, a quarter of a mile maybe. The water was cold and the high swell lifted him up and down in long regular beats. Though he knew it would bring him pain he could not help but look up to the Villa. The tide had yet to turn and though he could feel his body being pulled out ever further, it did not worry him; indeed, he encouraged this movement with the hidden paddle of his feet, for by doing so, the natural world became larger, omnipotent, and he a mere cork on its restless surface.

After smashing the pictures he had lain out on the lawn, drinking from a bottle of wine. After a while the Captain had come and stood over him.

'Do you know what you have done?' he shouted.

Lentsch had lurched to his feet, throwing his arms back at the house. 'Smashed a bloody picture, Rheinhardt! Smashed three bloody pictures!' He wheeled around and raised the half-empty bottle into the air. 'Bloody awful pictures too.'

Captain Zepernick grabbed his arm.

'You're a fool, Gerhard, an inconsiderate fool.' He pointed back to the Villa. 'Major Ernst is already on the phone. I am to place you under house arrest immediately. Tomorrow you will be escorted from the island to Jersey and then to the mainland. God knows what will happen to you there. It is not good, Gerhard, what you have done. Another time I might have been able to help you. But now!'

'Do they shoot you for breaking pictures now?'

The Captain had marched him to the far end of the garden, and stood shouting huge, incomprehensible words into his ear. He could not believe what the Captain was telling him. It did not seem within the realm of the real world, that such a thing could happen here. There was, the Captain had told him, a strict blackout on the news. On the island only he, Captain Zepernick and Major Ernst knew. That's why Ernst had looked so pleased with himself! They were His fortifications He would be coming to inspect. No wonder Ernst was beginning to treat this place as his own fiefdom.

'How long have you known?' he asked.

Captain Zepernick shrugged his shoulders. 'A month? I was not allowed to tell you,' he explained.

'Come here?' Lentsch repeated. 'But what will the islanders think?'

'The islanders?' Zepernick's mocking echo rang round the small bay. 'What have the islanders got to do with anything? Think rather of the propaganda. Here on British soil with British policemen saluting. British children waving flags.'

'They wouldn't.'

'Oh, yes, they would. Enough at least.'

'For how long?'

'Long enough for the cameras.'

Lentsch shook his head. 'I meant the visit.'

Zepernick shrugged his shoulders again. 'Two hours. Three?' He rubbed his hands together. 'There will be a lunch, I believe.'

Lentsch looked up to the house, as if he was going to be personally responsible.

'A lunch! And who will cook this lunch? Albert? He knows enough about vegetarian cooking, I suppose, thanks to the food shortage.'

'Gerhard, Gerhard.' Zepernick spoke softly. 'Calm down. Do not put your life at any greater risk. This afternoon I will have to write my report. I cannot deny what you have done, but I will tell them of the great strain you have been under, how much this girl's death has affected you. I will not tell them you wished to marry her. That would not help. I will stress that she was the daughter of our leading construction engineer, and with his presumed suicide you were worried that the defence projects might have been placed in jeopardy. That will sound good. Ernst might want to disagree but now that you are out of the way he will not bother much. He has won his battle. Bohde is a different story. He will remember every indiscreet word you have ever uttered. So now you behave correctly, understand? Do nothing more to hurt your cause. You will stay here tonight. In the morning a boat will come. You understand?'

'I understand, Rheinhardt.'

'No more little excursions to your tame Inspector's house.'

'You know of that?'

'I am Head of Security. Of course I know.' He looked at his watch. 'I must go. I am late.' He held out his hand. 'Goodbye, Gerhard. Good luck.'

Lentsch felt himself nodding stupidly.

He lay in bed that night unable to sleep. He could hear Bohde and the Captain talking into the early hours of the morning, Ernst too. Perhaps they were keeping watch on him. He was coming here! It would be a triumph, no doubt, for Him to step on British soil, a trophy to take back to the defeated battlefields of the other Europe. Medals would be struck. Those who escorted Him, served Him His meal of vegetables and rice, shook His hand, would be marked for ever. It was a rare event now, those hallowed meetings of master and men. Gone were the field lunches, the open-air car tours, the platform behind His train. Gone were the walks along mountain paths, the incidental meetings, the clasp of man and country. Gone too those hesitant, shape-searching speeches that had thrilled them all. He shivered now, not at the cold current pulling him out, but at the memory of that first one he had heard, to the Hitler Youth, the bare-kneed boys, thousands of them, washed and scrubbed, standing up on tiptoe or on one another's shoulders, jostling and jumping to see Him coming. He'd been given a ticket from his fiancée's father and had stood high up at the back. He could remember every word, every gesture. 'We want no class divisions,' He had intoned. 'You must not let this grow up amongst you.' His voice had faltered with that admonition, broken on the wheel of that profound longing, the crowd hanging in silence on the trembling space between His words. Lentsch had felt a gnawing pang of envy stir within him. What adult did not want to be a youth then, to grow up under such tutelage? How the boys roared when He stepped back. Is that what He had promised? Eternal youth, eternal pubescent strength, harnessed to an elementary world of work and play with no other reward except the nation's brimming health. Was that what had driven them into His embrace, the blind belief that the world could be that simple? He remembered that time, the only time he had come close to Him. It had been early on, in '33, or '34. He was on leave, back home, drinking as it happened on a Sunday afternoon with some fellows at the inn. He had joined the army only recently, his father's regiment, and though happy with his choice it had not been an easy decision. There were other things that life had called for him. It was hard to say, but he had thought to study ornithology, and had spent years learning natural history, first at home and then in Edinburgh, where

to the amusement of his landlady and fellow students he had learnt
to dance the reel. He had made friends there, some whose fathers
owned estates such as his own, who shot and rode as he did, felt
the call of heritage and duty as he did, and others who felt another
calling, a life of work rather than duty, and though he was
susceptible to that too, the call of his country had come winging
back. Yes, it had been a long time coming that call, like the slow
flap of the geese rising out of the damp swamp, but when it came
it was as if the sun had risen and cleared the mist and all one could
see was a country of great beauty and power, worked by a great
people. In those days, journeying to Munich or Berlin, the new
leader would try and cross the country unseen, his chauffeur, his
aide, his photographer and a small following staff car his sole
companions, but though He might fool the first town or village,
word of His coming spread ahead like a forest fire. Lentsch was
sitting outside when the news had come through, phoned to the
burgher by his opposite number twenty kilometres up the road.
There was no time to prepare, just a handful of hasty flowers
plucked from front gardens, flags unfurled and pushed out of top
windows. By the time the car turned the bend the whole village
was out, men with the smudge of work on their hands, smelling of
oil and horse liniment, children in straightened socks and brushed
breeches clutching their school slates, wives in short-sleeved dresses,
their elder daughters blushing in newly ribbed plaits, Dr Hascha
and the Pastor fussing at the front, Paul Koenig tightening the
threadbare stretch of his policeman's uniform. And yes He did stop,
first standing up in his dark-blue open seven-litre Mercedes, then
stepping out, smaller than they had imagined, hat in hand, His
brown suit a size too large and somewhat crumpled, his hair dry
and unhealthy. But as He looked out over them, His gaze never
faltering, it all became clear. Everything He saw belonged to Him!
When He looked up at the gables, He saw His flags fluttering from
His houses; when He held out His hands He placed them on the
heads of His children, and when He bent low to receive their gifts
they were His flowers He took, grown in His garden. He knew

them all, the schoolmaster, the blacksmith, the midwife, knew them all, in this village and the village after this and the village after that. He was their master, wanting nothing for himself, only to make them safe and their land secure. Frau Tobelman standing on the steps of the inn had stepped forward bearing the tray of cakes they all knew to be His one weakness; strudels with sugar and nuts, the chocolate éclairs, the marzipan fillings. He should not, they knew. To indulge would display a weakness, and weakness was to be shunned. And what about the next port of call and the one after that? Would He insult them by taking a cake here and refusing those? But then He caught her beseeching eye and, nodding as if He recognized the fatality of this lost cause, held a hovering hand over the display. He would sacrifice himself on the altar of her matronly art. This was the land of cakes and cake eaters, and was not He their representative on earth and in the mystical vaults of beyond? Reaching out He selected the biggest and took a bite, turned it in His mouth as they bit with Him, holding their breath as He savoured the balance of cream and pastry and the still German air. Handing the remainder to His aide He pronounced it the finest cake in the world! If He could choose another life for Himself, He would put His feet up on one of the tables in the inn here and spend the rest of His days eating plateful after plateful! How they had roared with merriment at the charm and absurdity of the idea. Then He had grown solemn and shaken Frau Tobelman's hand and murmured something soft, intimate, kissing the back of her hand. (The innkeeper's wife had spoken to Him! He had kissed her! For months afterwards she had been like a goddess or one of those figures out of Greek mythology, a bearer of great powers and great wisdom, transformed, not simply in her eyes but in the rest of the village's. Even his own mother, sophisticated, educated, had held her in awe after that.) Then He had turned, coming face to face with Lentsch. There was a wisp of cream on His moustache, a flake of pastry on his lapel. He looked at Lentsch as if He could hear the very fluttering of his past, as if He had lain by his side as a young boy, waiting for the geese to flap above, the soft grey of their bellies filled with warm and sacred blood. For a moment, terrible in its intensity, Lentsch had imagined that it was his destiny too, to be singled out that afternoon, that He would recognize in him an officer out of uniform, there to serve his country, and he had drawn himself up and stood to unmistakably military attention. But He did not seek him out. He did not draw him close. He looked. He saw. He turned away, plunging in the opposite direction with smiles and greetings, as if the sight of Lentsch had spoilt this uncomplicated treat. At the time Lentsch did not understand, but now came the tales of His great consuming hatred of His army and the secret admiration He held for Stalin, His Slavic enemy who had eliminated *his* troublesome officer class at one stroke. 'Would that I had done the same,' He had been heard to cry. Lentsch found it unimaginable that the nation's leader should utter such a thing. And now He was coming here if the war allowed, His own birthday present to Himself. The thought of Him strutting amongst these lanes filled him with revulsion. It was all very well at home. They deserved Him. These islanders did not, none of them. It was not their fault, any of it. Not Isobel's death, not the smuggling, not the broken families, the cheap love affairs, the bitter recriminations. None of it. This wretched traffic in misery was all their fault. His and Lentsch's and all the rest of them. They were devouring the island piece by piece, as though it were a house made of sweetmeats and they some monstrous army of Hansels and Gretels. And it came to him suddenly, a spoken voice that touched his heart. He must not come! He must not! Must not!

Fourteen

Albert runs up the graveyard cradling the small scrap of paper on which is written the message. It is creased and thumbed and the writing is smudged but it is the most sacred object he has ever held. He has shown it to everyone he has met, even those who barely know him. *Dearest Dad, Am in the best of health. Thinking of you always. Keep smiling. Kitty.*

For a while, fifteen, twenty minutes on the journey to the graveyard, he dropped his guard and shared his joy with whoever was at hand, showing them the folded letter with the printed lines and Kitty's childish hand, running his trembling fingers under the words, asking, as if he meant it, whether they had heard from any of their own. Without realizing it he has returned the island to its old ways, revisiting the discarded laws of easy familiarity and friendship.

'Am in the best of health' he had read with a pride that momentarily had quite overwhelmed his entrenched distaste, and there was no one who did not admire the note and wish him and his daughter well, those on better acquaintance vouchsafing that Rose would have been pleased too. 'That's where I'm off to now,' he told them, bringing his fingers up to his beret as he hurried off.

'Am in the best of health, Rose,' he repeats. 'Our own dear Kitty is in the best of health, thinking of us always.' He looks out across the graveyard, recalling all the folk he has known, friends, neighbours, a few enemies. He tells them too. 'She is safe,' he announces, 'as is my other little gift to the world.'

He is proud of his gift, proud how he engineered it, a length of cast-iron drainpipe dragged from its Hautville mooring, sawn to a manageable length and primed on that long mahogany table. It is irrevocably marked, that table, the ancient depth of its gloss scuffed and scratched, smeared with rust and iron filings and the fingers of a fanatic, for although Mrs H. does not realize it, that is what he has become. Mrs H. had protested at first at Albert's determined vandalism, explaining the history of it, the lines of nobility that had dined, quaffed and wenched across its burnished length, but he had brushed aside her complaints, telling her that these unexpected indentations too would find their way into guide books, how future generations would shuffle through the house to marvel at these historic scars, the cuts where he had sliced through the electric wire, the scratched circles where the drainpipe had been stood up on its end, the chip on the side where the claw-hammer had missed its mark. He did not tell her that there would be no such visitors, that the table and all the other contents of this house would be destroyed along with the rest of the island. All he had told her was King and Country and a war brought to a quick and righteous close. And she had believed him.

He has constructed this device in the same fashion that he used to make all his bombs, the only difference being that this one was bigger. They used to have such fun making them, him and his brother and young Ned, chucking them in, waiting for the earth to thud and bleeding rabbits dragging themselves out of the smoke-billowing holes. He has not been able to gauge the extent of this bomb's power, this mixture of sugar and weedkiller, these bags of six-inch nails and rusting bolts, clinking lumps all packed into jagged cans that once contained tinned peas and sweetened carrots, but it will make a mess of them, no doubting that.

How had it come to him, this plan which will bring about the finale of his world? Lidichy, Lidichy, that was the start of it, that haunting name. He had often wondered what it must have been like, this village that has been handed around the drawing room like a game of pass the parcel, perhaps like one of the hamlets here, a little street, a few farm buildings, a church, a close-knit huddle for a few hundred souls. Before all the kerfuffle, when the Major

311

was still in charge, they used to have this argument regularly about Lidichy and the bigwig that the partisans had killed nearby, blown up or shot, he could never quite work out which, though he took a week to die, he knew that. Whatever, the day he died they had surrounded this village, this Lidichy, sealed it off from the rest of the world and wiped it and those who lived there clean off the face of the earth. Didn't matter that the poor sods had nothing to do with it, it was like, 'Sorry, chum, you've got to go.' The Major used to get in a terrific bate about it, the crime of Lidichy he called it. The others had got fed up with him rabbiting on. The name had stuck in his own mind, Lidichy, and thinking of it, this Lidichy which used to exist in flesh and stone and now did not, he began to dwell on its demise, brought about not through military design or an accidental misfortune of war but for *example*. Leaning out of the Captain's window one morning, flapping his bedclothes against the brickwork, it came to him that this was what Guernsey deserved to become, an example. Wasn't that what the Germans had planned for it anyway, that the Channel Islands should be a model Occupation? That's what this kid-glove stuff was all about, and see what a model it had become, the shame his countryman had brought upon his home: married women lying abed with the enemy while their menfolk perished on the high seas; young girls strutting down the High Street, poxed or pregnant, it was all the same to them; men tipping their caps to them, queuing up to do their dirty work. Everyone had turned rotten. He can feel the start of it even in himself, softening his moral backbone, turning his stubborn will to sap. The island needs grubbing out, like he would a bed of diseased fruit canes. Husbandry they used to call it, dig the lot out and burn the earth; the spirit of Lidichy. He had put his hands on the window sill and looking out had seen, stretching out over the back lawn, a vision of Guernsey emerging out of the mist, a Guernsey overgrown, a Guernsey denuded, water swilling in and out of a harbour of abandoned moorless boats, the town deserted, packs of dogs scavenging among the rubble, whole streets blown apart, farmhouses burnt, a forbidden island with nothing but wild flowers and gorse enveloping the ruins. Then the mist had cleared and in the solitude of the sea below he imagined a rowing boat and cloaked men in black raising their oars as the craft glided in to shore – a new generation hoping to start afresh. He saw his Kitty standing in the prow, Kitty beside her man, Kitty with his grand-children in her arms.

During those weeks of the Major's absence, the Captain had thrown caution to the wind. All-night poker games, drinking sprees, lewd pyjama parties, Molly ensconced there permanent, young men smelling of hair oil and posing for Bohde's camera in bulging leather pouches. Ernst had invited himself over, putting his feet up on the drawing room fireguard, holding forth as if he'd just bought the place. He and the Captain had seemed rather hugger-mugger too, talking for hours in the Major's study behind a firmly shut door, glasses of Mr Hallivand's special brandy to hand.

Lidichy, Lidichy, Arrivaderchi Lidichy. It would be too much to ask. Then one morning Molly came skipping down the stairs singing 'Happy Birthday' and demanding breakfast in bed for her and the Captain. Half-naked she was, with those pimples that passed for breasts poking out underneath for all to see. There was something about that part of her body that he found almost obscene, as if she was not a proper woman at all, and the thought of a man enjoying her, touching those boyish things, kissing them, exciting them, had always disgusted him. Why she couldn't wear a dressing gown like everyone else he didn't know, except of course he did; to cause him maximum embarrassment that's why, to flaunt in his face the fact that she was the new mistress of the house and that he'd better remember it.

'We had the most wonderful evening last night, Albert,' she had said, starting up the careless humming again, and didn't he know it, his bloody boxroom rattling like he was strapped to a tramline half the night. 'Your birthday, is it, miss?' he had said, knowing full well it weren't, and she had stood on her toes and yawned, 'Oh no, not *mine*,' smirking at him like she'd just won the pools. 'Well, whose, then?' he had asked, irritated, not really listening to the answer, and she had come up close, closer than a woman should in that state, and tapped him on the nose. 'Never you mind, Mr Albert Nosey Parker. You'll find out soon enough.'

He knew all their birthdays, the Major's, the Captain's, Molly's, Isobel's. They all needed their little parties and their little birthday cakes, didn't they? Molly's twenty-seventh had been in June, a fancy-dress extravaganza down on the beach, with the lookout guards on the cliff opposite removed for the night so that they couldn't tell their mates the fun and games that went on, Albert standing by the French windows with cups of hot chocolate as they fell in at three o'clock in the morning, drunk as lords and twice as randy. So whose birthday, then? Some special toff from France no doubt, with more raids slated for the Villa's cellar. He'd thought no more about it, but later that morning, on his way to the barbers, he had passed by Hendy's the stationers and there in the window was this dirty great painting of Hitler himself, sitting on a horse with a lance stuck in his mitt, dressed up like some knight in shining armour and underneath *Mein Kampf* in magazine form. In English. To celebrate the Führer's coming birthday they were giving away ten complete sets. All you had to do was to fill in your name and address and wait for the draw. He had stopped and looked at the picture and the book beneath and thought again of Molly singing and smirking and Ernst's and the Captain's little huddles, one the man in charge of fortifications, the other in charge of security. If he *was* coming, that's what he'd be doing, wouldn't it, inspecting fortifications? He had walked into the shop and picked up the form.

'Never thought you'd be interested,' Mr Hendy had sneered.

'Aye well, might as well find out what the bugger's on about,' he had replied. 'When's the draw, then?

'When it says.' Mr Hendy was sniffy. 'April 19th. Winners to be announced in the *Star*, though I wouldn't like to find my name on that little list.'

'Many takers?' he had asked.

'Strangely enough you're the first,' and folding his arms Mr

314

Hendy had moved away to the back of the shop, where he glowered at him with displeasure. Albert had filled in the form and stuck it in the empty box.

Watching had been part of his livelihood, gamekeeper, gardener, gossip, they all needed sharp eyes and sharper ears, and since he has become their caretaker he watches all the time, keeping his face as natural as his masked duplicity allows. It does not do to be too stony-faced, for granite imposes a wariness on those in its presence, and above all he wants them to relax, to feel at home, to let their guard down. In that way the diary he has kept is an accurate portrayal of what they have done and what they have said, and such is the plasticity of his demeanour they rarely try to hide anything from him these days. He is wallpaper, he is furniture, he is part of the Villa's bricks and mortar. Molly had guessed right that morning when Ned had been round, for before the bomb he had thought it important that someone should record these treacherous cavorting years. When the house fell quiet he would go to his room and describe as best he could the arguments, the petty jealousies, the brazen lusts that he had witnessed the day, the night, the week before, and leafing through his record he has discovered how very predictable they have become, how easy it is to foretell their hourly inclinations, and how he has become the conductor of this deranged and deluded orchestra. By mastering the art of anticipation he has acquired the ability to direct movement and though neither the Major, the Captain, nor Bohde (his most suspicious foe) realize it, it is he, their stubborn and trustworthy caretaker, who they keep up at all hours, who is forced to listen to their private worries, who bears their humorous entreaties of goodwill with a stoic resistance which they can only admire, who runs this house, he who sets their rhythm and has them trotting up and down these stairs. He knows them all now, has learnt all their little secrets; alone in their rooms, dusting, shaking, sweeping, collecting their dirty washing, he has found them all out; the silver spoons and napkin rings that Bohde has tucked in amongst his underwear; the framed photograph the Captain has secreted underneath the lining of his sock drawer, of him in some vast American city, standing against a railing with skyscrapers in the background and a young woman leaning on his arm, confetti on them both and behind that photograph, a folded marriage certificate dated 1933 to one Marion Berger of Brooklyn Heights; finally there are the Major's pencil sketches; Isobel lying naked on his bed, sitting with nothing but a shawl wrapped round her staring out of the bedroom window, and though he disapproves, his disapproval is nothing compared with what the Major's superiors might think of the cartoons of their Führer and his leering cronies, drawings of what he takes to be the Major's homeland with the dark shadow of the swastika racing over the landscape.

All these things he knew but until that moment when he returned to the Villa with an idea of who the birthday guest might be he had not gone on the offensive and that was what was needed, for a plan came into his head, a design of such diabolical ease it made him feel giddy, like he had just stepped off a boat. He stood stock-still in the drawing room, the name Lidichy ringing in his head, thinking how it could be done. Lidichy. Lidichy, the spirit of Lidichy. If that was what they did in memory of one of his favoured sons, what would they do to an island which tried to assassinate the man himself? Even if he did not succeed, even if he merely maimed him, or killed part of his entourage, what a cruel and merciless fury would be unleashed? But first confirmation was needed, confirmation that this was not the imagining of an enfeebled old man. It came in drips and drabs, nothing definite; the Captain being fitted for a new uniform, Molly in an almost permanent state of sexual excitement, a sudden surge of activity down by the harbour. It was seeing the soldiers unloading a large foreign car, seeing the sweat and muscle of them, with the crane swinging, men shouting, that finally drove him to action of his own. Coming back to the Villa and realizing that Molly and the Captain had decided to take an afternoon bath, he stepped into the Captain's room and lifted his diary from the top pocket of his jacket, the sound of water gently slapping, the low mutter of voices, nervous assurance. Leafing through February and March, the pages were so thin he feared he might tear one in his haste, but then there it was, April the 20th, studded with exclamation marks, with a time, 11.30; the confirmation of his dreams. That was all he needed. He replaced the notebook quickly, unable to remember which way up it had been, and was halfway down the stairs before he remembered that he had not rebuttoned the pocket, shutting his eyes and pulling himself back up, only to meet the Captain coming out of the bathroom door.

'Yes?' The Captain held the towel tightly round his waist. It was a rule of the house that when they were there Albert did not use the main stairs.

'The water, Captain,' he said. 'I was concerned that there might not be enough seeing as there are two of you in there. I was wondering if you wanted me to burn some more of our fuel. We're quite low, though.'

'If I had wanted more fuel I would have asked for more fuel. You should not be here Albert. You know this.' He shook his hair and looked down at the gathering pool at his feet.

Albert coughed. 'I don't wish to sound impertinent, Captain, but that bath in there was not built for two. Britishers bath alone. We find it cleaner that way. What with you and Miss Molly and the water all in the bath together I am a bit worried about the weight. There's the billiard table underneath to consider as well as your safety. If you were to crash in on it, it would ruin the lie of the cloth.'

He hopped down the stairs, delighting in the Captain's silent rage. 'Get a hold on yourself, Albert,' he said, doubled up with laughter and fright, 'or you'll sink the boat before she's been bloody launched.'

So he formed his plan. Not a gun, not a knife, not a personal attack at all, nor a group of dedicated men hiding with rusty old rifles behind some drystone wall, but a bomb, a good and faithful bomb, certain in its effect, uncertain as to its origin, a bomb designed by traitors and partisans, built with lies and complicity, a bomb that would scatter shards of suspicion all over the island, covering friend and foe alike. And he could help there too. A packet of weedkiller in the boot of the Captain's car, a map of the island where X marked the explosive spot tucked in under the tissue in Bohde's drawer; something for some of the islanders too, a van Dielen container the bomb's packing case, one of the Captain's security passes slipped in Molly's vanity bag. What fun they would have with them all!

But he needed somewhere safe to make this bomb. The cellar? The lean-to at the back of the lodge? And then he saw Mrs H. on her way to Hauteville, and thinking of the house, though he had never been inside and never wanted to, he saw at last how it could be accomplished, where it could be assembled without fear of interruption, in Victor Hugo's house, with only Mrs Hallivand allowed through the front door, and he, the odd-job gardener, clipping the hedges at the back. And he went to Mrs H. that evening, brought her a fat rabbit and skinned it in the kitchen while he told her who was coming and what they must do. 'If we could cut the head off, Mrs H., think how it would bring all this to an end,' and gave her a lot more fanciful stuff, about the underground and short-wave radios and Commandos coming out of the sea to save them, and she, silly old woman that she was, saw herself in the centre of things again and agreed, briefly worried about bloodshed and killing, but placated, believing like all women that war could never be as bad as it is, never understanding its cruel and insatiable capacity until it rushed over them like a flood tide. 'Cut the head off, Mrs H.,' he said, holding down the skinned corpse, sawing through the bloody neck. 'That's what Winnie expects us to do. Cut the head off. Watch the body run round in circles.'

Hauteville House it was, then, with Mrs H. carrying the materials in her little basket; sugar, weedkiller, nuts and bolts nicked from the garage. It was good to keep her going; it stopped her thinking too much. She was Little Red Riding Hood on her way to see her grandmama. She could outsmart the Wolf!

He began to assemble his bomb. Clock, batteries, bits of Plasticine to hold the wires firm. But still he needed to determine where to place it. Though it was not necessary for him to plant it exactly where Hitler might be, it had to be close enough to activate that instinct for rage and retribution on which he was depending. Fifty feet would be enough. Every morning he walked into town sifting through the pavement gossip but he heard nothing of note. Every afternoon he chanced his arm and went through the Captain's room to see if he had left any papers, but he could find nothing there either. Every evening he stood, fighting back the yawns while he served them late-night drinks, for he had started on the stealing rounds by then. Weedkiller was not a problem, he had packets of it back in the Lodge, but he needed more sugar, once as plentiful as grains of sand, now as precious as the grit kernel of a pearl. By day he accepted invitations for morning coffees and high teas in the hope that he might discover whether it would be worth his returning, tyre iron in hand. By night he broke in.

The days grew closer. The Major was due to return. Licence to roam would be at a premium. Isobel had come round Thursday, asking about the party, complaining about that fat oaf Ernst, who was always hanging around her house, trying to engage her in conversation. 'I wish Daddy could deal with someone else,' she had said. 'They're just like Siamese twins!'

Of course. Van Dielen! They'd be preparing certain fortifications for his inspection – a gun emplacement, a lookout tower. Van Dielen's yard might have the details. That evening, with the Captain and Molly at the cinema, Bohde at the printers, he walked down to van Dielen's yard and under the noise of the clanking cranes and whistles of steam kicked in the wooden fence with the toe of his boot, and scrambled through. There had been a great pyramid of crates he had to climb over, and at one point he slipped, putting his foot through one of wooden lids. Jammed fast it were and though he didn't like it much he had to switch on his torch to free it. That's when he saw them, rows and rows of tins. Custard! He'd always known George had been involved in the black market but never on this scale! He'd taken a couple, thinking there wouldn't be many opportunities left for him to enjoy a bowl, thinking too that when the time came, he might try and arrange a little something for George in his plan.

The hut had proved a disappointment. Nothing there at all except blank order forms and bills of lading stuck on a nail next to a calendar of film stars. He'd scooped a handful of invoices in his pocket, appropriate confetti for his unsuspecting bride, taking the tin of tea and packet of sugar with him as well, to make it look like the foreigns again, messing the place up like they might. Poor bastards got blamed for everything.

He got back to the Villa to find Molly and the Captain having a flaming row upstairs. Thinking the house was empty, they were in full throat. Albert stood at the foot of the stairs and listened. He could hear it all. The Captain was getting jumpy. Suddenly it had dawned on him how serious this visit might be. 'Well, why not me,' she was yelling, 'if Isobel can, why not me? Afraid I can't hold a knife and fork properly?' 'You're not van Dielen's daughter, that's why.' The Captain was trying to explain. 'Her father was a friend of Dr Todt. It's out of my hands completely. You'll be there, Molly, but not at his table. It's the best I can do.'

A dinner! They're giving him dinner. He hotfooted it over to Mrs H. and told her invite Isobel for coffee the next day; Isobel came round and pretended not to know anything about it. He didn't know whether to believe her or not, but, as luck would have it, by that lunchtime it no longer mattered. He found out, going down to see to Mrs H.'s shoes. Up at the big school, St Elizabeth College, which had been empty for two years or more, a bunch of workmen were busy painting the place up. They had a big dining hall up there, probably the only place big enough on the island to get all the dignitaries in that would be coming, Guernsey's lot and those ferried over from Jersey too. But St Elizabeth College were no use to him. He'd never get within a hundred yards of the place. Then walking back, down the road from the police station, outside the Royal Court House, he saw a soldier carrying in that blessed picture. More work going on inside too, hammering and painting and hanging up their flag from a pole on the roof. The Royal Court. Guernsey's Parliament! They were going to be presented to him. Perhaps listen to one of his speeches, not that they'd understand a blessed word. Perhaps they'd have to swear allegiance to him, or give him a big key. A presentation at the Royal Court, lunch at St Elizabeth's. Maybe the other way around. Either way he'd have to go past the police station, have to be driven beneath the little room at the top where Guernsey's Amateur Dramatic and Operatic Society rehearsed; Mrs H.'s fiefdom. If he could get it up there he'd be in clover. He could set it off himself when he passed, or hang it out of the window perhaps, like a real drainpipe. The slate of Guernsey wiped clean, ready to start afresh. Whatever they said afterwards about what had gone on here, they couldn't deny what they had done in the end! He would be saving Guernsey's soul!

The bomb was almost ready now. All he had to do was to get it down there. So one afternoon he and Mrs H. wrapped it up in brown paper and stuck painted paper leaves in the top and made it look like a stage palm tree for one of her blessed plays. When the coast was clear he sneaked it out of the front door and marched it on his shoulder all the way through the town, like it were a rifle, the green paper leaves blowing in his face, getting all sorts of whistles and catcalls from people he knew and some he didn't. He'd even met Ned on the outside stairs, even got him to help him carry it up. And there it sits. At the top. By the window. Waiting.

He reads the letter out once more. '*Dearest Dad, Am in the best of health. Thinking of you always. Keep smiling. Kitty.*' For the first time he hears a tremor of uncertainty in his voice, as if by speaking of his daughter's life and her love for him rushing over the cold water, he has somehow placed it all in jeopardy. He holds the letter out, squinting at the squashed lines. It was Kitty's hand that wrote those words, Kitty's lips that kissed the envelope.

'Would that she could have written *Dearest Mum*, eh, Rose? Would that she could have written that.'

He wipes a gruff tear from his eye. He would like to see her again, just one more time. She would never see her mother again, she knows that, but, trusting soul that she is, she must hope that she might see him again one day. Is it right that he should leave her like this, cause her such grief? He presses the letter to his cheek. He wants to take it back to the Villa, to show it off to the Major and Mrs H., to smooth it out on his knee when his work is done and read it over and over again, but he dares not. He has set himself on another course and having Kitty's words to hand, his dear Kitty, who he misses more than the rain and the wild flowers, would only distract him. He picks up the small glass vase that stands underneath his wife's name and tucks the letter in between the green stems.

'You keep it, Rose,' he says. 'We'll be reading it together soon enough.'

Fifteen

At breakfast Bohde and Zepernick were nowhere to be seen, to save all of them from embarrassment, he supposed. He spent an hour in the study writing letters, one to the Captain, one to his mother, one to his sister, both short and falsely jovial, and finally one to Mrs Hallivand, which he found most difficult of all. He wished her luck and promised that when the war was over he would return and help rehang her pictures. 'Above all else,' he wrote, 'tell no one about the House. Keep it a secret. They are too busy on other matters to appreciate what is within their grasp. And I will not remind them.'

The clock in the drawing room struck seven. Two hours and it would be over, sent to the Russian front or arrested, either way stripped of his rank. And all because of a picture. He was not sorry for what he had done, but sorry that he could not prevent Him coming. He could hear Albert moving about upstairs.

'Albert,' he called up. 'Could you come down here, please?'

In a little while Albert appeared. He had a duster in his hand and wore an apron round his middle. On another man it would look ridiculous. On Albert it looked almost dignified.

'I am going now,' he said.

'So I gather, sir. I am very sorry to see it, Major. Very sorry. The house, we, Mrs Hallivand and I, all of us are.'

The Major handed him the key to his bedroom.

'There are some things there you might find of use. Hairbrushes, shoes, some good clothes. They are yours now.'

'Thank you very much, sir.'

'I wish I could have done more. The garden. Major Ernst. All those years of hard work gone.'

Albert shrugged his shoulders.

'We'll get by, sir.' He stood at the foot of the stairs waiting. For a gardener he was being remarkably sanguine about the destruction of his life's work. Lentsch turned and looked at the hall. The walls were bare.

They walked out onto the front porch. The starlings were gathering in jubilation on the lawn, pecking and probing every inch of the grass, preparing for their journey home. Lucky birds! Albert clapped his hands and Lentsch watched in awe as they rose in their hundreds, circling once before settling down again. Albert clapped a second time.

'See how disciplined they are, Albert,' Lentsch observed as they climbed once more. 'How none of them ever fall out of place or crash into one another. In Germany we regard them as the most independent of birds. And yet, they conform to the narrowest of spaces.'

'Starlings,' Albert said. 'I'd shoot the lot of them if I could.'

Lentsch turned. It was time to go. He held out his hand.

'I hope you will see your daughter soon, Albert.'

'There's only two ways that'll happen, sir, and she's not planning to die yet.'

'Nor you, I hope.'

'There's no telling, is there, how things turn out.'

'They say that is what makes God laugh, when men make plans.' He paused and looked the man full in the face. 'There is something I always wanted to ask you, but did not, for fear of offending you.'

'Oh?'

'Your beret. Underneath? Are you with or without hair?' He did not dare use the word bald.

Albert adjusted the blue felt cap.

'Not even my Rose knew that,' he said. 'If she went to her grave without knowing, so must you.'

Lentsch laughed. He was pleased in a way. 'Only the barber, eh, Albert?'

'And the undertaker.'

Wedel, standing by the car, offered to take his bag, but Lentsch waved him aside, telling him to take the day off. There was nothing in it, anyway. He was only taking a few things that mattered; a photograph of his mother and father and of his home with the turret window; his sketch pad with the watercolour of the bay, a figure drawing of Isobel and half a head of Albert, taken down hurriedly on an afternoon last autumn, as he set about cutting back the fruit bushes. Ah, the fruit bushes. He could hear the grind of a concrete mixer now. In a month's time the back garden would be gone and in its place would be another wretched gun to serve no purpose.

He walked down the path and knocked on the Lodge door, looking back up the potholed drive. The Villa would get its fresh gravel now. There was no reply. She was probably down at the theatre making last-minute arrangements to the variety show. He slipped the letter under the door.

He started for the town, through the lanes and woods. The air was delightful, warm and light. In the well-kept gardens the camellias were in full bloom, magnolias too. Cherry trees stood in swollen clouds of colour and by the roadside crowds of crocuses and narcissi and snowdrops covered the grassy banks. Overhead gnarled beeches filtered the climbing sun rays through their fresh green leaves, and with them came the dappled songs of the thrush and the blackbird, and far above, a lark's sonnet sung out over some empty field. Reaching the top of the road, where the postbox stood, he could see in the harbour the grey and battered naval control boat that would take him across to Jersey in an hour's time. He saw the men working on the quayside, saw the old machinery, the faded paintwork, the threadbare uniforms. He leant against the railing and looked inshore, to the tumbling lanes and steep, squashed houses, all propped up against falling into this overburdened lock of water. And in a few days a plane would land and out He would step. He must not come! He must not come.

Dropping the envelopes in the letter box he turned on his heel and hurried up the hill. Twenty minutes later he was knocking on the door. Mrs Luscombe stood in her slippers.

'Major. You're a bit early!'

'I am sorry, Mrs Luscombe. I must see your son. Is he here?'

He peered in. Through the kitchen he could see Veronica leant up against the kitchen sink, her head in her hands, crying. That boy Peter was there also, he thought. Ned came out of the kitchen, closing the door.

'Major.' He was stiff and awkward. He looked embarrassed. He must have heard the news of his dismissal.

'I am sorry to disturb you, Inspector.' The words were formal, polite. Not what he wanted at all. 'I am being called away. To somewhere colder, I think.'

'Called away?' The sobs behind Ned reached a crescendo, then died away again.

'I am sorry,' the Major repeated. 'I have come at a bad time.' He sighed and shut the front door behind him. 'I am to be arrested. I have done something foolish. It is too complicated to explain. But there is something you must know. Something I must tell you. A secret.'

'Oh?'

'A very dangerous secret. It makes me ashamed to tell you. If I could stop it I would.'

'Stop a secret?'

He told him.

'Coming here? Hitler's coming here?

'That is correct.'

'When?'

'His birthday. A morale booster. For Him as well as everyone else, I think.' He grabbed Ned by the arm. 'But don't you see, Ned, He must not come! It would be a sacrilege. Last night I imagined how I might prevent it.'

Ned diverted his train of thought.

'How long have you known?'

'Yesterday. At the moment only a few have this information. Captain Zepernick, Major Ernst, they have known for longer. But this is not the point.'

Ned interrupted again. 'How long have they known?'

'I do not know exactly. A month, I believe.'

'Before you came back from leave, then?'

'Yes, before I returned, why?'

'You'd better read this, then.'

He put his hand in his pocket and handed him the letter.

Lentsch's eyes were quick, unbelieving. 'This is Isobel's handwriting! When did you get this?'

'The day she died.'

'The day she died?'

Ned took a deep breath. 'This is very difficult for me, Major. Difficult for all of us. A lot of letters get sent to you, unpleasant letters, malicious letters, denouncing old enemies, settling old scores. They're quite easy to spot. We have them delivered to the police station, so we can weed them out before they cause too much trouble. It's something we've done all along, to protect ourselves.'

'And this came in such a consignment.'

'Yes, but hers was addressed to me, not you. That's what made it so odd. She'd written an anonymous note to me. I recognized her handwriting straightaway of course, like you have done, but that's what she was counting on. The point is she didn't want anyone else to know she wanted to see me. She was frightened of something.'

The Major read the note again.

'Why did you not tell me about this before?'

'I'd have thought that was obvious. Whatever it was she wanted to see me about was something she dared not tell you. Whether it was because you were involved or because it would compromise someone close to her, I didn't know. But I couldn't trust you.'

Lentsch turned on him. 'Couldn't trust me? I was the only one you could trust!'

For a moment Ned thought the Major was going to strike out. He beckoned him into the armchair. The Major sat down, reluctantly.

'Look, Major. You're German. I'm British. Whatever you might think, we're still at war. You are my enemy.'

Lentsch flapped the letter in his hand.

'And by this stupid deception we have been looking the wrong way. I did not think we were complete friends yet, but I did not think you would try and harm her in this way.'

'Isobel is dead. It was the living I was worried about.' The refrain ran through his head again. *She couldn't tell Lentsch, she couldn't tell Lentsch, she wrote me the letter 'cause she couldn't tell Lentsch.*

'Don't you see? She found out about something so terrible that she dared not tell even you, the man she was in love with. Because you were German.'

'You mean the visit?'

Ned shook his head.

'Not just the visit. Think about it. If she had found out, maybe someone else had too. An islander. A British patriot, Major. What do you think someone like that might try and do?'

'An assassination attempt?'

'Yes. She hadn't just found out that Hitler is coming. She'd found out that someone is going to try and kill him. Someone she knew, perhaps was close to. Her father?'

'Impossible!'

'Her aunt, then.'

'This is absurd! Mrs Hallivand trying to assassinate Hitler!'

'Well, someone is, I'd bet my life on it. That's why she was so nervous on the telephone. That's why she wanted to see me.'

Lentsch bit his knuckle and crossed to the window. 'Have you any idea what would happen if such a thing took place?'

'The war would end?'

Lentsch shook his head.

'Perhaps. Not immediately. But the consequences to this island would be terrible. It would be madness to try this. Madness.'

'But if it shortened the war.'

'They would destroy the island, Ned. Everyone and everything in it. Do you want that? Your mother shot. Veronica. Her mother. All of you shot!'

'No, but . . .'

'That is the price you would pay. Can you let that happen?'

'No. No. I don't think I can.'

'No! Then let others try and kill him. It would be better for our country's soul if we did it ourselves. But He must not come here, not for propaganda, not for an assassination attempt, not at all. And there is one way to prevent it. It rests on a simple equation, a strategic certainty. You are right about one thing. If the British knew he was coming here they would try and kill him. They would have to. It would be too great an opportunity to miss. And if He thought that the British knew of His intentions, He too would know they would make this attempt. Two years ago he would have cocked a snook at such a danger. But He is careful now, wrapped in suspicions of His own troubled destiny. The War needs him. Only He can win it. So He will not expose Himself to such unnecessary danger. He will stay at home, in one of his eastern bunkers with sandbags and sycophants for company.'

'I don't follow,' said Ned.

'I have thought of a way to lay a false trail. Make them believe I have managed to escape to England with this information. I have ranted and railed against Him, cursed his folly, and now, with his birthday hour approaching, I smash his picture and before I am put under formal arrest, I disappear.'

'Hide you here, you mean?'

'Yes. At first they will think that I have gone on a drinking spree. They will search the bars and the brothels and the out of hours drinking clubs. They might imagine I have committed suicide. But tomorrow the Captain will get a letter I have already sent. In it I have explained that my conscience demands that I betray my country, that I have defected to England, and that I intend to tell them everything I know. Everything!'

'And all the time you'll be here?'

'Of course. Just for a week, a month at the most, until the time has passed. Soon He will not be able to come. Soon fresh catastrophes will be occupying His great mind. Then it will be safe to come out of hiding.'

'Not for you, it won't.'

'No, not for me. For the island.'

Ned stared at him, not quite believing what he was hearing. It was a mad idea.

'So you want me to hide you, is that it?'

'If you please. But in a different chimney from your radio.'

Ned couldn't smile.

'It's not as easy as that, Major. It's been a busy night all round. You'd better come into the kitchen.'

Lentsch followed him into the kitchen. Veronica was sitting at the table now, holding the boy's hand. He started out of his chair when he saw the Major's uniform, but Veronica quietened him back down. Ned crossed over to the back door and lifted a jacket up from the one hook. He held it up to the light.

'Recognize this?' he said.

*

'I've been through it a dozen times with him,' Ned said. 'I still can't make sense of it all.'

'He saw the man who killed her?'

'That's what he told V. That's right, isn't it, Peter?' He held up the coat again and waved it in front of the boy's face. 'Coat? Girl?'

The boy nodded.

'Here we go again. Watch this, Major. Worse than a bloody pantomime.'

Veronica slung the jacket over her shoulders and lay on the floor. Ned picked her up and started to drag her across the room. 'This is what you see. *Ja?*'

The boy nodded again.

'And the jacket . . .'

V wriggled her shoulders. As the jacket slipped off the boy leant forward and snatched it up, clutching it to his chest.

'That's what he saw up on the cliff that night,' Ned explained. 'A man driving up in a car and dragging Isobel towards that shaft. Now. The man.' He spread his hands far apart. 'Big, *ja*?'

The boy nodded again and spread his fingers out.

'Big hands too, eh?' Ned pointed to his eyes and mouth. 'What about the face?' The boy shook his head.

'It was too dark. Now look at this,' Ned said, pointing to his own clothes. 'Like this?' He pulled at his jersey and his old trousers. The boy shook his head. Ned pointed to the Major's buttons. 'Buttons, cap.' He held himself upright, like a soldier, straightening an imaginary uniform. 'Uniform, yes?' He marched up and down. The boy clapped his hands. Ned turned to the Major.

'There you are. A big man in a uniform. You know of someone like that, don't you? Who lives opposite?'

'Ernst?' Lentsch sounded incredulous. 'You think it was Ernst all along?'

'I think it was Ernst all along.'

The Major fretted. 'You must take this boy to the authorities,' he insisted, 'to the Captain. Ernst must not be allowed . . .'

'You can't!' Veronica leapt to her feet.

Ned threw up his hands. 'V, I've already told you. I've no jurisdiction over him. It's out of my hands.'

'Out of your hands! Listen to yourself! You know what will happen to him if you do, don't you?'

'Veronica . . .'

'They'll beat him to death, that's what. Just because of who he is. Isn't that right, Major?'

Lentsch shook his head, not in denial but in despair.

'And even if they don't, he won't be fit to work after they're through with him. Which is the same thing in the end for him, isn't it? Isn't it?'

The Major looked down at the floor, ashamed.

'So what do you want me to do?' Ned asked.

'I don't know. Hide him. Lock him up. You're meant to be the law around here.'

Lentsch looked at them both.

'This is how it happens. The closer He approaches, the nearer His spirit draws, the greater the danger. You see how we are all being pulled into this crazy whirlpool. You still do not fully appreciate the truly corrosive quality of His name. Thank to my letter they will begin to worry that I am part of some conspiracy. They will start tracing back: me, Isobel, van Dielen. Her murder, his disappearance. There is quite enough there to unsettle them. Now there is this boy. It does not matter that none of us have anything to do with an assassination attempt. He has cast his shadow and that is enough. One of us might have been able to evade capture. But me, the boy? And what about Veronica here, who gave the Captain this information.'

Veronica bowed her head.

'They will come back for you,' the Major told her. 'They will talk to you not once, but twice, three times; all day and all night. And you will falter. And that will be the end.' He stood up. 'I have been wrong. If I go back, give myself up, perhaps these questions will be laid to rest. And you will have to try and find out the other matter before it is too late.'

Ned stopped him.

'There is another way, you know. To not hide but to cross the Channel. You and the boy, in the canoe. V too.'

'Tonight?' Veronica looked around, momentarily bewildered. 'But I'm on stage tonight.'

Ned began to laugh. 'Trust you, V.' He turned to the Major again. 'The sea's calm enough, if they don't catch you in the first couple of miles. There's a patrol boat out round the Casquets, isn't there?'

'Once an hour it goes. But I am not a sailor, Ned. I would probably end up sailing straight into Cherbourg.'

'A compass would set you straight.' He didn't tell them of the currents. They'd have to chance it.

Lentsch was thinking. 'What about you? I don't want you getting mixed up in this.'

'No one knows you're here, if that's what you mean.'

Veronica looked embarrassed.

'I'm afraid that's not quite right. Zep told me once that no one had any idea where the Major went every evening. So I told him.'

Lentsch sighed. 'So, Ned, now you are mixed up in this as well. They will come for you too. They will ask you what it is we talked about those nights, when I slunk away from the Villa.'

'I'll tell them.'

'And they won't believe you. They dare not. They could no more imagine that our evenings were innocent than they can believe that this boy has a right to life. They will see us all as threats to the fabric of his world; and in a sense they would be right. They would have to strap you to the block and squeeze it all out of you until you were broken into small pieces.' He looked around. 'Now, it is all of us.'

Silence fell upon the room. Four in a canoe. They'd sink before they'd got a mile out.

A sudden hooting noise outside disturbed their troubles. Ned ran over to the front window. The Captain could be seen walking down Veronica's front path.

★

Zepernick knocked on the door for the third time. He was becoming impatient. His face was unshaven and he looked dishevelled. The door swung open.

'Zep! Didn't expect to see you again so soon.'

The Captain looked her up and down. She was out of breath.

'You have been running.'

'I was in the back garden.'

He took off his hat. 'I'm sorry about yesterday evening,' he said. 'I have been busy. You know why.'

'Did you find him?' She tried to keep her voice as light as possible.

The Captain shook his head.

'We have been up all night looking for him. Every billet, every excavation site. Nothing.' He looked around. 'He is not the only one who has vanished.'

'Oh?'

'Major Lentsch. He should have reported to the harbour, but he has not.' He pointed to Ned's house. 'That is where he goes at night?'

'Used to, yes.'

'Last night he was at the Villa. This morning . . .' He puffed into the air. 'You have not seen him today?'

'No. I don't think Inspector Luscombe is there either.'

The Captain nodded. 'Good. Maybe the Major has done the proper thing. Perhaps in a day or two we will find him floating in the water with a bullet in his head. Still,' he looked at his watch, the smile returning to his face, 'everyone is searching for him. Everyone except me. No one knows where I am.'

'Oh?'

'All this time I have been thinking about yesterday in the Eyrie. It has been difficult looking for this *Zwangsarbeiter* with such pictures in my mind.' He reached out and touched the front of her dress. 'Some say the morning is the best time.'

'Zep! It's nearly lunchtime!' She pushed him back. 'Anyway, I can't,' she whispered. 'Mum's upstairs.'

'No matter. I know where.' He pulled her outside.

'Please, Zep. Not now.'

Grabbing her wrist he hauled her down the garden path. The shed door hung open, the set of garden tools, the workbench, the ornament dangling from the roof, all in place.

'This time I will not make the same mistake,' he said. Taking the wooden shoe from its hook, he placed it on top of one the boxes piled up at the side before lifting her up onto the bench. He pushed her dress back up to her hips.

'Zep,' she said, turning her head away, pushing his hands away. 'I don't think we should.'

'Don't think we should?' He was at her buttons now. 'Don't

think we should? What are you talking about?' He yanked the dress open.

'No, I . . .' She tried to talk but his hands were under her, pulling at her worn elastic, sending her sprawling back against the wall. 'Please, Zep. Not here. Not now.'

He pulled her up and hit her once, not hard, on the side of her head. She began to cry. He pulled off her underwear, slowly, methodically, looking her squarely in the eye. His fingers reached underneath.

'Now tell me again of this boy of yours.'

'What?'

'This boy of yours. Where did you say you saw him?'

Veronica kissed him quickly.

'We don't want to talk about that now, do we?'

'This is a new kind of interrogation, Veronica. Very good for me and very good for you.' He examined her with dispassionate interest. 'Where did you see him again?'

'I told you. Out of my surgery window. Climbing into one of those lorries.'

He unbuckled his belt and let his trousers fall.

'I don't believe so. I have found out all about this boy. His name is Peter. He is from a village in the Ukraine. He is fifteen years old. His father was shot for partisan activities. He is the wearer of Isobel van Dielen's jacket and has been wearing it since the time of her death. He is billeted in Saumarez Park and every day he marches to work from there to the tunnel. You did not see him climb into lorries and you did not see him from your surgery window. But you have seen him, that is true. Tell me where.'

She hesitated.

'If you do not I shall have your father shot.'

'What!'

'He has been trying to sabotage the airport runway. Mowing the grass too short. It is a very serious matter.'

'Oh, God!'

'I can prevent this, if you tell me all I want to know.'

335

'Oh, God!'

'You must tell me everything, Veronica, and then it will be all right. But before you talk, we do this . . .'

He took himself in his hand and looking down, slowly pushed himself in. She stared past him. There was a shadow in the doorway. She began to tremble.

'Oh, God, no.'

The Captain grinned.

'That's better. Just like old times, eh, Veronica?' He quickened his pace.

'No,' she said, struggling as the shadow moved quickly forward. 'No, keep away,' but the Captain pushed her back and held her fast, savouring the spectacle of her writhing hips and half-hidden sex, as the pleading cries which only made him more determined drowned the sound of the bare feet and the swing of the arc and it was only when he felt the breath of disturbed air and saw the look on Veronica's face as she tried to break free that he turned and saw the outline of the boy standing on tiptoe behind him with the dark shadow of the wooden foot coming out above his head. The boy swung with all the weight of all the pickaxes he had ever held, swinging the wooden foot by its short chain, true and sure, so that the heel landed in the centre of the Captain's head, cracking it open like a walnut, so hard that Veronica felt the blow jolt up through her womb as the Captain jerked first in then out of her, and dropped to the ground his knees on the floor, his hands trailing down over her twisting body, his broken head resting between her legs, blood seeping out of his mouth and his nose. She lay there, rigid, panting, unable to move. The boy stood before her, the foot and chain swinging back and forth. There was a sound of water running onto the floor and she could smell the sour scent of urine rising. She tried to move. The Captain's head bumped down onto the workbench, his hands on either side of her knees. The boy moved forward.

'*Kaput*,' he said, and pushed him over with his foot.

*

Ned and the Major carried the body through the back garden and out into the field, then pushed the car through the opened farm gate. They sat him in the front. Ned closed the gate and walked up the road. Lentsch looked down at the body of his friend. There was blood seeping out of his ears and down his nose. He leant in and wiped his face clean.

'You could have been a good man,' he said. 'Whatever you did, I am sorry for you.'

Ned returned. 'It can't be seen from the road,' he said. 'As long as no one finds it in the next six or so hours we should be all right.'

Together they tore branches from the hedge and laid them over the roof and against the boot. Lentsch stood back, and surveyed their work.

'We cannot leave it for long. When we go we must take the car down to the bay with us. That way when they find him, they will not connect his death with anyone here. It will be quicker for us too.'

'Won't they miss him?'

Lentsch looked at his watch. 'Everyone knows how the Captain likes to spend his afternoons. By nightfall, though, they will be worried. More so as I have disappeared too.'

'We'll be gone by then,' Ned promised. 'We'll row out to the Casquets, tuck up in one of the little inlets while the patrol boats pass, then head straight out. We'll be low in the water, so slow and steady, that's the trick. Slow and steady. You can do that, can't you, Major?'

*

Back at the house Veronica was shaking in spasms. Ned's mother was sitting with her, holding her hand.

'I'd have done the same myself if I'd thought it would save them.'

Veronica lifted her head. 'Where's the boy?' Her concern was dragging the fear out of her.

'Cleaning up. You picked a good one there.'

'Well, I was good at choosing, first time round, any road.'

Ned knelt down beside them. He'd never thought he'd see the day his mum and Veronica were holding hands.

'You know we've got to go, Mum.'

'It's where you would have been all along if Dad hadn't gone at such an awkward time.' She turned to Veronica. 'His father always was a difficult so-and-so.'

The Major returned with Peter following in his wake. Another unlikely couple, Ned thought.

'The outhouse is quite clean,' the Major said. 'We scrubbed the floor together.'

Veronica sat up and patted the arm of her chair. The boy sat down, shy at first. Through the open back door the first chill of the evening fluttered through.

'It's going to be cold out there,' Ned said. 'We should all be wearing waterproofs. I don't know if we've got enough spares.'

'Lard, that's what you need,' Veronica prompted. 'Before you set off, you should strip, the lot of you, and cover yourselves with it, head to toe.' She ruffled the boy's hair. 'And to think I've just given you your first wash in months. Couldn't have chosen a worse time if I'd tried.' She stood up to go next door. 'You'd best rub it on each other. That way you'll get a good covering all over.'

'I'll do yours, then, shall I?' Ned offered. His mother laughed.

Veronica cuffed him quickly. 'I'm not going,' she said.

'What?'

'You heard. As long as they find the Captain far away from here, I'm safe. Isn't that right, Major?'

'As far as I know, yes, but ...'

'That's settled, then. That canoe won't hold four and you know it. I could try and swim but I'm out of practice. Besides I've got a show on tonight. Damned if I'm going to miss out on my big number.'

Ned shut his eyes. He wanted to look to his mother, to Veronica, wanted to hold them both and tell them he would take care of them, but he could not. He was leaving them.

'We'll be needing some food, Mum,' he told her gently. 'Have you any spare? Just to keep us going.'

Veronica perked up. 'Take some of mine. I've been cooking all week.'

Ned's mum couldn't quite believe her. 'Cooking, V? You?'

'That's right. Proper little Mrs Beeton I am these days. Hang on a mo.'

They sat in silence while she ran next door again.

'You sure this is wise?' Ned's mother said eventually.

Ned patted her hand.

'It should hold us well enough, if the sea's not too big.'

'Not the canoe. Veronica's cooking.' She got up. 'Tell you what. I've got something that will fill you up before you go. I was saving it for the next time the Major came round to tea.'

They listened as she fussed in the kitchen. She was humming to herself as if she was almost happy. She had a son who loved her, a son with a girlfriend, a son who was escaping to safety. And she was making him tea.

Veronica returned carrying a bulging string bag.

'One potato and onion pie,' she said proudly, 'some oatmeal biscuits and three slices of carrot cake.' She nodded to the kitchen. 'Your mum's doing you proud too. Where did she get it from?'

'Get what?' asked Ned.

His mother called them in. She'd laid the little table with her best tablecloth, and on it stood her four best bowls, the ones with pictures of Westminster Abbey round the rim. There was a sweet scent to the air, a smell of childhood and warm spoons. His mother pointed to the steaming bowls.

'That's real custard in there,' she said. 'Stewed apple and real custard.' She lifted the tin high in the air. 'Bet you've see nothing like that in years. Bird's custard powder. You've got your uncle to thank for that.'

Sixteen

It's hard to believe that all these towers and gun emplacements and miles of tunnel have been built, not by fit young men with state-approved muscles and healthy assuaged appetites, but by men weakened by dysentery, who eat one bowl of cabbage soup a day, who sleep on planks of wood, who dress in discarded cement bags, who never wash, who shit in communal buckets, who are beaten with whips and chair legs, and who work twelve hours a day nonstop whatever their state of health. They have built this. They have.

He clambers down the rocky surface to where the machine lies, housed in a brick house, one storey high, long like a boat, unattractive like a urinal. It is a simple machine; a huge grey rectangular funnel at the top, into which are tipped the stones and granite, a long clanging chute, down which they fall, and at the bottom a row of great stone wheels, through which these stones are minced: Guernsey rock for Guernsey sand; Guernsey sand for Guernsey cement. There are two machines of this design on the island and through them Guernsey is producing the means of its own incarceration; eating its own tail. It is like one of those children's stories that his wife used to sing, yes, he remembers that, how she used to recite those English nursery rhymes on those long foreign nights, sitting under the mosquito net, looking out over the hot night air; Jack and Jill going up a hill; the man who looked like an egg; Old King Cole; the house that Jack built. That was her favourite, the house that Jack built, for Daddy was a builder, long ago, when he had a daughter to listen to such tales. Had he one? It was so hard to know, such an improbable possibility that he had a daughter and a wife and a construction called a family, with all the constituent parts that such a complicated entity would involve. No, he cannot imagine it, for he waved the boy goodbye, did he not, sent him running home before he began this journey to his. But whether he ever possessed one or not is of no consequence, for he is of the island now and this is where he must return.

It is not difficult to climb up the small service ladder and stare down into the heart of the machine. There is the loose tumble of rock churning above the slow grinding wheels, a whirlpool of granite and flint out of which flow grains of eternity. This is what he desires, to become an infinite speck of sand, to be swept along into the body of the island, to have the sea pounding him, pressing him. To be a rock! A stone! To have the sea and the sky and the wind calling you! He is a rock! He is a stone! He jumps into the grinding pool, one leg bent sideways, one foot immediately caught, the ankle taken down and squeezed so hard he cannot imagine it, his knee first cracked then flattened, and as his hands rise up and he is taken down, his soft body following, gut squirting through his mouth, he lets forth an unbearable scream. No man can hear him, not his fellow slave workers, unloading the next wagonload, not the overseers idling their hours in the cabin of their battered lorry, not the Spanish Republican engine driver leaning out of the cab of his dirty belching engine, not even Major Ernst, one hundred yards away, tracing plans with his stick. There is the grim crushing of the machine, there is the hissing smoke from the train's boiler, there is the rhythm of the labourers' spades and the wheeling call of gulls, but there is no van Dielen. Van Dielen is dead now, crunched and mixed and turned to wet, dusty powder. Van Dielen is dead but not buried. He will lie in a heap for a year or more, tufts of couch grass growing atop him. The wind will come and blow him over the pebbles and onto the sweeping sand. In later years he will be run upon by bare feet and shovelled into proud buckets. He will be hurled against curving walls upon which he once walked; luminescent specks of him will sparkle in the wet sheen of the seaweed; a bone in a shrimping net; grit in a sunbather's eye. Others will come and others will go but van Dielen will never leave. He washes in and out, in and out, lapping around the huge circumference of his family's grave.

Seventeen

Ned walked up the drive. Wedel was up at the top polishing Bernie's car. He looked up and grinned.

'Inspector Luscombe. You still have no auto?'

'I'm waiting for the matching suit.'

Wedel looked back at the house. 'If you have come for the Major he is not here. In fact, I do not think you will be able to see him again.'

'That's all right. It's my uncle I'm after.' He showed him his warrant card. 'It's official.'

He walked down the tiled corridor, putting his head round each door. All neat and tidy, except for the slight hole by the drawing room door. The dining room table was set for dinner, the drawing room redolent of cigars and hair cream. Beyond, through the French windows, he could see men and wheelbarrows and a great trench of freshly dug earth at the far end of the lawn. A couple of trees lay on their sides. At least they'd have fuel for the next winter. Above him he could hear an odd muttering, like a bad-tempered soliloquy. He climbed the stairs towards it. He recognized the voice now. On the second floor the door to one of the bedrooms lay wide open. Albert was on his knees going through the small drawer by the bedside.

'Uncle?'

Albert looked up. He held something in his hand.

'Spoons,' he said. 'Teaspoons, dessertspoons, and here, tucked in his fancy underwear, the fish knives that were stolen six months ago. He's been helping himself, the thieving bastard.'

'Who?'

'Bohde. This is Bohde's room. What are you doing here? If you want the Major . . .'

Ned held up his hand and looked around. Through the window smoke was coming out of the lodge's chimney. One law for the rich, he thought.

'Have you heard? The Major's leaving,' he said.

Albert put the spoons back in their place and pushed back the drawer.

'I know. Only himself to blame. Should have kept his mouth shut, whatever he felt. Bad enough at the best of times, but now.'

'Now?'

'The birthday boy.' He raised himself from the floor. 'They're very sensitive about Hitler's birthday. Don't like anyone to spoil the fun.' There was a sparkle to his eyes.

'You know, don't you, Uncle?'

'Know what?'

'Know that he's coming here.'

Ned took the tin of custard from under his jacket and put it on the dresser.

'Now tell me it wasn't you. Tell me it wasn't you who tipped Isobel down that shaft.'

Albert said nothing.

'I haven't quite worked it out, Uncle, which bit fits where, but then I'm not a very good policeman. You part of this smuggling ring, too? And how did it get mixed up in all this other business?'

'I don't know what you're on about. What other business?'

'However it is you're going to try and kill him. Isobel found out, didn't she? Who through? You? Her father? What do you plan to do? Stab him to death with a garden fork?'

'Don't talk daft.'

'Well?'

Albert stood defiant. 'We're at war, Ned.'

'So people keep telling me.'

'War means sacrifice. Laying down one's life if necessary.'

'When appropriate. What's the plan, then. Poisoned tarts for tea?'

'No!' Albert was shouting now.

'Well, what, then?'

'A bomb!'

'A bomb? Borrowed one of theirs, did you?'

'I made it myself. With nails and bolts, you know, like we did of old, weedkiller and sugar. Only a damn sight bigger this time.'

'You wouldn't stand a chance.'

'I'd get close enough for it to count.'

'How? Wrap it up in fancy paper? Christ Almighty!'

Albert held his ground. 'How many men get a chance like this? I had to take it.'

'And Isobel found out?'

Albert was sullen. 'Isobel found out nothing,' he said. 'I was there.'

'You were where?'

'When Mrs H. tried to get it out of her. They're giving him this lunch, see. Isobel were invited. Mrs H. asked her round that morning to see if we could find out where. She came up to the Villa first, to check on the party, then walked down. As soon as I saw her go through the Lodge door I followed. I wanted to hear it for myself. I let myself in. You could taste the sharpness between them, like when you bite into a sour apple. "How lovely you are looking," Mrs H. was saying, "quite captured the Major's heart," and I could hear the snap as she bit into a biscuit. She does love her biscuits, does Mrs H.'

'Never mind about the biscuits, Uncle.'

'No. "In fact between you both, you and your father have made the van Dielens quite indispensable," and Isobel said, "Oh, I wouldn't say that," already bored and irritated. I could hear the scrape of something, like Marjorie was trying to pull the chair closer. "I've heard something very *interesting*," she said, her voice hushed like she was afraid someone might be listening, "*very* interesting. A special visitor is coming, I hear, a very special visitor."

Isobel was hardly bothering to listen and Mrs H. hummed and hawed and poured herself a cup of tea, holding it God knows how high up, sounded like a man taking a Jimmy Riddle, and then she said, "I know you've been told not to tell anyone, and that's how it should be, but you can tell your old aunt, can't you? After all, it's not every day that a little place like this entertains a visitor of such *peculiar* stature," and Isobel got impatient, and laughed and said, "Who's coming then, Santa Claus?" and you could hear it in her voice that she thought Mrs H. had finally lost her marbles and I had half a mind to go in and stop it right there and then, but suddenly it was like Mrs H.'s feelings had got the better of her, this whippersnapper of a girl poking fun at her, lording it over her, and her voice went hard as granite and she spat it out. "Don't try and hide it from me, girl," she said, "I know who's coming. It's a privilege many of us would have liked to share, to have dinner with such a distinguished guest. Frankly I'm surprised the Major hasn't seen fit to ask me. I am after all about the only one left who's used to receiving heads of state." "Heads of state, what *are* you talking about?" she said, irritated. "Hitler!" Mrs H. screams. "Hitler, you silly girl. You and your father are dining with the Lord High Executioner Himself, here in Guernsey on his birthday. Don't tell me you didn't know," and Isobel started to stammer and said, no, that she didn't know, that she must be mistaken, that the Major would have told her. "The Major!" Mrs H. spat the word. "Yes, the Major. Gerhard tells me everything. After the war we are going to be married." "Married! You and Gerhard!" I thought she'd given herself an electric shock the way she screamed it and I heard her stand up, with a clatter of plates on the floor, and Isobel gave a little cry too, as if she'd been grabbed, by the hair or by the wrist I couldn't tell. "See that," Mrs H. said, yelling at the top of her voice, "see that picture there. That was me, Isobel, me! That was how I looked when I was your age. You wouldn't have thought it to look at me now, would you, but it's true. Russell just changed the face slightly so as not to cause my father too much embarrassment. It never crossed your mind that I could have once looked like that.

Well, let me tell you I had a better figure than you, I was better company than you, and most likely better in bed than you. Yet look at me now. I have his brains, his wit, and yet he barely notices me because of the one thing I have lost. And you hope to marry him! If he cannot look on me now and see me for what I am worth, imagine what he will think of you in years to come, when you will have nothing! Nothing! Not even a picture like this to remind him!" and with that she got up left the room and finding me in the corridor shooed me into the kitchen. "Best not push it any further," I said. "Let her think you're just jealous." Isobel popped her head round the door and saw me, so I gave her a little wave. The next thing we knew she was running down the pathway and out of the gates. Can't blame her of course, the way Mrs H. had carried on. But that's the last we saw of her.'

'And yet she ran back and wrote me the note.'

'Note, what note?'

'She wrote me a note, Uncle. She was frightened. She *must* have found out.'

He thought back to that time, when he sat in that little room of hers, with Mrs Hallivand eating her biscuits, her wicker basket at her dainty feet.

'Wait a minute. Did Mrs H. go to the house that day?'

'After she met up with Isobel, yes. That afternoon.'

'And what did she have in her bag?'

'The usual stuff.'

'Sugar and weedkiller.'

'That's right. Hidden under a cloth. It were the last lot.'

'That's how she found out!' He got up and looked down on the drive. Wedel was leaning against the car, smoking a cigarette. He looked up and held his cigarette out in invitation. Ned raised his hands and backed away.

'When Isobel got back home her father told me that she had ridiculed her aunt for having this embroidery she'd done, which she'd found tucked in her bag, of the Major standing by the bay or something. At the bottom of the bag, he said. Only it wasn't at the bottom. It was on top of all that other stuff, the sugar, the weedkiller. She sees the Major on this piece of cloth, lifts it up to take a better look and lo and behold, lying underneath, there they are. The next thing she knows there are voices in the kitchen and she comes out to find you and Mrs H. muttering together like a couple of amateur Guy Fawkes. She knows all about weedkiller and sugar and what you bloody do with them. I told her. Suddenly she realizes what you two are planning. She runs out of the house, forgetting her bike, and dashes home. She daren't tell the Major. She does the only thing she can, she writes to me, hoping that I can somehow save the island from your lunacy. Only someone gets to her first. Big hands, I've been told. And a uniform. How did you come by that, Uncle? Borrow one of the Major's?'

'What?'

'You were seen tipping her down a shaft!'

'I never tipped no one down a shaft. And I ain't no murderer.'

'Not much you aren't, trying to get us all killed.' He touched Albert on the arm. 'What would Kitty have thought of all this, Uncle? She'd have hated it.'

At the mention of her name, Albert grew contrite.

'I was seized by the wrongness of it, all the wickedness here on this one bit of rock.'

'You didn't kill her?'

'On my Rose's grave, I didn't. I'm not saying I wouldn't have if I had to. But I didn't. So.' He drew himself up, ready to be marched downstairs. 'What am I to do now?'

'Dismantle it. He's not coming.'

'Not coming?' Albert was indignant.

'He's got another engagement.'

'How do you know?'

'I'm a policeman. I've been told.'

'I suppose I'm under arrest, then. That'll be one for the record books. A nephew arresting his own uncle.'

'I can't arrest you for trying to blow up Adolf Hitler, can I?'

'No, I suppose not.'

'There's another reason. I'm taking your advice, making a run for it.'

'To England!' Albert gripped Ned's arm. 'When?'

'Tonight.'

'You'll be there by morning!'

'I bloody well hope so.'

'You'll go see our Kitty.'

'Only if you promise to keep out of mischief.'

'Look after her, Ned. She's all I've got.'

'If you look after Mum.'

'I'll move in with her, if you like. I've had it with this lot.'

Ned walked down the stairs. His uncle followed, rubbing his duster along the balustrade as he went. A few minutes ago he was prepared to blow Guernsey to ashes. Now he was back polishing the woodwork. He's going to escort me to the front door too, Ned thought, wish me good luck. Offer me some friendly advice.

'One thing, Uncle. I still don't understand where you got the custard from.'

Albert rolled up his trouser leg. There was a yellowish bruise and the line of a badly healed cut.

'It were me that broke into van Dielen's yard that night. My foot went through one of their containers. It were full of them. So I took a couple, sort of farewell treat. Gave one to your mother.'

'No more than two?'

'What would I want with any more? I weren't planning to take a bath in the stuff.' He looked up to the ceiling. 'Though I know of some as might.'

A picture came to Ned, of George Poidevin standing atop a pile of half-opened containers.

'Did you open any more crates?'

'Why should I do that?'

'To see what else you could find? To make it look like the foreigns had been there.'

'Foreigns wouldn't bother to open crates. They see enough of what's inside crates as it is. Anyway...' He stopped. 'Ah, what's the use. Go on, be off with you. And don't you worry about the bomb.'

'You won't try to blow up any Germans?'

'I won't blow up any Germans.' He wiped his hand on his apron. 'You row safely, now. The sea is a treacherous beast.'

'I'll row safely.'

'And be careful of the milk over there. It curdles in the stomach, the muck the English drink.'

*

They all tried to get some sleep for the rest of that afternoon, the Major and the boy sleeping on his mother's bed, Ned lying half awake on his own, listening to his mother and Veronica below. Then in the darkness the door opened quietly. Veronica slipped in under the blanket.

'V,' he whispered, 'Mum's downstairs.'

'I don't care. Neither does she.'

She snuggled in and wrapped her arms around him. 'I don't want to ... not after...'

'No.'

'I will in time, though. When you get back. You will be coming back, won't you, Ned? I couldn't bear it now, if you didn't.'

'V!'

'Sometimes I feel bad about it all, Tommy and the Captain. Gerald too, of course.' She sat up on her arms. 'Do you know, until just now I'd forgotten all about Gerald. And I thought he was going to be my passport to a better life. That's all I ever wanted, a better life.' She pulled his hair gently. 'Do you mind about the others?'

'I do a bit.'

'I had my eye on the Major too, you know.' She laughed and rolled over onto the pillow. 'God, you must have thought me a fool.'

350

'You just got carried away, V, that's all. Lost your sense of balance.'

'Well, I'm back on my feet now.'

'You're not on your feet at all.'

He made to lean over. Veronica pushed him back.

'Just you lie be. In my arms.'

When they woke it was dusk. She got up, lit the candle and bent to the mirror, running a quick line of lipstick round her mouth. She caught Ned's face in the mirror, watching her, his hands behind his head. It was like a marriage almost.

'I did what you asked,' he said.

'What's that?'

'Dreamt of you.'

She threw back the blanket. 'Come on, rise and shine. We've no time for that now. We best get that fat on you.'

She put her hands on her hips while he stripped, then rubbed the cold grease over his body.

'I could get to like this,' she said.

He needed help putting his vest back on. She pulled it down hard and turned him around. She stood on tiptoe and put her arms around his waist.

'Ned Luscombe,' she said.

'That's my name.'

'If I squeeze you too hard you'll pop out of your togs.'

'Well, we wouldn't want that, would we?'

'Actually we would.' She kissed him. 'I'd better go. It's the first performance tonight. We can't all do vanishing acts.'

She left without any further fuss, a kiss, a long silent embrace, another kiss, quick and wet with tears, and then a hurried clatter down the stairs. Ned watched as she half ran down the garden path, pulling her coat around her shoulders. He hoped she might turn, wave to him, blow him a kiss, but she did not. She shut the little wooden gate and, head down, set her face against the wind. Then the space where she had been was empty. Veronica was gone.

*

Albert climbed the stairs. He felt tired and stiff. The town was empty. He could hear the faint noise of the music hall band coming from the theatre a few streets away. Mrs H. would be there, half the town too. There was no one to disturb him here. All he had to do was to extract the detonator. The rest he could dismantle in dribs and drabs. He was glad now that he didn't have to do it. Since knowing Ned would be seeing Kitty, it was as if a boil had been lanced. He'd always hoped that Ned and Kitty would get together. Rose had maintained that Ned wasn't Kitty's type, she was too serious for him, too old fashioned. 'Wait till he settles down,' Albert used to tell her. 'He'll see reason. She's one in a million, our Kitty.' Yes. Perhaps in the months to come he'll get another letter from the mainland. He could just imagine what it might say. *Guess what, Dad. Ned and I are getting...*

He opened the door and walked over the creaking wooden floor. Beside the unwashed window stood his lovely dangerous bomb cloaked in its paper mask. It would have worked. He laid the drainpipe down carefully and fetched out the clockwork mechanism. The wires were still in place. His hands were trembling. Suddenly, at the far end, the door to the storeroom at the back was pushed open and a man's broad back emerged, with a snort and a rattle as he turned.

'Tommy?'

The big man gave a start. There was a crash and something metallic started to roll across the floor towards him.

'Mr Luscombe? What in blazes are you doing here?'

The object came to a rest against the toe of his boot. Albert picked it up. It gleamed in the dark.

'Might ask you the same question. Might ask you what you're doing with this lot.'

'Confiscated goods from the raid,' Tommy replied. 'We took so much stuff away we had to store some of it up here. I'm moving it back down for safe keeping.'

Albert weighed the tin in his hand.

'Just 'cause you're wearing a uniform, Tommy, don't mean to say that I can't tell a lie when I see one. My nephew has been looking all over the island for George Poidevin's missing custard. I bet he doesn't know it was up here all the time.'

'How do you know where it came from?'

'Cause I'm the bugger what broke in that night, Tommy. You didn't know that, did you? I was halfway out that hole when I saw you plodding up the street, flashing that torch about. Must have been like coming across Bluebeard's treasure, seeing this lot shining in the dark.'

Tommy laid the rest of his load carefully on the floor.

'It were no great surprise. Ever since Inspector Petty and the others were arrested the Poidevins have had a clear run of it.'

'And the temptation too great for you, was it?'

Tommy put his hands in his pocket and drew out a handful of coins.

'Two pounds nineteen and threepence is what I get a week. Used to be four before the invasion. When the Inspector were in charge, it weren't so bad. We all had a crack of the whip. But now! How do they expect us to get by on those sorts of wages? One hundred and fifty tins.' He nudged one towards Albert with his foot. 'You can share it with me,' he said. 'All of it, half and half. Christ Almighty, Albert, there's more money here than you or I would ever see.'

'Now, now, Tommy. I don't hold with swearing. Is that all you found? If we're going into partnership, like.'

'I jemmied up a few more, but that was it. It's enough. Near four pound a tin, you can get. You'd have to work a good many years to earn that sort of money.'

'You brought them all back here, then?'

'About twenty under my cape the first journey. Then on my bike, using one of our postbags. Daren't go far, not with patrols about. Half and half, Albert, I can't say fairer than that. I'll do all the work, you just count the pennies. Three hundred apiece if we're lucky.'

'I've taken two tins already.'

Tommy smiled. 'On the house.'

Albert passed his tin from hand to hand then chucked it across. Tommy clapped his hands together.

'You got big hands, Tommy,' Albert said. 'A uniform too.'

'So?'

'Ned said that this custard and Isobel's murder were somehow mixed up but the poor lad didn't know how. He got a witness who saw whoever it was chuck her down that shaft. A big chap it seems, with big hands, and a uniform too. Ned thought he meant a German uniform, not one of his own.'

'Half and half, like I said. Let's leave it at that. You could buy a bungalow with your share. A car as well.'

'Is that what I'm going to tell him, that his daft old uncle solved his murder for him? Don't know as I dare. He'd never live it down.'

'What about your daughter? Kitty, isn't it? Think of what three hundred pound could do for her. Forget about the dead, Albert. Think of the living.'

'Just tell me. If we're to be partners, I got a right to know. Then, whatever's in this room, we can share.'

'You're asking a lot of a man, Mr Luscombe.'

'Just tell me.'

Tommy sighed. He walked to the window and looked out.

'It was her bad luck really, coming up here that Saturday morning. I'd come back early, to move a couple of dozen back home, where I could start selling 'em. Up here were only temporary, what with all the rehearsals going on. I was loading them into my bag when Isobel bursts in, looking for some costume of hers. I drops what I have back in the trunk and slams the lid down hard. I don't think she's seen anything. I always liked Isobel, she was always friendly if we met outside or on the stairs. She told me she was going to a party that night, fancy dress. "It's all a big surprise, Tommy," she said. "I thought I might wear this," and she puts her hand in along the rack and pulls out this bit of nothing with tassels and fringes. She held it up against her close like, her hand flat on her belly. "What do you think?" she said, flirting with me a bit. "Very pretty, miss, though a bit cold for the time of year."

"I know," she said. "I'll have to wear something over it while I walk down, or I'll catch my death. Once in the Casino, though . . ." and she gave a little twirl, just to show what I'd be missing. I didn't mind that. I like a woman who knows the value of what she's got. So she puts the dress in some fancy bag she's brought along and hops off down the stairs. That unsettled me. There was no telling who else might waltz in. So I leave them be. I don't like it but there's nothing else I can do. I do me first shift. Then late afternoon we're called up to go through the mail. That was the best thing your nephew done, weeding out them bastard letters. The best thing he done. Well, he's stirring the pile when he goes, "What!" and pulls this letter out. It's from Isobel, asking to see him Sunday morning. *Must see you*, it said. *Must*. But not here, not at the police station, but somewhere else, as if she wants to tell him something without anyone here knowing. Well, it's obvious, isn't it. She saw what I'd been doing, saw them tins. She knows the history of this place as well as anybody else, knows how half of us were sent to prison. Your nephew were brought in as a clean broom, make sure it didn't happen again. And she was going to spill the beans, the two-faced little cunt. It would be the end of me. I know what's happened to those poor bastards what got caught last time. I worked with them, drank with them, aye and broke into those fucking stores with them. They were my friends. It was her or me, Albert, that's how I saw it, her or me. I had until Sunday morning. I knew she was going to the Casino and I knew she'd be walking. I'd got the Yellow Peril going by then, and about seven I went up there, parked at the top and waited. Half an hour later and her father hurried out across the road. It was now or never. I didn't quite know what I was going to do. Maybe I could get her outside without any fuss. So I eased the car down and knocked on the door, all friendly like. She was there in a jiffy, all dressed up in that pretty little dress, her legs half bare. Tight, it were. Saw the shape of everything, like it was drawn on a sheet of paper. She were a pretty piece, there's no denying it, and for a moment I wondered whether I couldn't work the charm on her.

Amazing what a good slice of pork can do to a woman's brains. If I'd had the time, who knows. "Yes?" she says, puzzled, but not suspecting that I know, and I think: Yes, that's it, you're just a little actress, that's all, like all the rest of them, 'cause that's what they are, Albert, the lookers of this world, actresses, in the mind and in the heart and down below too. She thinks she got the measure of me, but it's me what got the measure of her and I tells her that I've come with a message from Mr Luscombe, that he can't see her tomorrow like she wanted but could see her now, straightaway, like. "He's sent me with the car, miss," I said, "and tell you what, after he's done with you I'll give you a lift down to the front," and though she's nervous she keeps her head and grabs her coat. It's quiet in the lane and as I opened the back door and she ducked down I jumped down on top of her, pinned her down hard like against the seat, and she started to twist and heave, she can't cry out 'cause her face is all squashed against the seat, but she's giving me a ride I can tell you, bucking like a bronco, and I can't help thinking, 'cause it's not that much different, is it, her fighting for her life and her bouncing up and down on the end of my pole, and I grabs her head in both my hands, holding her down with my knees, grab it and twist it round hard like you would a rabbit, turned it right round so she's looking at me again. You could hear her neck snap all the way down the road, I reckon. She weren't quite dead but she were lifeless, and I propped her up and drove out to the headland. I was going to finish her off with a rock, make it look worse than it was, but when I got out of the car to do it I couldn't. Like I said, she was a looker. I like a good-looking girl, never lifted a finger to any of them, Albert, never had to, always a gentleman even with me chopper in my hand, but I had to shut her up. Well, there's no end of sandbags and cement bags up there so I scooped up a bit of both and mixed it all together in a bucket lying with a drop of water in the bottom, and stuffed it in her mouth and up her nose. They said I put it in other places but I never did, never. I just filled her up so she couldn't talk no more. She died quick then, heaving a bit in the back, and I was going to leave her on the grass, but then I thought I could try laying the blame on the Germans too, by tipping her down one of those shafts out there. I was careful, put her down feet first, so it wouldn't spoil her looks. I was thinking of her dad and the funeral. I didn't want to make it any harder on him. Then I drove back and had a bloody good drink, more than I should have probably but to tell you the truth I felt bloody marvellous. I'd done it. I'd won. I had one hundred and fifty tins to my name and no one was any the wiser. I went on patrol with Peter, down by St Sampson's again. Your nephew had asked us to make sure there were no further break-ins! When we got there, blow if there wasn't this Kraut bastard ranting up and down George's house, him or the whores next door I couldn't tell which, Mrs P. leaning out of the window screaming her head off, the whores as well, so we hauled him down the road and smacked him about a bit while we marched him back to his billet. I'd no idea who he was. If I hadn't nicked his wallet I'd have got clean away. Still can, despite all that's gone on. No one's any the wiser.'

'Except me. I know.'

'You're an old man, Albert. Everyone knows you work too hard.'

'I thought you said we could share it, Tommy.'

'Carrying things up and down the stairs at your time of life. Just asking for a broken neck.'

'Half and half, Tommy. You agreed.'

'I've changed me mind, Mr Luscombe. I'm a greedy bastard. Always have been. An old buzzard like you don't deserve three hundred pound. You probably would spend it on a bungalow. Bloody waste. Crack open a lot of young virgins, three hundred pounds. Sink a lot of pints on it too.'

Albert reached into the pipe.

'You're not the only one who's been busy smuggling,' he said. 'This'll make a bigger bang than your custard.'

'What's that, then?' Tommy asked.

He peered down. He couldn't see much, just a long black thing and a trickle of wire leading to Albert's hand.

'She's in the best of health, you know, Tommy,' Albert said.

'What?'

'My Kitty. She's in the best of health.'

*

The theatre was crowded. She stood in the wings while other acts came and went. A line of dancing girls, a juggler, a troupe of Girl Guides. She could hear the low growl of the German voices, joining in the sing-song. Six months ago these voices would have been loud and lusty, drowning out the islanders with the coarse confidence of victory, but now they were muted, hesitant, sung in memory of their friends and their families and their threatened homeland.

Veronica walked out on stage half an hour into the show. Though the lights in the house were dimmed, she could not fail to see Molly in the second row, dressed in fake fur, and in the seat next to her, his hand resting on her thigh, the fat figure of Major Ernst. Further down, Bohde sat next to an empty seat. She looked out across to the rest of the audience, the uniforms, the ironed dresses, the lost, expectant faces, thinking of the Major and the boy and Ned Luscombe on the cold and friendless sea.

She started to sing, twirling her parasol, dancing around the stage, but there were tears in her eyes and her voice started to break. She stumbled forward, tripping over her shoes, trying to swallow the emptiness growing inside. He had gone! Ned had gone! He was on the seas, rowing away from her heart. She couldn't remember the words.

'Bring back the Girl Guides!' someone shouted. 'They got better legs than you.'

'More of 'em too!'

A couple of lads began to whistle. Another hooted, like an owl. She stood facing them, unable to move, her parasol poised in mid-air. Then she heard the thump and felt the building shake. A siren went off and at the back a man jumped to his feet and started to scream.

'No need to get your knickers in a twist,' she bellowed out. 'Take a look at mine.' She lifted her skirt with both hands and let it drop. The crowd roared. 'Come on, Harry,' she cried down to the conductor. 'Down at the Old Bull and Bush!'

She began to sway to the rhythm, banishing the ache in her soul, stretching the smile across her face.

*

Ned's mother gave a start. 'What was that?'

'Gun practice.' He hugged her again.

'You best be off,' she said, brushing at his waterproof as if it was his best jacket.

'You'll be quite safe, then?'

'I'll be quite safe. V's just next door if I need anything.'

Ned looked her in the eye.

'Remember, tell them he took me at gunpoint. I've taken ours. V's got the wireless. They'll search the house thorough.'

'I better give it a clean, then.'

'No more sleepwalking, Mum.'

'I'm just trying to meet Dad, that's all. I miss the old bugger, I really do.'

'So do I.'

She sniffed and blew into her handkerchief. 'Do you?'

'Of course,' he said, but he wasn't sure if that was true.

They pushed the Captain's car out into the road and ran it down to the bay. Lentsch steered, with the Captain slumped next to him in the front seat. Ned and the boy sat in the back the canoe folded across their knees. Down by the bay Lentsch drove the car down the slipway and parked it under the shadow of the sea wall. As he got out Ned leant forward and, whipping the Major's cap from his head, slung it in on the Captain's lap.

'They'll be no doubting you now,' he said.

The Major looked back to the slow rise of the island. Now, when he was leaving, Guernsey seemed more remote, more mysterious than ever.

'I feel as if I am betraying her,' he said. 'Leaving her death unsolved.'

359

'You're not betraying anyone,' Ned told him. 'We'll be back for her, in time.'

They unfolded the canoe and carried it over the rocks. The tide was up. Together they slipped it into the water, the boy in the middle, Lentsch in the back, Ned in front. A hundred yards out the evening mist floated above the flat calm. They paddled quickly, silently. Ned felt strong and by the dip of the paddle, and the surging cut of the sea, the boy did too. The canoe was long and taut, the slatted wooden flooring creaking as it met the cold salt water. They reached the Casquets an hour later and paddled into one of the gulleys. They sat in a cleft of cave, rising up and down in the drip of the hollow cavern, not daring to speak and growing cold, waiting for the sweep of the patrol boat to pass them by. It came as expected at around half eight. Then, as the motor faded, all was quiet. Ned eased the canoe out. The night was dark, the sea running calm. For a moment the mist cleared and looking back he could see the outline of his homeland, silver and grey and wrapped in weightless reverie. He set the prow north and started forward. Out in the open a white swollen roller rose to greet them. He paddled hard, rushing into it, longing with all his heart.